PENGUIN BOOKS

Isabel's War

Rosie Meddon writes historical sagas that explore the lives and struggles of women living through times of war, the settings for which are often inspired by the dramatic scenery around her North Devon home. When not writing, Rosie is happiest working on her allotment or exploring the countryside and history of South West England – ever on the alert for inspiration for future novels.

Isabel's War

ROSIE MEDDON

PENGUIN BOOKS

PENGUIN BOOKS

UK | USA | Canada | Ireland | Australia
India | New Zealand | South Africa

Penguin Books is part of the Penguin Random House group of companies
whose addresses can be found at global.penguinrandomhouse.com

Penguin Random House UK
One Embassy Gardens, 8 Viaduct Gardens, London SW11 7BW

penguin.co.uk

First published 2026
001

Set in 12.5/14.75pt Garamond MT
Typeset by Falcon Oast Graphic Art Ltd
Printed and bound in Great Britain by Clays Ltd, Elcograf S.p.A.

The authorized representative in the EEA is Penguin Random House Ireland,
Morrison Chambers, 32 Nassau Street, Dublin D02 YH68

A CIP catalogue record for this book is available from the British Library

ISBN: 978–1–405–96484–5

In memory of Merle

I

St James's, London
7 September 1940

Damn. He was back. And half an hour earlier than usual, as well.

The need to kowtow to her husband first thing in the morning always got her day off to a bad start – and he knew it. It was the sole reason he went to the bother of coming home. To add insult to injury, to ensure she heard him arrive, he made a point of closing the front door so heavily against the frame that the pictures in the hallway rattled. It would have been bad enough had he done it to jolt her awake but, after twenty years of being forced to live by his ridiculous rules, he knew full well there was no chance she would still be asleep after six o'clock.

'From today,' he'd announced on the first morning of their honeymoon, at the same time taking hold of her wrist with a strength that had alarmed her, 'by the time I wake up, you will see to it that you have washed, dressed and made yourself look presentable. Slatternliness is something I will not tolerate. As my wife, it is your duty to ensure my day gets off to a smooth start, by which I mean that the appropriate cleaned and pressed set of my garments is laid out ready, my breakfast – which you are to ensure has neither grown cold nor been allowed to dry out – arrives at the table as I do, that my newspaper, along with the morning's post, is at my left hand. More generally, you are to run my household in such a manner that I am never inconvenienced by issues of a domestic or otherwise trifling nature. Confirm to me now that you understand my instructions because if I am forced to issue reminders, I guarantee you will not enjoy the consequences.'

No, her husband didn't come home in the morning and slam the door to wake her up; he did it to draw her attention to the fact that he hadn't spent the night in his adjacent bedroom – that he had instead been with Her. He did it to rub her nose in the fact that, after all these years, he was still being unfaithful, and to hammer home that she was powerless to do anything about it. Many was the morning she'd been tempted to tell him he could desist from the farce because she couldn't care less where he'd been – that she'd stopped caring years ago. But experience always checked her tongue; safer to remain silent and let him think he still had her nicely cowed than be called to account for her latest transgression or made to list her every shortcoming as his wife. The predictability of his routine did have one bright side: on the mornings when he didn't wake up in his own bed, she didn't have to be up with the lark to have everything ready for him. Today, however, with his timing adrift from the norm, she was about to get caught out.

Hastily pulling the bedclothes up over her shoulder, she braced herself for the door to fly open.

Three, two, one.

'Get out of bed and pack my things.'

When the canvas kitbag he tossed on to the bed landed on her feet, she winced under the weight of it but hauled herself upright anyway. She would never have thought it possible to detest someone quite so roundly. But it was, and she did.

'Good morning, dear.'

With his bulk filling the door frame, he glowered back at her. 'For the love of God, woman, hold your tongue and listen. Zero-seven-hundred a driver is to collect me. *Do not* make me late.'

Biting back the urge to do precisely that, she got out of bed, removed his kitbag to the floor and padded across to the easy chair for her robe. If the army was sending a driver, he had to be going out of town – not that she cared to know the details; military duties or otherwise, he went wherever he pleased. That said, on the handful of occasions when she'd been foolish enough to let him leave without enquiring as to his movements, she'd been left clueless as to when he might return. And having him show up without warning was a surprise she could do without.

'For how many days do I pack?' she asked, glancing up from tying the sash of her robe.

Already partway along the hall, he paused before turning to retrace his steps.

This morning, she detected from his demeanour an even greater distaste for her than usual, the telltale tic in his right temple suggesting he was close to blowing his top.

'Not that it's any of your concern, but I have been appointed lieutenant colonel of a battalion in Aldershot.'

A promotion? Her husband was being posted away? She doused a frisson of excitement; she'd got her hopes up before – many, many times before – only to have them roundly dashed.

'So –'

'I report this morning to Colonel Hyde-Llewellyn.'

'So, does that mean –'

'*Do not* mistake this for a discussion. My order to you was clear. *Pack my things.* By the time I'm dressed, I expect everything to be ready. And don't even *think* about leaving anything out.'

When he left to take care of his ablutions, Isabel turned back to her bedroom and sank into the easy chair. His assertion that his news didn't concern her wasn't true. While she didn't give a fig about his promotion per se, his announcement that he was being posted to Aldershot was nothing short of astonishing: Hector, promoted to lieutenant colonel in charge of a battalion – a *field* appointment, after so long comfortably behind a desk at the War Office? *That* can't have pleased him. Neither could the need to remove to somewhere as far from the capital as Aldershot, the two, together, constituting inconvenience on an unprecedented scale. His secondment to a cushy job in Whitehall, about three years previously, had provided him with all manner of perks, not least of which was working within a fifteen-minute stroll of the apartment in the Holborn mansion block where he'd installed his long-time mistress, Audrey Deacon-Jones. No wonder he was crabby; being promoted to a distant field battalion was definitely not the type of leg-up for which he would have spent the last year or so jockeying. But it served him right. He was in the army, and there was a war on. And she, for one, couldn't be more delighted that his luck had finally run out. The one or two female acquaintances with whom she still occasionally crossed paths remarked how fortunate she was to still have her husband at home; little did they know how deeply she wished he wasn't. Either way, make it through the next half an hour and she would be rid of him, at least for now.

She shot to her feet, the enormity of his revelation sinking in: her husband was being sent away – and for more than the odd few days. Her prayers had been answered. She must make haste and be rid of him.

Grasping his kitbag, she carried it along to his dressing room. Then she shuttled between various drawers, assembling on his leather-topped bench the requisite undergarments. From the rack in the bottom of the closet, she retrieved his dress shoes and PT plimsolls, which she stuffed with paper and then forced into separate linen bags; she folded briefs, vests, and rolled pairs of socks in precisely the manner in which he liked to find them. From where he'd cast them off, she scooped up what he'd worn to last night's black-tie dinner, catching as she did so a whiff of patchouli, vanilla, carnation – of Tabu – the heady scent favoured by his mistress, the woman's choice of fragrance always striking her as rather *on the nose*.

Quelling amusement, she plunged the garments into the linen bag for the dry-cleaner. From the wardrobe, she retrieved an identical outfit and then fell still to listen. In the bathroom, he was running water into the wash-basin, which meant she had about ten minutes before he would reappear and expect to see everything mustered and ready.

Taking marginally greater care with his newly laundered outfit, she slipped it inside the canvas suit carrier that bore his initials. The sight of them, stitched in gold thread, jogged a memory of how she'd once let him go away without his hip flask – a gift from his mother and similarly emblazoned – the recollection leading her to dart across the hall to his study. Spotting the flask alongside the decanters on the galleried silver drinks tray, she snatched it up, the lightness of it telling her it was empty. Despatching him with a flask devoid of whisky was as heinous a crime as failing to pack it at all.

Removing the stopper from the decanter of his single malt, she positioned the little silver funnel and carefully topped up the flask to a level she knew to be precisely three-quarters: *I said three-quarters, you dolt; had I wanted it filled all the way up the neck, I would have said so.* His exasperation, on that very first occasion he'd instructed her to fill it, was still sharp in her mind today: the depth of his scorn; the extent of his loathing; the fury with which he had grasped her arm. No matter how often she attempted to rid herself of such memories, the shock and the hurt never dulled. They hadn't even finished their honeymoon before she'd found herself wondering what life must be like for the poor soul he'd picked to be his batman. She hadn't needed to wonder for long, her own experience at the wrong end of his temper giving her a pretty good idea. Still, very shortly now, he would be gone. All she had to do was obey him a moment or two longer.

With his final requirements assembled on the floor of his dressing room, she set about packing them into his bag. If she'd found his behaviour that first time abhorrent, it was a good job she'd had no idea what else lay in store, especially given that, around eighteen months into their marriage, Audrey Deacon-Jones had been divorced by her own husband on the grounds of her adultery — specifically, the affair she'd been carrying on with Hector. Hector, of course, like the rat that he was, had strenuously denied any and all transgressions. Yes, it might have taken her less than a month of marriage to realize that making him happy was going to be an uphill task — and that was *before* she had failed to become pregnant — but it had been Audrey's divorce that had ultimately sounded the death knell for her loveless union; as far as Hector was concerned, from that day forward, by the simple act of being his wife, she stood in the way of his happiness; from the moment Audrey had become a divorcée, every time she'd thought his behaviour couldn't become any worse, he would deliver a new humiliation and prove her wrong.

Packing his cashmere scarf and kidskin driving gloves, she shook her head in dismay. As she had pondered so very many times — and, on occasion, had even dared to ask him outright — why, if she made him that unhappy, hadn't he simply left her? With next to no effort on his part, he could have fabricated grounds for throwing her

out. Instead, since he apparently had what he wanted –
a subservient wife running his home and the thrill of a
mistress for his pleasure – he'd chosen not to give her
the satisfaction. Despite spending at least five nights each
week in Holborn, he still got up every morning and came
back to their apartment in St James's. And the only reason
he continued with the charade – at least, that she could
think of – was either because it gave his assignations with
Audrey an illicit edge or, more likely, because he enjoyed
rubbing his wife's nose in it.

She supposed an outsider might ask the same question of *her*: why, once it had become clear what sort of
man he was, hadn't *she* divorced *him*? The answer was
straightforward. Firstly, she lacked the means; she had
very little money of her own and certainly nowhere near
enough to pay for a divorce. Secondly, while a wife was
now allowed to petition her husband for a divorce on the
grounds of his adultery or cruelty, the onus fell upon the
woman to prove it. And with Hector having long since cut
her off from her friends, what was left of her social circle
comprised almost exclusively his acquaintances and their
wives, not a single one of whom would speak out against
him: how dare she complain that her husband kept her
in her proper place? Even if a court did somehow take
her side, a divorce wouldn't bring an end to her problems
but rather present her with a whole new set. She had no
family to speak of – her father having died while she'd
been away at school, her mother having remarried and
gone abroad twenty years ago, her only brother having
been lost in the Great War. No, Hector had her so cut

off that she had nowhere to go and no means by which to survive on her own. She was exactly where he wanted her – firmly under his control. Why had she married him in the first place? Because, although she hadn't seen it at the time, her widowed mother – anxious to marry the wealthy Argentinian she had snared for herself – had schemed and manoeuvred and manipulated her into it.

Realizing with a jolt that the splashing of water in the bathroom had given way to the sound of his humming – her signal that he had reached the point in his routine where he oiled his hair – she knew she had just two or three minutes to have everything ready. With a wry smile, she got to her feet; if she was really fortunate, once he had things as he wanted them in Aldershot, he would install Audrey somewhere close by and forget that he had a wife at all.

The recognition triggered an idea. Grabbing the pile of handkerchiefs she'd set aside to pack, and with a quick glance towards the closed door of the bathroom, she stole back to her room. There, she spread out the starched linen squares, snatched her bottle of Joy perfume from her dressing table, and treated every one of them to a light misting of jasmine and rose. Granted, it was a criminal waste of good perfume, especially since she had no idea when she might be able to replace it. But picturing his irritation at being forcibly reminded of her every time he plucked a handkerchief from his pocket more than compensated for the profligacy.

Back in his dressing room, the handkerchiefs slipped in among his garments, she got to her feet.

'Done?' He dumped his shaving kit and wash bag in front of her.

'Done.'

As she watched him adjust his collar, she realized she never had managed to work out what Audrey found so irresistible about the man; she doubted it was his thinning hair and shiny forehead, the combination of which his mother insisted upon referring to as his 'noble brow'. Since the description implied honourable qualities, it could hardly have been less appropriate. She also thought it unlikely Audrey had fallen for his eyes, which, unlike those of heroes in novels, were less *dark soulful pools* and more *seething pits*. Of late, he was also starting to develop a paunch, which made her think that even Audrey wasn't brave enough to suggest he consider cutting down on the claret.

As she watched him survey his reflection in the cheval mirror, she wondered whether it was the sight of him in dress uniform that attracted the woman. It seemed unlikely; something so superficial couldn't possibly account for Audrey Deacon-Jones not only destroying her own marriage by pursuing an affair with him but also enduring the humiliation of being dragged through a public court hearing for adultery. Perhaps that was it – perhaps she thrived on humiliation. Hector certainly knew how to dish it out. And it did take all sorts to make the world go round.

'Two minutes to spare,' he announced over his shoulder as he stood fastening his wristwatch; having one day found a handwritten card inside its box, she knew it had been a gift from Audrey on their tenth 'anniversary'. When she handed him his hip flask and he stowed it in his pocket, he added, 'Rather late in the day to finally have come good.'

Feeling her fingers twitching at her side, she fought the urge to slap him. 'If you say so.'

'You know, had you given me offspring – sons, in particular – it might have worked out. You might have made the grade. You weren't unattractive, in your own girlish sort of way.'

It was only the ring of the telephone that prevented her from delivering an unwise retort.

Jaw clamped, she went to answer it.

'That was the doorman,' she returned to inform him. 'Your driver is outside.'

He checked his wristwatch. 'Precisely on time.'

When he lifted his bag, she handed him his suit carrier. 'Might I enquire when to expect your return?'

'In case it has somehow escaped your notice, woman, we're at war, which means that, even were I of a mind to tell you, I couldn't.'

He couldn't resist, could he? Even a perfectly civil enquiry brought sarcasm.

'But you'll be coming back, as the need arises.' Her concern, as she asked, was that, purely to spite her, he would tell his mother – by whose gift they occupied the mausoleum of an apartment in the first place – that he no longer had need of it; several times over the years, he'd threatened to put her into a rented bedsit. While she didn't think he'd go through with it – largely for fear his friends might think him a cad to treat such an apparently docile and compliant wife in such a degrading manner – it was a humiliation she couldn't risk. On occasion, she'd found herself wondering whether such a fate would actually be so awful – at least she would be away from him – but that was the other reason why he would never make good on the threat: to avoid giving her the grain or two of freedom and independence such a move would provide.

'I haven't yet decided,' he replied to her enquiry.

She regretted asking; his response was worded to give him the whip hand one final time, before his removal to Aldershot put her beyond daily reach.

'I see.' Part of her was tempted to add, *Well, that's all right because* I *haven't yet decided whether or not I shall stay.* As she knew to her cost, though, trying to sound clever was never wise. *Besides*, a tiny corner of her brain urged, *be patient: you are mere moments from having him belittle you no more.*

When he opened the apartment door and stepped out on to the landing, from force of habit, she went ahead of him to call the lift. As she pressed the button, from the bottom of the shaft came the clank of the mechanism rousing itself into life, the subsequent whirring as it ascended soberly towards them echoing around the otherwise silent marble stairwell.

'Oh, and by the way,' he said when the lift car arrived and he was sliding back the scissor gate to step inside, 'I've cancelled the daily. No sense paying staff to skivvy for a woman who spends all day doing nothing, is there?'

Practised in the art of concealing her emotions, she held her expression and watched as he latched the gate and stabbed a finger at the button marked 'G'. When the lift motor sent up a whine, and the car began its clunking descent to the ground floor, she continued to hold firm. Only when his sarcastic grin disappeared from view did she allow herself to turn and walk away. In truth, she couldn't give a hoot about the daily woman – she was more than capable of maintaining the upkeep of the place by herself. But no matter how desperately she longed to set him straight, she would bite back her frustration; no matter the depth of her pent-up rage, she hadn't let him see her cry in twenty years of marriage and wasn't about to start now, on the day he was being posted away.

Back in the apartment, she went to the drawing room window, where she pulled aside the curtain and stared down at the forecourt below. Standing to attention alongside a black motorcar was a corporal who, upon sighting his passenger, saluted, and then stepped forward to relieve him of his luggage and briefcase; in mere seconds, her bully of a husband had gone from giving orders to one subordinate to issuing them to the next, it never occurring to him to treat her any differently from anyone else he considered in some way his inferior.

Waiting until she'd seen his vehicle negotiate the exit on to the street, she turned away from the window and let out a dismayed sigh; at the precise moment she should have been dancing around the room, singing at the top of her voice in celebration, two decades of keeping her emotions in check prevented her, her loathsome husband sucking the joy from the occasion even after he'd left. But he wouldn't be doing it for much longer because she had a plan. And it was a plan that was going to completely change her life.

Yes, she thought, as she finally allowed herself a smile, what *she* knew, but Lieutenant Colonel Hector Maximus Alexander Thaxley did not, was that, if things later this morning proceeded as she was hoping, his parting salvo just now was the last she would ever have to bear.

2

Oh, what bliss. What pure, unadulterated bliss to feel so gloriously alone, to wallow in the bath for as long as she liked – even if it was in just the regulation five inches of water – with no one to complain about her rose-scented bath salts. *I told you to get rid of those God-awful things. I told you I can't bear the smell.* Had Hector not berated her every time she used them, then once her last lot had run out, she might not have spent an hour scouring Bond Street for more; but for his complaining, she would have been perfectly content pouring Epsom salts into her bath.

She stared up into the steam and inhaled deeply, unable to believe he was gone – and for what could be several weeks at a time, maybe even months, if she was lucky. Of course, at *some* stage he would be back, she mustn't forget that. But, until he was, she was free; for the moment at least, there would be no bracing herself for the slamming of the door; no creeping about for fear of unwittingly appearing in his line of sight and, for no reason other than that she wasn't Audrey, igniting his temper. There would be no watching him go out, only to be left unable to relax for wondering when he would be back. The thorn had been removed from her side, the pea of gravel from her shoe. To her incredulity and delight, the opportunity she

15

had thought would never come had dropped right into her lap. And she wasn't about to waste it.

The novelty of being able to relax in the bath eventually fading, she got out, dried herself and tried to decide what to wear. Most of her outfits were dull, verging on matronly, Hector maintaining that she shouldn't draw attention to herself with flounces and prints.

'You're too plain to carry it off,' he had remarked of a floaty lawn frock with pale pink roses on a soft green background that she'd bought last summer, intending to wear it to the wedding of his godson. 'Take it back and change it for something more befitting – something in beige. Or grey.'

She hadn't taken it back. But she had obeyed the spirit of his instruction in so much as, on the day in question, she had worn her serviceable navy-blue two-piece and matching hat. Later today, though, if all went well, she would have the perfect reason to wear the delightful garment. Mid-thought, she swung about and went to the window. Peering up at the sky, she noted the lightest film of hazy cloud veiling an otherwise unbroken spread of blue. She pushed open the casement; already, the air felt too warm for autumn – dare she hope they were in for an Indian summer? A week or two of fine golden days would be lovely. Either way, later on, she would wear the lawn frock. And she would be anything but plain.

Until then, though, she would pull on her burgundy pleated skirt – another garment Hector could never abide, deriding the sunray pleats as frivolous – and her cream-coloured sweater with the openwork around the neckline. She would make herself some toast, brew some of Hector's expensive coffee – coffee that, in his presence, she purported not to like but drank when he wasn't there, and which she would now miss his having delivered. When she'd asked him recently if he thought the government would add coffee to the list of rationed foodstuffs, as they had recently done with tea, his reply had been *not if I can help it*. As though *he* had any sway over the Ministry of Food.

In the kitchen, she toasted two slices of bread, spread them thinly with margarine and then, to disguise the taste of it, covered them with gooseberry jam, two jars of which she had been given by an elderly neighbour with family in the countryside. Marge really was no substitute for butter, no matter how hard government posters tried to convince people otherwise.

In the bathroom, which was still steamy and fragrant from her bath, she wiped a hand across the mirror and examined her reflection. Her hair was badly in need of a set; had she known earlier in the week that Hector would be leaving, she would have made an appointment for this morning to have it done. She supposed it was possible Kitty might be able to pop round and see to it. She would check with her later. In the meantime, since she was only going as far as the telephone box on the corner, she would make do with quickly combing it back into place.

That done, she scooped up her handbag, let herself out of the apartment and cantered down the four flights of stairs, it usually proving quicker than waiting for the lift.

'Morning, Mrs Thaxley.'

'Good morning, John,' she greeted Wilson, the liveried doorman.

'Major Thaxley been posted off somewhere, has he?'

Despite her eagerness to reach the telephone box, Isabel slowed her pace. 'Now, John, you know very well I'm not at liberty to disclose that. Although I don't suppose the major would mind me letting slip that he's been made up to lieutenant colonel.'

Wilson straightened himself up. 'Has he now. Do you know, when I saw that motor pull up, and the serious look on the major's face as he got in, I said to myself, John, that man's being sent somewhere important. You see if you're not right.'

Isabel turned on a charming smile. 'No flies on you, John.'

'I like to think not, Mrs Thaxley.'

'Just off to see to something. I'll only be gone a moment or two.'

'Right you are, Mrs Thaxley.'

Exiting the grounds of Warbone Gate on to Cabendon Street, Isabel took the shortcut through to Palace Street, on the corner of which stood a pair of telephone boxes. Slipping into the first of them, she put her handbag on the shelf, plucked from her purse a couple of coins, lifted the receiver to listen for the dialling tone and fed her money into the slot.

At the other end, the telephone was answered by a voice she had come to know well. She pressed button 'A' and waited while her coins chinked down through the mechanism.

'Good morning, Alphonse. This is Isabel. Forgive me for troubling you this early but would it be possible to speak to Vincent?'

When Alphonse confirmed that it was no trouble, Isabel pictured the old man placing the receiver on the counter before going through to the back. She'd never telephoned Vincent at the bistro before – had to hope, somewhat belatedly, he wouldn't mind the interruption while he was at work – but she couldn't wait to tell him her news. After five or six months of arranging clandestine meetings, they might be on the verge of having their dream of her escaping her husband become a reality; thanks to Hector being given his marching orders, she and Vincent might finally be together – not married, of course; in that regard, Hector would forever remain an obstacle, the respectability that came with a new wedding ring denied her. But, with Vincent already planning to help her go into hiding, they could at least be together. And in the longer term, who knew how circumstances might change?

'*Chérie*, what a lovely surprise.'

Hearing Vincent's voice, she pressed the receiver closer to her ear and dived straight in. 'I'm calling with news.'

'Yes?'

Aware of all that hinged on what happened next, she didn't allow herself time for second thoughts. 'Hector has been posted away. Aldershot. He's been made up to lieutenant colonel of a battalion there. He left early this morning.'

'Does this mean you are free to come to the bistro for lunch?'

In the stuffy little telephone box, Isabel pictured delight softening Vincent's expression but, mindful not to sound like a schoolgirl excited by her first crush, she paused before replying; with Hector gone, there was no urgency.

'I am, yes. Although perhaps not too early. I want to get my hair done.'

'Very well. I am not free until after two o'clock because the bistro has a booking at midday for a wedding breakfast. But can you be here after that? Perhaps . . . two thirty?'

'Two thirty will be perfect.'

'Then I will see you later.'

'Yes, you will.'

In the grubby little telephone kiosk, Isabel gave herself a hug. When she'd woken up this morning, she'd had no inkling the day ahead of her would turn out to be different to any other – even less so when Hector had come storming in. Now, however, not only was today going to be joyous, but her entire life might soon be more wonderful than she'd thought possible.

'I hope you have a little room for dessert.'

Isabel sighed. 'Even if I had, I should really decline.'

Reaching across the table, Vincent took hold of her hand and grasped it tightly. 'Isabel, *chérie*, have you forgotten we agreed just now that your days of saying *should* are almost over?'

Slowly, Isabel shook her head. 'I haven't forgotten, no.'

'The moment you are away from your husband for good, then as long as you are careful, you will be free to live as you please. I know it is not perfect – not as either of us would wish. I know we would both rather it was . . . *official*. But at least *you* will be free, and *we* will be together.'

'I know. And that by itself feels like a miracle.'

While 'miracle' might indeed describe this morning's turn of events, for Isabel, it was already becoming clear that old habits were going to be hard to break; a lifetime of conditioning – first by her mother, and then by Hector – didn't feel like something she could simply shake off. Even the freedom to make small changes felt momentous, her arrival there this afternoon a case in point. For the first time ever, she had walked straight up to the restaurant, gone purposefully in through the door and submitted to the warmest of embraces, not only from Vincent but also from his grandfather, Alphonse. Before this morning, she would have lingered a few doors along the street, checking several times in all directions before sidling up and slipping quietly inside. She would still have been checking over her shoulder when Vincent came through from the back to greet her.

As arranged earlier, Isabel was having lunch with Vincent at Bistro Durand, the restaurant and its adjacent patisserie opened by Alphonse when he'd arrived in England after fleeing the German advance on Paris in the September of 1914. The first time Vincent had invited her there, she had been astonished by how quickly she'd felt at home, her ability to converse with Alphonse in French – albeit in embarrassingly rusty fashion – only adding to the warmth with which she was subsequently welcomed back.

Where Vincent was concerned, she had taken great pains to be honest – had made it plain from the outset that she was married. Alphonse, however, clearly looking forward to the day when he might become a great-grandfather, they had decided to keep in the dark. It was a regrettable state of affairs that had come to weigh on her more heavily as time had gone on.

'So, from today,' Vincent said, leading her to realize she had been miles away, 'when you are offered dessert, your only concern should be which one you would like first –'

'*First?*'

'– and then to imagine how you will devour every morsel as though it is the last one you will ever taste.'

'Truly,' Isabel said, 'wonderful though Mireille's pastries are, at this precise moment, I would be unable to do it justice.'

Still holding her hand, Vincent grinned. 'Then later, yes?'

Unable to disguise a smile, Isabel conceded. 'All right. Ask me again later.'

'Better still,' Vincent said, letting go of her hand and getting to his feet. 'Let us make a picnic. It is such a warm afternoon, we should stroll to the park to sit on a blanket and take afternoon tea.'

The idea sounding delightfully normal, Isabel laughed. Today, as long as they were discreet and didn't attract attention, she was free to do with him what couples everywhere did on sunny afternoons. 'I should like that.'

When Vincent crossed to the display of desserts, she followed him with her eyes. It was wonderful to feel so at ease; to no longer have her shoulders knotted with tension, her brow furrowed, her lips pressed together in a straight line. This afternoon, she felt tranquil, content and at least ten years younger, although that last sensation might have more to do with the fact that she was wearing the lawn frock – the one she'd bought because, the moment she'd tried it on, she'd been astonished by how feminine and attractive it made her feel.

She was also hopeful. From now on, she had no need to scurry back to the apartment by five thirty in case Hector came straight home from work; as a rule, he rarely did – just sufficiently frequently that she could never take the chance of not being there for fear of getting caught out. And that, of course, was why he did it. For twenty years, he'd had her on an invisible lead, one he need only twitch and she would appear at his side and await his command. *To do as you're told*, he was quick to point out if she ever had the temerity to complain, *is your sole purpose on this earth.*

While her thoughts were elsewhere, Vincent had reappeared with a rug and a small wicker basket in which she could see one of the patisserie's distinctive white boxes, tied with lilac ribbon, and a bottle wrapped in a linen cloth.

'Come,' he said. 'We will go along Queen Anne's Gate, across Birdcage Walk and into the park that way. We will find ourselves somewhere to put the blanket – somewhere overlooking the lake. But not too close to the bridge – it will be busy with servicemen asking passers-by to take photographs of them with their sweethearts.'

He wasn't wrong; at weekends, the park quickly became crowded. 'Here,' she said, 'let me carry the rug.' Accepting it from him, she tucked it under her arm. 'And let's not go too close to Horse Guards, either.'

'Agreed. This end of the park is much nicer.'

'I was remembering,' she said, once they had negotiated the gate into the park and were trying to pick their way through the throng of couples and families, all seemingly drawn to St James's Park to enjoy the lovely weather. The majority of the men, she noted, were in uniform, on their arms young girls done up to the nines. In most cases, she was old enough to be their mother.

'Remembering what?' he asked. 'Here, let us go this way. There are not so many people.'

Her hand in his, she followed closely behind him. 'The afternoon we met.'

He squeezed her fingers. 'It was March . . . no, it was April. You were the other side of the lake.' With his head, he gestured across the park. 'It was a windy day. You were watching the pelicans. I had seen you there before.'

She turned to regard him. 'You'd been watching me?'

His expression changed to one of consideration. 'Not watching you but watching *for* you. You did not come every day.'

'I didn't.'

'Look, there is a space over there. What do you think?'

She followed the line of his finger to a few square yards of unoccupied grass. 'Just right.' Her mind still on the discovery that he had been looking out for her, she said, 'So, you had seen me there before.'

'I noticed you because you looked . . . sad. No, not sad. Lonely.' He put down the basket and held out his hand for the rug. 'This is all right here?'

Looking about at the grass, splashed yellow and white with daisies, she nodded. 'This is perfect.'

Once settled upon the blanket, she eased off her shoes. Who would have thought something as simple as sitting in the park on a sunny September afternoon could bring such pleasure? Even as she was thinking it, though, she knew her contentment owed little to the park and the weather and rather more to the company. Without this serene and tender man, into whose orbit she had so unexpectedly fallen, she wouldn't be there. Back in the spring, she'd spent dozens of afternoons on that bench, trying to decide whether defying Hector and joining one of the voluntary organizations appealing for help would be enough to stop her from going quietly mad, or whether the better answer lay in more drastic action, such as finding a way to leave him altogether. The former, she had come to conclude, would amount to nothing more than pressing a sticking plaster over a gaping wound; the latter, akin to amputating the entire limb.

Beside her, Vincent reclined, legs outstretched, his weight supported by his elbows, his eyes directed across the lake. While he was thus occupied, she studied his profile. From the moment he'd caught her eye, she'd suspected he wasn't English. There was something about him that said 'other': his chestnut hair and its tendency to curl, untamed; his eyelashes – longer than she had seen on a man before and drawing attention to his eyes in a manner that would make most women green with envy; his lean physique, his proportions those she imagined couturiers picturing when designing an outfit. And where most Englishmen's complexions tended towards pallor, Vincent's always suggested health and vitality.

'I think I shall open the wine. We must drink it before it grows too warm.'

Tucking her feet beneath the skirt of her dress, she leaned towards him in disbelief. 'You brought wine?'

'The only civilized accompaniment to sweet pastry.'

'I thought pastries were accompanied by coffee?'

'Coffee is for morning pastries. For afternoon pastries, I say we have wine.' He proffered the bottle so that she might inspect the label. 'Are we not worth it?'

'Loupiac,' she read aloud. 'I don't know it.'

When he eased out the cork, it left the bottle with a pleasing *cloop*.

'Few people outside of France know of it. It comes from a small wine-growing area on the northern bank of the Garonne. The other sweet white wine from the area is Barsac. Please, hold the glasses for me.' Reaching into the basket, Isabel complied and watched as he filled them halfway. 'Of course, the chances of getting more wines from France now – let alone white dessert wines from Bordeaux – are nil. Before much longer, our stocks will be gone. Those of our wine merchant, too.' He raised his glass. '*Santé.*'

She acknowledged the toast. '*Santé.*'

The sip she took filled her mouth with a riot of summer – peaches, marmalade, almonds, honey – tastes that transported her back to her year spent finishing in Lausanne; in particular, to her final glorious month, when she'd teetered on the verge of succumbing to the charms of a different young Frenchman. The taste was sweet and full and luscious. She loved it.

'Now,' Vincent broke into her thoughts to announce, 'I have brought a single slice —' He turned back to the basket.

'Of?'

'Of Paris-Brest, of course. Is it no longer your favourite?'

Isabel laughed out loud. 'Only a Frenchman could think it a good idea to carry a slice of delicate dessert, filled with cream —'

'Mousseline.'

'I do beg your pardon — filled with *mousseline* — to a picnic on an unexpectedly warm English afternoon.'

When he pulled on one end of the lilac ribbon securing the pastry box and it unravelled, he tugged it clear. 'Hold out your wrist.'

She frowned. 'Which one?'

'Let me see —' she offered both wrists — 'you do not wear a wristwatch.'

'Only when I need to be on time for an appointment.'

'Your right wrist, then —' she withdrew her left hand — 'in case our assignations in the future require that you be punctual.'

When his fingers brushed the soft skin on the underside of her wrist, she almost snatched back her hand. If he noticed — and she was certain he couldn't have failed to — he simply continued winding the band of lilac satin around her wrist until the remaining ends were the right length to tie into a bow.

'It's such a pretty colour,' she said, her voice barely a whisper.

'My mother chose it for the patisserie because it is the

colour of renewal. For her, coming to England was a new beginning.'

'Then it shall serve to remind me of my own fresh start.'

With a light sigh, she turned her attention to the patisserie box and the portion of Paris-Brest nestled inside. It looked far too large for just the two of them.

'It is large,' Vincent explained when she remarked as much, 'because we are going to eat it together.' Leaning across to place a napkin in her lap, he selected a fork and sliced it sideways down through the top of the pastry. 'Now. Open your mouth.'

'No, seriously,' she protested with a shake of her head. 'That's far too much.'

'*Pardonne-moi.*' Returning the pastry to the box, he halved the amount and offered it up. 'Better?'

She stopped shaking her head. 'Far more suit—' When the filling started to dissolve on her tongue, she groaned with delight. 'This is wonderful,' she said once she'd swallowed the last of it.

With his own mouth full, Vincent gestured with a wave of the fork. 'The flavour of hazelnut is one I adore.'

'Me, too. Along with almond.'

'Ask most Frenchmen,' Vincent went on, momentarily setting the fork back in the box, 'and they will tell you it is impossible to get good Paris-Brest outside of Brittany – that only a Breton can make the perfect choux. But I disagree. After all, the secret is not just in the pastry but in the filling. The taste you should experience first, and the one that should also linger with you at the end, must come from the mousseline – the flavour of hazelnut and almond. When made correctly, it is sublime.'

'Utterly.' She loved the way Vincent spoke of the things he enjoyed, but especially the way he expressed his passion for flavours – for food in general. She had never known anyone wax in such heartfelt fashion about humble ingredients. In fact, she'd never come across anyone in England who talked about food with anything close to his enthusiasm.

'Of course,' he picked up the fork again, scooping more of the dessert on to it and offering it in her direction. 'We do not know for how much longer we will be able to make such things . . .'

Unable to respond with her mouth full, Isabel frowned.

'It is true that, for the moment, we have supplies of eggs, cream, butter . . . but I do not believe that will continue. And nor should it. If ordinary foods are rationed, it does not seem right that the wealthy should continue to buy and consume whatever they like.'

Finishing her mouthful, Isabel took a sip of her wine. Vincent had been right to say that it would quickly grow warm. Even in the shade of the tree, the air was balmy.

'So, what will you do – when you can no longer make pastries?'

'If we can, we will bake loaves and rolls. If not, Papi will close the patisserie to save the restaurant, and we will offer meals that are simple and homely. Even without the scarcity of the ingredients, it is likely we will lose Yves and Alexandre soon anyway. Waiters and kitchen hands are not exempt from call-up. And both are itching to serve.'

Isabel nodded. She could understand two young Frenchmen being desperate to fight for their homeland. 'I suppose so.'

'Do you know that I applied to join the army?'

His disclosure left her reeling. 'I . . . didn't. No.'

'They turned me away. It was my own fault. On the application, I wrote that my occupation was a baker. And to be a baker is to be in a reserved occupation. "Go back to your business, Mr Durand," the officer said. "Feed the people." On my way home, I realized I should have written "waiter" or "restaurateur". But if I had –' he sent her a mischievous grin – 'I would not have met you . . .'

Into Isabel's mind shot the expression *close shave*.

'So, for now at least, I am an ARP warden.'

'ARP wardens are vital. At least, they will be if the Germans start bombing us in earnest, as most people expect them to.'

'In France –' leaning towards her, he lowered his voice – 'I have two cousins in the *Résistance*. The Durands have a long history of rising to our country's defence. In the last war, my father was a member. At times, I cannot help but feel I should be there to join them.'

Recalling him once telling her that, in the last war, his father had been caught and executed by the Germans, she tried to think how to move away from the subject without appearing disrespectful. To that end, she asked, 'Do you remember much of France? You must have been young when you left to come here.'

For a moment, he didn't reply. Then he said, 'I remember school. I had a friend there, Jean-Fernand, and he had a dog he called Coquin.' Seeing her puzzlement, he explained, 'It means something like scamp or rascal.'

'Ah.'

'It was a good name for him. But anyway,' he said. 'No more talk of France. Let us talk about *you*.' When he pulled her towards him, she rested her head against his shoulder. 'Last week, when I told you I was trying to find somewhere you might stay if you could find a way to leave your husband, you said you would pack a suitcase – to be ready should the chance arise when you were not expecting it. Did you do that?'

'I did. I filled it with as many clothes as I could fit into it. Mainly for wintertime but a few garments for summer, as well. Then, while Hector was at work one day, I followed your advice and took it to left luggage.' She remembered how good it had felt to finally be shaping her own destiny; when Vincent had first mentioned finding somewhere for her to stay, she'd worried that the chance to flee might come about in a rush – perhaps under cover of darkness one night when Hector was with the Deacon-Jones woman – leaving her little chance to prepare. Now, though, with him posted away, she could take her time, ensure she covered her tracks.

'And your husband,' Vincent continued, 'if he comes back in the next few days, he will not notice these things are missing?'

'It would no more occur to him to look in my wardrobe than it would to clean the bath or take the rubbish to the chute.'

'Good. If there is anything else you would not wish

to be without – important papers, family jewels – bring them to me and I will place them in our strongbox for safekeeping.'

In her surprise, she pulled away and studied his expression. 'So, your plan for me to leave Hector is almost ready?'

'Almost. There are many important things to consider. Once you leave him, you must go far away from St James's.'

To Isabel, that made sense: many of Hector's acquaintances lived close by. And once she'd finally left, she couldn't afford to be spotted by any of them – let alone be seen with Vincent.

'From what you have told me, once you are gone, your husband will search for you –'

'He will. He'll be incensed.'

'– alert friends to your disappearance, appeal to them to look out for you.'

'Almost certainly.' Yes, swept along by the news that Vincent was almost ready for them to be together, she had overlooked just how much her life would need to change – the extent of the precautions necessary to prevent her from being found.

'You will remember, perhaps, I mentioned that my cousin, Jean-Pascal, has a restaurant, too?'

'I remember, yes.'

'It is in a small street, some distance from here. Jean-Pascal is older than me and trying to find a way to get back to fight in France. Even if he does, his family will remain here, at his restaurant. But in his building there are rooms they do not use. My idea is to see whether he would agree to let you stay there, at least until –' He shot to his feet.

Around them, other people were doing the same. On the air was a low thrum.

'What is it?' When he tugged on her hand, she scrambled to get up. 'What's going on?'

'It is an air raid. Quickly.'

Thinking he was directing her to gather up the picnic things, she bent down, knocking over her glass as she did so and rueing the loss of her wine.

'Then why is there no –'

Multiple air raid sirens wound up their wails.

'Leave it. Leave it all. Come on.' With one hand he gathered the blanket; with the other, he scooped up her handbag, thrust it into her arms and then, grabbing her free wrist, began to run, pulling her after him. 'The shelters in the park will fill up. I will take you to one near the restaurant. Businesses in that street are closed at the weekend. You will be fine.'

When they reached Birdcage Walk, he darted straight across.

'What about you?'

'I am ARP. I must report to my command post.'

'Yes . . .' she replied, already panting from running. 'But you're not . . . on duty.'

'No matter. They will need all hands.'

'Couldn't I go home? It's only just across the park. The basement has a proper shelter.'

'No, look, we are almost there.'

Her throat tightening with fear, she had to force a swallow. 'But –'

'Quick. Down here.' Along the side of a grey stone building, on a street corner she was struggling to recognize, a door stood wedged open by a chair. Painted on the wall above were the words 'Public Shelter' and, beneath that, a black arrow pointing downwards. 'Take the blanket. You will need it later to keep warm.'

Past them dashed two young women who looked to be in their twenties.

'How long do you think –'

'I do not know. Stay here until the all-clear. Then return to the restaurant. I will be there as soon as I can. Tell me you understand.'

She'd never known him be so insistent. 'I understand.'

'Good. Now, go inside. I must report for duty, to see where I am needed.'

Suddenly, she had the urge to tell him something she'd so far kept to herself.

'Vincent, I love you.'

'Isabel, *je t'aime, moi aussi.*'

With that, he darted back around the corner. She was on her own. And how she was going to last until the all-clear sounded, without knowing whether he was safe, she hadn't a clue.

3

Isabel pulled the rug more tightly about her shoulders. It was fortunate Vincent had pressed it upon her because the basement air raid shelter was cavernous and, after the warmth of the afternoon outside, distinctly chilly. Even the folding wooden chair upon which she was sitting struck cold through the thin fabric of her dress.

The speed with which she had lost track of time since descending the stairs from the street was unsettling. If pushed to guess, she would say she had been there about an hour. For most of that time, the world beyond the four walls of the shelter had been largely quiet. In fact, since the warden had closed the door on the outside world, she hadn't heard a single aircraft. Perhaps this would turn out to be nothing more than another of those 'nuisance raids' that had been blighting the East End this last week. Either that, or the bank of aircraft they'd seen had only been after the docks and now, their mission complete, they'd gone home. *Home in time for tea.* Sometimes, the business of war felt utterly deranged.

For want of anything better to do, she took to eaves-dropping on the two young women sitting nearby. They appeared to be dressed for an evening out.

'There are *some* gentlemen out there,' one of them said to the other. 'They're not *all* only after a quick bunk-up

35

round the back of the King's Head. It's just that sorting the decent ones from the rotters can't half be tricky.'

Isabel smiled. The young woman was right; not *all* men were only after one thing, Vincent being a case in point. Although, what did *she* know about men? Married to Hector in the same week she'd turned twenty – and without what might even pass for a courtship beforehand – she hardly qualified as an expert. From the moment she'd met Vincent, though, she'd known he had none of Hector's tyrannical traits; in fact, he'd been nothing but patient and kind, and respectful of the fact that she had a husband, and that their home was not somewhere they could 'be together', even though being with him was something she had begun to crave more than she would have thought possible. Still, once she left Warbone Gate, Hector would have no idea where she was; Vincent had said he would make sure of it. Not long now and she would have a fresh start. *They* would have *their* fresh start.

When she looked back up from her musings, it was to see that one of the girls was filing a fingernail and grumbling about the light. The atmosphere in the shelter was certainly depressing. As places to wait out an air raid went, it did nothing to bolster spirits or inspire optimism.

By now dreadfully uncomfortable on her wooden chair, she got to her feet and cast her eyes about the room. Vincent had been right to say the shelter wouldn't be busy; apart from herself, she counted just a dozen other souls.

To stretch her legs, she walked the few yards to the foot of the steps leading up to the street and then turned back. Twice more, she did the same. Then, as she was about to sit back down, a noise like the tremendous rushing of air culminated in an explosion of such force that the ground shook beneath her and plaster from the ceiling fell in lumps to the floor. Overhead, the light bulbs flickered. Heart hammering, she stumbled to a nearby pillar and pressed herself against it. Almost immediately, there was a second blast, followed by a third but more muted *crump*. Clearly, she had been naive to think the Luftwaffe done, but with St James's having so far escaped previous raids, what did she know?

'That were close,' an old man sitting in the corner announced. Until then, he appeared to have been asleep. 'Stick of four, I shouldn't wonder. Means there'll be another one somewhere that hasn't gone off. Least, not yet.'

His announcement did nothing to help.

'What do they want with bombing 'round here?' the young woman with the nail file looked up to ask. Beneath the flickering light, her face had a grey-tinged hue.

At that moment, another of the ceiling bulbs went out altogether. In the even murkier light, she sent the young woman a shrug. 'I don't know. I wouldn't have thought there was anything in St James's of interest to bombers. Perhaps one of them strayed off course.'

'Buckingham Palace,' the old man piped up. 'That's what he'll have been after. Something of a triumph to hit that.'

'Bomb our king?' The girl's expression was a mixture of horror and disgust. 'They wouldn't ruddy dare.'

Isabel wished she shared the young woman's conviction.

But the old man was right: laying waste to Buckingham Palace would be a major coup. Not only would the audacity of such a strike dent the nation's morale but, having pulled it off, the Germans would believe they could get away with anything. Their tails would really be up.

'I'm sure the King will be safe.' There was no need to alarm the poor girl in the same way that she, herself, had recently been terrified by Hector.

'If Germany decides to launch an all-out raid on the capital,' her husband had come home one day last week to announce, 'current estimates for the first twenty-four hours are that sixty thousand will be killed. And if Göring can find the capacity to keep up attacks for weeks on end, the number of dead could run into millions, and that's without counting the seriously wounded. Take a couple of hospitals out of action and most of the injured would quickly become fatalities anyway.' When she'd looked at him, her expression one of shock, he'd laughed. 'Yes. You absolutely should turn pale – even more so when I tell you how the government is preparing the authorities to deal with such an eventuality.'

'And how is that?' she recalled asking him. She really should have known better.

'How? By instructing officials to identify sites to dump the dead in vast lime pits. There simply won't be sufficient timber for the number of coffins. There aren't even the men to bury that number of dead, let alone the space for the graves. All is not lost, however. You'll be comforted to know that the government's preparations include making sure a million burial forms will be available.'

Sarcasm, she had long since learned, was stamped through Hector like the word 'Hastings' through a stick of rock. That he'd told her at all had been not solely to frighten her but to demonstrate how powerful and 'in the know' he was. Most husbands in his position would shelter their wives from bad news – and, yes, it could be argued that, in its own way, that was just as bad – but Hector positively delighted in filling her with terror. He'd always had a callous streak, and a pompous one as well, but since being seconded to Whitehall, he'd become thoroughly evil, coming to take even greater delight in feeding her fears. In a way, now that the raids he'd threatened had begun, she wished she'd paid more attention because she might have been better prepared for whatever was coming next.

Seeing no value in tormenting herself with the hypothetical, and at the same time desperate to stop thinking about Hector, she looked about the shelter for a clock. Unable to see one, she rued not wearing her wristwatch. Not that it mattered; they would be there for as long as remained necessary. She wasn't even sure what time the sirens had gone off. Shortly after five, perhaps?

From there on, it became steadily more difficult to gauge the passing of the hours, the shelter quiet apart from the soft snoring of the old man in the far corner who, despite the uncomfortable little chairs, had somehow managed to fall asleep. The stillness around her grew so deathly that when the raiders returned sometime later, the cacophony of activity seemed all the more vivid: the thrum of aircraft engines; the boom of the anti-aircraft guns in Hyde Park; the thunder and rumble of distant explosions, sometimes for minutes on end without respite – sounds that made her sit permanently braced against another near miss.

Trying not to picture what might be happening above ground, she prayed Vincent was out of harm's way. While she had no desire for him to lie low like a coward, she would prefer he didn't take unnecessary risks.

Fingering the lilac ribbon around her wrist, she distracted herself by wondering about the location of his cousin's restaurant – the place he had suggested she might be able to stay. No doubt her new life with Vincent would be a simple one but, with him by her side, she would happily live anywhere; picturing their future together was the one thing keeping her going.

The other thing she was looking forward to was having friends; through the patisserie and the bistro, Vincent seemed to know dozens of people. And his family had welcomed her with open arms. His mother, Mireille, had been less effusive than his grandfather, which struck her as perfectly understandable; there could hardly be a mother on earth who wasn't protective of her son. Vincent attributed his mother's reticence to the fact that she struggled to express herself very well in English. Perhaps, Isabel thought, she could help her to become more proficient. Not straight away, of course; that would be presumptuous. But, once she and Vincent had shown everyone how committed they were to one another, all manner of things might become possible. She wasn't blind; she knew full well they couldn't marry, and that the only avenue open to them was what most people considered *living in sin*.

In her exhaustion, she exhaled heavily. Despite the nature of her marriage to Hector, until she'd met Vincent, she'd never been able to actually envisage leaving him. She'd certainly never expected to become one of those scandalous women who, out of the blue one day, simply upped and left, never to be seen again; how often had she overheard someone besmirch the character of a runaway wife by branding her *no better than she should be* – in other words, deserving of everything she had coming to her. She also didn't need it pointed out to her that the future she and Vincent were planning was being built upon rather precarious foundations – that, when it came to pitfalls or things going against them, they ran all manner of risks. But if the reward for taking those chances was a life with Vincent – in any way, shape or form – then having to spend it quietly, in the shadows, was a price she was more than willing to pay.

Her impatience to be back with Vincent now mounting, she glanced about. Against one of the walls stood a long wooden form. Since the raid appeared to have moved further away, she might see if she could get comfortable enough upon it to close her eyes. Even if she only napped for half an hour, she might get a second wind for when they were released.

Crossing to the bench, she took the rug from her shoulders and draped it in a double layer on the form's wooden top. Then she lowered herself on to it, scrabbled about for the free end of the rug and pulled it over her body. The resulting discomfort was acute, the bench unforgiving against shoulders, hips and knees. She closed her eyes anyway and hoped to sleep but, with her head resting upon the hard surface, the distant droning of aircraft seemed merely amplified. All she could do, she concluded in worn-out fashion, was try to put everything out of her mind – and pray for exhaustion to do the rest.

Was that a siren? Unable to work out where she was, Isabel opened her eyes and tried lifting her head to look about – only to find her neck so badly cricked she could scarcely move.

'Hey, miss?' She squinted at the figure bending over her. It was a young woman. 'Miss, that's the all-clear. We can go home.'

Of course. She was in the air raid shelter. 'Right . . .'

The woman held out a hand. 'Here. Let's help you up.'

With unbelievable difficulty, Isabel manoeuvred upright. 'Thank you,' she said, reaching to rub the back of her neck. 'I don't suppose you know what time it is?'

'The man over there said it's a little after six.'

'Six. Thank you.'

'You had a good sleep.'

'Good' wasn't the word she would use for it; at that precise moment she felt as though she'd fallen under a steamroller. 'I must have done, yes.'

'Got far to go?'

She shook her head. 'Not far, no.'

'Well, you be careful.'

'You, too.'

Having struggled to her feet, Isabel pulled the rug from the bench, folded it in half to form a triangle and draped it about her shoulders in the manner of a shawl. Next time she went out with Vincent, no matter how warm it was, she would take a cardigan or jacket and make sure to put a few essentials in her handbag – such as a comb and her powder compact. Hopefully, she would never spend an entire night in a shelter ever again; hopefully, having come over and dropped a few bombs, Hitler would think he'd made his point and decide that coming back for another go carried too great a risk. If they *were* destined to suffer more raids, she would like to think that, by then, she and Vincent would be settled somewhere with a shelter of their own – one she would already have made comfortable for them with pillows and an eider-down. Maybe she should get herself one of those siren suits, as well. Or, at the very least, since she wouldn't have to worry about Hector's disapproval, a pair or two of slacks.

In the meantime, she thought, as she made her way up the steps to the street, unless Vincent was already out there waiting for her, she would pop home, freshen up and change out of her crumpled dress. Once clean and tidy, she would go to Bistro Durand and wait, with a lovely reviving coffee, for Vincent to return and tell her more about the plans he was making for their new life together.

4

After such a desperately uncomfortable night, she'd been counting on some fresh air to clear her head. But, as Isabel trudged up the stairs from the shelter and stepped on to the pavement, she was greeted by smoke so thick it made her eyes water, and a stench so foul it turned her empty stomach.

A couple of yards from the exit, she paused in alarm to fan a hand in front of her face and glance about. Until yesterday evening, the Luftwaffe's attacks had amounted to little more than 'nuisance raids' – the odd railway bridge destroyed, a gasometer set ablaze, a few craters disfiguring a park – the resulting casualties minimal. This morning, however, the smokiness of the air suggested that, while the buildings in the immediate vicinity might *seem* undamaged, somewhere close by must have taken a direct hit, the power of those first explosions surely responsible for fatalities.

The recognition that she might only have been spared by the narrowest of margins – when others wouldn't have been so fortunate – engulfed her in a wave of guilt. To make matters worse, with Vincent apparently not there, waiting for her, she was beginning to feel concerned for his safety. But she mustn't succumb to fear; rather than torture herself by imagining the myriad reasons why he hadn't been able to get there yet, she would choose instead to picture him helping the injured from ruined buildings, and remind herself that, unlike some this morning, she had the luxury not just of being safe but of being able to return to home. In fact, since it could be a while before Vincent came off duty, she would take the chance to pop back there now and freshen up.

Imagining Vincent eventually returning, tired and ravenous for something to eat, she allowed herself a smile. But, as she stepped from the kerb to cross the deserted street, a glimpse of something away to her right made her turn sharply; in the distance, a wall of khaki-brown smoke towered so high that even the tallest buildings looked like toy models. Clearly, the worst of last night's attacks must have been around the Isle of Dogs.

'Take it from me,' she recalled Hector taunting. 'In terms of an attack on London, it is now very much a case of *when* as opposed to *if*. The moment Göring is done with the airfields in Sussex and Kent, he'll go after the wharves and the factories of the East End. And trust me, when he does, he won't stop until everything below Tower Bridge has gone up in smoke – warehouses, docks, vessels, depots crammed with our supplies of everything from timber and rubber to sugar and soap.'

Was this it, then? Had Hector's nightmarish prophecy come true? While it galled her to admit he could so accurately have foreseen such a thing, it seemed now that he had. No wonder the air smelled foul – all those goods, burning out of control.

Unease deepening, she forced her feet across the road

and on towards Cabendon Street. Those few bombs that had fallen on St James's had been frightening enough but it now seemed that, this morning, as little as five or six stops away on the underground – barely two miles from St James's, where that pillar of smoke was still billowing upwards – entire communities would be coming up from shelters to find their homes destroyed, their sole remaining possessions just the clothes on their backs. Their plight made the luxury of being able to return home for a bath feel obscene. But what could she do? As she'd been reflecting on that park bench, on the afternoon she'd first met Vincent, when it came to an emergency, she was of no use to anyone. Dolefully, she continued on her way. What was the point of nations' rulers proclaiming the Great War as *the war to end all wars* if, little more than two decades on – barely a generation later – wasted lives and suffering were once more the order of the day? Did the world's leaders really have such short memories? Well, for the moment, she would try not to dwell on the matter. But, later, with Hector no longer there to stand in her way, she would give proper thought to joining one of the voluntary organizations always appealing for help. In fact, with Vincent being a member of the ARP and presumably well placed to understand what they all did, she would ask him which of them might put her to best use.

With an exhausted sigh, she rounded the corner on to Cabendon Street. Yes, she would explain to him what she had in mind to do, and then –

She teetered to a halt.

What on earth . . . ?

Grasping the railing for support, she glanced up to the street sign. No, she wasn't in the wrong place: this *was* Cabendon Street — meaning that over there ought to be Warbone Gate. All of it. But where the central wing should be — five storeys of people's homes, her own included — was just a mound of rubble and a clear view straight through to the street beyond. The wings to either side were still standing but, with every pane of glass blown out, drawing rooms, bedrooms and kitchens gaped wide, their inhabitants' furnishings crudely exposed. Of her own home, on the fourth floor of the main wing, there was nothing to suggest it had ever been there.

Her insides knotting, she crouched low and clung even more tightly to the railing, a wave of nausea flashing upwards from her stomach to leave her feeling hot and faint. But for her illicit picnic with Vincent, she would have been at home in her bed, the wail of the siren sending her scurrying to the basement along with whichever of her neighbours had been home at the time. Last year, the building's owner had installed props and reinforcements to make the unused space into a proper shelter, but would that have been enough? Upon hearing the bomb, whistling down towards her, doubtless she would have frozen, rigid with fear. But would she now be lying trapped and injured beneath the rubble, or would the explosion have claimed her life so quickly that she wouldn't have known what was happening? It was a question she would rather not dwell on.

Raising herself gingerly back up to standing, she turned to survey the scene. Alongside the entrance gates stood a fire engine; beyond, on what was left of the building's forecourt, an ambulance. Clambering over the debris were figures in all manner of uniforms. From the pavement, an elderly couple, swathed in blankets, looked on.

She cast her gaze wider; further along the street, seemingly transfixed by the activity, stood a newspaper boy, his bicycle propped against a lamp post.

She went towards him.

'Forgive me, but do you know when this happened?'

Without moving his eyes, the boy shrugged. 'Supper time. Jerry plane dropped a stick of HEs. Two landed back there –' with his head, he gestured over his shoulder – 'another one come down in the King's garden –'

'The grounds of the palace?'

'Didn't go off, though. Likely a dud. Or one of them delayed action ones.' *Dud.* With that, Isabel remembered the old man in the shelter. 'Now it's light,' the lad picked up again, 'they say the army's gonna try an' defuse it.'

'So, the bomb that fell over there –' she indicated Warbone Gate – 'was an HE?' She had no idea why she was asking; either way, she'd had the most incredible escape.

The child nodded. 'If it'd been an incendiary, there'd be black everywhere from the fire – charred wood and everything. But there ain't none. No, this were a big 'un. *Pow.*' With his hands, he mimed the force of an explosion. 'Shame. All them people's homes, gone, just like that.'

Isabel fought a renewed urge to be sick. 'Yes,' she said, willing the moment to pass. 'Thank you.'

With her thoughts darting all over the place, she

wandered away to stand on the corner; she'd often gazed at this spot from their drawing room window. But when she tried to picture the front of the building, her mind went blank. After a moment, fragments of an image slowly came together, slotting into place like the pieces of a jigsaw: red-brown brick, solid and rather severe, oversized, cream-painted casement windows on the half landings of the central staircase, the fenestration to either side symmetrical but otherwise plain. But what did it matter about the building? Surely, the more important consideration was what to do now. She supposed she would have to try and get hold of Hector – tell him what had happened and own up to the fact that she was homeless. Or should she spare herself the agony and simply call his mother? The apartment did belong to her, the furniture as well. Ghastly stuff. Ghastly place all round. She could honestly say she wouldn't miss a single inch of it.

With no idea what to do for the best, she stood, immobile with disbelief. She would prefer not to have to break the news to either of them. When Hector realized he would have to come back and sort things out, he would fly into a rage and curse her for being too incompetent to be trusted to act on his behalf. His mother would be no kinder, making out that she, Isabel, was somehow to blame for their loss. *What do you mean, you don't know what happened because you weren't there?* There or not, the Luftwaffe would still have dropped their bombs.

She supposed it was the shock, but earlier nausea was giving way to the urge to giggle. But she mustn't. As it was, she was going to have the devil's own job explaining why she hadn't been at home in the middle of the night – why she had only arrived back, wrapped in a picnic rug, the morning after.

But wait. Wait a minute. But what if she *didn't* explain? What if, rather than try to get hold of Hector . . . she simply crept away?

Casting a glance over her shoulder, she fought to calm the torrent of possibilities suddenly swirling in her head. As she stood there now, in the immediate aftermath of this terrible event, there was no one apart from a paper boy who could claim with any certainty that she had survived the explosion. In fact, apart from Vincent, there was no one to attest to her whereabouts either way. For all anyone else knew, when the air raid siren had gone off, she had been in bed and slept through it; at the first sound of a warning, the night porter made his rounds – hammering on doors and calling out – but had no way to check whether or not an apartment was empty. Moreover, were her husband to be asked, he would have to admit that, yes, his wife *was* in the habit of taking pills to help her sleep.

From her gradual realization emerged the vague outline of a plan. But could it work? Could this be her chance to flee? If she was careful about what she did next, could she simply disappear? Surely, when she explained to Vincent what had happened to Warbone Gate, he would agree that this was the perfect opportunity for her to escape – to bring about what they'd been planning for her to do anyway.

Yes, she could go to Waterloo, collect her suitcase of clothes, and start over. By the time someone eventually got hold of Hector or his mother, she would be long gone, safely hidden away. And the extent of the devastation to Warbone Gate had surely to mean it would be ages before the authorities could account for every single resident – dead or alive – especially as there was no record of who would have been at home at the time and who wouldn't. In the generally confused state of affairs, they wouldn't even be able to rule out that she'd been killed by a bomb elsewhere in town.

Her plan seeming too good to be true, she tried – but failed – to spot the flaws. To get away with it, though, she would need to be clever. For a start, it would be wise to change her appearance, perhaps alter her hair – something Hector would never countenance, his only concern being to have her look as plain as possible. She also regretted now that she hadn't had time to spirit away a second suitcase of clothes, especially since, just the other day, Hector had suggested that, before much longer, clothing was likely to be rationed.

'Then,' he'd said triumphantly, 'you'll regret not having bought more of the sensible woollens and hard-wearing tweeds I constantly tell you to wear – but which you steadfastly dismiss as matronly.'

She remembered thinking at the time that, if he was right, she should stock up on everything from undergarments to a new winter coat and a pair of boots. Her problem, now, was that she would be unable to draw money from the household account to buy any of those things without alerting Hector to the fact that she was still alive. Thankfully, last summer, when it had become clear war was unavoidable, she'd taken to squirrelling away a few pounds from the small allotment she received each month from Hector's salary for the purposes of covering day-to-day household expenses. Fortunately, just this week, she had moved her ill-gotten nest egg from the empty cold-cream tin in her sweater drawer to her purse; her intention had been to ask Vincent to keep it safe for her. In addition, she had the quarterly interest from her grandmother's trust. She hadn't drawn on it in years, which must mean that, by now, it would amount to a worthwhile sum. Best of all, Aunt Elvira – the account's trustee, and the only relation Isabel had ever been able to rely upon to keep a confidence – after taking a dislike to Hector from the off, had not only kept the trust a secret from him but had arranged for correspondence to be sent 'care of' her own address in Salisbury. Thank goodness she'd agreed with her aunt on the matter – not because she had foreseen one day deceiving Hector, but rather because she'd had no idea how controlling he would turn out to be. Had she now found herself unable to draw the interest without him knowing, her plan to escape would fail before it even got off the ground.

Redirecting her eyes to the ruins of Warbone Gate, she exhaled heavily. While she might wish there was something she could do to help those residents now made homeless, she was at a loss to know what; apart from being in the same boat as them – meaning she couldn't even offer to take them in – when it came to their neighbours, Hector had forbidden her to do any more than exchange polite greetings, meaning they had only ever been on nodding terms. So, while her conscience was telling her she couldn't simply walk away from those in need, this was one of the few times when she knew she had to put herself first.

In two minds, nevertheless, she looked all around. Could she really find the courage to make all this happen – to finally leave Hector by such audacious means? If she genuinely wanted to be free of him, she would have to seize the moment. First, however, she must go to Vincent and hope that, like her, he would see this as their chance to act.

The shock of losing her home would have been bad enough. But to turn the corner and find that another of the raid's bombs had struck Petty France brought the sensation that she might faint. Reaching out to grab hold of a lamp post, and steeling herself for the worst, she craned her neck to peer along the street. No, thank God; the bistro was still standing. The Durands were probably safe.

Further along, she spotted ARP wardens with long metal spikes, probing the debris where a bomb must have come down, and a team of firemen and council employees clearing aside the rubble. *Vincent. Vincent would be one of the wardens.* Eyes filling with tears of relief, she picked her way along the pavement towards them, shards of glass snapping and crunching beneath her shoes. No wonder he hadn't been waiting for her – his family's restaurant, and their home above it, had suffered a perilous near miss.

Ahead of her, from the doorway to the bistro, she saw Alphonse appear, a broom in his hand.

'Alphonse!' she called and hastened her pace further. '*Tout va bien?*'

The old man looked up. 'Isabel, *c'est toi?*'

'Yes, yes, it's me.' In her relief, she threw her arms about him. 'You are all right? And Mireille and everyone else?'

'We are all right. When the bomb comes, we are in the –' He tapped the ground with his broom.

'The cellar?' She wracked her brain. '*Le sous-sol?*'

'Yes.'

She ran her eyes up the front of the building: the sign that had hung above the door had been blown to the ground; the down pipe from the gutter hung at a precarious angle. But by far the greatest damage was to the windows. Not a single pane of glass remained at any of them, the curtains upstairs hanging limp and torn, the interior of the restaurant on the ground floor exposed for all to see. The patisserie, accessed from the side street, appeared to have fared no better, the large window, and the glass display cabinets, all shattered. She could only think that the narrowness of the alleyway had served to intensify the effects of the blast. Poor Alphonse; poor Mireille. Poor Vincent. What a tremendous amount of expense and hard work they now faced. And that was before considering the setback to their livelihood.

'And Vincent?' she asked. 'Is he all right?'

'He is with the ARP.'

'Down there?' She gestured along the street.

'No. Not there.'

'He . . . he hasn't been home yet?' When Alphonse shook his head, she tried to recall what Vincent had said to her as they'd parted; he'd mentioned having to report to the ARP command post – but had he said where that was? 'His ARP post,' she said to Alphonse. 'Do you know where it is?' *Why couldn't she remember where it was?*

Alphonse picked his way over the debris and went inside. Through the glassless window, she watched him go to the corner by the telephone at the end of the bar and ferret about. He returned with a page torn from a notebook.

'This is the place.'

She ran her eyes over the address: the school on Palace Street. That made sense – it was barely three minutes' walk.

She handed him back the piece of paper. 'I will go and see if they know where he is.' Alphonse nodded. 'And I'm so sorry about –' turning to set off, she waved her arm at the restaurant – 'this.'

'*Fais attention*, Isabel.'

'*Vous aussi*, Alphonse.'

The school, when Isabel arrived and went in through the gate, was eerily quiet, but seated at a wooden table inside the entrance was an elderly gentleman filling in a document she could see was entitled 'Warden's Report Form'.

When he didn't immediately look up, she cleared her throat.

'May I help you, madam?'

'Good morning, yes. I'm hoping you can tell me the whereabouts of one of your wardens.' He stared expectantly back at her. 'His name is Vincent Durand.'

The warden pushed back his chair and got to his feet. 'French chappie.'

'That's right.'

From a cabinet on the side, the man picked up a hard-bound ledger and returned to the desk. Having opened the cover, he flicked through the pages, stopped at one bearing yesterday's date, and ran his finger down a list of names. 'Here he is. Reported for duty at seventeen twenty-five last evening.'

'Do you know where he was sent?'

'A call for assistance came in from another post. He went along but came directly back. Not needed, I suppose. Then, eighteen thirty –' the man ran a finger back across the page – 'he went on fire watch, up on the roof. Twenty-three fifteen, a call came in from Victoria Railway Station. He and another chap went along.'

'And after that?' Fingering the lilac ribbon, Isabel held her breath.

'No record of him coming back so I'd say he's likely still there.'

She exhaled. Victoria Station. She could be there in ten minutes. 'Thank you. I'll go and see if I can find him.'

The man met her look. 'By all accounts, the incident was on quite a scale. I doubt you'll be allowed anywhere near.'

She suspected he was right. 'Maybe not. But I need to find him. I'm worried. And his family home has been damaged by the bomb that fell in Petty France.'

'Then might I suggest, before you go all the way down to Victoria, you leave a message for him here? In case you miss each other on the way.'

'Thank you, yes. I'll do that.'

On the notepad the warden handed her, Isabel quickly wrote Vincent's name, followed, in brackets, by the words 'ARP Warden', and then his address at the bistro. In the space beneath, she wrote: *Bistro damaged. Everyone fine. Am homeless after HE. Hope you are all right. Will return to bistro to see you later.* After a moment's hesitation, and aware that the old man was watching her, she signed her note 'Bel'. If she was going to disappear with Vincent, the last thing she needed was to leave a trail of breadcrumbs for Hector to follow.

The walk to Victoria Station took her longer than she'd anticipated – a lot longer. In part, she blamed her shoes; clearly never designed for covering long distances, they'd quickly started to rub her heels. But there was nothing she could do about that; thousands of people had awoken this morning to far worse problems than uncomfortable shoes. Some hadn't awoken at all.

In contrast to how easily she had been allowed to pick her way through the rubble of Petty France, when she arrived at Victoria Station, she found police constables manning barricades at the entrances.

'Sorry, madam,' one of them said as she went towards him. 'The station is closed until further notice.'

'Yes,' she replied, craning to see beyond him. 'But I'm trying to find my fiancé.' Vincent wouldn't mind her calling him that; call him her 'man friend' and she was in danger of coming across as a floozie, leaving officials less inclined to put themselves out to help her. 'He's an ARP warden. He reported to Palace Street yesterday evening and was sent here. The thing is, he hasn't come home yet. And I really need to find him to tell him that his own home has been damaged.'

Surprised that the constable had allowed her to ramble on for so long, she raised a hopeful smile.

'ARP warden, you say?'

'Yes. So, while I have no wish to cause a fuss, if you could direct me to whoever is in charge of the ARPs, I would be terribly grateful.'

The constable turned to look across the street. 'Well, normally, the ARP command post is down the side of the station there, in Wilton Road. But last night it had to be evacuated and so they set up a temporary command in the doorway of that shop over there.'

Isabel followed the line of his finger. 'Thank you. Thank you very much.'

In the doorway of the shop in question sat a man who appeared to be in his sixties.

'Durand, you say?' he checked when she had explained about Vincent.

'Yes. He would have arrived a little before eleven thirty last night.'

'From St James's.'

'That's right. From the command post on Palace Street.'

'Aha. Yes. Here's your chappie. Twenty-three thirty. But I'm afraid there's no record of where he is now.'

Isabel's heart sank. For a moment, she'd genuinely thought she and Vincent were about to be reunited. But, having now drawn yet another blank, it was becoming

increasingly hard to bury her fear that something un-
toward really had befallen him – something she'd rather
not contemplate. 'So –'

'By rights there should be a record of him leaving. That
said –'

'So, he *could* still be here, then?' All the while there was
hope, she would cling to it.

The man shook his head. 'When daylight broke, the
police cleared everyone from the site, bar railway survey-
ors and maintenance workers. And before you ask, no,
no reports of ARP casualties have been raised – and I've
been here since midnight.'

'So, he definitely left.'

'To the extent that it's possible to say for certain, yes.
Those wardens still here at the end were signed out and
either went home or to help colleagues still assisting elsewhere. There should be a record of who left before that
point but, such were the conditions last night, with several
calls a minute coming in from the docks, wardens who
weren't needed here dashed off to help where they could.'

Isabel's heart sank further. 'So, what you're saying is
that he could have gone anywhere.'

'I'm afraid that's about the measure of it.' With a look
that suggested he genuinely pitied her plight, the man
went on, 'The only way I can think to assist you would
be to enter a message in the log. Should he return to
report going off shift, he'll see it. Although, if you want
my opinion, after all this time, it's more likely he'll simply
return home.'

Having watched the man write 'Please Go Home'

against Vincent's name in the log, Isabel turned away. She had done all she could. Vincent had been there but had left. Left for where, no one knew. She could only hope the warden was right and that, eventually, Vincent would make his way home.

Having tramped back to Petty France, she arrived at the bistro troubled – but not entirely surprised – by the news that there was still no word of him.

'I have sent Mireille to my nephew,' Alphonse greeted her. 'He also has a restaurant. If I can make safe this place, I will go there, too. If not, I must stay.'

Yes, Isabel thought, the poor man would have to keep guard against looters.

With a sense that she was getting in his way and taking up his time when he had enough problems to contend with, Isabel bade him farewell. Ironic, she thought, as she wandered away, that in the whole of St James's only four bombs had fallen – one of those apparently a dud. And yet while, of the remaining three, the one that hit Warbone Gate had put freedom within her grasp, the one that had wrecked Petty France looked to have nudged it away again: not only were the whereabouts of the man she was counting on for help currently unknown, but his own home had been so heavily damaged that the place he'd been thinking might serve as a refuge for her was now to be occupied by his family instead. Rightly so, of course; their problems were greater than hers.

Perhaps, she surmised as she wandered, directionless, the heavens were trying to tell her something. Perhaps, after contemplating leaving her husband for another man, she was being punished. It certainly felt that way. As to what she did now, on a crisp September morning, wearing nothing more substantial than a flimsy summer dress, she hadn't the faintest idea. The only thing she *could* do, she supposed, was keep checking the bistro for Vincent's return and rely on the fact that, when he did reappear — because, while she was aware of the danger of false hope, she was far from ready to believe he wasn't simply going to turn up — he would find somewhere else for her to stay.

What did it say about her, she went on to wonder, that, in a time of crisis, she couldn't even stand on her own two feet — that all she could think to do was wait for a man to come to her aid? Clearly, it spoke volumes.

Well, once she and Vincent started their new life together, she would stop being *the little woman* — charming but dutiful — and develop some spine. The prospect might seem daunting now but, with Vincent by her side, she would summon the courage to tackle all sorts of new things, the first of which would be to follow his example and volunteer her labours for the good of the realm. Once Hector was no longer able to forbid her to go out, or to mix with whomever she liked, she would be free to do her duty — and, in so doing, to make both herself and Vincent proud.

5

'You all right, dearie?'

Slowly, Isabel looked up. No wonder she felt cold; in the half hour or so she'd been sitting there, numb to anything but her deepening fear, it had grown almost dark.

'Do you know what time it is?' she asked the woman in the WVS jumper who'd stopped to enquire after her well-being.

The woman checked her wristwatch. 'Five-and-twenty to eight, dear. You live 'round here?'

Isabel glanced up and down the street as though seeing it for the first time. Where was she? Where was *'round here*? Unable to recognize a single building, she wasn't even sure how she'd got there. All she could recall was walking for hours, hope gradually losing ground to distress as she followed one suggestion after another in her search for Vincent – or for anyone who had seen him since the raid. Of all the wardens she'd spoken to, only one remembered him. Where Vincent might be now, though, he'd been unable to say, which – coupled with his description of Vincent as *that nice French chappie* – had seen her turn away and dissolve into tears.

'You want to check the police stations,' someone else had said to her. 'They're starting to put up lists of casualties.'

Casualties. Clearly, the stranger had meant well but being forced to check lists of the names of the dead, while peering over the shoulders of other women in an equal state of distress, had been almost more than she could bear. Even when there was no trace of him on any of the noticeboards, mounting trepidation made it hard to keep putting one foot in front of the other. Somehow, though, she'd pressed on because, as she had gone on to discover, each police station only posted the fatalities from their immediate vicinity, meaning that, with no idea where Vincent had ended up, she had no choice but to check every constabulary she could find; she owed him no less. As it turned out, some of the lists had contained as many as forty or fifty names, others fewer than half a dozen. That Vincent wasn't among any of them did little to stem her increasing alarm.

By late afternoon, the mixture of creeping exhaustion and deepening despair had given way to a sort of stupor; at one point, she'd even found herself thinking it might be better if she *did* discover him on one of the lists because not knowing whether she was still looking for Vincent, or for confirmation that he was dead, was torture.

'Love? Can you hear me?'

With a frown, Isabel looked up. 'Yes?'

'I asked if you live around here.'

'Oh, yes. Sorry.' She got up from the bench and tried to pull herself together. 'No, I don't.' But then after what had happened to Warbone Gate, where exactly *did* she live now? 'I've been looking for someone. An ARP warden.

He was supposed to meet me this morning but, during last night's raids, he was sent over here to help out and no one has seen him since.'

'Most likely he's back home by now, then.'

Biting back fresh tears, Isabel shook her head. It wasn't the first time some well-meaning soul had suggested the same thing. 'He isn't. I've been back there to check. Three times now.'

'Then perhaps it's time you went home yourself. Any moment now, it'll be pitch-black. If your chap still hasn't turned up by morning, you can start looking for him again then.'

Isabel stared along the darkening street. 'Well, yes, but –' remembering just in time not to disclose where she lived, she changed tack – 'the place where I've been staying was destroyed by an HE.'

'Listen, love, when did you last have something to eat?'

Looking up to meet the woman's kindly expression, Isabel tried to remember. 'Yesterday afternoon. We had a picnic in the park.'

'And you've had nothing since?'

Only then realizing it was true, Isabel shook her head. 'Nothing.'

'Right, then. You're coming with me. If nothing else, you shall have a cup of tea and a sandwich. And I might register you for a bed – unless you can convince me you've somewhere else to go. Come on, before you catch your death of cold.'

The woman's suggestion seemed the answer to Isabel's prayers; after something to eat and a night's sleep, she could resume her search – having checked in the mean-time that Vincent wasn't already back at the bistro.

'Thank you. You're very kind.'

At the rest centre, reached after a few minutes' walk, another WVS volunteer pointed to the columns on the pages of a ledger and told Isabel to enter her details. 'Name, address, next of kin.'

Isabel paused. As she'd reminded herself more than once over the last twenty-four hours, she mustn't leave a trail for Hector. So, what should she write in this book?

Having whittled down the possibilities, she picked up the pen and, without further ado, wrote *Bel Smith. Chalk Hill Lodge, Salisbury.* But who to give as her next of kin? It was one thing to claim as her residence a corrupted version of her Aunt Elvira's address in Wiltshire but . . . Grasping the pen more firmly, she wrote *Mrs Elvira Castillo*, followed by the word *grandmother.* There was, she thought as she stared down at the trumped-up details, sufficient resemblance to the truth that, if challenged, she would be able to recall what she'd written – but insufficient for Hector to make the connection. He'd never met her Aunt Elvira and certainly wouldn't recognize her maiden name.

'Salisbury,' the woman remarked as she took back the pen. 'You're a long way from home, duck.'

'I am. And I've lost my lodgings here in London.'

'Maybe you'd better head back to Salisbury, then.'

'Yes,' Isabel replied. 'I might have to.'

'But since it'll be morning now before you can find out what trains are running, we'll get you a bite to eat and a cup of tea. Then we'll find you a blanket and somewhere to sleep.' Looking her up and down, the volunteer went on, 'And since you'll catch your death if you go about like that, maybe a jacket or a cardigan. You'd be surprised how generous folk have been with donating clothing.'

'Thank you,' Isabel murmured, and followed the woman through the doors into a noisy and crowded hall. 'Thank you very much. I'm truly grateful.'

Yes, once she had eaten, she would try to get some sleep. And then, at first light, she would go straight back to the bistro and pray that, when she got there, Vincent would be waiting to wrap her in one of his warm and reassuring hugs.

The two slices of toast were as thick as doorsteps and the cup of tea so strong that even a sip of it made her shudder. But it was, Isabel realized, precisely the sort of sustenance she needed to face the day ahead. Throughout the night, she'd struggled to sleep, partly down to the discomfort of the make-do bed, partly because of the unfamiliar and never-ending noise going on outside, but mainly through worry; with Vincent still unaccounted for, and despite her worn-out brain knowing she couldn't search for him in the dark, she'd felt guilty even contemplating closing her eyes.

It was now the following morning, and Isabel knew that her first task had to be to find her way back to the bistro as swiftly as possible. If Vincent was there, then she needed to know without delay. Her feet had complained when she'd had to force them back into her same pair of shoes but at least the sticking plasters she'd obtained at the First Aid post were helping; once she found Vincent – despite accepting in the cold light of day that she might not, she couldn't give up – she would go to Waterloo and fetch her suitcase, in which were not only her winter boots but the pair of navy-blue court shoes that were rather more suited to walking. In any event, she was desperate for some warmer clothes. But for the kindness of strangers, she wouldn't even have a cardigan to keep out the early morning chill.

When she arrived back in St James's and, with some apprehension, turned into Petty France, the first thing she noticed was that much of the masonry and glass from the explosion had been cleared into piles. And when she craned her neck in the direction of the bistro and saw Alphonse and two other men carrying planks of wood, her pulse quickened. But no – it was plain even from a distance that neither of them was tall enough to be Vincent.

She hastened towards them anyway. 'Alphonse!'

Lowering the plank he was carrying, Alphonse turned round. 'Isabel. *Ça va?*' The other two men looked on. 'My cousin,' Alphonse said, indicating the elder of the two. 'And his son.'

Struck by the resemblance of the elder one to Alphonse, Isabel acknowledged the pair with a polite smile. 'Vincent,' she said, rueing the need to ask; clearly, had he returned, he would have been out there, helping. 'Is he back?'

Alphonse gave a slow shake of his head. '*Non.*'

'And . . . he hasn't telephoned?'

Again, Alphonse shook his head. 'The telephone, it does not work.'

No, she'd overlooked that the lines would be down. 'And Mireille?'

'She cries. She fears. You know . . .'

Yes. She knew all too well.

Through the bistro's doorway, she could see that the broken glass had been swept up and the few pieces of undamaged furniture righted, but the extent of the loss was still heartbreaking. 'Then,' she said, turning back, 'I will go and look for him. As soon as I have news, I'll come back and let you know.'

'God bless you, Isabel.'

Over the following hours, Isabel retraced her route from the previous day – at least, those parts of it she could remember. Since yesterday, the ARP command post at the school on Palace Street had been packed up; in its place, teachers were preparing for the start of the new term. At Victoria station, railway workers were carting away rubble, and a small number of train services appeared to be running again; outside Rochester Row police station, the list of casualties on the board contained new names – none of which was Vincent's. If he *had* perished, he didn't appear to have done so anywhere close to his home.

'You want to check St Thomas's Hospital,' a constable on duty at the door of one police station suggested. 'That's where they're treating the casualties from the bombs that fell on Victoria Railway Station.'

She thanked him and trekked across Westminster

Bridge, arriving at the hospital only to find that, no matter how many times or how slowly she checked the list of those who had been admitted, Vincent's name wasn't among them. As discoveries went, this was oddly disappointing; while she was desperately relieved to have no confirmation he had been injured, finding his name would at least signal the end of her search and the start of helping him to recover.

Unable to summon the energy to traipse all the way back to the emergency rest centre, she returned to the bistro.

'Any word?' Each time she arrived back, it became increasingly hard to ask.

Alphonse appeared equally weary. 'There is no news. But here, you must eat.'

In a basket of provisions evidently brought over by Mireille was a Thermos flask of coffee, a couple of baguettes, halved and spread with potted meat, and several pastries. 'Please,' Alphonse urged her. 'Eat.'

'If you are sure you can spare this, then thank you.'

At the bar, on the only stool to have survived the blast with all of its legs intact – and which Alphonse dusted off for her to use – Isabel sat, forcing herself to take small mouthfuls and to chew slowly; she hadn't realized how famished she was. Eating by the light of a single candle – the boarded-up windows now excluding all but the odd ray of daylight, the electricity supply having gone off with the explosion – she decided it could only be nervous energy keeping her going.

When she had finished eating and was wiping her

fingers on the corner of her handkerchief, Alphonse came in.

'I worry,' he said.

She saw no point lying to him. 'So do I.'

'I know my grandson. To him, family is everything. His mother is everything.'

'Yes,' she said. 'I know.'

'He would not let us worry like this. He would send word.'

Isabel had long since arrived at the same conclusion. If Vincent was in a hospital ward somewhere, his first thought would be to ask someone to contact his family. That they'd had no word troubled her more deeply with each passing hour but, somewhat contrarily, strengthened her determination not to give up.

Poking her handkerchief back into her handbag, she slid from the stool. 'Do not lose hope, Alphonse.'

'No.' After a moment's hesitation, the old man said, 'Your family, Isabel. They know you are safe? You have sent word?'

A rush of guilt made her stiffen. By now, news of Warbone Gate would doubtless have reached Hector; not only was he named as the apartment's occupant, but their doorman, along with most of the building's residents, knew he was in the army, making him straightforward to trace. Whether any of their neighbours would have survived the bomb to explain that to the authorities, she didn't know. But she couldn't take the chance; upon receiving word, Hector would surely be granted at least a day or two's leave to deal with matters. He could be on his way back there right now – might even, she realized with another start, already have arrived, meaning she could bump into him at any minute; on foot, the distance between Warbone Gate and the bistro was only seven or eight minutes. After all of this, she couldn't bear it if her plan to leave him failed simply because the two of them walked into one another on the street. Getting caught out through her own carelessness would be a catastrophe she could never forgive.

Realizing that Alphonse was still waiting for an answer to his question, she met his look. 'The people who matter to me know I am safe.' It wasn't too much of a lie.

'It pleases me to know this.'

When she'd given him a hug and turned away, her thoughts returned to the matter of what to do. Despite the risk of bumping into Hector, she couldn't go into hiding, not with Vincent still missing. And, clearly, asking Alphonse if she could stay with him at the bistro was out of the question. It seemed, therefore, that she would have to spend another night at the rest centre, even though, before much longer, the people running it would surely want to know why she hadn't gone back to Salisbury. Giving it as her address had seemed a good idea at the time but now she worried it might trip her up – and there were already enough things waiting to do that.

There was also, she realized, the question of how long she could keep searching for Vincent anyway. When she had awoken this morning, only to recall the events that had brought her to sleeping in a church hall, she'd tried to imagine what life would be like without him, but the only thing she'd been able to picture was emptiness. *Nothing.*

At the street corner, she stood for a moment and stared blindly ahead. No, Vincent was alive. He had to be. She was simply not ready to give up on the chance of a life filled with love – especially given how long it had taken her to find in the first place.

6

'Looks like the council have arrived. Maybe now they'll start to get us sorted out.'

Having awoken from another night of patchy sleep, but grateful once again for the sustenance of tea and toast, Isabel got up from where she'd been perched on her camp bed and followed the woman's gaze. Although it was barely eight o'clock, traipsing into the hall was a stream of officials who, under the direction of a supervisor with a clipboard, immediately took to arranging trestles and unpacking cardboard boxes of ledgers, documents, ink-pads and stamps.

When the woman from the adjacent bed went to investigate, Isabel sank back down again; since she couldn't have it on her conscience, accepting anything to which she wasn't entitled, she had to get back out there and resume her search for Vincent. Not only did she need to find him but, if the council was starting to rehouse people, it was possible she could come back one afternoon to discover the rest centre was being wound up. And then what would she do?

Pulling her borrowed cardigan more closely about her body, she picked her way between the rows of camp beds to the entrance, pushed open the door and stepped out on to the pavement. Today, she would be methodical in her approach. She would start at the bistro. If, when she got there, Alphonse still hadn't heard anything, she would check once again at the police stations and the hospitals. If Vincent's name hadn't appeared on any of their lists, she would return to St James's, find whoever was responsible for ARP wardens and explain to them that, on Saturday evening, Vincent Durand had reported for duty and hadn't come back. Then she would demand they look for him. And she wouldn't be fobbed off with excuses about telephone lines being down or the prevailing state of confusion. She would simply insist he be traced. And if they didn't immediately mount a search, she would threaten to stay there until they did.

The morning striking her as cooler than of late, she quickened her pace; since she was still underdressed, striding along seemed the best way to work up some warmth. Last night, one of the WVS volunteers had announced that more boxes of donated clothing had arrived, but her conscience hadn't allowed her to do as others had and rifle through them for something more substantial to wear; unlike the other women in the rest centre, she had a suitcase full of clothes waiting for her at left luggage. She also had a modest amount of money in her purse. But to use either for anything other than what she and Vincent had been planning felt tantamount to accepting he was lost.

As she turned the corner, and glanced about to check where she was, she spotted a man arranging items on a trestle. Beyond him, the sign above what had once been a plate-glass storefront read *Lawley & Sons, Purveyors of*

Travel Goods. As she drew closer, she could see holdalls, wash bags, and tiny alarm clocks in leather cases; on the pavement beneath sat a cardboard box brimming with patterned cloth. She bent to look. The fabric, silky to the touch, had been hemmed into large squares.

'Are these headscarves?' she enquired. A scarf would be useful not just to conceal her unwashed hair but also to disguise her identity.

The stallholder looked her up and down.

'By rights, love, they're offcuts.'

She fingered one with a paisley pattern on a navy background.

'How much are they?'

'For you, love, one-and-six.'

'I'll take this one, please.' From her purse, she picked out a half-crown.

'Mind how you go,' the trader cautioned as he passed her a shilling change.

Wasting no time, she folded the scarf into a triangle, threw it over her hair and tied it under her chin. Further along the same street, where the occasional shop window still had its glass, she stopped in front of one to check her appearance. Just as she'd hoped: dowdy and unremarkable. Coupled with the rather shapeless donated cardigan, she doubted anyone – much less Hector – would give her a second glance.

When she eventually approached the bistro, she saw that every window was now barred with rough-sawn planks. For the comfort it brought her, she fingered the lilac ribbon about her wrist. *Please, Lord,* she willed as she spotted the door standing open and went towards it, *let him have come home.*

'Alphonse?' she called from the doorway. '*Vous êtes ici?*'

From the direction of the kitchen, Alphonse arrived and kissed her on both cheeks.

'He is not back.'

The news no better than she'd been expecting, she reached for his hand. 'And there has been no telegram?'

'None.'

Gently, she released his fingers. 'I see. But we still must not give up hope.'

'We must not.'

From there, she once again traipsed her now-familiar route around the six or so police stations. Each of their lists contained new names. None of them was Vincent's.

When she had drawn a blank at the hospitals as well, she turned away and stood for a moment in despair. Seemingly, then, there was only one thing left for her to do.

The cup of tea she'd been given had gone cold. It was no great loss; it had been so weak and milky she'd struggled to face it anyway.

After making a nuisance of herself at the only ARP command post she'd come across that was actually manned, Isabel had been directed to the address of the sector headquarters. When she arrived, however, she had been forced to stand firm and insist that, as far as she was concerned, promising to *do their best* to look for a missing warden wasn't good enough. It was then that she'd been shown into the office of the chief warden himself – the man responsible for the entire sector and where, finally, her concern for Vincent was taken seriously.

'I assure you, Miss Smith,' the chief warden looked across his desk at her to say, 'now you have brought to my attention that Mr Durand is missing, no effort will be spared in the making of any and every enquiry to establish his whereabouts. As you rightly point out, the onus is upon us to find him. I also assure you that, the moment we have word, I shall personally send a telegram to Mr Durand's family. As I am sure you appreciate, though, a search of this nature takes time.'

Raising her gaze from her insipid cup of tea, Isabel met the warden's look. 'All I ask is that you find him.'

Utterly drained by the persistence required of her to be taken seriously, Isabel left the chief warden's office feeling as though, for the moment at least, she really had done all she could; the search for Vincent was now in the hands of people far better equipped to find him than she was. The only sensible thing she could do was go back to the rest centre and pray the ARP succeeded where she had so far failed.

'You all right there, love?'

Slowly, Isabel nodded. 'Fine, thank you.' It wasn't true of course: here she was, back to sitting on her camp bed in the church hall, feet worn out from traipsing around, head pounding from having to remonstrate with members of the ARP, and yet it was barely even eleven o'clock. How she was supposed to pass the rest of the day, she had no idea.

'I'm Ruby Jones, by the way,' the woman from the adjacent bed introduced herself.

'How do you do? I'm Isabel,' she replied, concerned not to give too much away. Shaking the woman's hand, she nodded towards the clusters of people crowding around the officials. 'Have you found out yet about being rehoused?' From the look of things, it seemed unlikely.

'Chance would be a fine thing. Turns out there's a pecking order, and with me being on my own, it would be hard to rank much lower. No, I'm resigned to being here a good while longer yet, duck. What about you?'

'Well . . .'

'Look,' Ruby went on when Isabel hesitated, 'tell me it's none of my business and I'll shut me trap, but I've heard you, these last two nights, sobbing your heart out. I mention it not so as to pry but simply because, well, it's times like these we'd turn to our nearest and dearest. But you seem to be all on your own.'

The woman's mention of *nearest and dearest* brought Isabel to ferreting about in her handbag for her handkerchief. 'Sorry,' she mumbled and dabbed at her eyes.

Ruby moved to sit beside her.

'No need to be sorry, love. Although, since neither of us would appear to have anywhere else to be, how about you tell me what's up?'

In the face of Ruby's kindness, Isabel crumpled; with only the barest of consideration to the wider consequences, she poured out the story of Hector – to whom she referred simply as her husband – the bombing of Warbone Gate, which she took care to describe only as 'home', and then about Vincent, and their plan, seemingly now in tatters, for the two of them to start a new life. 'So, you see,' she said between racking sobs, 'if he's lost, then I don't know what I'll do because my hopes for a future with him are dashed.'

'Oh, love —'

'But anyway,' Isabel rushed on, mortified to be disclosing her private business to a stranger. 'Pay me no heed. You have problems of your own.' Glancing up, she looked about the crowded hall. 'As does everyone else in here.'

'Look,' Ruby said, nevertheless, 'bottling things up never helped anyone. So, if what you need right this minute is to have a good cry and get it all off your chest, then you go ahead.'

'You're very kind.'

'And while I'm not one to spout advice unless it's asked for, and I've no time for false hope, I *will* say this. Were it me in your shoes, then one thing's for certain. Even if my chap *was* missing, I wouldn't sit around waiting for my husband to show up. I'd leave word with someone I trusted and get myself away. And, by that, I mean *far* away.'

'Which,' Isabel said flatly, 'was Vincent's plan. But now I'm on my own, I've no idea where to start. *You* might be a woman with the fortitude for such a thing, but *I'm* not.'

Ruby's amusement erupted in a wry laugh. 'That's not fortitude, love, that's just a thick skin.'

Spotting a smudge on the gold-coloured clasp of her handbag, Isabel reached with a finger to rub it away. 'I always thought *I* was thick-skinned. After twenty years of my husband and his ways, I thought I'd grown the hide of an ox and that, if anyone did manage to pierce it, all they would find inside of me was steel. But then, back in the spring, I met Vincent and, gradually, over the weeks, as I got to know him, he opened my eyes to what was possible in life, made me dare to dream about what might be. When I was with him, for the first time in decades I felt warmth and hope. The revelation was so powerful that, one afternoon, as we sat holding hands and watching the ducks, I knew, without doubt, that I wanted to spend the rest of my life with him, no matter the difficulties, no matter the risks. And to find he felt the same way about me . . . well. To my pain and my sorrow, though, barely had I got used to the idea than here I am, our future together hanging by the finest of threads. But I suppose,' she went on, her tone a mixture of despair and resignation, 'since I might yet have to go cap in hand back to my husband, a thick skin might once again serve as my salvation.'

'This husband of yours,' Ruby said, lowering her voice and turning to regard her. 'Quick with his fists, is he?'

Isabel pushed aside her handbag. 'He makes as though to lash out, but no, his method of ensuring my obedience relies more on humiliation and fear.'

'One of the sly ones.'

'And relentless with it. Which is why I've started to worry how, without Vincent to help me stay hidden, I'll avoid him potentially tracking me down and dragging me back. You see, having had more time to think, it occurs to me that, at some point, the authorities will dig down through the ruins to the basement shelter so as to recover the bodies. And if, when they do, they are able to identify all the remains – and mine aren't there – well, the question in Hector's mind will surely become one of whether I was even there to start with. And if that happens, trust me, he won't rest. He might have had another woman these last two decades, might not actually *want* me, but he'll come after me all the same. I mean, *his lowly wife, escape from his control?* Over his dead body.'

'Even more reason, then,' Ruby said, 'to get yourself away while you still can.'

Isabel scoffed. 'But get away to do what? To spend the rest of my life continually looking over my shoulder in fear?'

'Take it from one who knows, girl, the fear of being found is a good deal less crippling than the fear that comes from staying put.'

'Perhaps.' Even were that true, how could *she* – forty years old, alone and with no significant means – entertain starting over somewhere new? Moreover, how could she even consider it with Vincent still missing?

'Listen, dearie. I only mention getting away because, if you *are* minded to, I know someone who might be able to help.' Curious to hear more, but wary of what might be involved, Isabel sat perfectly still and willed Ruby to continue. 'See, some years back, *my* brute of a husband – Frank, he went by – came at me with the leg of a chair he'd just smashed into the wall. It wasn't the first time he'd come at me like it, not by a long chalk. But that particular night turned out to be the last because, next day, a neigh-bour took me to this woman who ran a refuge – who still does. Connie, her name is. She takes in women, their kids, too, and gives them somewhere to stay until she can help them escape more permanently from the likes of your husband and my Frank. The only reason I'm back here now is because, one night, not six months after I fled, someone stuck the bastard with a knife, and that was the end of him.'

Isabel met Ruby's look. 'So, what does Connie actually do to help women get away?'

'Depends, love. Some who find their way to her door need a doctor and urgent refuge, others just need pointing in the right direction. Even with Connie's help, though, I'll be honest and say that getting away takes strength. It ain't the sort of thing you do on a whim. At the very least, you got to change your name and be prepared to start over somewhere completely foreign. And unless you've got private means, you need to find work, too, and trust me, that can be harder than it sounds. But, for a lot of women, none of that is anywhere near as hard or as risky as staying put.'

For a moment Isabel sat, deep in thought. Could she really do this? Vincent *had* already been planning for her to leave St James's, although not, of course, to go away from London altogether – and definitely not on her own. And she had always known she would have to change her name. As for work, well, she had no idea how she would fare on that front. Besides, even if the cast-iron opportunity for her to get away from Hector was put within her grasp, did she really have what it took to survive by herself – even just until Vincent was found?

'So, supposing,' she began, the prospect nevertheless begging to be explored, 'if I *did* want to change my name, how does it work?'

Leaning towards her, Ruby lowered her voice. 'Trickiest part, nowadays, is that you've got your identity card and your ration book to think about. You can change your name and move away easy enough but, if you don't tell the authorities, then, sooner or later, like when you're due a new ration book, you'll come a cropper.'

She might have known there would be a catch.

'I hadn't thought about that.' She didn't believe Vincent had, either.

'That's where Connie comes in. She knows a woman in the records office who can help with the forms and whatnot.'

'Above board?'

Ruby nodded. 'Only downside is that you have to lie low for the twenty-one days it takes while the notice is in the newspaper.'

'*In the newspaper?*'

'As I found out when *I* was in your shoes,' Ruby continued calmly, 'the law says you've got to give notice in this paper called *The London Gazette* to state that you're changing your name . . . and what you're changing it to.'

'So, there's no way for me to become Isabel Smith without announcing it to the whole world?'

'Oh, there's a way, all right. But neither Connie nor her friend will break the law and risk going to jail to do it, not for you nor anyone. No, that way would mean putting yourself in the hands of criminals and forgers. And even if that's a risk *you're* prepared to take, don't look to me for help doing it. I don't need that sort of trouble.'

'But if my husband can find out I've changed my name,' Isabel said, her earlier optimism dissolving into despondency, 'won't he be able to see my new address, too? And if so, why go to the bother when he'll just hunt me down anyway?'

'That's where Connie comes in. We put on the forms that you're staying at her place. Given you've been bombed out, no one will ask questions. So, even if he *does* eventually discover what you've done, with a name like Smith, and with you moving away to start over somewhere new, his chances of finding you are all but non-existent.'

'I suppose.' While Ruby made a good point, could this truly work? Could she really escape?

'But that does mean,' Ruby went on, 'that when you're thinking about a place to go, it's got to be somewhere he wouldn't know to look for you.'

'A place to go.' And there was the rub; she didn't have anywhere. If she had, she would probably be there now.

'Look, I know you said you ain't got family, but you must have friends. Maybe away from London, somewhere your husband might not know to look?'

Friends. She pulled herself upright. Of course.

'I do, yes.' In fact, of her two long-standing schoolfriends, Ronnie – as she was known to most people but, more properly, Veronica Claremont – was in Sussex, and not much more than an hour away by train. On the downside, Ronnie's in-laws were acquaintances of the Thaxleys. Indeed, it was through them that she and Hector had been introduced in the first place – which meant that expecting Ronnie to conceal her presence in their home would put her friend in a difficult position. And friends didn't do that to one another. Conversely, Julia was all the way down on the north coast of Devon – sufficiently far away to be safe from Hector, but hours and hours away from Vincent when he was eventually found. Still, what price a lengthy railway journey compared to staying in town to try to find Vincent, only for Hector to find *her* first?

'Thought of someone?' Ruby looked expectantly back at her.

'I have a friend in Devon. We've somewhat fallen out of touch of late, but I'm sure she wouldn't turn me away.'

'Then seems to me, we ought to go and see Connie.'

'But what about Vincent, what about –'

'Love, listen to me,' Ruby said. 'For certain you'll feel guilt. But leave word with his family and then, when he's found, if he's the man you say he is, he'll come for you.'

That Ruby continued to make sense was hard to dispute. 'Even so . . .'

'Look,' Ruby went on, 'maybe ask yourself which puts the fear of God up you the most – not being with your Vincent the instant he's found, or having your husband march you back home so you never get to set eyes on your new feller ever again.'

There was no question: being found by Hector would render Vincent's whereabouts academic. Nevertheless, wary of the speed with which this was coming together, Isabel paused before asking, 'And how much do I pay

Connie for doing this?' She couldn't imagine such a service would be cheap.

'Well, since most of the women who find themselves on her doorstep arrive without a farthing to their name, the arrangement is that, once you get on your feet, you send however much of a donation you can scrape together, to help keep her refuge going for the next woman who needs it.'

'And where is she?' Isabel asked, the arrangement seeming generous. 'Where do I find her?' In fact, the whole thing suddenly seemed such a godsend, she didn't want to dally a moment longer; within reach was an answer to at least one of her prayers.

'Well, first things first. Once we've filled in the papers, you'll need to lie low until your new documents can be issued, meaning you need to think hard about any business you have to take care of beforehand – especially with regard to money – and about telling anyone you trust what you're up to. Like your chap's family, for instance.'

Isabel scrabbled to think. 'Yes, yes. I need to telephone and check my friend will have me. And go and see Vincent's grandfather and give him her address.'

'Then, in which case, love, if you're of a mind to do this, I suggest you go and make a start.'

When Alphonse placed a hand on each of her arms and kissed both of her cheeks, Isabel felt her eyes fill with tears.

'Isabel, please, do not cry. When there is news, I will telephone. Or send to you a telegram.'

On the slim chance that Vincent had shown up there since her visit barely two hours earlier, Isabel had hurried straight from the rest centre to the bistro. It was hard to believe she was contemplating abandoning Alphonse with Vincent still missing but, despite having no way of knowing how things would eventually turn out, she knew Ruby was right: for the time being at least, it made sense for her to get away.

'Thank you, Alphonse. I hope to see you again very soon.'

'*Bonne chance, ma fille.*'

From there, Isabel hurried, head down, to the post office, where, from a concealed compartment in her purse, she pulled a slip of paper upon which were written several telephone numbers. Dismayed to find all of the telephone booths occupied, she joined the queue and, the moment one of them became available, darted in and closed the door.

'Yes, good morning,' she said when the operator came on the line. 'I should like to place a person-to-person call to Mrs Julia Nance.'

'The number, please, caller?'

Smoothing out the slip of paper, Isabel peered at her faded handwriting and read out the number.

'Please hold for Mrs Nance.' When the line went quiet, Isabel drummed her fingers on the little shelf. Surprisingly quickly, the operator was back. 'I'm sorry, caller, but all trunk lines are busy. I suggest you try again later.'

Deeply disappointed to be thwarted so early in her endeavour, Isabel replaced the receiver and vacated the booth, holding the door for the elderly lady who was next in the queue.

After five minutes spent waiting to try again, she got the same response. Ten minutes on from that, the situation still hadn't changed.

'I'm sorry, caller,' a different operator said, 'but with one of our exchanges having been bombed, we are operating with reduced trunk lines.'

When she replaced the receiver for the third time, something Alphonse said gave her an idea: she would send Julia a telegram. Surely, the telegraph lines had to be working.

Locating the appropriate form from the rack on the wall, she wrote her message and then handed it, along with the fee, to the clerk behind the counter, who read back to her what she had written.

'*Bombed out. Homeless. Need refuge. Isabel.* And you've indicated that you wish to await a reply.'

'I do.'

'I'm afraid I can't say how long that will take. As you might expect, we are experiencing delays.'

'Thank you, but I will wait nonetheless.'

Her message taken care of, Isabel retreated to a vacant chair by the doorway. If Julia replied that it was all right for her to go there, she would hurry back and ask Ruby to take her to Connie's friend. Then she would go straight to Waterloo, reclaim her suitcase from left luggage, and get on a train. She had no idea of the route, or the number of changes necessary to reach Julia's village, but she would worry about that later.

She hadn't been sitting there all that long before the discomfort of the wooden chair forced her to get up, stretch her arms above her head and take a few paces across the floor. With a glance to the clock – why couldn't time, just this once, go any faster? – she retraced her steps and sat back down. After the last few days of wandering, endlessly, lost to know what to do for the best and fearful of being spotted by Hector, the speed with which her departure from London was coming about was unnerving.

After a further hour's wait, and just as she was beginning to fear that her plan was destined to fail at the first hurdle – after all, Julia could be anywhere – the clerk who had taken her message came scurrying towards her.

'Madam, I have your reply.'

Fingers trembling, Isabel unfolded the slip of paper. Then she let out a sob. Julia's message read simply, *Come at once*.

7

Slipscombe Sands, North Devon

'Well, good morning. Did you manage to get much sleep?'

Isabel stifled a yawn. 'I dozed a little, on and off.'

'Better than nothing.'

Julia was right. After a couple of days with next to no sleep at all, even a couple of hours might have cleared her head. 'Definitely.'

'Perhaps, this morning, you might like to go out for a walk, get some fresh air, find your way around. It's not like you can get lost. As I always say to my guests, being up here on the cliff top means we're visible from even the furthest corner of the village.'

'Yes,' Isabel said, so utterly displaced that she didn't really know where she was, let alone the situation of the house in which she'd woken up. 'Some fresh air and a walk would be good.'

It was the morning after Isabel's late-night arrival at Fairlight – the guest house in Slipscombe Sands owned by Julia Nance, one of her two closest friends from her time at Havenham House School for Young Ladies. The journey from London had been one of unbearable tedium: the train from Waterloo had been packed even before she'd boarded; at Exeter, her expected wait of twenty

93

minutes for her connection had turned into an hour. By the time she'd eventually reached Barnstaple, the ancient and rickety connecting service to Ilfracombe, from which she would have alighted at Wichin Moor, had long since finished for the day, leaving her forced to wait while the station master found a taxi driver willing to bring her the eight or nine miles to Julia's.

'Won't be many a-wanting to go all the way out there at this time of night,' the station master had informed her. 'It's the blackout, see. And the bother of having to find their way back.'

Even when a driver had eventually been persuaded to take her, and they'd spent over an hour crawling along pitch-black lanes to arrive in the village, her problems weren't over; seeking directions from a local out walking his dog revealed that Julia's guest house wasn't in Slipscombe Sands at all, but was up the hill, in a hamlet called Anzy Cross, the lane leading to it only accessible from back out on the main road. For the taxi driver – as unfamiliar with the area as she was – it was an inconvenience too far. For Isabel, it was the moment when the generous tip she'd intended giving him had shrunk to a couple of pennies. To her astonished relief, though, a chap in a van, who had apparently seen her being abandoned on the esplanade – and who introduced himself only as John but knew both Fairlight and Julia – offered to take her the rest of the way and then refused to accept anything from her for his trouble.

'My goodness,' she'd exclaimed when Julia had greeted her with an enthusiastic hug. 'Is everyone down here so obliging?' Her knight in shining armour had even carried her suitcase along the side of the house and up the steps to Julia's front door.

'You're in Devon now, maid,' Julia had replied, her chuckle precisely as Isabel remembered it. 'None of your London stand-offishness down here.'

'Anyway, it's so good to see you. I feel terrible about not writing much these last twelve months or so.'

'I haven't exactly kept in touch either. But yes, after all this time, and in spite of the sad and awful circumstances that bring you here, it's lovely to see you.'

For Isabel, though, waking up this morning to remember how distant she was from St James's had brought on all manner of feelings. Part of her was simply relieved to have somewhere to stay, and grateful for the company of a friend. A far greater part, however, felt traitorous; try as she might, she couldn't rid herself of the sense that leaving London without finding Vincent was unforgivable. If nothing else, what if, without her there to chivvy them along, the authorities simply stopped looking for him? Further playing on her mind was the realization that, for the next three weeks, while she might introduce herself to everyone as Isabel Smith, officially, she was still Thaxley; to her mind, having to place that notice in *The Gazette* to announce she was changing her name seemed to defeat the reason for doing so in the first place but, as Ruby had said, the law was the law and, at least now, it was done, her period of notice counting down.

Feeling utterly overwhelmed by her situation, she turned to see Julia emerging from the pantry, in her hands a tray bearing a china butter dish, a honey pot and a bowl of fat brown hens' eggs.

'Can I lend a hand?' she asked. Perhaps having something to do would still her confusion and numb the rawness consuming her insides.

'Thanks, but no, I'm fine.'

'So, how have you been finding it down here since war broke out?' she asked, her aim being to distract herself from thoughts of Vincent and London.

'What,' Julia said, her tone weary, 'apart from trying to keep a guest house with no guests from going under, you mean?'

Immediately, Isabel regretted not stopping to think before asking; it should have been obvious that Julia's business would be struggling.

'Well, yes. I suppose I rather meant –'

'It's all right,' Julia said, her response accompanied by a dismissive wave. 'I won't deny it's been fraught at times but, just this last week, I received the news that four teachers from a school evacuating from Bristol are going to be billeted with us. Ordinarily, given how badly we need the money, I'd be overjoyed. But it doesn't sit easy – the thought that I'll be profiting from their misfortune.'

'I don't think you've anything to feel bad about,' Isabel replied. 'By providing them with a home and food, you'll be doing your bit to ensure they stay safe.'

Julia sighed. 'That's the hope. This whole business of war's been peculiar at times, though, hasn't it? In those first few months after Chamberlain's broadcast, before the fear of an enemy invasion started to take hold, you could have thought the newspapers' description *Phoney War* had been invented for Devon, maybe even specifically for Slipscombe. Elowen reckons the person who came up with it must live here. Seriously, ask anyone in the village and, pound to a penny, they'll tell you that, until Easter time, apart from having an identity card and a gas mask, and some of the menfolk having taken themselves off to join up, you wouldn't have known there was a war on at all. Those first seven months or so, the place was much the same as ever – simply without the holiday-makers spending their money to keep us all afloat.'

'I suppose until last week,' Isabel said, 'the same could have been said of London. Until recently, it all felt like a lot of fuss for nothing. There were still buses to catch, tube trains to travel on. In fact, the biggest upheaval was right back at the beginning, with the evacuation of all the children, and the setting up of shelters and so on. But after all the initial fear and that first flurry of activity, so little seemed to happen that some parents even started fetching their children *back* from the countryside, finding the separation far more of a worry than the risk of them being in harm's way at home. And I have to admit, at the time, I appreciated their point.'

'Hm.'

'Even on the occasions when the sirens did go off, the alert generally turned out to be a false alarm. The odd raid that did happen was usually over the East End, and rarely of any real significance. For most people, life went on as normal. Women still frequented Regent Street to browse the latest season's fashions, the conversations I overheard suggesting they were all simply *keeping a stiff upper lip* and *standing by*. They always seemed especially eager to let everyone know they'd just finished doing something worthy, such as training to drive an ambulance, or a refresher course in first aid, only to then play down the fact by pointing out that, *really, though, it's absolutely nothing*. Which is all very well until, in their next breath, they'd go on to bemoan the call-up of everyone from waiters and hairdressers to porters and delivery men as being *such a nuisance*.'

At the kitchen table, Julia scoffed. 'I know the sort.'

'But I suppose that's how change happens, isn't it?' Isabel went on as the thought occurred to her. 'Slowly, gradually, until, without noticing it, we're so far from where we started, we can no longer recall what life was like before.'

'If you say so.'

Was that what would happen with her and Vincent? Isabel wondered. Would she – if he never came for her, or if she never found him and they were never reunited – slowly come to forget him? Would she one day find herself unable to remember his face; would she forget the way he looked at her, as though actually seeing the person within; forget how it felt to have him listen when she spoke? And what about the sensation that ran down her spine when he took her hand? Would she forget that, too? Perhaps it would be worse if she *didn't* – if she simply couldn't; if she never saw him again but her mind wouldn't let go. Surely that would be the very definition of torture.

The prospect was enough to make her sob.

'Hey, hey.' Wiping her hands on her apron, Julia hastened to Isabel's side.

'Sorry.' Tugging her handkerchief from the sleeve of her blouse, Isabel dabbed at her eyes, the kindness of Julia's embrace making her feel even more tearful. 'It's just that –'

'It's all right. No need to explain. You've every right to feel weepy. You've lost your home.'

'Yes.' In her case, though, Isabel reflected amid a flush of guilt, her tears had nothing to do with the loss of Warbone Gate. Too tired last night to explain to Julia about Vincent, she'd refrained from mentioning him at all, saying merely that she welcomed the chance to get away from Hector. And Julia, who couldn't have failed to suspect there was more to it, hadn't pressed.

'But we'll get you sorted out.'

'That you've even let me come here has eased my worries.'

'Think nothing of it. Just try and take one day at a time.'

Unfortunately, having Julia suggest she take one day at a time didn't help. But what had she been expecting? What could anyone possibly say or do to lessen the fear gnawing at her bones and the anxiety shredding her nerves? The only thing that would douse either of those would be answering the telephone and hearing Vincent's voice at the other end. But for Julia to understand that, it required that she, Isabel, be honest with her.

First, though, she needed to work out how best to explain. After all, when Julia learned about Vincent, she might not approve.

'Would it be all right if I were to go and catch a breath or two of air?'

'By all means. Rodney – he's the baker's lad – will be up any minute now with the loaf. Can't start breakfast until then anyway. There's no bacon this morning but how about an egg?'

Isabel nodded. 'An egg would be lovely.'

'Scrambled? Coddled? Boiled? Poached?'

'Poached, if it's no trouble.'

'Right you are, then. Soon as Rodney's been, I'll make a start.'

On the front doorstep moments later, Isabel drew a long breath of the cool morning air. For the sake of her sanity, not only did she need to find a way to cease constantly crying but also to stop imagining the worst. There was still plenty of time for Vincent to turn up – especially if he'd been injured and taken to hospital. As Ruby had reminded her, she had ages before she would need to accept they weren't going to be reunited. Plenty of time. Weeks. Months, even.

When the early morning breeze raised goosebumps on her skin, she folded her arms across her body and stared out across the bay. Having arrived in darkness and been unable to familiarize herself with her surroundings, the view from her window this morning had come as a delightful surprise. Instead of drawing back the curtains to stare out at the grey marble and brown brick of neighbouring buildings, as she would have done in Warbone Gate, before her was an expanse of sea and sky and a curve of pale sand backed by undulating dunes, in turn set off by the autumnal shades creeping across the gently rolling hills beyond. Apart from the shrieking of the herring gulls wheeling like children's kites, the only sound had been the repeated flop and rush of the low swell. She'd been to the coast before, of course: a week on the Isle of Wight to stay with a distant relation when she'd been about nine, and a school trip by charabanc to Minehead with the art mistress, to immortalize in watercolours the pier and wider scenery of the Bristol Channel. There had been the most beautiful lake in Lausanne, too. But all of that had been long before she'd spent twenty years hemmed in by the crowded thoroughfares of London, where her focus rarely extended beyond the modest horizons of the royal parks.

Keeping her arms folded against the breeze, she let her eyes travel over the scenery, only halting when a particular detail captured her attention. Beyond the lawn to the front of Julia's delightful Edwardian villa, and those of her two neighbours, a ragged line of gorse appeared to mark where the land dropped precipitously to the sea. To the left, the hillside sloped less dramatically, but still sufficiently steeply that, according to the chap who'd given her a lift last night, the path, in ascending from the promenade, had to make a series of sudden switchbacks. Beyond that, in the sweep of the bay, nestled the village itself. She could see what drew people to holiday there, especially those more used to life in a town or city.

She stepped from the veranda down on to the path and looked back up at the house. It was larger than she'd imagined, stretching further back than the front elevation alone suggested. The bay windows to either side of the front door were wide, she supposed to give the best possible view of the bay, those of the two bedrooms on the floor above the same. The walls were of stone, which, in the early light, was a soft grey colour. The roof was slate, with dormer windows for what Julia had said were the smaller rooms in the attic; at full stretch, she'd mentioned accommodating sixteen plus two cots and a handful of youngsters on truckle beds.

Hearing the sound of wheels on gravel, she went to peer along the side of the house to see a boy in a flat cap leaning his trade's bike against the wall. Supposing him to be the baker's lad, she went towards him.

'Morning, ma'am,' he greeted her.

'Good morning,' she replied. With her head, she gestured towards the loaf he was lifting from the basket on the front of his bike. 'Shall I take that from you?'

Acknowledging her request with a brief touch of his cap, he handed her a tin loaf.

Perhaps, she thought, the bread still slightly warm, being forced to await news of Vincent in such tranquil surroundings would provide not only a distraction from her fears but a buffer between her old way of life and the start of her new one. In fact, perhaps she should try to look upon her stay with Julia as an *entremet* – a palate-cleanser between leaving Hector and starting afresh with Vincent – a small but diminishing corner of her mind steadfastly refusing to give up on their dream.

Back in the kitchen, she placed the loaf on the table. 'Feel better for some air?' Julia enquired.

'A little, yes.'

'It's certainly put a spot of colour in your cheeks.'

'I don't doubt it.' That was another thing of which she should try to take advantage – the apparently endless fresh air; there was little enough of it in London. In fact, she remembered reading in a women's magazine that, as long as one avoided an excess of direct sunlight, sea air was a real tonic for the complexion.

'Well, anyway, poached egg on toast coming up, then.'

Poached egg – *fresh* poached egg – what luxury, she thought as she watched Julia set a pan of water on the stove and then add a dash of vinegar.

In fact, were it not for her worries for Vincent's well-being and her concern that, at any moment, Hector might show up and drag her back to London with him, then a chance to catch up with an old friend at her comfortable seaside guest house amid the fresh air and scenery of Devon might ordinarily have made for a very enjoyable break indeed.

'So, are you ready to tell me why you were so anxious to get away from Hector?'

It was later that same morning, and the two women were in the scullery, Julia washing up, Isabel drying.

'Tell me to mind my own business, if you'd rather,' Julia went on. 'But you know what they say about a problem shared being a problem halved.'

If only that were true, Isabel thought. But when she explained about Vincent, even Julia might have to accept that nothing could possibly halve her worries for him.

Picking up the plate Julia placed on the drainer, and for the umpteenth time since leaving Waterloo, Isabel found herself trying to decide whether to disclose as little as possible or to be completely open, her resolve on the train journey down flip-flopping between the two. She didn't *think* Julia would disapprove of Vincent; after all, this was the woman who, on a holiday in Cornwall to get over the death of her first husband, had married a fisherman she met while there. *I cannot tell you how*, she recalled deciphering from the message Julia had scribbled on the reverse of the postcard she'd sent to announce the fact, *but I just know he's the man with whom I want to spend the rest of my life.* Such had been Isabel's astonishment that, even now, she could recall both the sketch of fishing boats marooned on the low tide at Bude on the front of the card, and how she had reeled from shock when she'd read the message on the back. It surely meant, though, that, if anyone, anywhere, was going to understand her situation, it would be Julia. Moreover, by telling her about Vincent, she might also clarify her own thoughts – perhaps even come to accept that abandoning her search for him wasn't as unforgivable as it felt.

'Well,' she began, at the same time shooting a wary glance back over her shoulder to the kitchen.

'It's all right,' Julia said. 'Elowen's at work –'

'At work? I can't believe she's old enough. When I picture your stepdaughter, she's just a little girl.'

'And according to her, that's how I still treat her sometimes. But, as I said to her just recently, by blossoming into womanhood, she's left me struggling to keep up. She even has a young man, now. She won't let me call him her *boyfriend*, but he's lovely. Police Constable Gregory. *Greg*. Quite new to the village. Real handsome. Anyway, where was I? Oh, yes, well, since all our bookings dried up, Elowen does a few hours each morning down at Jennings' Private Residential Hotel. But that's a tale for another day.'

'Very well.' For Isabel, such was her feeling of displacement this morning, she suspected she wasn't going to remember much of what Julia had been telling her anyway; as it was, her own story, when she eventually went on to relay it, hardly came out in the most orderly fashion. But, once she got going, she found that she didn't actually want to hold anything back. In fact, it was a relief to finally have someone in whom to fully confide. Apart from Vincent, who obviously knew *about* Hector but had clearly never met him, and the few details she'd related to Ruby, this was her first chance to properly bare her soul.

'This Vincent sounds like a good man.'

Isabel sighed. 'He is. He's everything Hector's not.'

'I'm so sorry you're having to go through this. It must be agony – not knowing what's happened to him. But I suppose all the while there's no news, there's still hope.'

'Yes,' Isabel said softly. 'That's how I'm trying to look at it.'

'And if there's anything I can do to help, you must tell me.'

'You're already being a help by letting me come here.'

'Any chance you have a picture of him – Vincent?'

Rueing that she had no memento other than the lilac ribbon, Isabel shook her head. 'I wanted one – desperately – but couldn't risk Hector finding it. Vincent has one of me, along with one of us together, taken by someone in the park.' Glancing across, she tried to read her friend's expression. 'Are you greatly shocked? About Vincent, I mean?'

Julia shook her head. 'Shocked? Me? When you arrived, and I saw how upset you were, I guessed there had to be more to it than you'd let on.'

'It was that obvious?'

'There was really no other conclusion.'

'To be clear,' Isabel said, blushing at the nature of what she felt bound to confess. 'We haven't actually – I haven't – what I mean is, I haven't broken my wedding vows.'

'I'd say that rather depends.'

Since it wasn't the answer she'd been expecting, Isabel met her friend's gaze with a frown. 'Upon what?'

'Upon how closely you define your vows. It might be *your* view that because you haven't been to bed with this Vincent, you haven't done anything wrong. But for some men – and by *some* I mean pretty much every chap on earth – even as little as looking at another man constitutes infidelity. And while I obviously don't agree with that view, pound to a penny, that's how your Hector would see it, even if he *has* been carrying on his own full-blown affair these last twenty years.'

'Double standards,' Isabel muttered. Gathering a handful of knives and forks from the drainer, she set about wiping them dry.

'Course it is. You know, given all you've just told me about Hector, I'm left wondering why you never said anything before now – about the way he treated you, I mean.'

Under her friend's scrutiny, Isabel looked away. As an outsider looking in, Julia could picture an alternative to putting up with the man. The truth of her situation, though, had been considerably more fraught. But how to explain that without appearing feeble?

'I never breathed a word to anyone. I daren't risk him discovering I'd talked about him. And trust me, he would have done. Many was the time I tried to see my way to leaving him, but my inability to even *picture* summoning the courage only ever left me feeling angry and frustrated. But allowing Hector to see that, well, it would only have strengthened his power over me, so I perfected a front of indifference. Even when he repeatedly rubbed my nose in his infidelity, I showed no sign that I cared. But then that was easy – because I didn't. On that particular matter, I couldn't have cared less.'

'I can't imagine how awful it must have been, living like that. You should have come here sooner. You must have known we would have taken you in, no questions asked.'

Isabel lowered her gaze. 'To be honest, I never thought to ask. Eventually, though, I stopped even contemplating running away for fear that, once he'd found me and dragged me back, my life would have become even worse. The man has a long memory. *And* he holds a grudge. No, in the end, I thought it better to simply go on as I was and just . . . wait.'

'*Wait?*' Julia laughed. 'Wait for what? For him to die of old age?'

Julia's tone made Isabel smile. 'No, just until something

happened one day that meant I could genuinely see my way clear to leave.'

'Well, anyway,' Julia said, 'you're free of him now. And yes, I know your plan wasn't to come here but to disappear with this Vincent chap, but at least you've got yourself away.'

'For the most part, I have, yes.'

'And if Hector is the bully you say he is, then, as far as I'm concerned, he had it coming. The way I see it, rather than waste any breath stewing over *him*, you'd be better served getting clear in your mind whether the reason you want this Vincent feller is solely because he's offering you the chance to escape from Hector – or because you want him, full stop.'

'I want him. I want a life with him.' In Isabel's mind, there wasn't a shred of doubt; the thought that it might not come about was terrifying.

'Then that's all that matters. Now we just have to pray Vincent's safe somewhere, and that, someday soon, you'll be back together. Oh, and I suppose it couldn't also do any harm to hope that, when Hector can't find hide nor hair of you, he looks upon your supposed disappearance in the same way you do – as a God-sent stroke of good fortune.'

Yes, Isabel reflected, as she picked up the last item of crockery to dry; being reunited with Vincent might *feel* like the most important thing in the world right now but it would only be the answer to her prayers if, at the same time – and new name or not – she managed to evade any attempt Hector might now make to find her.

*

It had seemed a good idea. Unfortunately, Julia's suggestion – that she keep busy by helping her to make up the guest bedrooms – wasn't the distraction it could have been; the tasks of putting pillows into their slips and tucking sheets under mattresses were so mundane that Isabel found her mind continually returning to Vincent. Had he been found yet? Was he back with his family? If he was, when would he telephone her? Or send a telegram? She'd left clear details of where she could be contacted and had stressed to Alphonse that, the moment he sent word, she would be on the next train back to London to oversee his grandson's recovery. And no, she hadn't forgotten the need to avoid Hector, but, since helping Vincent would be her priority, she would just have to be jolly careful.

'Hey, dolly daydream. I said give it a bit of a tug, will you?'

With a jolt, Isabel looked down to find herself holding the corner of an eiderdown. 'Sorry. What?'

'Pull it towards you a bit. There's far too much over this side of the bed and next to none over yours.'

'Sorry. Yes. I was miles away.'

The final two beds made, and a rug for warmth set over the linoleum between them, Isabel went to the dormer window and raised herself on tiptoe to look out.

'Listen, Issy,' Julia said, arriving to stand beside her. 'Take it from someone who knows, the best thing for worry really is an occupied mind.'

Isabel sighed. 'I don't doubt it. But while I don't mean to appear ungrateful for your concern, it's only now sinking in quite how much joy and happiness and fulfilment I stand to lose from my life if Vincent isn't found. Don't misunderstand me, I'm over the moon to have got away from Hector. But now I've met Vincent and seen what life can be like, what life *should* be like, and having got up my hopes for the future as a result, I can't see how I will go on without him. And I don't solely mean how will I live? Obviously, having run away from the man who put a roof over my head and brought in the money to feed and clothe me, I won't deny that I've landed myself in a fix. At the very least, I'm going to need a job. But doing what? I don't have a single useful skill. And if no one will employ me, how will I get by? I mean, for heaven's sake, I'm forty years old. My best years are behind me. Even if, somewhere down the road, my most sensible course of action became to find a new husband, I couldn't remarry anyway – not with Hector still alive.'

'Look,' Julia said and moved away from the window. 'I'm not pooh-poohing your concerns – they're all perfectly reasonable. But working yourself into a lather over things that might never happen is plain daft. Yes, where Vincent is concerned, it would be reassuring to have heard something of him by now, of course it would. But you've got to stop meeting trouble halfway. If something *has* happened to him, you have me. You also have a home with me for as long as it takes you to work out what you're going to do. I promise you.'

'Thank you,' she said. 'You're being unbelievably understanding.'

'I say it because I mean it. But for now, how about you do something practical to try and calm some of your fears? How about, you go downstairs to the telephone and ask the operator for Vincent's place. It could be there's news of him but that, for reasons we can't see from here, no one has been able to get in touch.'

Julia's suggestion wasn't without merit. The trouble was that even the prospect of picking up the telephone knotted her stomach.

'Just yesterday, the line to the restaurant was still down.'

'And since then,' Julia said, 'it might have been fixed.'

Picturing the mess in Petty France, Isabel doubted it.

'So, come on, fetch the telephone number, and I'll come and wait with you while you call.'

Moments later, having realized that Julia wasn't going to take no for an answer – and, in any event, knowing in her heart that it was the sensible thing to do – Isabel drew a deep breath, dialled the operator and asked to be connected to the bistro. As she waited, her fingers went to the lilac ribbon, deliberately concealed by the sleeve of her blouse but still damp from her bath. This morning, the feel of it brought scant comfort.

A click on the line signalled that the operator was back. 'I'm sorry, caller, the number you have given me is out of order. Is there another you would like me to try?'

Isabel hung her head. 'No, no other number, thank you.' With a weary sigh, she replaced the receiver and turned to Julia. 'The number is still out of order.' Wishing she hadn't tried in the first place, she began to cry. 'I'm so sorry. Having me . . . bawling my eyes out . . . must be the last thing you need.' Feeling Julia's arms close around her, Isabel simply cried harder. 'But it's breaking my heart. Truly . . . without him . . . I can't think how I'll go on.'

Reaching into the pocket of her skirt for her handkerchief, she moved aside from Julia's embrace and blew her nose.

'Would you like me to ask Dr Locke to pop up and give you something? Something to help you feel calm, maybe even let you get a proper night's sleep?'

Isabel shook her head. 'Kind of you, but no, thank you. For the last ten years, I've taken pills to help me sleep. But I promised myself that once I left Hector, I would never take another one ever again.'

'Well, if you change your mind,' Julia said, 'let me know.'

'I will. You have my word.'

'In the meantime, I prescribe coffee. Come on, even the bedmaker gets to sit down for a moment.'

Bedmaker, Isabel reflected; if Vincent really was lost, and Hector didn't find her, at least she would finally be free to try her hand at work of some description – even if it was bedmaking. She would also be free to volunteer for the war effort, something she'd been considering doing that afternoon when she'd first met Vincent.

Slipping her fingers back inside the cuff of her blouse to find her lilac ribbon, she turned to follow Julia through to the kitchen. Comforting herself with tentative plans was all very well but, if what she feared in her heart turned out to be true, would making beds and volunteering, no matter how useful, really give her reason to get up every morning?

But then, without Vincent, would anything?

8

No one would guess Elowen wasn't Julia's daughter. For two people related only by marriage, Isabel found their resemblance to one another uncanny: similar dark hair with a tendency to wildness; same chestnut-coloured eyes; same bubbly manner.

It was late morning on the day before the expected arrival of the evacuating school party from Bristol and the women were in the kitchen, taking a break from preparing Fairlight to receive four of the school's teachers as lodgers. And as Isabel continued to listen to Elowen and Julia discussing the matter, she realized the two of them even sounded alike, Julia's West Country burr identical to how she remembered it from their schooldays at Havenham. At the tender age of eleven, Julia Day had stood out like the proverbial sore thumb; Miss Padget, mistress of literature, Classics and history, had striven, with negligible success, to teach the poor girl to speak the King's English.

'That's *rahs-berry*, Miss Day. Not *raz-berry*.'

It wasn't just their looks and voices that Julia and Elowen shared, though, it was their mannerisms, too. She'd already noticed how, when pausing to reflect, or when about to laugh, they pursed their lips in identical fashion; when they did laugh, they raised their chins and

113

chuckled. She supposed it was no surprise they were so similar; when Julia had apparently horrified everyone by so hastily marrying Jago Nance, his motherless daughter had been barely a year old. When, less than two years after that – around fifteen years ago now – Jago had been killed in an accident with a gun, then not only did Julia become the only mother Elowen had ever known, but the only parent, full stop. Studying them together now, they could even be sisters, their relationship joyous to watch.

It was precisely the sort of moment when sorrow at her own childlessness still caught in her throat – not that, as things had turned out, she would have wanted Hector as the father of her children anyway; offspring would simply have become one more thing on the long list of topics for them to disagree about, her capacity as a parent further grounds for him to find fault and berate her. Once or twice, she'd even come to think her barrenness might have been a blessing in disguise.

'You know, Mrs Thaxley,' Elowen said as she carried a glass of milk to the table and sat down, 'since your telegram came, Mum's told me more about her schooldays than she ever has before.'

Wondering whether that was because her friend rarely had reason to recall their time at Havenham, or because she preferred not to, Isabel studied Julia's expression. Being a scholarship pupil, the poor girl hadn't had an easy time of it – certainly not in the early years.

'Please,' she said to Elowen, 'call me Isabel. And since,' she continued, realizing that, despite her preoccupation with the matter, she'd so far failed to mention it, 'we're on the matter of names, I should probably tell you both that I've taken to using the surname Smith.'

'Smith it is,' Julia responded with neither surprise nor concern. 'We get quite a few guests by that name, don't we, Ellie?'

'A surprising number. And a good many of them seem to come just for the weekend, as well. At least, they did until recently. I suppose now all the Mr and Mrs Smiths are busy being at war. Come to think of it, rather a lot of them *were* in uniform.'

Isabel smiled. If she and Vincent had managed to escape to somewhere like this for an illicit weekend, she supposed they would have registered as Mr and Mrs Smith, too.

'So, what about the name on your identity card and your ration book?' Julia asked.

It was a matter Isabel knew she should have raised with Julia before now.

'Well, for the moment, while the necessary notice for my change of name is given, and until my application is granted, I have neither. But, in a couple of weeks, the woman at the refuge, who helped me to sort everything out, will forward my new papers in the name of Smith.'

'Official new papers?' Julia enquired. 'Or would you prefer I didn't ask?'

'No, no, all completely above board. Although, once they do arrive, I'll need to notify the authorities of where I am and register here for my rations. I should really have asked you this before, but will you be able to manage until then – without any coupons for me, I mean? These days,

I really don't have much of an appetite anyway and rarely eat bacon or ham . . . nor much of any other meat, really. What's more, I'm happy to drink coffee instead of tea, and I don't take sugar.'

'If it's just for a couple of weeks, we'll find a way to get by.'

Isabel's shoulders relaxed and her stance softened with relief. 'Thank you. Thank you so much.'

'So, anyway –' But whatever Julia had been on the point of saying was cut short by a sharp rap at the front door. When Elowen showed no sign of going to answer it, Julia hauled herself to her feet. 'I'll just go and see who that is, then.'

'Hardly likely to be for me now, is it?' Elowen called after her stepmother's departing back.

With Julia gone, Isabel gathered their coffee cups and was about to carry them through to the scullery to wash up when she stopped dead, her hand hovering above the table: the caller at the door was male, his tone commanding. What if he wasn't there for either Elowen *or* Julia, but for *her*?

Her breathing swift and shallow, she lifted the tray of crockery and made for the scullery from where, by craning to listen, she heard Julia call to Elowen.

'Love, come here a minute.' When Elowen got up and left, Isabel stole back across the kitchen and, holding herself rigid, peered through the crack between the door and its frame. What she saw made her shrink backwards in horror. A policeman? What was Julia thinking, bringing a policeman indoors? 'Inspector Childe, this is my stepdaughter, Elowen. Elowen, this is Inspector Childe, who has most thoughtfully come up to introduce himself.'

Isabel retreated further, her heart pounding harder for the fact that, by the sound of it, Julia didn't even know the man. What if he'd been sent to see whether Julia was harbouring her? Or, what if he wasn't a real policeman at all but a private detective commissioned by Hector to find her? Struck by the absurd direction of her thoughts, she gave a despairing shake of her head; nobody, even Hector, could have tracked her down this quickly. It simply wasn't possible. Furthermore, was this how she was destined to carry on – regarding every figure of authority with mistrust? Look at her, skulking in doorways. Of course, the poor chap was a real police inspector. And while a modicum of caution was essential, letting suspicion rule her days was no better than when she'd spent her every waking minute trying to gauge Hector's mood in order to avoid accidentally provoking him. She had got away from the man. She had assumed a different name. For now, at least, she was safe. And she would do everything within her power to ensure she remained so until she heard from Vincent, and he came up with a new plan – preferably one that saw them now making their fresh start somewhere other than in London.

Deciding nonetheless to remain out of sight, she returned to watching through the crack to see Elowen and the inspector shake hands.

'How do you, Inspector Childe? I heard from Constable Gregory that you'd arrived.'

'Constable Gregory,' Julia said, 'is my stepdaughter's –'

'Friend,' Elowen said sharply. 'We're friends.'

Isabel switched her attention back to the caller. From what little she could see of him, he had an open expression and a surprisingly gentle face. Apart from that, he was singularly unremarkable: medium height and build; upright stance; on his face, the first etchings of middle age.

'You know, Inspector Childe,' she heard Julia say, 'I'm glad you've come up because I never did get around to thanking you for recommending us as a billet for the evacuees from Bristol. And that's remiss of me because we truly are grateful.'

Isabel saw the inspector smile. 'Since it was Sergeant Edworthy who put forward your name, and I believe Constable Gregory who thought of you in the first place, I shall pass your gratitude on to them. Sergeant Edworthy speaks highly of you.'

'Goodness. Anyway, Inspector, would you care for a cup of tea and a biscuit – a spot of refreshment after your climb all the way up here to see us?'

Cup of tea and a biscuit? Had Julia forgotten she was there – let alone supposed to be in hiding?

'As tempting a prospect as that is, Mrs Nance, I really should get back to the station. If I am absent much longer, Sergeant Edworthy will think I've become lost and send out a search party.' With the conversation seeming to draw to a close, Isabel allowed herself to relax a little. 'Although, one last question, if I may.'

'Ask away, Inspector.'

'Aside from the schoolteachers you are about to billet, is it just the two of you residing here?'

Behind the door, Isabel tensed afresh.

'Well, we no longer have paying guests. And no doubt Sergeant Edworthy told you I'm widowed. But I do have a friend staying. She's a voluntary evacuee.'

Now what was Julia doing?

'I see. Well, please, do remember, both of you, that my station and I are at your service. Day or night, should need arise.'

'Good to know, Inspector.'

'It was a pleasure to meet you, Mrs Nance.'

'You too, Inspector.'

When Isabel heard the front door close, she exhaled in relief. 'I thought,' she said when the two women returned from seeing the inspector out, 'he might have been someone sent by Hector.'

'What, even though you've made it nigh-on impossible for him to find you?'

Isabel lowered her gaze. 'Nothing guarantees my safety from that man.'

'Either way,' Julia said matter-of-factly, 'not inviting him in would have looked suspicious.'

'I suppose it would, yes.'

Returning to the scullery and turning on the tap to start the washing-up, Isabel tried to slow her breathing; all the while Inspector Childe had been standing in the hall, her heart had been thudding as though preparing her to flee. On a more welcome note, her fear that Hector had tracked her down had at least brought her to appreciate that, even after just a few days of living beyond his reach, she had been right to take Ruby's advice and seize the chance to leave. Moreover, had she ever been uncertain whether a life with Vincent was what she really wanted, she knew now that it was. How she would get over her grief if that didn't come about, she had no idea. But since, to her unabating distress, there was nothing – other than pray – that she could do to hasten Vincent's return, she would direct her efforts to living as quietly as possible. How long her nerves would allow her to exist in this state, she didn't know. It would simply have to be for as long as it took.

At the sound of the Greenwich time signal on the wireless the following morning, Isabel checked her wristwatch: eight o'clock precisely.

'Sorry I'm late coming down,' she said when she reached the kitchen to find Julia already busy. 'I opened my eyes and couldn't believe the time.'

'No matter. You're clearly still catching up on your sleep.'

'Yes. I don't think I woke up all night.' She gestured to the wireless set. 'Is this news of London?'

'Sorry. Couldn't say. Haven't really been listening.'

'Mind if I –'

'Be my guest.'

In the capital, the newsreader's voice intoned as Isabel turned the volume knob to the right, *enemy attacks continued. On Thursday, during the second of three daylight raids, Buckingham Palace was struck by a number of high explosive bombs. Two of the devices exploded in the palace quadrangle, rupturing a water main and blowing out windows. A third struck the*

Poor old Buckingham Palace again. Clearly, Isabel thought, the Luftwaffe were trying to finish what they'd started in those attacks that had destroyed Warbone Gate. The speed with which she'd become out of touch with what was going on back in the capital pricked at her conscience; where she'd had the fortune to escape and leave it all behind, few others would have been so lucky. Alphonse, Mireille and their staff would be enduring the infernal raids and surviving in any way they could. And then there was Vincent. What business did she have sleeping soundly through the night with him still unaccounted for? What right did she even have to leave London – to stop looking for him?

'I should be there,' she blurted.

'What's that?'

At one end of the kitchen table, Julia was weighing out flour, apparently to add to a bowl of what Isabel assumed to be cake mixture. She went towards her.

'I should go back to London.'

The metal pan settled in equilibrium with the brass weight on the other side of the scales, Julia folded over the top of the bag of flour and, with a frown, met Isabel's look. 'Has Petie been, then?' She tipped the flour into the mixing bowl.

'Petie?'

'The postman. Has he brought word of Vincent?'

Isabel shook her head. 'I didn't see anything on the mat.'

Taking a large spoon, Julia set about folding the flour into the batter. 'Fatless sponge,' she remarked. 'Mrs Black from the WVS was looking for volunteers to knock up a cake for when the school arrive. She said the little 'uns are bound to be famished. Since I had sufficient sugar, I told her I'd make a sponge and fill it with jam.'

'That's kind of you.'

'Well, these things make you stop and think, don't they? In a different life, it could have been me putting a child of mine on a train this morning. One measly cake seemed the least I could do.'

'Do you need a hand?' Not for the first time since arriving, Isabel felt awkward, simply standing there, watching. Unlike the way so much of her own time in Warbone Gate had been spent languishing, aimlessly filling her days, Julia was hardly ever still.

With her head, Julia gestured to the assortment of utensils on the table. 'Spot of washing-up wouldn't go amiss. Once this thing's in the oven, I'll get us some breakfast. But you still haven't explained the urgent need to go back to London.'

Watching Julia divide the cake mixture between two sandwich tins and then level the tops with the back of her spoon, Isabel shifted her weight. 'According to that news broadcast, the Germans are persisting with their attacks. And Vincent's family is still there. Even with their home badly damaged, *they* couldn't just leave.'

'No, but, from what you said, they had other family to go to. You also said there wasn't room for you to go with them.'

'Well, no, there wouldn't have been.' As far as she could tell, they hadn't even known Vincent was intending for her to take refuge there, let alone that the two of them were planning a future together.

'So, even if you did go back, where would you stay? And what about the risk of bumping into Hector? Don't forget, I saw how panicked you were when our new inspector showed up. More to the point, while going back there might make *you* feel as though you were doing something useful, you run the risk of becoming a nuisance for the poor man's family when they already have problems of their own. No, as far as I can make out, none of the reasons why you went to the bother of changing your name and coming all the way down here in the first place have gone away.'

Julia was right; there were myriads of reasons why going back would be foolhardy, all of which only made her feel worse. 'The reasons haven't gone away, no.'

Her kitchen timer wound to thirty-five minutes, Julia set it on the window sill and then turned to stand, hands on hips. 'Issy, I know how much you must be pining for Vincent – and how worried you must be for his well-being. It's only natural you should want to go back there and look for him. But, surely, as you said yourself, the best people to search for him are the ARP.'

From where she'd been absently trailing a finger across the surface of the table, Isabel met her friend's look. 'Then why haven't they found him?'

'We don't know for certain they haven't. But I'm a firm believer in the saying that no news is good news. You told me Vincent's family are lovely people. So, when they know something, I'm sure you will be the first person they think of.'

Julia continuing to be right did nothing to ease the nagging of Isabel's conscience. 'While everything you've said might be true, it doesn't make me feel any better.'

'I don't suppose it does. I doubt there's much that will. So, come on, let's get this lot cleared up and have some breakfast. Everything always looks bleak on an empty stomach.'

At least, Isabel reflected, feeling guilty on an empty stomach didn't also make her feel sick. But she couldn't keep on disagreeing with Julia. 'Very well.'

'Good. Now, then. We've been told to expect the school around three o'clock.'

'And that will be the children and their teachers, all arriving together?'

'That's right. Down in the village, there's a rambling old house called Foxbeare. Until a few years back, it was the holiday home of Sir James Sackville and his family. Anyway, when war broke out, he gave it over to the government to use as they saw fit, and so it's going to be used as the school. The headmaster's going to live there with his wife, along with a few of the youngest children and their mothers. Up here, we're taking four schoolmistresses, and the rest of the children are being billeted with local families.'

'Gosh. What an ordeal for them all.'

'Indeed. By all accounts,' Julia went on, 'the poor mites will have had quite the journey, which is why, thanks to the generosity of folks hereabouts, we're laying on a welcome tea. And why it's a case of all hands to the pump.'

'Of course.' As Isabel needed to keep reminding herself, she wasn't the only one having to contend with upheaval and distress. 'Obviously, I'll do what I can – hand round sandwiches or whatever.'

When Julia threw back her head and laughed, Isabel frowned.

'Far be it from me to turn down help, but tea with the ladies' circle this most definitely won't be. More likely, you'll be trying to prevent the older ones eating everything in sight at the expense of the tiddlers.'

Recognizing her own stupidity made Isabel feel foolish. 'Yes, well, either way, I'll try to be useful.'

'Then let's see what there is for breakfast. I've a feeling that today is going to take every ounce of stamina we have.'

While she knew what Julia meant, Isabel felt she needed every ounce of her stamina simply to get through any sort of a day. Living with so much uncertainty – continually having to try and keep a lid on her fear for Vincent and the direction of her own future – was fraying her nerves and consuming her energy to a degree she'd never thought possible.

Following Julia from the scullery back to the kitchen and the sweet, eggy aroma of the baking sponge, her thoughts returned to the children in Bristol, whose poor mothers would, just a couple of hours earlier, have been packing them up, ready to entrust to the care of strangers in a village more than a hundred miles away. How awful for all of them, children and parents alike. With no thought for the justness of it or otherwise, war was spreading terror and heartache far and wide; no one had the monopoly on fear, few were untouched. And perhaps, every time she thought about Vincent, and felt the cold hand of dread fasten its bony fingers about her heart, she would do well to remind herself that, for some, their plight was even worse.

'I *want* to see a cow.'

'Not sure I can manage a cow, my 'andsome. How about some sheep instead? Got plenty o' they.'

'But I want to see a *cow*. They said there'd be *cows*.'

It was late that afternoon and Isabel was with Julia and the women of the WVS in the church hall, welcoming the evacuated teachers and children from Bristol.

Acknowledging the woman waiting to take the young boy home, Isabel bent down to the level of his screwed-up little face. From his size, he appeared to be about six years old. From the luggage label looped around the top button of his coat, she read the name Malcolm Baker.

'Hello, Malcolm,' she said, taking care not to sound stern. 'Shall I tell you something I haven't told anyone else?' The child regarded her with mistrust. She pressed on anyway. 'Like you, I had to leave *my* home and come all the way here on the train. And just like you, *I* was hoping to see a cow, too. But *you're* lucky, because *you're* going to see some sheep and although I've been here a few days now, I haven't seen even *one* sheep yet. So, how about, if you go with this nice lady, Mrs –' She looked enquiringly up at the woman.

'Bale. Mrs Gladys Bale. Beacon Farm.'

'If you go with Mrs Bale to her house, where she's going to look after you for a while, I'll keep my eye open for any cows. And if I see some, I'll tell Mrs Bale where they are. How about that?' His mistrust still plain, the child nevertheless nodded. 'Good. And Mrs Bale will keep a lookout for some, too, won't you, Mrs Bale?'

'I certainly will. And when we get 'ome, we'll ask Mr Bale if *he's* seen any.'

When adult and child left the church hall, Isabel sighed. The evacuated school had arrived in the village a little before four o'clock, some of the children boisterous, most of them fretful, their teachers appearing simply relieved the ordeal of their journey was behind them.

'Thank you so much for this,' one of their number had said to Isabel when the children were tucking into a modest spread of paste sandwiches and sponge cake. 'We couldn't have had a better welcome.' Unable to claim any of the credit, Isabel smiled, nonetheless. 'I'm Elizabeth Anderson, by the way. Deputy to the headmaster, Mr Lawrence.'

'How do you do?' Isabel said as she shook the woman's hand. 'Isabel Smith. I believe you're billeted with us at Fairlight.'

'Then please, do call me Elizabeth.'

And it was with Miss Anderson that Isabel once again found herself chatting that evening.

'When we were leaving school this morning, I said to Mr Lawrence that I was going to miss my bicycle – I cycle to school and back, you see. But I rather think climbing that hill every day will do more for my calves and lungs than any bicycle ever could.'

'I haven't got the hang of it yet myself,' Isabel admitted. 'I've only been here a few days – I'm a voluntary evacuee from London. Julia – Mrs Nance – is an old friend.'

'London, goodness. I should imagine you couldn't wait to leave. Have the raids there been as terrible as we hear on the wireless?'

Isabel paused for a moment while she considered what to say. Already, she regretted mentioning London. 'Those first air raids recently did rather take us all by surprise. We knew attacks were imminent – we'd already had a few, although, in reality, they'd been little more than nuisances. So, the scale of the bombardment did come as something of a shock.' In a bid not to be drawn further, she asked, 'What about you?'

'Our very first raid was back in June – the night of the nineteenth if I remember correctly. They went for the docks at Avonmouth. That was when Mr Lawrence started talking to the school's governors and the council about everyone's safety. In evacuation terms, though, the government considered Bristol a neutral area and recommended we stay put. Then came more alerts – thankfully, a good number of them false alarms.'

'But it's always the case that the next one might not be.'

'Precisely. In fact, when they came back for the Bristol Aeroplane factory at Filton, Mr Lawrence decided enough was enough. Thankfully, by then, the governors and the council were of the same mind and the ministry agreed that we should evacuate.'

'And now you're here. And safe.'

Elizabeth nodded. 'We hope so.'

Detecting the melancholy in the woman's tone, Isabel realized that being safe was something no one should ever take for granted. That said, to flourish rather than wither – even amid that safety – she had come to appreciate that what one also needed was love and fulfilment. Until a week ago, she had been close to having all that and more. But now what did she have?

With a sidelong glance at Elizabeth, she withheld a sigh. The only thing she could do, she supposed, was keep praying that, somehow, despite what would now appear to be very low odds, Vincent was still alive and that, before too much longer, they would be back together, those precious necessities of love and shared purpose once again within their grasp, the prospect of a life of warmth and fulfilment unfolding ahead of them.

9

'So, tell me, what exactly does your preparedness committee do?'

It was now a morning in early October and, with Elowen gone to work, Isabel had been making herself useful by pressing pillowslips. She was finding it surprisingly satisfying to take a crinkled cotton case, smooth away the creases and add it to the growing stack on the table. Moreover, not only had she so far avoided burning herself on the smoothing iron but she'd been finding out how, in the absence of her usual stream of guests, Julia had taken to occupying her days.

'To be honest,' Julia replied to her enquiry, 'we do anything we think might help us to survive under the enemy's rule. When those government leaflets came through the door back in the summer – you know, instructing us all what to do when the invader comes – I went to the parish council and asked what they were doing to prepare the village as a whole. When they said they saw no need for anything more than the government's advice, well, Elowen will tell you, I saw red. If it was obvious to me that the best way to prepare for enemy occupation was to band together, pool reserves and ideas, why was it not plain to the parish councillors? Anyway, as is usually the case with these things, having been the one to put forward the idea, I got saddled with the job of setting it up.'

When Julia went on to list aspects of everyday life that might become difficult under enemy occupation, Isabel realized she'd never given the practicalities of life *after* the invasion a thought.

'That sounds like an enormous undertaking,' she said. The final pillowcase pressed, she folded it to match the others and put it on the pile.

'It was. Keeping the thing going still is. Anyway, since you look to be done there, fancy coming down the village with me? I need a length of knicker elastic.'

Wrestling with the ironing board in an attempt to fold it, Isabel smothered a laugh. 'Oh dear. Please tell me you were sitting down when it snapped.'

'Mercifully, on this occasion, I was.' Arriving beside her and, with two deft manoeuvres, folding the board flat, Julia grinned. 'So, anyway —' But at the clatter of the letterbox, Julia disappeared through to the hall, returning moments later with a brown envelope. 'For you,' she said and handed it to her. 'Postmarked London.'

Dare she hope, Isabel wondered, heart racing as she scanned the unfamiliar handwriting, that inside this envelope were her new documents? Holding her breath, she ripped open the flap and tugged out the contents. Then she exhaled with relief: official registration document; identity card; ration book. All showing the name Smith. Ruby and Connie had worked a miracle. She was no longer Thaxley. More than three weeks of existing in a state of limbo were over.

In her relief, she started to cry. 'It's done,' she said. 'I can inform the authorities of my new address and register here for my rations.'

'Then, how about,' Julia suggested as she put an arm around Isabel's shoulders, 'we walk down to the village for my elastic and see to your business while we're there?'

'Good idea.' Turning away, Isabel dried her eyes. 'Then I'll have one less reason to fret.'

New documents wouldn't bring Vincent back, she knew that, but their arrival did mean one less lie to catch her out. She was now Isabel Smith and, although not in the situation or location of her choosing, deeply grateful, nonetheless.

'So,' Julia said as they left the draper's. 'That's your affairs seen to and my length of elastic bought. Anything else you need while you're down here?' But before Isabel could reply that she didn't think so, Julia elbowed her in the ribs. 'Look. Over there.'

She glanced as directed; on the other side of the street was the new police inspector. 'I suppose,' she muttered, feeling her pulse speed up, 'it's too late to avoid him.'

'Avoid him? Why would we want to do that?'

'Because I'm —' But because she was what? Did being in possession of a new identity card mean she was still in hiding or not?

'Surely,' Julia said, 'now you have new documents, you can stop skulking about in the shadows and go about your business like anyone else.'

By the time Isabel realized Julia had a point, the

inspector had raised a hand in recognition and was diverting towards them.

'Ladies, good morning.'

They responded in unison. 'Good morning, Inspector.'

'Nice little burst of sunshine,' Julia went on to observe.

'Most welcome, yes.'

Anxious not to appear stand-offish, Isabel said, 'Tell me, Inspector, how are you settling in?'

'Very well, thank you. I don't believe we've met but instinct tells me you're Mrs Nance's evacuee friend.'

Bother. What an idiot she was. In her desire to do as Julia had suggested and come across as normal, she'd overlooked that they hadn't yet been introduced; *she* might know about *him*, but he knew nothing of her. 'Isabel Smith,' she said and extended a gloved hand. 'How do you do?'

'How do you do, Miss Smith? A pleasure to meet you.'

'Likewise, Inspector.'

With a polite smile, the inspector returned his attention to Julia. 'I trust all is well with your evacuated teachers, Mrs Nance?'

'All good so far.'

'Excellent. Well, then I mustn't detain you —'

'Actually,' Julia said, 'I was wondering, Inspector, whether you would care to join us one weekend for Sunday lunch?'

Isabel flinched. The prospect of having to face a police inspector across Fairlight's dining table was disconcerting; concocting tales to conceal her tracks from Hector was one thing, misleading an officer of the law quite another.

'That's a very kind invitation.'

As the inspector replied, Isabel felt certain he flicked her the tiniest of glances, although it could easily have been down to her imagination and heightened state of alert. On the other hand, perhaps instinct told him she was hiding something. It wouldn't surprise her; Hector always had said she was a hopeless liar.

'No standing on ceremony,' Julia went on. 'Just the chance for me to thank you for recommending Fairlight as a billet, and for you to get to know some of us.'

'Sounds delightful.'

'This Sunday might be difficult but perhaps the week after?'

'Perfect. What time should I arrive?'

'Shall we say . . . one o'clock?'

'One o'clock. And may I bring something? A contribution in these straitened times?'

'Just yourself, Inspector.'

'I shall look forward to it.'

When Inspector Childe continued on his way, Isabel set aside her momentary irritation to pull her friend's leg. 'You know, the eagerness with which the man accepted your invitation for lunch suggests to me he's a bachelor.'

'He may well be. But before you accuse me of flirting – or some such nonsense – that's not why I asked him.'

'No?'

'Having him recommend us as a billet really did save our bacon. I'm also of the opinion that you can't befriend too many police officers. The man's predecessor didn't have much time for a woman employed on her own account. This one seems different.'

'Even so,' Isabel said as they began walking, 'I shall probably spend the entire lunch in a flap, worried that he'll detect I'm hiding something.'

'Which is precisely why we should all be on first-name terms. The more we welcome him, the less cause he'll have to regard you with suspicion.'

While she couldn't dispute Julia's reasoning, Isabel remained unconvinced; the man might have friendly eyes, but he clearly hadn't risen to the rank of inspector without being shrewd. That said, she could hardly insist Julia stop entertaining in her own home.

'If you say so.'

'I do. Besides,' Julia went on, 'it will only be for an hour or two. You can act normally for that long, can't you?'

Isabel laughed. 'I'm not sure I know what normal is. It's a long time since anything about my life qualified as that – since *I* was normal.'

'Then pretend. Play a part. By your own telling, it's what you've been doing these last twenty years anyway.'

Julia was right. Her role as a wife had indeed been one long performance: in the company of Hector's friends, she'd acted gracious and convivial; in private, she'd acted immune to the humiliation and belittlement. In fact, the only times in the last two decades when she hadn't been acting was when she'd been with Vincent.

Vincent.

The dull ache of loss swooped back in.

She didn't have time to dwell, though, because as they started up the zigzag path, Julia took her arm and said, 'Who would have thought, all these years after we left

Havenham, you an' me would be back to muddling along together?'

Recalling the warmth of their friendship at Havenham made Isabel smile. 'Oh, to have had the wisdom and experience then that we have now.'

Yes, if only. Through the intervening years, Isabel had often found herself with cause to reflect upon how the simplest incident – seemingly unimportant at the time – and one's reactions to it, could change the entire course of a life. Had she never persuaded her mother, Leonora, to accept an invitation to a polo match – purely to be rid of her for a weekend – then Leonora would never have met the Argentinian she'd subsequently been in such a rush to marry, and would have had no need to push her only daughter into marrying Hector. Equally, had she, Isabel, the summer before that, simply dared to kiss that astonishing young Frenchman in Lausanne – had she experienced whatever he was offering – then she might have returned home more certain not just of her own mind but of what she wanted from life, as well. She would definitely not have allowed herself to be herded into marrying Hector. But she *hadn't* kissed him. And she *had* been herded, the result being that it had taken twenty years, and the chance arrival into her life of a different Frenchman, before she'd truly come to understand not only what she'd been missing, but what she no longer wanted to live without.

So, yes, whether she was ever reunited with Vincent or not, she knew now that she would be eternally grateful to him for opening her eyes – for showing her it was never too late to see what was possible and, perhaps, just as importantly, to grasp the opportunity to bring it about.

'Oh, my goodness. Here's a surprise.'

It was now a couple of days later and, from where she was busy at the stove, Isabel glanced over her shoulder to see Julia, leaning against the door frame, reading a letter she'd just collected from the doormat.

'What's that?' Turning back and raising herself on tiptoes, she peered into the stock pot of soup she was stirring. She was in two minds about chopping up a couple of potatoes to add in the hope that, as they cooked down, they would thicken it up. The idea of trying to remember how to make the recipe she'd grown up knowing as 'Granny's Autumn Broth' had come to her as she'd been hanging her smalls on the washing line and noticed the size of the pumpkins growing behind the outhouse; according to Julia, Elowen had been given a handful of seeds by Alf Nott and, in a burst of enthusiasm, had sown them, watered them meticulously for a week or so, and then promptly forgotten all about them. Clearly, the plants hadn't suffered for their neglect, producing between them half a dozen bright orange fruits, some almost large enough to fill a wheelbarrow.

'It's a letter from Ronnie,' Julia replied.

Fetching a spoon, Isabel tasted the soup. Hm. It needed a dash of salt and a pinch more nutmeg and cinnamon; Julia's spices were so ancient they seemed to have lost their potency. Otherwise, apart from the thinness of it – simply remedied – it tasted surprisingly good.

'Heavens, that is a surprise,' she said of Julia's news before putting down the spoon and reaching for the grater. 'How is she? It's ages since I dropped her a line.' In fact, Isabel thought, the last time she'd written to her would have been back in the spring; it was certainly before she'd met Vincent.

The extra spices grated into the pan, she went to the pantry to fetch a couple of potatoes.

'Same here. Terrible how easily we fall out of touch.'

When Julia continued reading but didn't immediately go on to share any of Ronnie's news, Isabel surrendered to curiosity. 'Is she well?' She stared down at the size of the potatoes: two should suffice. Now, where had Julia's peeler got to? Ah, there it was, in the sink.

'She seems fine. She says that Philip – you remember her son, don't you? – has proposed to his girlfriend.'

'Is the young lady anyone we'd know?' It wouldn't surprise her; the Claremonts were 'County', and it was rare for their set to be infiltrated by anyone who wasn't – certainly not where potential marriage partners were concerned, social climbers, in particular, quickly rooted out.

'Unlikely to be anyone *I'd* know. Once we finished school, I was dropped like the proverbial scalding-hot spud. I don't mean by Ronnie herself,' she hastened to add.

'No.' Julia wasn't wrong; most of the girls' families had been inveterate snobs.

'Even at school, Ronnie had to fight to get me invited down for a weekend. And even then I could always tell I was only there under sufferance.'

'I remember, yes.' The potatoes peeled, Isabel chopped them into cubes, putting them into the colander as she went.

'Wrong accent, wrong clothes. Wrong father.'

What had made it particularly galling, Isabel reflected, as she rinsed the potatoes under the tap to remove some of the starch, was that Ronnie's own family, the Veaseys, had been rather 'fringe' themselves – at least, they had until Ronnie had bagged Ralph Claremont. Their status had gone up in leaps and bounds after that. 'Anyway, who's the girl?'

In the interim, Julia had been reading on and had to turn back a page to check. 'Alexandra Groves.'

Carefully, Isabel dropped the potato cubes into the simmering pan. 'I don't recall any Groves.'

'Ronnie says they're what her mother-in-law would have dismissed as *nobody much*, and that she is probably now turning in her grave, but that times have changed and it's down to Philip to choose who he marries.'

'Sounds like the sort of thing my mother would write when she didn't want to go on record as disapproving of someone.'

'Although, as it happens,' Julia said, 'that's not the reason for her letter.'

Rinsing her hands under the tap, Isabel turned to regard her friend. 'No? It's not Ralph, is it? He's not ill?' It wouldn't be too much of a surprise; at twenty-five years her senior, Ronnie's husband, Ralph, had to be somewhere in his mid-sixties.

'Not as far as I can tell.'

'That's a relief.' As she stood, drying her hands, she watched Julia lower the sheet of notepaper and then move to the table to sit down.

'No, she's actually enquiring about *you*.'

'*Me?*' With a quick glance at the soup pot, Isabel went across and pulled out the seat next to her.

'She writes that, about a week ago, they had a telephone call from Hector.'

Thoughts scattering in all directions, Isabel landed heavily on the chair. So, Hector *was* looking for her – for him to resort to telephoning Ronnie, there could be no other reason. Ralph Claremont was one of the few people Hector looked up to, a man he would feel he could rely on for discretion – all that old-boy regimental nonsense. In Ronnie, though, he'd met his match, which was why he'd always forbidden Isabel to visit the Claremonts without him. Since the morning she'd stood, staring at the ruins of Warbone Gate and determining to seize the chance to leave him, she'd become beset by the fear that he would look for her; he was, by nature, a thoroughly suspicious and mistrustful man, who never could bear to think someone might outmanoeuvre him. So, when no one was able to provide him with definitive proof that she had been lost in the bombing, all her instincts decreed that his nature would quickly get the better of him, leaving him unable to rest for fear she had somehow managed to escape his grasp. It was why she'd been wary of having to put that notice in *The Gazette* about her intended change of name; even though she'd given Connie's lodgings as her address, Hector was nothing if not resourceful and knew people everywhere. He also wasn't above using intimidation to get people to divulge what he wanted to know.

'Does she say why he telephoned her?' It seemed wise to make sure she wasn't jumping to conclusions.

'To know whether she'd heard from you – specifically, it would seem, if she knew where you might be.'

Isabel exhaled; then thank goodness she'd decided against leaving London for Sussex, or Ronnie would have ended up in a real jam. 'Does she say what she told him?'

'She says –' Julia checked the letter – 'she told him she hadn't heard from you in quite a while and assumed you were in town.'

Isabel relaxed slightly; by coming to Julia rather than going to Ronnie, she had definitely made the right choice. 'Doesn't mean he won't still find me, though.'

As usual, Julia was more pragmatic. 'Don't see how. Not only have you changed your name, but you said you'd never mentioned me.'

Isabel tried to think back. 'I'm bound to have spoken about you at some point. Although, such would have been his lack of interest that, after all this time, he would be extremely unlikely to recall where you live.'

Julia set Ronnie's letter on the table. 'Then without knowing that, there's no chance of him suddenly showing up here, is there?'

Isabel wished she shared Julia's conviction. 'In theory, no. But you don't know Hector.'

'I don't, no. But I do know even he can't do the impossible. And so, I really think,' Julia said as she refolded Ronnie's letter and pushed it back into the envelope, 'there's no need for you to panic. I, for one, shan't give you away – not even to Ronnie. I'll simply write back and say something vague.'

Isabel tensed; *something vague* wasn't terribly reassuring. On the other hand, she couldn't expect Julia to tell outright lies. 'How vague?'

'Oh, I don't know. How about something along the lines of "It does sound as though it's been terrible in London these last few weeks, doesn't it? People there must be desperate to get out. As for Isabel, she hasn't written in a while." No word of a lie there.'

'I suppose not.'

'Truly,' Julia said, and reached to squeeze Isabel's hand. 'Even if Ronnie reads between the lines, she wouldn't give you away – you do know that, don't you?' Slowly, Isabel nodded. 'Loyalty runs through her veins. However,' Julia went on, 'since it's clear Hector *is* now spreading his search for you, I feel duty-bound to point out quite how foolish you would be – should you feel so moved – to go back and resume searching for Vincent.'

Julia was right. If Hector was making a concerted effort to locate her, she'd be a fool to make his job easier. Not that her husband would actually be hoping to find her; more likely, he would be after having her declared dead. Ironic, really, that it was an outcome that would, for once, suit both of them just fine.

Unfortunately, Julia's mention of Vincent once again put him at the forefront of her mind – along with an altogether darker recognition. 'You don't believe Vincent is still alive, do you?'

Julia returned her look with a sigh. 'Since you would want me to be honest, I'll admit to thinking it unlikely. Despite my belief that no news is good news, were he alive, then, by now, I would expect you to have heard – either from him, or about him.'

'So, you think he's been dead from the very beginning.' She was surprised at how calmly she was able to say it. Did that mean she thought the same?

'I'm afraid I do.'

'You think I'm wasting my time, continuing to telephone the ARP and trying to get through to the bistro.'

'I do. That said, if you want to keep on trying, I won't think any less of you.'

Isabel sighed. 'I simply can't find it in my heart to give up on him – not without knowing for sure what's happened.'

'Understandable.'

'So maybe –' with that, she had a thought – 'maybe I'll have one last go. But this time I'll send a telegram. And I'll pay for a reply. That way, whatever the situation turns out to be – either with him or with his family – I surely stand a better chance of finding out.'

'No harm in one last try.'

'Then I'll go down to the post office and do it right now.' *Before my last scrap of courage deserts me for good.*

If it wasn't for the fact that Julia would want to know how she'd got on, Isabel suspected that, by now, she would have chickened out of going through with it. Earlier, her idea to send a telegram – spurred on by a desire to stop careering between a state of hope for Vincent's safety one day and the depths of despair the next – had seemed sensible. After all, once the thing was sent, the range of possible outcomes was limited: she could receive the joyous news that Vincent had been found alive, irrefutable proof he was dead, no further information either way or, given yesterday's news of yet another Luftwaffe *Blitzkrieg* on the capital, the return of her message with the notification that it couldn't be delivered.

Behind the counter, the postmistress double-checked the number of words in Isabel's message, totted up the price, accepted her money and passed her a penny change. 'There you go, then, dear. I'll get this sent straight off. And the moment your reply comes in, Petie will run it up to you.'

'Thank you, Mrs Crabbe.' Dropping her change into her purse, Isabel turned for the door. She had done all she could. What happened next was beyond her control. All she could do now was try not to let worry eat her up while she awaited her reply.

Back outside, wondering nevertheless how to distract herself in the meantime, she spotted a young boy, arms swinging determinedly by his sides as he came striding along the pavement. Despite being tidily dressed, the way the collar of his shirt poked out from the neckline of his grey V-neck pullover suggested he'd been in a hurry to put it on. But why, on a school morning, was he out on his own to start with?

As he drew closer, she recognized him as one of the children evacuated from Bristol.

She stepped into his path.

'Hello. You're Malcolm, aren't you?' Forced to come to a halt, the child stared back at her, lips pressed together in mistrust. 'Don't you have school today?'

Lowering his eyes back to the pavement, he dodged around her and continued on his way. 'I'm going to find the trains.'

She turned and fell into step beside him. Presumably, he'd managed to slip out of school without anyone noticing, meaning that, if she were to persuade him to go back, it would help to know what had driven him to abscond in the first place.

'Do you know the way?' she asked. 'To the trains?'

The child kept up his pace. 'I'll find 'em. I'm good at finding stuff.'

'That's a clever thing to be able to do. I'm hopeless at it.'

He slowed a fraction. 'You got to use your eyes.'

'Yes. Perhaps that's where I'm going wrong.'

'And you got to look really hard. Sometimes, I help Mr Bale find his sheep. They get through the fence and go in the wood.'

Picturing the woman who had been waiting to collect him on the afternoon of the school's arrival, she asked, 'Do you like living on the farm?'

'Uh-huh. There're foxes. And badgers. But I ain't frightened of 'em.'

'No, you don't seem as though you would be. You seem very brave.'

'I am. Mrs Bale says so.'

At least he didn't appear to be running away because

of problems at his billet. 'Mrs Bale sounds like a very wise lady. Do you like her? And Mr Bale?'

'Uh-huh. At bedtime, Mrs Bale gives me warm milk. Milk comes from cows.'

'It does.'

'And if I've cleaned behind my ears and got into my 'jamas by seven o'clock, she reads me a story. Mr Bale got me a stick like his so I can go over the field with him. He says sometimes you need a stick to lean on. And to go up a hill when you get old.'

Isabel smiled. 'I see.'

'And he lets me play with Jess.'

'Is Jess his dog?'

Malcolm nodded. 'She's a girl dog. But she's still good at making the sheep go through the gates.'

Again, Isabel smiled. 'So, tell me, why are you going to find the trains?'

When he unexpectedly looked directly back at her, she was taken by surprise.

His frown suggested the answer was obvious. 'To run away.'

'But I thought you said you like Mr and Mrs Bale. And Jess. And the farm.'

'I do like them. But I *don't* like Big Barry. He calls me *Squirt* and says I'm stupid. But when I tell Miss on him, he says he didn't.'

'Big Barry is a boy in your class?'

Malcolm's eyes darted about as though checking he was safe. And when he replied, it was softly, as though fearing he might be overheard. 'At playtime just now, he told everyone not to talk to me because I was telling lies about being allowed to play with Jess. Then he thumped me and said from now on, I have to do what he says or else watch out. So, I'm going to find the trains cos I *don't* tell lies and I shan't *ever* do as he says.'

'I see. Well, I hope you told Mr and Mrs Bale you were going to run away. That's what they teach you at school, isn't it – to always tell a grown-up where you're going?' Although he continued walking, Isabel noticed his gaze drop to his feet. 'Otherwise, they'll worry about you, won't they? In fact, poor Mrs Bale might be *so* worried that she'll cry and be awake all night, fretting. And without you there to help, Mr Bale might not be able to find his sheep in the wood.' To her surprise, the boy came to a halt and stood, hands on his hips, brow furrowed in thought. 'So, how about, before we go too much further – because it's a very long way to the railway station – you and I go back to school and tell your teacher about Big Barry? After all, if he's being mean to you, he's probably being mean to your friends as well.' When she looked at him for confirmation, he merely kicked the toe of his shoe at a flint. 'That way, you needn't run away and cause Mr and Mrs Bale to worry that you've come to harm. Or miss helping Mr Bale or playing with Jess. What do you say?'

The child regarded her doubtfully. 'Teacher will really make Big Barry stop being mean this time?'

'I'm certain of it – and not just stop being mean to you but being mean to everyone else, as well. And that will happen because *you* chose to be brave and stand up for yourself. You see, Malcolm, when you get older, you'll understand that it's the duty of brave people not to look the other way when they see something that's not right, but to say something – not just for their own benefit but for others who might be even more frightened or scared by it than you are.'

Unexpectedly, her mention of looking out for others triggered a picture of Vincent; dressed in his ARP uniform, he was helping people from the ruins of a bombed-out building.

She fought back tears.

'If I stand up for the other children, they won't be frightened any more?'

'Nowhere near as much as they would be without you. Especially if you tell them you'll keep an eye on them and be ready to help if they do feel afraid.'

'And I can tell them not to listen to Big Barry saying I tell lies about Jess because I *am* allowed to play with her.'

'You *can* tell them that, yes. But, to do that, we need to go back to school, don't we?'

Malcolm huffed. 'S'pose. But you'll come with me? You'll help me make Miss believe me about Big Barry? I won't have to tell her on my own?'

'Of course I'll help you tell her. As a brave person myself, it's my duty.'

'Then you'd better hold my hand, or you might get lost because this school I go to now isn't like my old school. My old school's got a sign outside, so you know where it is. *This* school is inside an old house that doesn't look one bit like a school at all. It hasn't even got a proper playground. It's got big trees, but we're not allowed to climb them and there's —'

When Isabel took the hand Malcolm was holding expectantly towards her, she was unprepared for the tenderness she felt — or for the tugging ache in her chest. In the early years of being married to Hector, her distress over her failure to become pregnant was something she'd done her best to keep buried; it was enough to have the man trot out her failure in that regard every opportunity he got. But, with the passing of time, disappointment had given way to resignation and, since she had no siblings to provide her with nephews or nieces, her life had ground on, devoid of children altogether. She'd never stopped wondering, though, whether, despite the tyrannical and intolerant sort of father Hector would have become, she herself might have made a good mother. It was, of course, impossible to know. But she didn't need to be a parent to recognize that here, today, was a small boy, far from his family and everything he knew, in need of her help to defeat his own Hector. And if that required her to divert to Malcolm some of the bravery she was trying to cling on to as she waited to hear about Vincent and the Durands, she had a feeling that, with Vincent being the man he was, he wouldn't mind in the least.

IO

The envelope trembled in Isabel's hand. 'Gosh,' she said, turning to Julia, standing beside her in the hallway. 'I hadn't expected this so soon.'

'Me neither.'

Isabel's hand continued to quiver. 'Do you think that means it's good news or bad?'

'Well, since we'll only know that by opening it,' Julia said, and gestured towards the drawing room, 'I suggest you come through, sit down and find out.'

It was after lunch on the same day Isabel had sent her telegram to Bistro Durand. And, with her pulse pounding in her ears, she did as Julia said and went to perch on the edge of the sofa, her eyes roving the words *Post Office Telegram* printed in black at the top left-hand corner of the flimsy brown envelope. How she was going to find the courage to open it and read what it said, she had no idea. All the while it remained sealed, then the outcome for which she'd spent these last weeks praying – that Vincent was alive – was still possible; remote, yes, but possible, nonetheless.

With another glance at Julia, she held out the envelope. 'Would *you* open it?'

'Very well.' With no wish to watch her friend's expression while she read the contents, Isabel drew a breath and

151

looked away. She still hadn't breathed out when she heard Julia say, 'They couldn't deliver it.'

She turned sharply. 'That's what it says?'

Julia handed her the slip of paper. On it was her original message, along with the words *Undelivered. Address Bombed Out.*

Precisely the outcome she'd feared.

'Well,' she whispered as the lump in her throat turned to tears. 'If it's all right with you, and there's nothing else you'd like me to help with for a moment, I think I'd like to go out and get some air.' There were only so many times she could break down and sob in front of Julia.

'Take as long as you want. And when you're ready to come back, you can help me make a start on supper.'

Slowly, Isabel rose from the couch. 'All right. Then I'll see you in a while.'

For October, the sunshine had real warmth to it, the sky the clarity of crystal. Unusually, given the exposed location, there wasn't even a breath of wind.

In two minds about which direction to take, at the bottom of the front steps, Isabel paused to look around and then turned right along the gravel path. At the gate, she let herself out, latched it behind her and turned to the left. This afternoon, since there was no need to seek shelter from salt-laden winds, she would explore the path out on to the headland. The ground underfoot felt reasonably dry but, if the going became too rough, she could always turn back.

For the first hundred yards or so, she followed the

tarmac lane, part of her mind pressing her to address the tumult of her thoughts without delay, the other part wanting to do nothing of the sort. When the lane started to curve away to the right, a path – in reality, little more than a track worn through a waist-high stand of bracken – continued ahead. She followed it. And where the crispy brown bracken began to thin, a short stretch of tussocky grass gave way to a sloping expanse of turf that felt dense and springy beneath her feet. There were rabbit droppings and evidence of sheep but the path, whose course across the sward was becoming increasingly difficult to pick out, appeared to continue towards the first of two promontories. Realizing they were the jagged finger-shaped outcrops she could see from her bedroom window, she swung round and looked back. This low down, all she could see of the three villas were the tops of their first-floor windows, the grey slate of their roofs, and the fancy brickwork of their chimney stacks.

She turned back and followed the route trodden into the turf, the crash of the waves and the drag of pebbles on the narrow stretch of beach at the foot of the cliff growing louder the further she went. Until a few weeks ago, she'd never realized how the sea could be so noisy, nor that it was so relentless. Of the man-made clamour that normally filled her ears, there was no sound; without the sea and the wailing of the gulls, the place would be silent.

Away to her left, she spotted what appeared to be a bench and turned towards it. Positioned in a slight depression, and facing the bay, it was a simple plank, worn smooth from use, the ground in front of it a dimple of scuffed-bare earth. From force of habit wiping a hand over the surface and then inspecting her palm, she sat down. As she had thought a while ago, with Hector no longer able to forbid her, nor her mother to pronounce them unbecoming, she should probably try to buy a couple of pairs of slacks. They would certainly be more practical than a skirt and, no doubt, warmer through the winter. She'd already noticed that Elowen wore a pair, as, on occasion, did Julia. But that was beside the point; she hadn't brought herself there to think about clothing; she had come to try to decide what to do.

With no idea where to start, she let her gaze drift where it chose across the bay. Aside from what the troubling result of her telegram suggested about Vincent, his family, and their fate, she had a husband to avoid and, apart from the quarterly interest on her trust, no proper means of support. Julia was being immensely understanding and had said she could stay at Fairlight for as long as she needed. But, despite Elowen taking two jobs to help keep them afloat, and Julia receiving a billeting allowance for taking in evacuees, she could tell that her friend's financial situation was tight. Besides, a middle-aged woman shouldn't be scrounging from friends, no matter how long-standing their relationship. On the other hand, as she had recently reflected, what sort of age was forty to be contemplating starting over? Were it anyone else, she would pronounce them hare-brained, tell them they needed their head examined. How could anything good come of a woman of her years throwing everything up in the air? When Ruby had said that making a fresh start would be hard, she clearly hadn't been exaggerating.

Continuing to gaze ahead, she sighed. The sorry truth was that she was ill-equipped for life on her own, her entire existence as an adult having depended upon Hector for support. But then Vincent had come along. The fact that there was no comparison between what the two men offered her was neither here nor there; of greater significance was the fact that the only reason she had been able to even contemplate leaving Hector was because Vincent had been prepared to provide for her.

By contrast, there was Julia, who, it could be argued, by coming into a generous inheritance, had been extremely fortunate. However, rather than sit back and fritter it slowly to nothing, she had seized the initiative, believed in her own innate abilities and, in order to provide for herself and her stepdaughter, had gone into business. And when it came to overcoming hardship, Elowen, no doubt spurred on by her stepmother's example, was following suit. Even the schoolmistresses billeted on Julia earned their way in the world; none of *them* relied upon a man. And they weren't radical emancipation types but ordinary women taking responsibility for their own well-being.

Was it too late for her to do the same? Common sense suggested it was. But common sense might have to yield, because the only alternative to standing on her own two feet was to go crawling back to Hector. Unfortunately, getting by on her own would require a plan – or at least an idea from which to start building one – but she simply couldn't picture its shape or form.

Maybe you can't, the more rational part of her mind reasoned, *but you could stop clinging to the dream of a life that is clearly no longer going to come true.* Last week, when the telephone operator still hadn't been able to get through to the bistro, she'd asked her for a list of other telephone numbers in the name of Durand. When she'd called each of them in turn, no one had known of either Vincent *or* Alphonse, the only sensible conclusion being that his cousin didn't share the same surname, thus bringing that particular line of enquiry to a dead end; even had the Durands survived this latest round of air raids, wherever they were now, she was unlikely to find them. Moreover, on the occasions when she'd telephoned the ARP and insisted on being put through to the office of the Chief Warden, one of his subordinates had come on the line to inform her that their search for Mr Durand continued and that, as soon as they had anything to report, not a moment would be wasted in letting her know.

In her despair, she sighed. With Vincent now missing for five weeks, she had to accept he was unlikely to simply turn up one day, let alone do so completely unharmed. But whenever she'd so far paused to reflect upon the fact, she'd inevitably ended up in tears, the absence of definitive news simply hardening the terror she'd spent the last month trying to quell.

Perhaps, now, though, with her telegram undeliverable, it was time to be truthful and admit that, in all probability, Vincent was lost and that, lost with him, was not only the warmth and reassurance she had found in his love, but the hope she'd had for the future they'd been going to pursue. Accepting the fact wouldn't be easy; she would have to summon the sort of strength she wasn't even sure she possessed. At least, thanks to Julia, there was no rush; she could take things one step at a time. Besides, before doing anything further, she should at least make one last call to the ARP and insist they tell her the state of their search, because only once that final glimmer of hope had been extinguished would she be able to sit down with Julia and ask for her help determining what to do next.

But first, since the tears were already in her eyes, she would have one last cry: she would mourn the loss of the man for whom she had been going to risk relatively little to gain so much; mourn the loss of her one chance of love and happiness, the loss of her dream. Julia had lost Jago and survived. Somehow, she would have to find a way to do the same, without Vincent.

Isabel stared into her lap.

'That's it, then,' she said when she felt the warmth of Julia's hand covering her own. 'I have no idea where his family is, and the ARP have been unable either to locate him or even to be certain of his last movements.'

'My condolences, Miss Smith,' the Chief Warden had said when she'd just telephoned, 'but it would appear we have done all we can. I have personally notified the police that Mr Durand must now be presumed dead and have asked that they attempt to notify his family via the details he gave us when he joined. I truly am sorry. Those I have spoken to from his command tell me he was both compassionate and dedicated. Again, my condolences for your loss.'

Yes, heartbreakingly, Vincent's status as a casualty of the raids was official. It was the last thing any of them had wanted but the only outcome that made any sense.

'Remember,' Julia said as they sat together at the kitchen table. 'You have no need to decide anything in haste. Take your time. Grieve. It will be no consolation to hear this – I know that, even before I say it – but, once someone has been a part of your life in the way that Jago was a part of mine, and Vincent was a part of yours, they never really leave you.' Pressing her fingers to her chest, she went on, 'They stay with you in here.' She moved her fingers to her temple. 'And in here. Memories of things you did together remain. For certain, you'll feel pain. But, eventually, you'll feel peace, too. Even now, I still draw strength from those brief years I had with Jago. I won't go so far as to say that I feel him watching over me, but I understand when people say they sense their departed loved ones close by. When someone has been a profound part of your life, their presence never entirely disappears. You're still guided by them, even when they're no longer with you in body.'

It was a sensation Isabel had recently started to feel about Vincent but was only now, having heard Julia say what she had about Jago, beginning to comprehend.

'One thing I do know for sure,' she said, suddenly confident of the fact, 'is that I shall never go back to Hector. I'd rather go to the poorhouse than that.'

Julia grinned. 'Announce that you were going back to Hector, and you'd have to get past me first. And I have the stubbornness of a mule and the heft of an ox.'

Isabel grinned back. 'You might be right about the mule but you're wrong about the ox.'

'Huh.'

'By not going back to Hector, though, I must accept that I shall never be able to return to London at all.'

Julia shrugged. 'Is that any great loss?'

'Apart from our time at school, and that year in Lausanne, it's pretty much all I've known.'

'Happen it is,' Julia said. 'But it's not where you live that makes you who you are. You've only got to look at me to see that. I moved from Wiltshire to Cornwall driven by passion. I came *here* on a cloud of grief, but also because I saw an opportunity to pay my way in the world and, I hoped, find fulfilment of a different sort.'

'And that's what I need to do, isn't it?'

'Work out what fulfils you? Or stand on your own two feet?'

'Both. I shall never be a mother, but I should like to know fulfilment. I could have stayed married to Hector for a hundred years and still never felt a moment's purpose – unless you count the satisfaction to be had from finding ever more inventive ways to creep about behind his back and to avoid incurring his wrath.'

'That's hardly fulfilment.'

Isabel scoffed. 'Trust me, I know. But then there's a lot I understand now that I didn't when I was twenty – or even a year ago. Anyway, I'm starting to ramble.'

'It doesn't matter,' Julia said. 'If rambling around in circles helps you sort out in your mind what you're going to do, I'll listen 'til the cows come home.'

'Do you know what truly needles me, though?' Isabel asked with a sigh.

'Tell me.'

'That having spent two decades in one long and uninterrupted attempt to meet the standards of a man who was beyond pleasing in the first place, I finally get to walk away . . . but with nothing – no home, no money, no security. He, on the other hand, his livelihood and his reputation intact, gets precisely what he wanted all along – to be with Audrey Deacon-Jones, unencumbered by the small matter of already having a wife.'

'You get your freedom.'

Isabel met Julia's look. 'Don't misunderstand me, I'm well aware of what I've finally shed, as well as everything I ought to now gain. But freedom, by itself, neither feeds nor clothes me.'

'Well, the only other thing you can do is leave hiding, sue him for divorce on the grounds of his adultery, and hope to get some sort of settlement.'

'I couldn't. He'd do everything he could to ensure I failed. He'd line up witness after witness to speak to my folly. Besides, the courts always take the man's side. How dare a woman claim she's been wronged?'

'So, if walking away with nothing is the price of your freedom, only you can decide whether or not it's worth paying.'

She didn't have to think about it. 'It's completely worth it. It's just hard to swallow.'

'And it'll stick in your craw forever if you let it. So, how about, instead of allowing the unfairness to eat away at you, you remind yourself that, despite all that you've lost, you've escaped the man's control. And although the outcome might not be working out how you envisaged when Vincent appeared in your life, you're free – not just to start over but to finally go after that fulfilment, make up for lost time.'

Julia was right. She was free. But what exactly that meant, and how she would find the courage to make a go of it, alone, in the longer term, she had no idea. She could only hope that, when the chance arose for her to make something of herself, she would recognize it for what it was, take tight hold and do everything within her power to see it through.

Isabel studied her reflection. It was Sunday and, any moment now, Inspector Childe would be arriving to join them for lunch. And while she understood Julia's comments about making a friend of the man, knowing she might need to lie to a police officer about the circumstances that had brought her there – a subject she just knew was bound to come up – was leaving her fidgety and unable to relax.

Taking a step back from the mirror, she smoothed a hand down the front of her navy wool dress and adjusted the pink-and-navy patterned scarf she had arranged to brighten up the rather plain neckline. All she had left to do was clip on her pearl earrings, change her slippers for her court shoes, make a quick application of Antique Rose to her lips and, as Julia had said the other day, assume the role of recently-bombed-out Isabel Smith.

Returning her lipstick to her cosmetics purse, she spotted her bottle of Joy perfume. But when she went to reach for it, she stopped; catching the scent of it might lift her spirits, but it would be nice to keep what precious little of it she had left to wear for Vincent.

Vincent. How quickly she'd forgotten her resolve to accept he was lost. But if the pain that had just seared through her chest and sent her fingers reaching into her sleeve for the comfort of her ribbon was anything to go by, resolve alone wasn't going to be enough. Perhaps, if she was to accept he wasn't coming for her, it would help to remove the ribbon. Distractedly, she traced the tip of her forefinger over its satiny surface. No, it was too soon – felt disloyal, traitorous, even. One day, yes. But not just yet. For a while longer, it felt only right to keep wearing it, just in case . . .

'Well, isn't this nice?' When everyone had helped themselves to vegetables from the enormous china serving dishes, and Elizabeth had said grace, Julia looked about the dining room with a satisfied smile, her remark bringing murmurs of agreement.

'Lovely, yes.'

'Very homely.'

Alongside Isabel, Inspector Childe reached for the cruet.

'Might I offer you the salt and pepper, Miss Smith?'

'Thank you.' Moments earlier, having arrived at the table to realize they were short of a serving spoon, she'd popped back to the kitchen to fetch one. Upon her return, she'd been dismayed to find that the only vacant seat was alongside him. As a result, she wasn't sure which was making her more jumpy: being so closely under his scrutiny, or having to listen to him keep addressing her as Miss Smith – a reminder of her deceit that she could do without. 'Please, Inspector,' she said, grateful to spot a way around one of those worries at least, 'call me Isabel.'

With a smile, the Inspector nodded. 'When I am not in

uniform, I should be delighted to address you as Isabel if, in those same circumstances, you will call me Harrington.'

She smiled back. 'Harrington. Very well.'

When he took to sprinkling pepper on his potatoes, she made a discreet study of his profile. His precise age was difficult to pin down; in civilian clothing, his features had a softer air than when she'd seen him in uniform. This close to, she could also see that he was beginning to grey at the temples, albeit in a manner that gave him an air of worldliness and wisdom. She supposed that made him a few years younger than Hector, who would soon be fifty.

Not wishing to think about Hector, she glanced up from her meal at the identical moment that Miss Anderson, seated directly across the table from her, did the same. Finding her thoughts on Malcolm, she said, 'I keep meaning to ask, Elizabeth, about young Malcolm Baker. And how he's getting on now.'

Elizabeth smiled. 'I'm pleased to report that Malcolm is doing well – still a little wary in the playground on occasion but otherwise fine. As the headmaster often reminds us, a classroom of young children isn't so different from a household of siblings, each one developing their character and abilities at their own pace and in their own ways. The result, more often than not, is the butting of heads, even in the most settled of surroundings, let alone as our children find themselves here, amid so little that is familiar.'

Relieved to hear that Malcolm was all right, Isabel nodded. 'And what about Big Barry?'

'Contrary to how it might have appeared at the time, Bartholomew Weekes is a bright boy. Unfortunately, he struggles to concentrate – especially when it comes to sitting still to read. As a result, at the end of the summer term, the headmaster decided not to move him up with the rest of his class, but to hold him back for a term in the hope that, rather than fall even further behind, he might be helped to catch up.'

'But that didn't go down well with Bartholomew.'

'I'm afraid it made Bartholomew angry and unsettled. So, after the incident with Malcolm – and a couple of con-tretemps with other children – it was decided he should rejoin his peers in the next class up but, rather than do art and craft with them on Friday afternoons, have extra reading lessons instead. Not surprisingly, now he is back to no longer being the biggest child in the class, the nat-ural order of these things has been keeping him rather more in check.'

'All's well that ends well.'

'Indeed.'

For a while after that, the meal proceeded in silence until, just as Isabel was racking her brain for a topic of conversation, Edna Price, the eldest of Julia's schoolmis-tress lodgers, looked across to Harrington to ask, 'Are you from Devon originally, Inspector?'

'I'm not, no. Ever since the summer my parents first brought me here on holiday, though – when I became enchanted by the beaches and the dunes – I always hoped to one day live here. In fact,' he went on, turning to Julia, 'I was wondering, Mrs Nance, about your surname. I enquire only because one year, we went to Bude, and I recall a family with your name running pleasure-boat trips there. Would there perhaps be a connection?'

'Possibly a member of my late husband's family.'

At the tautness of her friend's reply, Isabel frowned; was there something about the Nances Julia hadn't told her – or didn't want known?

'What a coincidence,' the Inspector said, unperturbed.

'And please, do call me Julia.'

When the table once again fell to silence, Isabel was about to resort to commenting upon the tastiness of the pie when the Inspector beat her to it.

'If I may say, Julia, this pie is delicious. But I can't quite decide what's making it so tasty – a secret ingredient in the sauce, perhaps?'

Julia smiled. 'That'll be the cider.'

'And do I detect mustard?'

'You do.'

'Ingenious.'

'These days, having to rely on rabbit and vegetables for a filling, rather than chicken or beef, I find it helps the flavour.'

'Well,' Isabel whispered to Julia a while later when, at the end of the main course, the two were ferrying plates and empty serving dishes to the scullery, 'despite the odd nerve-jangling silence to begin with, I think it's going well. Your pie was certainly a hit.'

'Not *too much* mustard? Or too many leeks for the amount of meat? Only, since the rabbits were on the small side, I had to find ways to eke them out.'

'If all of these clean plates are anything to go by, I'd say it was just right.'

Back at the table shortly after that, with Elowen serving baked apples from a large enamel dish, and a jug of custard making the rounds, the Inspector expressed interest in Julia's invasion preparedness committee and applauded her foresight.

'She worked jolly hard,' Elowen pointed out as everyone was tucking into their dessert. 'I've lost count of the hours she put into that.'

'Several people I've met have told me the same,' Harrington said.

Julia, though, simply shrugged. 'Someone had to do it.'

With the matter of the war unavoidably back in people's minds, it was no surprise when conversation moved from there to the German threat more generally, the inspector responding to questions about the likelihood of an invasion in only the broadest of terms; if he was privy to plans for meeting it, Isabel reflected, he was keeping them close to his chest.

A while after that, over coffee and a digestif – Julia having searched her drinks cabinet and found an unopened half-bottle of port and the dregs of some Grand Marnier – Isabel once again found her thoughts returning to Vincent. It was only when she heard laughter that she snapped her attention back to the discussion at the table.

'You do know, don't you, Ellie,' Julia was saying and setting down her liqueur glass, 'that most of what's said over a few drinks in The Ship bears little relation to the truth? At the very least, it's exaggerated for effect.'

'With my police inspector's hat on for a moment,' Harrington interjected, 'I would have to disagree. An excess of ale might indeed produce a good deal of braggadocio but, equally, *in vino veritas.*'

'Never was any good at Latin,' Julia responded with another laugh as she reached to retrieve her glass. 'Couldn't see the point of a language no one spoke. Although I do seem to recall *vino* having to do with wine.'

'You remember correctly,' Isabel said. 'It translates as *in wine there is truth.*'

'In other words,' Elowen went on, 'I'm right. What the old codgers spout when there's a line of empties in front of them is far more likely to have a basis in fact than when they're sober and wary of the repercussions.'

'An astute observation,' the inspector said. 'You know, Miss Nance, with reasoning and deduction like that, you have the makings of a woman police constable.'

'Tease me all you like, Inspector —'

'I assure you, I wasn't teasing.'

'— but I happen to think it a worthy occupation for any woman.'

'I don't think I've ever seen a female police constable,' Edna Price commented. 'Although, I daresay there must be some in Bristol.'

Isabel nodded. 'I used to see them in London. And I recall reading in the newspaper recently that they're becoming a common sight in other towns and cities now, too.'

Beside her, Harrington nodded. 'They are. There's

a growing appreciation of the fact that women officers bring compassion –'

'And then have to resign when they get married.'

'Lamentably, Miss Nance,' the Inspector said, 'at present, that is indeed the case. However, once this war ends, it is my belief that outdated restrictions like that particular one will become hard to continue to defend.'

Elowen's expression softened from scorn to interest. 'Truly? You're not just saying that to mollify me?'

'Miss Nance, I wouldn't do you the disservice. No, assuming we triumph over evil, then I firmly believe things will change.'

'They said that about the last war.' The observation this time came from Julia.

'They did.'

'But if anything,' Julia went on, 'when *that* one ended, life for women went backwards. Women who had answered the call and stepped up to play their part were simply dismissed and told to go back to their homes.'

'Also true. But, a year or so afterwards,' the Inspector said, 'the Sex Disqualification Removal Act was passed, leading the way for women to become appointed to judicial posts such as barristers and solicitors, as well as to civil posts such as mayors.'

'The new law also permitted them to join the civil service,' Isabel said, as she recalled the fact, 'but, even today, they still have to resign when they marry.'

'And for society to insist they cast aside years of training,' Harrington observed, 'solely because they do, is not only absurd but a waste of good minds.' In her surprise at his words, Isabel straightened up. 'If the husband and wife are comfortable with their domestic arrangements – prepared to accept having no one at home all day to mind the hearth or, indeed, happy to pay someone else to do that for them – what right does the law have to overrule them?'

'So, you think the marriage bar will eventually be removed?' Elizabeth asked.

'With the emphasis on *eventually*, I do, yes. You see, I feel the momentum for change at the end of *this* war will be considerably greater than last time. And it will arise largely through the sheer number of women who, either by voluntarily joining one of the women's services or else completing some form of compulsory war work, as yet to be introduced, will have experienced the freedom that comes with earning a wage.'

'I hope you're right,' Elowen said.

Taking in her expression, Isabel could see that, in keeping with her own feelings on the matter, the girl was only partially convinced. But to come across a man holding such an enlightened view in the first place was encouraging – inspiring, even.

She met Elowen's look. 'What was it you were going to tell us – before we became side-tracked by the matter of female police officers? If I recall, it was in connection with something you'd overheard in The Ship.'

Elowen frowned. 'Oh, yes. Well, it's not that far removed from what we've been talking about.'

'Come on, then,' Julia urged her stepdaughter. 'Spill the beans.'

'All right. But I shan't be mentioning names. Although, when I tell you what I overheard, you'll most likely guess anyway –'

'Is this the point at which I tactfully leave the room?' Inspector Childe asked, making as though to stir from his seat. When Elowen regarded him uncertainly, he hurried to add, 'Now I *am* teasing you. Please, do go on. You have me intrigued.'

'Well, anyway,' Elowen began again. 'All I was going to say is that, apparently, when women down on the south coast were refused admission to the Home Guard, just as you were up here, Mum, they got together and set up their own.'

Inspector Childe nodded. 'I've heard the same.'

'*See*,' Elowen said, staring pointedly back at her step-mother. 'I saw you looking at me as though I was making it up. Anyway, the feller who was telling the story thought it a joke. Sat there, sneering, he was. And the rest of them were laughing. *Madness,* one of them piped up. Course, that got the others going. "Women should stay in the kitchen." "Whatever next?" You can imagine the com-ments, can't you?'

'Back in the spring,' Julia explained to Inspector Childe, 'after Mr Eden had been on the wireless asking for vol-unteers for his LDV, Amelia Plumley and I – at the time, she was a long-term guest here – went along to try and sign up, only to meet with disdain.'

'Unfortunately,' Isabel said, finding herself on famil-iar ground, 'with most men remaining firmly set against the idea of a woman making her own decisions, let alone holding a position of responsibility and earning her own money, new laws alone are unlikely to change the situation – at least, not in the short term.' The others, she realized, perhaps drawn by the directness of her tone, were regarding her with interest. But, while she knew better than to mention her own circumstances, she nevertheless felt bound to speak out. 'All the while their wives, daughters, sisters have neither money nor independence, many men feel . . . powerful . . . in control. Beyond threat or challenge. At the inkling of a woman gaining even a grain of freedom, they simply place her under even greater constraints, press her even further down.' *Mete out punishments. Humiliate her. Remind her that her opinion is of no value.* 'And I mean you no offence, Inspector. It is just my opinion.'

Harrington met her look. 'Miss Smith, never apologize for holding an opinion. Be prepared to have it challenged, yes. Be ready to defend it – even to back down if another argument convinces you to change your mind. But never apologize.' Under his gaze, Isabel felt herself growing warm. 'A certain type of man does indeed see a woman of independent means as a threat. And I'm inclined to agree with you that it will be a while before we see the back of such individuals – if ever. But that should not deter any of you from acting in accordance with your conscience and doing what you believe to be right – as long as, in so doing, you do not endanger yourself or others.'

'Hear, hear,' Julia agreed.

'You, Julia,' Harrington continued, 'through feeling unable to sit by in the belief there was nothing you could do but accept your fate, chose to set up the invasion preparedness committee. On the south coast, women felt similarly moved about the situation with the Home Guard. That said, I fully understand why, in the first instance, the government's call to join the Local Defence Volunteers did not extend to women. Men, in their thousands, exempt or unfit for call-up, had been clamouring to be allowed to help out. To the government, they represented an untapped source of manpower. Nevertheless, the sheer weight of the response to Mr Eden's broadcast left the authorities overwhelmed. There wasn't the capacity to deal with the weight of male volunteers, let alone cope with women wishing to apply. Aside from that –' with a smile, he turned back to Elowen – 'please be assured, Miss Nance, that not all men hold the same view as your regulars at The Ship. That those individuals feel as they do, should not deter you in your ambitions.'

'Oh, I don't take no stick,' Elowen said hotly. 'I let them have it straight. I told them I'd far rather be shown how to use a rifle to defend myself – and Mum and this place – than entrust our well-being to a handful of old sots like them.'

Julia banged her fist on the table. 'That's my girl. Drunken old fools.'

'Course,' Elowen picked up again, 'that only made them laugh even harder. They were too stupid to even realize that without me and Mrs Nott working there, rather than sitting at home darning socks, they wouldn't have anyone to draw their pints. You know, Mum,' Elowen went on, 'we should get up our own defence force. You'd be good at that. Look at how quickly you got the preparedness committee up and running – despite the chairman of the parish council trying to scupper the idea before even putting it to a vote. Pretty soon had egg on his face, though, didn't he? Turns out, loads of women shared your concerns and were only too glad to pitch in.'

'They were. But you can't have forgotten the pain we went through to get it done.'

'Forget? Hardly.'

'And it's still not easy keeping the bloomin' thing going, even now. So, much as I share your dismay that no one thought about women wanting to sign up, I already have my hands full. And worse than doing nothing would be to take on the task amid a rush of hot-headed indignation, only to quickly discover we've bitten off more than we can chew, and have the whole thing fall apart around us. Do that and we would simply be adding fuel to the fires of those who don't want us to succeed in the first place.'

'It's unlike you to admit defeat, Mum.'

'I'm not admitting defeat,' Julia said, 'rather I'm recognizing there are only so many hours in a day. Should someone else see fit to take it on, I'll be first in line with both my gratitude and my support. But now we have our lovely boarders, I really don't have it in me for anything more.'

'And perhaps, therein,' Edna Price observed, 'lies the crux of the arguments against women remaining in work once they marry.' When the others at the table turned to regard her, she continued, 'Please, don't think, any of you, I support the view that women should never hold positions outside of the home at all – on the contrary, right here, in this room, is proof that women excel in occupations within the realms of pastoral care. That said – and I realize I am in danger of being called an old fuddy-duddy who refuses to move with the times – the fact remains that a home does not look after itself. *Someone* must see to the housework, the meals and the raising of the children. And whether we like it or not, that isn't going to be the husband. In that same vein, you will also struggle to convince me that war is any business for a woman. Unmarried girls who go into nursing to help wounded soldiers are to be commended and admired – it's not a job for the faint-hearted. Moreover, wearing my pragmatic hat for a moment, since the wheels of industry must be kept turning, I also understand the need for single women to fill factory jobs vacated by men who have enlisted. But anything more than that – especially the idea of women forming into armies and training with weapons – and I genuinely fear for what will become of us as a society.'

'There is also, perhaps,' her colleague Elizabeth took the chance to add, 'a certain comfort to be drawn from the fact that people *can't* just band together, willy-nilly, setting up groups to go about protecting or avenging their particular set of beliefs. Surely, if that is allowed to happen, we risk the breakdown of law and order. And I hold that to be true, despite having lately come to accept that these particular desperate times do indeed call for desperate measures.'

When, in the wake of Elizabeth's impassioned remarks, the room fell quiet, Isabel sat in reflection. Being party to a discussion where women expressed their views without fear of being shouted down had ignited something within her. She agreed, wholeheartedly, that a woman's place shouldn't be where a man told her it was – that it should be where, after level-headed and respectful discussion, the couple in question agreed it best suited *them*. But, for every man like the inspector, who questioned the right of the law to rule against such freedoms, there were men like Hector, and Elowen's customers in The Ship, openly mocking women who chose to act on their own authority. Dare she hope Harrington was right – and that with the end of this war would come far-reaching change? Even if it did, what of the meantime? War was plunging women into a state of limbo – on the one hand encouraging them to step up, on the other severely restricting how they might do so.

Realizing that, beside her, the inspector was setting down his empty port glass, she once again brought her attention back to the room.

'Well,' she heard him say, 'while I could happily sit and discuss these topics with you for the rest of the afternoon, a considerate guest knows to depart *before* wearing out his welcome. Julia,' he said, as several of the women made to get to their feet, suddenly mumbling about clearing up or else generally aghast at the slipping away of the afternoon, 'thank you, most sincerely, for the invitation to join you. Lunch was delicious, a real treat. And I have been made to feel most welcome.'

'Inspector,' Julia said, 'I'm glad you were able to come. And if you're always so complimentary, I might have to invite you again.'

'Madam, I would be honoured.'

'Harrington,' Isabel turned to him to say as she rose from her chair and gestured towards the hall, 'allow me to show you out.'

'Thank you.'

Encouraged by the discovery that he appeared singularly enlightened, she waited while he donned his coat and collected his hat and then, before she could think better of it, followed him out on to the veranda, quickly pulling the door shut behind her. 'Forgive me,' she said upon seeing his puzzlement, 'but I was wondering, these women on the south coast, do you know what it is they're actually doing?'

'In forming a defence force, do you mean?'

She nodded. 'Between Elowen and yourself, you have me intrigued.'

'All I recall is that, rather than be left to watch as only men were trained to defend the home front, they set up their own group – including, I believe, in some instances, attempting to procure training in the use of weapons.' At the mention of weapons, Isabel flinched. 'That said, while I don't know who commands the platoon – if that is even the correct term for it – I do know that, at some point, Lady Virginia Scott became involved. If I describe her to you as being something of a local dignitary, I'm sure she wouldn't mind. Until recently, her husband was an MP, which afforded her access to an extensive circle of contacts.'

'I see.'

'But, since it is you who now has *me* intrigued, might I enquire as to the nature of your interest?'

Isabel paused. It was a good question. 'At the risk of sounding quite batty, I'll be honest with you and say that I'm not really sure.'

'But there's a chance you might be moved to explore something similar here?'

'Would it be such a bad thing if I were?' She couldn't recall the last time anything had quite so roundly captured her interest – nor quite how forward she was being.

'Isabel, if you're asking me as a police inspector, then it behoves me to dissuade you from doing anything rash. However, if you are asking me as a guest in your home, I might hint that you could do worse than write to Lady Virginia and request that she acquaint you with the facts.'

'I see.' Was she crazy to even be considering getting involved in such a thing? What did she know of defence forces and weapons? Nothing whatsoever. What she *did* know, however, was how it felt to be deliberately ignored, to be cast as invisible and powerless.

'You know, were I to make a telephone call or two, I might even be able to supply you with Lady Virginia's address. What you chose to do with it after that, of course, would be down to you.'

'And we could keep it between the two of us?' she asked, folding her arms against the chilly wind. If she was going to become tangled up with something like this, she would prefer to do so of her own volition and not because Julia and Elowen tried to talk her into it.

'If that is your wish.'

'It is. At least until I find out more.'

'Then I'll see what I can do.'

Once she'd watched the inspector turn along the side of the house in the direction of his motorcar, parked in the lane to the rear, she opened the door and stepped quietly back inside.

When, just the other day, she'd agreed with Julia about needing something to occupy her mind, she'd pictured lending a greater hand with the housework or, perhaps, being of rather more help with the shopping and cooking. Instead, to her own bewilderment, buoyed by this afternoon's discussion, she appeared to be considering something about as far removed from either of those as it was possible to imagine. But *why not* throw herself into something with vigour and purpose, something that might make a real difference to women like her? She had no ties, no one to inconvenience through her involvement – not unless Vincent was found. Even if he was, and the time came for her to leave Fairlight, there was nothing to prevent her from handing the whole thing over to someone else to continue. Moreover, she had no one to point out the folly of *her* attempting to take on a task that would clearly require single-mindedness and pluck. She could hear Hector's derision now: *You? Do something like that? Preposterous. Put such lunacy out of your head, right this minute, or I warn you now, I won't be held responsible for my actions –*

Yes, by being out of her husband's reach, there was no one to demand she desist; no one to scoff at her audacity. Moreover, if, after learning more, she genuinely concluded that she was out of her depth, then she need take it no further, with no one but Harrington any the wiser. But, if she continued to feel as she did now – driven not just to prove herself but to finally stand up and be counted – then she would give it a go. And if she was right about Vincent being lost, and he never did come for her, then she would go about it in his memory and as a show of gratitude for the new life he had so unexpectedly placed within her grasp.

'Inspector, good morning. Would you like to come in?'

'That's very kind of you, Miss Smith, but I'm afraid on this occasion I must decline.'

It was now several days on from the Sunday lunch and when Isabel had gone to the drawing room window to check who was knocking at the front door ahead of going to answer it, it was to see Inspector Childe on the step.

'You won't even stop for a cup of coffee after that steep climb?'

'As it happens, I'm returning from police business in Lynmouth and so I came by motorcar. Regrettably, I must get back to the station.' He withdrew a slip of paper from his breast pocket. 'But I didn't want to miss the opportunity to bring you the details of Lady Virginia Scott.'

'In which case,' Isabel said, 'thank you for going to the trouble but I won't delay your return.'

'No. But please, do let me know how you get on.'

'I shall.'

Once she had watched him descend the steps and turn along the path at the side of the house, she closed the door and turned back to see Julia appearing from the kitchen.

'Who was that?'

'Inspector Childe. He —' While she hadn't intended

telling Julia what she'd felt moved to investigate, she realized it would be poor form to keep it a secret. 'He brought
me an address for Lady Virginia Scott – you remember,
in connection with the women's defence force?'

'And you didn't invite him in for a cup of coffee, poor
man?'

'No, I did,' she said, going towards her. 'But he couldn't
tarry.'

'So, come on, then. Since you clearly only enquired
because you felt sufficiently moved to do something, what
is it you've got in mind?'

'Well, don't laugh but, after our discussion on Sunday,
I've been considering setting up a women's home guard.
But now that I have in my hand the means to do so, I find
I have no idea where to start.'

'Only natural. When I took on the preparedness committee, no matter how driven I felt, I had no earthly idea
what I was doing. I'd never done anything like it and was
convinced all I was going to do was make a fool of myself.
I'll also admit that it took a number of meetings before I
even *began* to feel as though it was me in charge, and not
the chairman of the parish council. So, I understand your
hesitation. I already had plenty on my plate and a dozen
good reasons not to get involved. But I did it anyway. And
do you know what?'

Isabel shook her head. 'I've a feeling you're going to
tell me, though.'

'I'm glad I put myself out and gave it a go. People often
say the first step to anything is always the hardest. Turns
out it's true. The more I got involved, the easier it became

and the more it put everything else into perspective. I got my confidence back. I also found that whereas, at the beginning, the threat of invasion made me feel power-less and angry and afraid, getting stuck into preparing for it gave me back a sense of control. It also forced me to find ways to get along with people I'd previously had down as miserable or cantankerous or only out for their own ends.'

'The difference,' Isabel said, 'is that you're naturally confident. You've spent the last fifteen years fending for yourself, raising Elowen, running a guest house . . .'

All the while Isabel was speaking, Julia was shaking her head. 'You're confusing confidence with my tendency to be rash and bull-headed.'

Isabel laughed. 'I don't think I am. Timorous people couldn't act rashly or stand firm if their life depended upon it. Trust me, I know.'

'Isabel, you forget, I know you of old. At school, you were everything I wasn't – and I don't just mean dainty and polished and petite. I mean bubbly and outgoing, as well as naturally bright and quick to learn. In examina-tions, you were always in the top two or three places. You had an aptitude for remembering facts that made it look to me as though you never even had to try. More than anything, though, you were warm and kind and honour-able and fun.'

Recognizing a grain of truth in her friend's words, Isabel gave a deflated sigh. She *had* been fun, once upon a time – outgoing, too. 'School was a long time ago. A lot has happened since then.'

'Yeah. Hector bloody Thaxley came along and suffocated the life out of you. Do you know, when you sent me that telegram, I didn't even stop to think. I simply gave Petie my reply. Not only was I excited by the prospect of seeing you, but I looked upon it as a chance to repay some of the kindness you'd shown me at school. When everyone else shunned me, *you* didn't. You didn't care that my father ran a stationery shop, nor that my uniform was second-hand. You never made me feel in any way lesser. I also wanted you to come here because things for me and Ellie had been rotten, and I told her you would cheer things up. Obviously, when I said that, I didn't know about Vincent. To see you so upset broke my heart. And to then learn how Hector has been mistreating you made me want to hunt him down and run a skewer through his privates.'

Isabel rocked with laughter. 'You haven't changed a bit.'

'See, now that's the Isabel I remember – gay and fun and giggling at the daftest of things.'

'My giggling was the bane of Miss Greenwood's life,' Isabel said. 'Do you remember? "No man, Miss Walcot, wants a wife who giggles. Such behaviour is juvenile and unbecoming." She despaired of me, truly.'

'Bit rich, wasn't it?' Julia said. 'Her, a spinster – and Miss Snow, her deputy, likewise – lecturing *us* about the qualities that made a good wife.'

'I never thought of that.'

'And anyway, she was wrong. Jago loved it when I laughed. Even William said it cheered him to hear it.'

'Yes, well, I'm sure those two old women were wrong about a lot more than just laughter.'

'But my point,' Julia picked up again, 'before we digressed, was about you getting back some of your old self. I know the burden of losing Vincent weighs heavy, of course it does. But even if he was only half the man you say he was, he wouldn't want you to remain miserable. Surely, he would urge you to make the most of it. Make up for lost time, be the woman he saw – the one Hector wouldn't allow you to be. She's still in there, you know. All you have to do is encourage her to come out. And this women's home guard business might be just the lure.'

Isabel stared down at the address on the slip of paper. 'You truly believe that?'

'Truly.'

'I must admit,' Isabel said as she reflected upon her friend's statement, 'I do find the idea of women taking responsibility for their own safety stirs something in me. Although, perhaps, before I go troubling this Lady Virginia, it might be wise to test the waters first – see whether any of the women in the village might be moved to join us.'

'It couldn't harm. Although, I can tell you now, there will be plenty. The government might no longer be bombarding us quite so often with warnings about the imminence of an invasion, but you've only got to listen to the news broadcasts to know the threat hasn't gone away, not in the slightest.'

'It doesn't seem to have done, no.'

And in which case, Isabel thought, perhaps she really should stop prevaricating and take that first step.

'Good heavens, this looks like Ronnie's handwriting again.'

It was later that morning and, as Isabel stood running her duster along the dado rail, from the corner of her eye she saw Julia retrieve the envelope that had just dropped on to the doormat and then peer at the postmark. If Julia was right, and it was another letter from their friend so soon after her last one, then it could really only be about Hector again. Perhaps, disbelieving Ronnie's claim that she knew nothing of Isabel's whereabouts, he had turned up at the Claremonts' home in the hope of catching them out in a lie; she wouldn't put it past him. His continuing failure to find any trace of her had to be making him livid.

Reminding herself not to fly into a panic nonetheless, she raised her duster to the hall mirror and watched Julia's reflection as she withdrew the sheet of notepaper and began to read. 'What does she say?'

'She answers my question about Ralph by saying that he's fine, which is good news.'

'It is, yes.'

'And then she goes on to write – Hang on, let me read a bit further first.'

Struggling to bury her impatience, Isabel shifted her weight and folded her duster into a neat square. Then she screwed it tightly into a ball. Golly, she wished Julia would get on with it. 'What is it? What does she say?' *Please don't keep me in suspense like this.*

'Probably best,' Julia eventually replied, 'that I read it

aloud. So, she writes, *I've had another telephone call from Hector. He still has no firm word of Isabel and wished to enquire whether I could think of any friends with whom she might be residing. When I learned that she is still unaccounted for, my reaction was one of deep and immediate sadness to think her lost. However, when I offered my condolences, Hector advised that, thus far, no proof had been found to confirm she has perished. He also said that, with the situation in town being one of considerable chaos, although the police have listed her as "missing", they do not have the manpower to set about a search. Consequently, in order, as he put it, "to move forward with my life", he must continue to make enquiries of his own.'*

Having listened with growing concern, Isabel lowered herself on to the nearest of the hall chairs. 'Damn the man. He's going to find me, isn't he?'

'I really don't see how – they might not have found your remains but where would he even start to look for you? Anyway, do you want to hear what else Ronnie says?'

'If it's still about Hector, then as much as I'd really rather not know, I suppose I must.'

'Very well. Then she goes on, *Since there would appear to be no way of knowing whether Isabel truly is dead – nor what might have come to pass between the two of them to lead her to disappear, if not – might she have left him, do you think? I came down in favour of not giving him your details in case Isabel has been in touch but wouldn't wish Hector to know. It's a curious business, isn't it? Rather than sound distraught when he telephoned, the man came across as irritated, going so far as to say that, if he didn't soon find out what had become of her, he would have no option but to go to the bother of engaging a private investigator. As Ralph quite rightly observed when I subsequently told him, irritation is hardly the normal reaction of a husband who believes his wife might have been killed by a bomb.'*

Clearly, Isabel reflected when Julia finished reading, Hector was convinced she was still alive and that either the Claremonts were hiding her, or else they knew where she was; his threat of engaging a private investigator was designed to have them give her up rather than become mired in scandal. And she didn't know which ate away at her more: the knowledge that, six or seven weeks on, Hector still seemed determined to find her and drag her back, or the realization that, if she came clean and let Ronnie know she was alive, then both of her only two remaining friends would be ensnared in her deceit.

'Oh, dear Lord,' she said as the recognition dawned. 'What have I done? What do I *do*?'

Her lips pressed together in thought, Julia shrugged. 'Nothing in haste, that's for sure.'

'But what about Ronnie? If we tell her I'm here with you, it will have to be on the understanding that she keeps the news to herself and then, if challenged, lies about it. But if I *don't* tell her, she'll go on thinking I'm dead.'

'Which, for now,' Julia said, 'while not something you'd allow by choice, strikes me as the lesser of the two evils.'

In her despair, Isabel hung her head. How on earth had she thought she would get away with this — certainly without any consequences? In truth, beyond seizing the chance to flee, she'd given precious little thought to the longer term at all.

Well, she would have to think about it now because, if one thing was clear, it was that she had no intention of going back to Hector. And if that meant hiding away every time there was a knock at the front door and jumping out of her skin every time the telephone rang, then so be it. If that, and the continual pricking of her conscience every time she thought about Ronnie, was the price she had to pay, it was one she would have to bear.

'What have you got there?'

It was later that afternoon and, from where she'd been sitting at the kitchen table, Isabel looked up. 'Well, at the moment, it's just an idea. But, as I said to you earlier, before I bother Lady Virginia Scott, I should probably find out whether anyone in the village is even interested in forming a women's home guard in the first place. To that end, I thought I would put up some notices.' Looking down at her effort so far, she picked up the sheet of paper and passed it to Julia. 'At the moment, it's only rough but, what do you think? Am I on the right lines?'

She waited while Julia studied the details.

'It's good,' she said. 'I like how you've put "Volunteers Required". That makes it clear it's not a paid job.'

Isabel frowned; it had never occurred to her that anyone would think otherwise. 'And the rest of it?'

Julia squinted. 'Any day now, I'm going to need spectacles. "Slipscombe Women's Guard", that's a good name – to the point.'

'I thought the word *guard* more likely to strike a chord with women than *defence force*, which might make it sound too much like the army. But the idea of guarding one's home and family –'

'Definitely.' Julia read on. 'I like the way you've put "Interested Women" should come to the meeting.'

'I had something different to start with but thought this better conveys the fact that it's purely an idea at this stage. I suppose all I'm hoping is to make enough women sufficiently curious to come along and find out more.'

'Well, anyway,' Julia said, 'I think you've made a good job of it. Where are you thinking of displaying them?'

'To be honest, wherever anyone will let me.'

As it was to transpire later, the act of persuading people to display one of her notices was more difficult than Isabel had anticipated.

'It's in aid of *what*, love?' If the postmistress's stiff response was anything to go by, the very thought of females taking matters into their own hands and defending themselves filled the woman with horror. It wasn't a good start. Even after she'd explained all over again, Mrs Crabbe's expression didn't change. 'Well, I have to say, I find the idea abhorrent but, if you think there's some as would be interested, well, I'll take one for the window. It's your money. But since it's twice the size of a postcard, I'll have to charge you double.'

At the vicarage, Mrs Pugsley was equally appalled. 'Women? Fighting?'

'Well, no, not fighting –'

'*Women* shouldn't be *fighting*.'

'As I said, we wouldn't be –'

'No, dear, that's not what the Lord intended for women at all.'

About to remark that she didn't think the Lord had

intended for *anyone* to fight, regardless of their sex or the gravity of their dispute, she instead changed tack. 'I assure you, Mrs Pugsley –'

'A woman's place is at home –'

'And, for the most part, that's where she would still be.'

'– not out grappling with the enemy. Miss Smith, you've evacuated here from London, haven't you?'

Isabel frowned. 'I came here after my home there was destroyed in an air raid.'

'And I thank the Lord he saw fit to spare you. But what you need to understand is that, down here, we don't hold with London attitudes. We're decent folk who live according to God's word. And anyway, haven't we already got the preparedness committee?'

'We have, yes. And under Mrs Nance's auspices, that will continue. But the two are quite different things. The aim of the preparedness committee is to help the village survive under German occupation, whereas this would be women coming together to learn how, as a last resort, they might defend themselves and their homes.'

'Well, I can say with all certainty that Reverend Pugsley wouldn't want a notice about a female home guard on display in the church porch. But I suppose I *could* put one on the board in the parish hall if you like. Although, I have to say, I think you're wasting your time.'

'I might well be,' Isabel said, all the while trying to maintain her smile. 'But unless I can find a way to draw women's attention to it to start with, I'll never know.'

The reception she received from the secretary in the doctor's surgery was altogether more eager; barely had the woman scanned the details before she was out of her chair, heading to the noticeboard in the waiting room and driving a drawing pin through the top of the flyer to secure it dead centre.

'If I were you,' she said, 'I should ask in the library, as well. There's a noticeboard right inside the door. I'm sure Miss Marshall would be more than willing. Oh, and you should try Mayfield's Grocer's. Vera Mayfield is well known for getting stuck in.'

'The library and Mayfield's. Right. Thank you for your help. I'll do that.'

'Good luck.'

Since the library was at the far end of the High Street, Isabel decided to make Mrs Mayfield her next call. But first – she glanced at her wristwatch – she just about had time to get to Foxbeare House before the children left school for the day, because there was something she was hoping to witness.

When she rounded the corner, she found Mrs Bale already waiting at the gates. Crouched down a couple of yards in front of her were Malcolm and Jess, surrounded by a group of children.

With a smile, and lightly breathless from her eagerness to get there, she went towards them. 'Thank you for agreeing to do this,' she greeted Mrs Bale. 'I realize Jess isn't a pet dog – I know she has to earn her keep on your farm – but I thought it would be nice for Malcolm if his classmates were to see her.'

'She likes to have her ears tickled,' she overheard Malcolm explaining to the knot of six-year-olds keen to see the animal, 'but only by one of you at a time so she don't go getting overexcited. Only, she's a Welsh Collie. Too much attention and she gets a bit daft.'

Mrs Bale smothered a laugh. 'The way he said that, then, was the spit of my husband. Uncanny likeness. But anyway, when I explained your idea to Mr Bale, he was more than happy for me to bring her down here. Anything to help the poor mite. As I remarked just yesterday, despite everything the lad's going through, he's given us no trouble whatsoever. Obedient. Nicely mannered. And I popped a note in with his last letter home to tell his mother the same. Poor woman. How must she feel, her husband at sea – and her, a hundred-odd miles away from her only child?'

'I can't begin to imagine,' Isabel said. 'Anyway, thank you again. And please pass my thanks on to Mr Bale, too.'

'Will do. Right, then, Malcolm, a couple more minutes is all I can manage or Mr Bale will be a-wondering where we've got to.'

But when, shortly afterwards, she signalled that the extra few minutes were up, there were still groans of disappointment.

'Oh, please, missus. Just a bit longer. Jess is so lovely.'

Mrs Bale was unmoved. 'Now then, young man,' she said when the children nevertheless began to drift away, 'if I let you hold her lead, do you think you can keep her under control and nicely to heel all the way home?'

Malcolm beamed. 'See,' he said with a nod and then a solemn look at the two friends still lingering nearby. 'I told you what I said about Jess was true.'

Yes, Isabel thought as she watched them go, she was glad she'd thought to nab Mrs Bale the other day and explain what she'd had in mind.

Turning back in the direction of the High Street to finish distributing her flyers, she smiled. Rather late in life for her to feel a surge of maternal instinct but, well, when she'd actually needed it, there it was. Strangely, the recognition brought her a sense not just of validation but of peace, too.

At the grocer's a few moments later, precisely as the doctor's receptionist had suggested, Vera Mayfield was indeed keen to find out more about the women's guard. 'Count me in, love. I've already whittled a broom handle to a nice sharp point, just in case some Jerry invader should chance his luck. I'll put your notice in that side window there, where customers queue to be served. An' I'll tell me daughter-in-law, too – not that she needs a broom handle. Cut them dead with her tongue alone, that one could.'

It was while making her way from Mayfield's to the library that Isabel noticed a smartly dressed female coming towards her.

When the two drew level, the woman came to a halt. 'Forgive me,' she said. 'We haven't been introduced but I imagine you must be Julia's friend.'

Isabel faltered. The woman was stylish and immaculately made-up; as to her identity, she hadn't a clue. 'That's right. Isabel Smith, how do you do?'

'Pleased to meet you. Alma Jennings, of Jennings' Private Hotel.'

Jennings. 'Yes, of course. Elowen works for you.'

'She does. And most reliably, too.'

'So, a private hotel . . .' Was there any value in offering her a flyer to display?

'Long-term residents. Some of whom have been with me almost a decade.'

'Goodness. Any ladies among them?'

'Four at present.'

'I don't suppose they would be interested in joining a women's home guard?'

Alma laughed. 'While a couple of them would be frighteningly eager, I'm afraid, given their ages, you would find them something of a liability. Why? Is that what you're setting up?'

'More a case at this stage of exploring whether there might be any interest.'

Leaning closer, Alma gestured to the flyers Isabel was clutching. 'May I?'

'Of course.' Handing Alma the topmost leaflet, Isabel watched her read the details.

'You know, I helped out with a little task for Julia's preparedness committee – a very minor one – but I was surprised by how satisfying it felt to be so directly aiding the war effort. Tell me, have you had much interest thus far?'

Isabel angled her head in thought. 'To be honest, reaction has been mixed. But I suppose the enthusiastic responses do just about outnumber the incredulous.'

Alma laughed. 'I should imagine I could name every one of the incredulous. If you think Julia wouldn't mind, though, I should very much like to come along.'

Unsure why Julia should mind, Isabel nodded. 'Please do. The more, the merrier.'

'Then it's fortuitous we should meet,' Alma said before handing her back the leaflet and, with a polite smile, taking her leave.

When Isabel arrived at the library, she found Miss Marshall to be the most enthusiastic recipient of all.

'Goodness, yes,' she said, making her way to the board immediately inside the entrance. 'Of course I'll pin one up. I'll put it right here. And I'll make sure I draw it to the attention of every woman who comes in. And should you need a second-in-command, or even a third, don't be shy to ask.'

'Thank you. I won't.'

As Isabel made to leave, she noticed Miss Marshall glance through the doors to the porch as though appearing to remember something.

'Nearly forgot,' she said, and trotted back to the counter. When she returned, she was struggling under the weight of a stack of newspapers. When Isabel held open the door, she set them heavily on top of a pile already stacked outside. 'For the new National Salvage Campaign,' she explained. 'Today's collection day.'

Isabel surveyed the teetering stack. 'That's a lot of newspapers.'

'I know. And that's just from the last day or two. Anyway, don't let me keep you. I'll see you at the meeting.'

'I do hope so.' As she stood easing her gloves back on, ahead of the walk home, Isabel congratulated herself on a morning well spent. Of her twelve flyers, she had just two left. But, as she stood considering whether to add them to the salvage pile or keep hold of them, she found her eyes drawn to the topmost newspaper on the stack: folded open at the Personal column, the title of one of the notices, printed in bold type, read MISSING WIFE.

Heart racing, she snatched it up.

> Information sought. Any person with knowledge of the whereabouts of Araminta Wooding (née Grant), aged 44, dark hair, brown eyes, last seen 7th September 1940, at her home in Worcester Sq., Pimlico, is requested to contact Corning & Crouch Investigators, SW1.

Exhaling in relief, she thrust the newspaper back on the pile; she wasn't the missing wife – not this time. But, if Hector had done as he'd intimated to Ronnie, and engaged a private investigator, then one day there might easily be a notice in relation to her own disappearance. And then what would she do? For a start, the whole thing felt sordid – thousands of people across the land, sitting at breakfast, speculating over their tea and toast as to her fate. Maybe her husband had secretly done away with her – *if he discovered her with another man, she had it coming*; or she had taken her own life – *perhaps he wouldn't grant her a divorce to marry another*; or she had run off with a lover – *it's always the quiet ones*. Thankfully, apart from Julia and Elowen, no one in Slipscombe knew her real name. But imagine if she hadn't gone to the bother of changing it? Thank goodness she'd met Ruby – and how fortunate that, while she wouldn't wish a violent husband upon any wife, the woman had turned out to be not just kindly but someone who'd gone through something similar and knew what to do. Without Ruby, the sort of difficulties she might now be facing didn't bear thinking about.

Her thoughts all over the place, she descended the library steps and turned stiffly along the High Street. Despite the anonymity afforded by her new name, she would use this morning's shock as a timely reminder not to let down her guard – not even for a minute.

'Your tuppence change, Miss Smith.'

'Thank you.'

Clutching the copy of the *Daily Telegraph* she had just bought, Isabel left the newsagent's and headed swiftly around the corner to the shelter of the side street. In the lee of the blustery wind, she drew a long breath, thumbed through the pages until she reached the Personal column, scanned its length and then exhaled in relief. After spotting the private investigator's appeal for information about a missing wife the other day, she'd felt obliged to check every morning since for anything similar from Hector. By chance, Edna Price bought a copy of the *Daily Telegraph* on her way to school each morning and usually – but not always – brought it home afterwards to finish reading. However, the task of retrieving it, once Mrs Price had consigned it to the kindling basket, required Isabel to apply stealth.

'What on earth are you doing?' Julia had asked just last night, when she'd come across her in the scullery, smoothing out the badly crumpled page printed with the day's notices.

'Oh, nothing,' she had mumbled. 'Just after a sheet of newspaper to put down to polish my shoes on.' Thankfully, Julia had been too engrossed in her own business to challenge her further.

As a result, though, this morning, Isabel had gone to the newsagent to arrange to have her own copy delivered. It was an expense she had hoped to avoid, requiring that she now make economies elsewhere, but it couldn't be helped; she had to remain alert. If Hector carried out his threat to engage a firm of private investigators, it was quite possible they would appeal for sightings of her. If they did, she would need to know straight away.

Her newspaper refolded and tucked under her arm, Isabel looked up to see Malcolm coming along the pavement, by his side a girl of similar height.

'Good morning, Malcolm,' she greeted him.

'Hello, miss.'

'On your way to school?' Since he wasn't in the company of an adult, she felt it best to check.

Malcolm adjusted the weight of his satchel on his shoulder. 'Mrs Bale says she only needs to come with me as far as Joy's house now. And then we're allowed to walk the rest of the way together.'

'That's good, isn't it?' The two children nodded. 'Well, I mustn't make you late. But please be careful crossing the roads.'

'Look left, look right,' Malcolm said.

'Then left again,' Joy went on. 'And if all clear, quick march.'

'That's right. Well, goodbye, then. I hope you have a good day at school.'

'Bye, miss.'

Watching the two youngsters skip along the pavement towards Foxbeare House, Isabel smiled and turned her thoughts to her own day ahead, specifically the matter of the women's home guard. In readiness for the meeting she'd called to gauge opinion, she needed to prepare for questions, the most obvious being the matter of how the group would actually operate, day-to-day. She already had quite a number of ideas but, as she looked up to cross the road and saw the police station, she had another one: why not save herself trouble later on by checking now whether anything she had in mind could lead them into trouble with the law?

Despite arriving unannounced, Inspector Childe seemed delighted to see her.

'May I offer you coffee?' he asked once she had settled into one of the two chairs in front of his desk and was removing her gloves.

'Thank you, but no, please don't put anyone to the bother.'

'Very well. Then in that case, Miss Smith, how may I assist you?'

'Well,' she said, 'the reason I am here, taking up your valuable time, is that if I am to set up a women's home guard, it would help me to know whether, in your pro-fessional capacity, there are activities you would advise us against undertaking because, clearly, I would prefer that you didn't turn up one evening and arrest us all.'

The Inspector's smile suggested the prospect amused him.

'Miss Smith, without knowing *precisely* what it is you are proposing to do –'

When Isabel opened her mouth to enlighten him, he

held up a hand. From the way he then raised an eyebrow and angled his head, she understood why: at some point in the future, and with his inspector's hat on, he might need to deny all knowledge.

'— it is difficult for me to know whether anything you propose would be unlawful.'

She smiled. 'Of course.' Clearly, then, she would have to rely on her own judgement.

'However,' the inspector went on, 'I feel obliged to point out that, by the letter of the law, these women's defence units, as set up elsewhere in the land, are, by their very nature, illegal. With their status not recognized by the Crown, it could be deemed that their leaders were running a private army, the distinction even less debatable in cases where they bear arms.'

The depth of her disappointment took her by surprise. 'So, are you telling me not to go ahead?' Surely, having been the one to provide her with the details of Lady Virginia, he wouldn't, would he?

With a glance at the door, he lowered his voice. 'Isabel, I'm telling you not to get caught.'

Not to get caught. Rather different from *don't go ahead.*

'I see.'

'Thirteen months into this war, it has become plain to me that, unlike last time, considerable German attention will be aimed directly at us here, in Britain. The upheaval, and the country's response to such attacks, will create a situation where the lines between what might or might not once have been considered dutiful or patriotic are likely to become more blurred the longer it goes on. Even our government, in issuing us with those instructions entitled "Stay Where You Are", went so far as to state that it is the right of every man – *and woman* – to do what they can to protect themselves, their family and their home. And so, surely, it wouldn't require too much of a leap to convince someone that all your group was doing –'

'Was following government advice.'

'Indeed.'

Returning his somewhat conspiratorial smile, she rose to her feet. 'Inspector, I won't take up any more of your time. You have been most helpful. And I do hope that, before too much longer, we will see you again at Fairlight for lunch.'

'I should very much like that.'

Moments later, as she stepped back out into the blustery autumn morning, she was glad she'd thought to talk to him, her determination to go ahead with her idea having simply deepened. And in which case, should enough women feel the same way, she would proceed. In fact, her only regret now was that Hector wouldn't be there to witness her doing so.

'Oh, there you are.'

Struck by the uncharacteristic wariness to Julia's tone, Isabel looked up from her darning; yesterday, she'd caught the pocket on the front of her housecoat – well, more accurately, one of Julia's housecoats – on the handle of a drawer and had ripped a hole. Thankfully, it wasn't sufficiently torn to require patching, but it did need a repair. 'What is it?' she asked.

'Captain Richardson is here and asking to see you.'

Isabel frowned. 'Captain Richardson . . . ?'

'You haven't met him yet but he's in charge of Slipscombe's Home Guard.' Moving closer, Julia lowered her voice. 'He has a superior with him – older, sour-faced chap, with a whole paint palette of medals on his chest.'

Her hand hovering over her darning, Isabel continued to frown. 'Did he say why on earth he wants to see *me*?'

'Only that it's in connection with your flyers. He has one of them in his hand.'

Setting her darning on the table, she got to her feet. 'Then I'd better not keep him waiting.'

'Want me to come with you?'

She shook her head. 'Thanks, but I'm sure there's no need.'

In the drawing room, Isabel found the two men, hands behind their backs, staring out of the window. In the fingers of Captain Richardson's right hand was a copy of her flyer.

She went towards him. 'Captain Richardson, good morning.'

Both men turned sharply.

'Miss Smith. How do you do?'

She shook his hand. 'Very well, thank you.'

'May I introduce to you Colonel Harling, Group Commander, Home Guard.'

'Colonel Harling, good morning. How do you do? Please, won't you both have a seat?' The moment they appeared settled, she said, 'So, how may I be of assistance?'

It was the captain who replied.

'Miss Smith, we are here in relation to this.' He held up her handbill. 'I'm given to understand it is your handiwork.'

Under such direct scrutiny, she tensed. 'That's right. I'm hoping to establish the views of the women of the village about a home guard.'

'For women.'

The tone of the colonel's observation deepened her wariness.

'That's right. Although not, of course, with weapons and patrols but rather to give women skills that might be useful should we find ourselves in a position of last resort – by which I mean, needing to defend our homes and our loved ones against the enemy.'

'Miss Smith, had you thought to consult me first, I might have saved you the effort. You see –'

'Goodness, Colonel,' she said, surprising herself with the forcefulness of her interruption, 'I was unaware that I needed permission from the Home Guard to gauge the feelings of my peers.' What was it about this man that instantly had her hackles up – his patronizing manner? Or had Hector simply soured her against any man in khaki? 'Only, even though we are at war, you must admit, such a requirement would seem draconian. However,' she went on, 'to allay your concerns, I assure you that all I wish to do is establish whether there exists among the women of Slipscombe a desire to take greater control of their own safety. Should it transpire that no such interest exists, then, clearly, the matter will go no further.'

'Miss Smith, regardless of any interest you might identify, you cannot take the idea anywhere at all. The War

Office has made it quite plain that women *may not* be admitted to the Home Guard.'

'Colonel, forgive me,' she said. 'I fear you misunderstand. We have no intention of attempting to enrol in the Home Guard. We are well aware that we would not be welcomed. No, this would be our own distinct endeavour.'

From the colonel exploded a snort of derision. But, with his having sunk down into the cushions of Julia's settee, rather than appear intimidating, he looked shrunken and squashed, comical, even.

'Madam,' he said, hauling himself more upright. 'The idea is absurd. No one, other than the War Office, can sanction the setting up of a military unit.'

Isabel bit back irritation. 'This will not be a military unit. We are not proposing to wage war.'

'Miss Smith,' the colonel snapped, 'the view of the War Office is clear. Women may play no part in combat, unarmed or otherwise.'

Unable to help it, Isabel sighed; here she was, trying to reason with yet another individual in military uniform who, rather than trouble himself with the facts, was concerned simply to talk over her, browbeat her into submission. Well, having broken free from two decades of Hector forbidding her to do anything on her own account, she was in no mood to yield. That said, if she let this man, seated in front of her now, see how incensed he was making her, then, no doubt as had been the case with Hector, he would simply dismiss her, claiming that, as was typical of her sex, she had fallen prey to her emotions and was in danger of becoming hysterical.

Swallowing the sour taste rising in the back of her throat, she wondered about the captain's view of the matter. However, since taking a seat, he had said very little, which suggested there was no point trying to appeal to him for support. Either way, now that the colonel had set out his objections, what should she do? Reiterate that, in practical terms, it really would be just a few women watching out for one another? As a line of reasoning, it hadn't won him over so far. Or, since she had no intention of ceding to his demands, should she hear him out and then simply go ahead as planned – even if that did court trouble later on? Neither choice was ideal but, if she truly believed in what she was trying to achieve, shouldn't she at least make a robust attempt to defend it?

It was finding her eyes coming to rest upon the expanse of khaki straining across the colonel's chest, and then wandering over his buttons, no doubt polished to gleaming by some overworked and downtrodden subordinate, that a renewed image of Hector helped to make up her mind.

'Colonel Harling,' she said, her tone as polite as she could hold it, 'I am aware that, when it comes to the role of women in this war, a good many men feel as you do. I will also concede that *some* of their objections are not entirely without merit.' Commencing one's counterattack with a concession was a trick that, over the years, she'd honed to perfection – if only to momentarily throw her opposition. 'But women today are taking on all manner of roles that would once have seemed inconceivable. As you don't need me to tell you, they are joining the services, working the land, filling the factory jobs of men who've been drafted away. However, there are also women who, while unable to serve their country in such fashion, still wish to do their bit. You will be aware, I am sure, that when Mr Eden broadcast his appeal for volunteers for the LDV – as it was at the time – women also came forward. They did not necessarily wish to fire a weapon or to engage, hand-to-hand, with the enemy. But neither did they wish to tidy up or make tea –'

'And I commend their eagerness to be of use, Miss Smith. But, when it comes to women, the law does not allow for them to do anything else.'

'The law does not allow Hitler to invade,' she said, rather more pointedly than she'd intended. 'And if he did not consider himself above it, this discussion today wouldn't be necessary. I don't doubt the number of women who would willingly engage with the enemy, or knowingly put themselves in harm's way, must be small. Equally small, however, must be the number prepared to sit meekly in their parlours and await whatever atrocities the German armies see fit to commit as they rampage their way towards them.' Pausing only briefly to draw breath, she continued, 'And I hope that no man would expect that of *any* woman. I am happy to convey to any ladies who show an interest in the idea that you are against it. However, I should prefer to advise them that, while Colonel Harling does not directly support our aims, he does recognize the premise from which they arise and that, provided we do not get in the way of the Home Guard, or other public or military body, he will not go out of his way to prevent us taking whatever measures we deem necessary to defend our families and our homes.'

'Well, naturally, Miss Smith –' Finally, Captain Richardson had something to say.

Perhaps, then, she thought as she sat, trying to recover her breath, she'd at least given *him* pause for thought.

'– one wishes one's womenfolk to feel safe, which is, in good part, the role of the Home Guard – and one that my men take seriously. But that does not alter the facts as conveyed by Colonel Harling. Women can neither join the Home Guard nor set up a platoon of their own.'

'Captain –'

'Madam,' the colonel barked, attempting to raise himself up as he did so. 'Even were I inclined to sanction your idea, I am prevented. The situation is clear. The law forbids the setting up of private units – by *either* sex. Thus, were you to go ahead, your little band of housewives and spinsters would be committing treason.'

Treason?

When Inspector Childe had pointed out that her group would be illegal, he'd made reasonably light of the situation. He certainly hadn't mentioned treason – and surely, had he thought it pertinent, he would have. Could the colonel be using it as a threat to simply scare her into submission? He seemed the sort of man who might.

Either way, having argued her case thus far, she was reluctant to give up – not while she felt there was still a chance for her to prevail.

'Since, as I said, Colonel, we would not carry arms, and are exceedingly unlikely to have uniforms, the prospect of us being considered a threat to the King is hard to imagine.'

'In times of war,' the Colonel said, 'even more so in the heat of battle, there is little time to pause and draw distinctions.'

'But, as I said –'

'Miss Smith, need I remind you that treason is a felony offence?'

Isabel tensed. While she didn't know precisely what that meant, she could tell it was serious. 'No, of course not.'

'Or that, under the new law, passed just this summer specifically to cover the war emergency, the mandatory penalty for committing it is death?'

It was then that the facts of her situation hit home. If she went ahead with her group, and Colonel Harling one day took it upon himself to report them, she could argue all she liked that they hadn't been doing anything treasonous, but who were the authorities more likely to believe: her and her women's guard or an army colonel? She knew from Hector's threats that men in officialdom always stuck together, which, at the very least, meant she would end up in serious trouble. In any event, the laws of the land existed to protect people, all people. So, what gave her the right to go against them – even more so to urge others to do the same? Despite her conviction that a band of women, coming together to ensure their own safety, posed no threat to anyone, she couldn't advocate breaking the law, certainly not for something as grave as treason; nor, no matter how unlikely she considered the risk, could she lead other women into trouble. There was also the fact that, if she was arrested, then despite her new name, a check of the national register would bring to light that she was married – meaning that Hector would be traced and informed. And no matter how fervently she believed she was in the right, was she really prepared to risk her hard-won freedom to prove it?

Needled by the prospect of backing down – especially under pressure from a man like Colonel Harling – but fearful of the risk of Hector finding out, it pained her to concede. But, faced with no choice, she might as well get it over and done with.

'Colonel Harling,' she said, her jaw tense as she spoke. If she had to climb down, she refused to do so in a manner that made her appear to simply be doing as a man had instructed. No, she would blame something else, something bigger than the colonel. The outcome might be the same but at least she wouldn't simply have cowed to a man. 'It is plain to me that you are merely concerned to prevent me from breaking the law.'

'Miss Smith, that is indeed my aim.'

'In which case, I will take down my flyers and cancel my meeting.'

'You will desist? Dismantle any arrangements already in place?'

She unclamped her jaw. 'I will.'

Alongside the colonel, Captain Richardson got to his feet, his look one of relief. 'Then the situation would appear to be resolved.'

When the colonel also stood up, she rose from her

own chair, pulled back her shoulders, affixed the air of indifference she had always assumed in front of Hector in similar situations, and turned for the door.

'You know, Miss Smith,' Colonel Harling said as he followed her through to the hallway, 'from the moment we shook hands, I knew you would be persuaded to see sense. A lady of breeding knows to admit when she is wrong.'

Knows to admit when she is wrong? How dearly she wished the man could read her thoughts!

Regardless, she held her smile for as long as it took to show them out. But the moment she'd closed the door, she doubled over and, hands curled tightly into fists, bellowed with rage. She'd guessed at the outset that a women's home guard would prove thorny to bring about; it was, in part, why she had sought counsel from Inspector Childe – to be clear in her mind about the risks involved. She had even been prepared for the odd warning salvo from those who would oppose her. What she hadn't been expecting was to be subjected to a barrage of shelling before she'd even marshalled her troops.

That she'd seen no choice but to capitulate – especially to a man in army uniform – stuck in her throat. But, since this was where she found herself, she would do as she did whenever Hector had triumphed or lorded it over her: choke back her bile and refuse to allow it to eat away at her for a second longer than necessary.

14

'You're calling it off? Oh, that's a real shame.'

'It is.' In fact, Isabel thought as she offered Miss Marshall a thin smile, it was more than a shame; the way she'd been talked down to yesterday by the colonel had been intolerable. Worse still, her disappointment with herself for backing down refused to abate.

'I'd been looking forward to learning what you had in mind.'

Miss Marshall wasn't the only one; if the reactions from the women who'd already watched her write the word cancelled across her posters this morning was any indication, the idea of a women's guard had struck a chord.

Having now cancelled the last of her flyers, Isabel was left feeling cheated and dismayed – not to mention regretful at what she saw this morning as her cowardice. Still, what was done, was done.

'I've had similar comments everywhere I've been,' she said, trying to keep the bitterness from her tone. 'Well,' she corrected herself with a half-hearted scoff, 'apart from the post office. When I asked to amend the poster in the window there, Mrs Crabbe couldn't have been more gleeful. "I told you so, dear," she said as she went to fetch it for me. And I daresay Mrs Pugsley would have done likewise had the copy she pinned to the board in the village hall not mysteriously disappeared.' She'd never doubted the flyer Captain Richardson had brought to Fairlight had been given to him by the reverend's wife. Still, when it came to a woman's place in this war, every individual was entitled to her own opinion; it was just regrettable when she tried to foist it upon others.

'So, it's definitely off?' Miss Marshall asked. 'Not just the meeting but the whole women's guard idea?'

'I'm afraid so.'

'Do you mind if I enquire why?'

'Well . . .' As Isabel conveyed the gist of her contretemps with the Home Guard, she watched Miss Marshall's expression turn to thoughtfulness.

'Have you solicited Inspector Childe for his view?'

Isabel nodded. 'I have. His *official* word on the matter matched the line taken by the Home Guard. However, rather than try to talk me out of going ahead, he merely suggested that, if I thought the idea worth pursuing, I walk a careful line and try not to get caught.'

'But that's not sufficient to convince you to go ahead?'

'Sadly,' she said with a sigh, 'now that the Home Guard has ordered me to desist, I suspect they'll be watching my every move.' *Watching her every move.* But what if she gave them nothing to see? *Try not to get caught*, the Inspector had said. 'You know,' she began, 'maybe there *is* a way for us to go ahead.'

'Truly?'

As the idea began to unfold before her, Isabel felt a quiver of excitement. What if she simply let the Home Guard *think* they'd won? In the short term, she could remain true to her word – deflect further scrutiny by calling off her meeting and allowing them to think she'd given up – only to then proceed behind their backs. Furthermore, if she genuinely believed that what she proposed risked neither breaking the law nor committing treason – if she stopped short of setting up anything that could be construed as an army – then her conscience would be clear. After all, what right-minded judge would jail ordinary housewives for simply trying to keep themselves and their families safe? At worst, they would be told to cease their activities. So, perhaps, rather than look upon her decision yesterday as surrender, she should view it as a tactical withdrawal – one designed to give her time to rethink.

'Miss Marshall –'

'Please, call me Geraldine.'

'Geraldine,' she said, aware of the dangers of getting ahead of herself. 'I've just had an idea. But, before I get carried away, I need to give it more thought.'

'Sounds intriguing. You'll let me know what you decide?'

Reining in the urge to explain there and then, Isabel nodded. 'The moment I know whether it might be made to work, I'll pop down and see you.'

'Excellent. Then I very much hope you succeed.'

As Isabel left the library and trotted down the steps to the street, she checked her glee; did she have it in her to convince others to operate in defiance of the colonel's order? In truth, she had no idea. But she was coming to the conclusion that, unless she wanted to spend the rest of her life being cowed by the same sort of man from whom she'd just escaped, the time had come to find out.

'I've shown her through to the drawing room.'

'And what's she like?'

In response to Isabel's question, Julia shrugged. 'Immaculate. Formidable.'

'Now I wish I hadn't asked. My stomach is already in knots. *And* my palms are clammy.'

It was later that week and, in response to Isabel's telephone call to her, Lady Virginia Scott had arrived at Fairlight to talk to her about the women's home defence groups.

'Look,' Julia went on, 'I know you haven't got off to the best of starts with your idea, and that your confidence has taken a knock. I also know that, when it comes to doing anything new, it's natural to feel out of your depth. You've already had a lot of upheaval and upset to deal with and now, here's something else. Not so very long ago, you were blithely going about your life in London, thoughts of leaving Hector little more than a pipe dream. Since then, you've lost Vincent, escaped both London and your bully of a husband . . . oh, and, despite changing your name, have taken to spending every morning pacing about, waiting for the paperboy to arrive so as to snatch up the *Daily Telegraph* the second it drops on to the mat –'

Isabel grew hot with embarrassment; she'd hoped no one had noticed her obsession with the Personal column.

'– no doubt in a bid to satisfy yourself that Hector

hasn't tasked a private investigator with tracking you down.'

'You guessed?'

Julia's expression was one of despair. 'It seemed the only explanation.' When Isabel made no attempt to deny it, Julia went on, 'Happen, in your shoes, I'd do the same. But it's also why, despite your setback with the Home Guard, you really do need something to distract you. So, rather than worrying you won't live up to this Lady Virginia's expectations, just go in and listen to what she has to say.'

Julia was right; the only way to know whether she was up to the task of organizing a women's defence force – in plain sight of the Home Guard – was to pick the brains of someone who knew what was involved.

As it turned out, the moment Isabel entered the drawing room and saw her guest admiring the view, she felt her shoulders drop by several inches and the tension soften from her shoulders.

'Good morning, Lady Virginia,' she said, hand outstretched in greeting as she went towards her, 'and thank you for coming so far out of your way to talk to me.'

'Nonsense, my dear. A trifling diversion.'

She could see why Julia had described this woman as formidable. In her tweed two-piece, and with an expensive-looking silk scarf in the neck of her blouse, Lady Virginia exuded what Isabel's mother would have called 'Old Money'. She didn't, though, exhibit any of the stand-offishness that came with it. In fact, on the strength of their exchange of greetings alone, Isabel already had her down as precisely the opposite. Moreover, when Julia came quietly in to set down a coffee service and a plate bearing fingers of pumpkin cake, it didn't even occur to her to request that she stay for moral support.

Instead, swallowing to clear her throat, she said, 'Lady Virginia, may I pour you some coffee?'

'Yes, please, dear. And I don't mind admitting to having my beady eye on those slices of cake.'

'Then I should perhaps warn you,' Isabel said with a smile, 'that while it might look to all the world like carrot cake, it is in fact pumpkin.'

'How terribly inventive.'

The formalities of coffee seen to, Isabel sat back in her chair and listened to Lady Virginia explaining what had drawn her to support the idea of a women's defence group in the first place.

'When war broke out, a good friend of mine in Surrey found herself left with all of her female household staff but scarcely a handful of her men. She'd seen it happen before, of course, in the last war. In those days, however, there had never been any real threat of Germans landing on our shores. Now, though, she was forced to accept that the house and grounds stood defenceless.'

'So, she mobilized her female staff.'

'She did.' From there, Lady Virginia explained about the similar banding together of women on the south coast of Devon, outlining how each group, generally known by a title along the lines of Women's Defence Force or Women's Home Defence, chose for themselves how they wished to operate.

When her visitor then took a dessert fork to her slice of cake, Isabel made a further study of her appearance: the neat set of her hair displayed any number of greys; her lips were losing some of their plumpness and, at the corners of her mouth, she had more than a few deep creases. Her eyes, though, glittered with defiance – or was that mischief? Her age was hard to place, her looks putting her somewhere in her late fifties.

'I don't suppose you would happen to know,' Isabel said as Lady Virginia set down her plate, 'whether any of these groups in south Devon have run into trouble with the authorities?'

'You know, I must say, this cake is terribly moreish. I don't suppose you could furnish me with the recipe?'

Recalling how she'd had to guess at the number of eggs to use, how many teaspoons of baking powder, and the proportion of flour to pumpkin, Isabel smiled. 'I'll try and remember how I made it and write it down for you.'

'Thank you. But to answer your question, the snippets I hear from those groups would suggest they've had to deal with all manner of challenges. But I believe they've also found it useful to seek out the more supportive elements of authority and then draw upon their advice as to the best way forward. One woman I know counts among her friends a retired army officer. I believe he's proved to be very useful.'

Fearing that might be the extent of Lady Virginia's suggestions, Isabel decided to come clean. 'There's a retired army captain in the village. He's also platoon commander for the Home Guard. Regrettably, he and his superior have already made plain their opposition to a women's equivalent. In fact, the colonel in command informed me that, should I go ahead with the idea, I would be committing treason . . . and instructed me to desist.'

'Well,' Lady Virginia began after pausing to chuckle, 'technically, he's not wrong. But, as I said to someone just recently, all one can do is weigh the risks. So far, I am unaware of official action being taken against any woman in that regard. The authorities generally have far greater concerns than small groups of housewives attempting to protect themselves. Sadly, though, your experience isn't unusual. Too often, military men, in particular, believe a woman's role should extend no further than managing the home with the same precision that they, themselves, employ to run their battalion, all the while losing none of her fragrance or charm. And if that's the path a woman chooses *for herself*, that's perfectly fine. We don't all aspire to be warriors. But, in many quarters, there is deep-seated opposition to those women who *are* capable of doing more choosing to do it.'

Isabel smiled. 'Regrettably, yes.'

'I sense, though,' Lady Virginia said, pausing to meet her look full-on, 'that even were I to tell you your chances of being arrested for treason are infinitesimal, this colonel chappie has rather put a dent in your enthusiasm.'

Isabel was taken aback; did she really give off such a pronounced air of resignation?

'He has rather, yes. But, since then, I've given the matter a good deal of thought and decided not to allow myself to be intimidated. Indeed, should we go ahead with our own group, my thought is to do so under the disguise of meeting about something else . . . a needlework circle seeming an appropriate choice.'

Lady Virginia raised an eyebrow. 'That's the spirit. But to go back to your earlier question about assistance, who's the landowner here?'

'I don't know. I would have to enquire.'

'Sympathetic police official? Always good to have one of those in your pocket.'

Picturing Harrington, Isabel smiled. 'It just so happens a throwaway comment from our local inspector was what spurred me to act in the first place.'

'Cosy up to him, then. Of course, what we're trying to bring about in the longer term is either a woman's right to join the men's Home Guard on equal terms or, if not, then parity for an operation of our own. As you have discovered, though, resistance to both is deeply entrenched. That said, there is a certain female MP – wrong side of the House but, on this occasion, we won't hold that against her – who never tires in her efforts to gain women recognition. So, it might only be a matter of time.'

'Which, while encouraging news,' Isabel said, 'is something we might not have.'

'Speed *is* of the essence. And I'm encouraged you should see that. The War Office's opinion might be that Hitler's *best* window for invading has passed but that doesn't mean the risk has gone away. And one should certainly never trust to fate.'

'One should not, no. These women's groups,' Isabel said, recalling another obstacle she was having trouble seeing beyond, 'how have they managed to become trained?'

'My dear, I should like to tell you that there exists a common approach. Alas, that isn't the case. I doubt it will surprise you to learn that many women who join a group do so with the hope of being trained in combat and the use of weapons in order to fully defend themselves and their family. I also doubt it will come as a surprise to hear that training of such a nature, certainly in any meaningful fashion, is incredibly difficult to bring about, most of it highly dependent upon both goodwill and local resources. But, as you have demonstrated with your idea of a needlework circle, we women are an inventive breed, are we not?'

Heartened that her guest appeared to approve of her plan to adopt subterfuge, Isabel smiled. 'Dreadfully devious, when needs must.'

'You know, my dear,' Lady Virginia said and smiled back, 'I can see you being a tremendous asset. However, as I have just noticed the time, I am afraid I must take my leave.' Rising to her feet, Lady Virginia extracted something from her handbag. 'On my way over, I jotted down a list of points you might find helpful as you get started.'

With a glance to the heading written at the top, Isabel accepted the sheet of notepaper. 'Thank you. Thank you very much.'

'And finally, please don't take offence at what I am about to say but, the moment I am gone from here, it would be entirely human of you to decide you could do without the trouble of setting up a group that has no legal standing and could end up the subject of much ridicule. Please do not give in to that urge. You will be surprised at the number of ordinary women who have planned what they will do should Germany invade – anything from making themselves look hideous in the hope of avoiding being raped, to shooting themselves in the head with their grandfather's ancient service revolver or, for those with children, to gassing their little ones and then themselves in order to spare all manner of possible horrors.' Clearly reading her shock, Lady Virginia went on, 'Yes, Miss Smith, that any woman should feel the need to even consider such action is appalling. So, those feelings of abhorrence you have right this minute? Use them. Harness the energy of these terrified women. Build on your anger at Hitler for making them fear as they do. I do not believe you will regret it.'

When Isabel had shown Lady Virginia out, she turned to find Julia coming along the hall.

'All right?'

'Well, she's certainly a force of nature. But I fear she overestimates my abilities. Despite how we're planning to make it appear to the rest of the village, this won't be like organizing a group of women to darn socks. Now that I've learned more, I can see it's going to be a serious undertaking.'

Julia regarded her sternly. 'Well, of course it's a serious undertaking – that'll be the war's doing. But who better to get womenfolk together and ready to defend themselves than someone who not only has the time but, more importantly, knows the pain of loss?'

'Well, yes, but that doesn't –'

'*Yes but nothing*. You agree that you need to do something meaningful. You also despise Hector for crushing your spirit. So, what better way to use your resentment for him, and for the Germans who took Vincent from you, than to equip yourself and others like you to take a stand against them?'

'But –'

'No, no "buts",' Julia said, her tone still firm. 'In the face of the enemy, *whoever* that may be, there's no room for prevarication. Trust me, Issy, if for no reason other than your own sanity, you need to do this. And the rest of us need you to do it, too.'

Julia was right. For far too long, Hector Thaxley had ridden roughshod over her every wish. Not only that but, as Julia had also pointed out, she'd had her plans for a future with Vincent wiped out by a German air raid. So, yes, what more of a spur could she possibly need? And as for Colonel Harling, well . . .

'So, you can do that? Spread the word?'

Geraldine Marshall grinned. 'Of course I can. I know which women I saw reading your flyer, and who from among them came in to ask what more I knew about it. First opportunity I get, I'll explain that it's back on and urge them to come.'

'Pressing upon them the need for secrecy, though, and that, if they can, they should bring their knitting or darning – cross-stitch, if that's all they have.'

'Leave it to me.'

'Wednesday,' Isabel reiterated. 'Seven o'clock, at Fairlight.'

'Understood. Anyone else you're enlisting to put out the word?'

Isabel lowered her voice. 'Well, clearly not Mrs Crabbe – not after *her* reaction. Nor the reverend's wife. But, when I was trying to persuade people to put up my flyers in the first place, Mrs Mayfield seemed keen. And Julia says we can trust her to be discreet. So, I thought I'd go and talk to her.'

'Good idea. There can't be a woman in the village Mrs Mayfield doesn't know.'

'It's a terrible shame I can't put up new notices,' Isabel said. 'But I'm hoping word of mouth will get us started.'

'I'm sure it will.'

'Right, then,' Isabel went on, heartened by Geraldine's support, 'I mustn't keep you from your work. See you Wednesday evening.'

Yes, she thought as she turned away, recalling previous occasions when she'd been filled with doubt and trepidation, it was true what people said: the first step towards anything new generally was the hardest to take.

'The cheek of the man.'

'Who do they think they are? That's what I'd like to know – forbidding us to defend ourselves. The audacity of it.'

'What right does *any* man have to stop us looking out for one another? How would *he* feel if *we* told *him* to desist?'

Isabel allowed herself a smile. It was now the following Wednesday evening and, having introduced herself to the women, and explained that she was an evacuee from London, who had lost both a loved one and her home to separate bombs in the same air raid, Isabel had got straight down to business. By relaying the reaction she'd received from the Home Guard to her idea of a women's unit, she seemed to have fired her audience's indignation in the same way the colonel had fanned hers. Indeed, with his tactics now garnering support for her aims, she felt a perverse sense of satisfaction.

But, while she couldn't have hoped for a better start, she was anxious to direct the women's energy to the matter of how they should respond.

Her chance arose from a question put by an older woman she didn't recognize.

'So, this women's guard, how would it be different from the invasion committee? I'm Mrs Vye, by the way.'

'Good evening, Mrs Vye,' Isabel replied. 'It's good to make your acquaintance.' The matter was one she had previously sought to clarify with Julia.

The different purposes of the two groups explained, she met with a second question.

'So, we would set up the same as the men's Home Guard?'

'Having learned what is being achieved by women in the south of Devon, I see us more as a group of equals, with everyone free to contribute anything they feel might advance the common aim, rather than as an organization with all the cumbersome titles and ranks men seem to find it necessary to adopt.' At this, there was laughter.

'So –' Geraldine raised her hand – 'without formal ranks, how would we organize?'

'I suppose,' Isabel said, 'I picture us perhaps having a unifying pledge.' From the corner of her eye, she noticed Julia nodding encouragement. 'Something along the lines of "Faced with the enemy, I shall do all I can, with whatever means at my disposal, to keep my home and my family safe."'

To her astonishment, there was a round of applause.

'Well said.'

'Nicely put.'

Swallowing a gulp of surprise, she shot a glance at Julia, from whom she received a grin.

'But how would we go about doing that – keeping our families safe, I mean?' another woman asked.

Isabel relaxed a little further. So far, her audience seemed keen. 'Well, much of what I envisage is probably no more than most of us would do if faced with an intruder ordinarily –' From there, she forgot what she had rehearsed and spoke instead from her heart about securing their homes, teaching their children what to do, looking out for elderly neighbours.

'Will we have weapons?' another asked. Her question raised a keen murmur.

'If there are weapons to be had, then it occurs to me we should certainly know how to use them. We should equip ourselves to be of maximum use.' The murmur rose in volume – generally, she felt, favourable in tone. 'But only,' Isabel said, finding it necessary to raise her voice, 'for those of us who feel comfortable with that. I wouldn't envisage anyone being forced to use a weapon against her will.'

'A few of us have fashioned weapons for ourselves.' The speaker was Vera Mayfield, seated, balling yarn from a loose skein of it at her feet.

'And that's something I believe we should very much encourage – even among women unable, for whatever reason, to join our number. I feel we shouldn't rest until every woman in Slipscombe has something in her home with which to defend it.'

'Hear, hear.'

'When it comes to actual arms,' Isabel went on, the subject one she knew nothing about, 'we would, in any event, need to find someone willing to train us.' Feeling unexpectedly drained, for a moment, she let the discussion carry on around her. As far as she could tell, consensus had been reached; enough women were sufficiently interested to warrant further effort.

'So,' Julia said and got to her feet. 'What do we think? Despite being threatened with treason, do we want to do this?'

'Maybe a show of hands,' Geraldine suggested.

'All those in favour?'

Every woman present raised her hand.

'Then I think,' Isabel said, scarcely able to believe what she'd started, 'we are agreed. In which case, I propose we meet again next week to decide precisely what we'd like to achieve, and how to go about it.' When there was further agreement, she added, 'And I urge you to remember, everyone, that we cannot let anyone outside of our number know what we're planning.'

'So, don't forget to bring your knitting,' Julia quipped.

'Nothing guaranteed to lose a man's interest faster,' Mrs Mayfield observed as she put away her yarn and, with a chuckle, heaved herself up from the settee.

'Well,' Julia remarked once she'd closed the front door behind the last of the women and drawn across the black-out curtain. 'I thought you ran that very calmly. But then I expected no less.'

'Hm. It's all very well being calm now,' Isabel said, 'but I suspect we have no idea what we're letting ourselves in for. It's going to require a lot of careful thought – more so for the need to operate in secret.'

'I don't doubt it for a moment.'

'And next time I cross paths with Captain Richardson, I shan't be able to look him in the eye for fear he'll read from my face what we're up to.'

Moments later, though, as she climbed the stairs, intent upon trying to have a relaxing soak in a disappointingly shallow bath, she recalled how, as Hector had left Warbone Gate to take up his appointment in Aldershot, he'd called her *a woman who spends all day doing nothing*. After tonight, though, if she ever found herself doubting her ability, she would take his disparagement – particularly since her worthlessness had been of his making in the first place – and use it as a spur to bury not only all thought of him but also to ensure that, from now on, she was anything but *a woman who did nothing*.

15

After fifty-seven consecutive nights of bombing since the current wave of air raids began, yesterday, the third of November, Londoners passed their first night without German attacks.

The voice of the newsreader coming from the wireless in Julia's kitchen made Isabel pull up short. *Fifty-seven consecutive nights* – when she'd struggled to cope with just three? How could anyone live through that and not be driven mad with worry and fear? It was no wonder the ARP hadn't found Vincent, and equally no wonder she hadn't been able to trace his family; in two months of nightly attacks, their cousin might easily have lost *his* restaurant to bombing as well. And if that was the case, who knew where they might all have ended up? As she'd recently had cause to reflect, Vincent's entire family might have left London altogether.

Her loss of Vincent was still no easier to bear. Sometimes, even simply picturing his face or recalling a snatch of his voice was enough to bring back such searing pain that she would be left clutching her midriff or doubling over, her only recourse being to remind herself that it would pass.

Fortunately, this afternoon, she had matters with which to distract herself.

'Sorry I have to dash off like this,' she said, looking across at Julia.

'Truly, Issy, it's fine. I managed to get the guests' meals on the table before you turned up.'

Buckling the belt of her raincoat about her waist, Isabel nodded. 'I appreciate that. But since I'm not paying you any rent, and barely covering the cost of my food, I said I'd help you to keep house.'

'And you are. But, right now, you're doing something more important.'

Adjusting her hat, Isabel regarded Julia doubtfully. 'You know, I'm still never quite sure when you're poking fun.'

Blowing a long strand of hair from in front of her face, Julia put down the fork with which she'd been mashing swede. 'Trust me, if I was poking fun, you'd know it. Getting the women's guard set up is important. You weren't here when I was trying to get the preparedness committee off the ground so you wouldn't know this but, as Elowen will tell you, the bloomin' thing took over entire weeks of my life. It's the way of these things. So, go on with you.'

'All right. But I'll try to be back before supper.'

'Fine. But don't fret if you aren't. I'll keep a plate warm for you.'

It was now the week after Isabel had decided to proceed with her Slipscombe Women's Guard and, yesterday evening, while discussing the idea with Elizabeth, she'd learned that the headmaster of the evacuated school was a practitioner of something called ju-jitsu.

'Picture it,' Elizabeth had explained, 'as a form of self-defence that doesn't rely upon the use of a weapon. Since you've told me you're hoping to give yourselves the means to defend your homes and families, I think you would find an understanding of the basics useful. You should have a word with Mr Lawrence. You remember our headmaster? He's a real advocate.'

When she arrived at Foxbeare House – where the head-master, his wife and the school's youngest pupils were billeted – Isabel relayed to Mr Lawrence what Miss Anderson had told her about ju-jitsu, and her suggestion that she approach him to find out more.

'Please, Miss Smith,' he said, his expression betraying unease. 'Allow me to show you into my makeshift office.'

When he gestured her through a door leading off the heavily panelled entrance hall, she went ahead of him and glanced about. His desk, such as it was, com-prised a short length of plywood resting upon two rough wooden trestles. Behind the rickety construction was an uncomfortable-looking ladder-back chair and, in front of it, one not dissimilar.

'Before Sir James gave up the house for war purposes,' Mr Lawrence went on to explain as he waved a hand over the spartan set-up, 'he had most of his furniture removed and placed in storage. Can't say I blame him. But the result does rather require that we be inventive.'

When he gestured her to the chair and she sat down, his remark about the need to be inventive gave her a thought. 'I'm beginning to understand how that feels. Not unlike your own circumstances here, when it comes to work-ing out how we might defend ourselves and our homes, other than enthusiasm and ingenuity, we women are similarly placed, having precious little else at our disposal.'

'Tell me, Miss Smith,' Mr Lawrence said after a moment's thought. 'What do you know of ju-jitsu?'

'Just what Miss Anderson said about it being a form of self-defence not reliant upon weapons, and that to master the basics, one need be neither male nor athletic.'

'You know,' Mr Lawrence said, 'many's the time I've told Miss Anderson she should have been a saleswoman – although I'm eternally glad that she chose instead to teach.' Isabel smiled back. 'Fundamentally, what she has told you is correct. But I am forced to wonder how you envisage yourselves using the art. After all, engaging in any form of combat carries risks.'

About to reply, she stopped herself. She mustn't tell him about her women's guard; as far as he was concerned, they were just a small group of women eager to feel less vulnerable. 'I suppose,' she said, 'I picture it being of use in situations of imminent danger, say, where there is an intruder in our home, threatening our safety and that of our children, and we have no other deterrent to hand.' Studying his thoughtful expression, she got the impression he was keen to reassure himself they would only use anything he taught them as a last resort – and not for dealing with an overly fresh boyfriend or the advances of a drunken husband. Although . . .

'Then I suppose it *might* suit. You see, the underlying philosophy of ju-jitsu is that, rather than meeting an attack head-on, one takes one's opponent's force and uses it against him.'

'Which is why,' Isabel said, the penny dropping, 'Miss

Anderson was so keen to stress that even a slight person can use it to good effect.' In fact, the headmaster's own modest build and advancing years seemed illustration of the fact.

'That's correct.'

Recognizing then not only its power generally but its value to them as women, Isabel couldn't help herself. 'So, you would be willing to teach us?'

Mr Lawrence rested his elbows on the desk in front of him. Then he brought the fingertips of each hand to meet their opposite number and paused before continuing.

'Miss Smith, my primary concern stems from the fact that I am not used to teaching women. I'm not even sure the nature of the contact required would be appropriate.'

Isabel's spirits sank. But she was determined not to give up. 'I do see your point. Although Miss Anderson tells me that it was you who instructed *her*.'

The headmaster continued to look thoughtful. 'It's true. I did. But that was different. I knew her family and was teaching her brothers. What's more, at the time, she was just a slip of a girl. By contrast, grasping a woman I have never met and encouraging her to manoeuvre me to the ground is rather harder to envisage.'

He made a fair point; most women would need considerable coaxing to do anything of the sort. Well, apart from Mrs Mayfield; catch Vera Mayfield at the end of a trying day and the poor man might not live to tell the tale. In fact, Vera Mayfield probably didn't need teaching how to counter an attack anyway; she suspected even pillaging Vikings would have met their match in Vera.

It was a thought that nevertheless gave her an idea.

'What if we were to find a man to take part? Could you not demonstrate the technique on him, thus enabling we women to practise with each other?'

'I can see how that *might* work.'

Discreetly, Isabel glanced at her wristwatch; she'd told Julia she would be back in time for supper.

'Perhaps, Mr Lawrence, I should leave you to consider my request in more detail. While our chat has been heartening, I must not monopolize your time.' As she rose to her feet, however, she realized that leaving without some form of commitment from him would be a wasted opportunity. 'But would it be fair to say that, should I manage to conscript a male volunteer, you would be willing to provide us with basic tuition? Perhaps one evening a week for two or three weeks? And yes, before you set me straight, I'm sure it does take years of practice to become anywhere close to proficient in the art. But we don't have that long. Time is of the essence.'

'Come back to me when you have your volunteer, Miss Smith. In the meantime, I will give some thought as to how the principles – the "basics" as you called them – might be mastered in so little time.'

When Isabel relayed this outcome back at Fairlight, Elowen burst out laughing. 'Greg! He'd be just the fellow.'

'For throwing to the floor?' Julia said and turned to her stepdaughter to check. 'Or were you thinking more of having *him* manhandle *you*?'

'I merely thought,' Elowen said, her tone one of exasperation, 'given the reason for us learning in the first place, he wouldn't mind doing us a good turn. And we can rely on him not to go blabbing about it afterwards.'

Isabel raised an eyebrow. 'Then would *you* like to approach your young man or should *I*?'

'He's on duty tonight. I'll pop in and see him before I start at The Ship.'

'You could always telephone,' Julia suggested to her step-daughter's departing back. 'Save going out of your way.'

'I think,' Isabel said as she donned a pinafore and tied the strings in order to help with the dishing up of dinner, 'you're rather missing the point.'

'Trust me,' Julia replied with a grin. 'Where those two are concerned, I don't miss a thing.'

To Isabel's astonishment, Mr Lawrence's first ju-jitsu lesson, held one evening later that week in Julia's draw-ing room, was remarkably well attended – almost too well.

With the women seated in a circle, their bags of knitting and needlework pushed out of the way, the headmaster proceeded to demonstrate how, when PC Gregory approached from behind and reached an arm around his victim's throat, he could be thrown to the ground.

'The most important thing to remember,' Mr Lawrence explained, extending a hand to help PC Gregory up from the mattress – removed from Julia's bed earlier that evening, dragged down the back stairs and placed to cushion his fall – 'is that while your assailant might have surprise on his side, so will you. When he approaches, he is unlikely to be expecting you to do anything other than freeze or try to pull away from him. With this particular manoeuvre, however, by lowering your knees and thus placing your centre of gravity below his, then pulling strongly down upon his arm as you bend sharply forwards, you will bring his bulk over the top of you and on to the ground, giving you time to get away.' Looking around the room, Mr Lawrence said, 'I shall demonstrate again, step by step. Please, observe carefully.'

'*Oof*,' PC Gregory exclaimed when he once again landed with a thud.

Isabel winced.

'Would anyone like to try for themselves?'

At least half a dozen hands shot up. Julia, though, went one further and got to her feet. 'May I?'

His disquiet palpable, PC Gregory took a step backwards. Watching from the floor, Isabel thought his subsequent grasp around Julia's neck a touch apologetic. She felt his anguish.

'Now, Mrs . . . er . . .'

'Nance. Julia Nance.'

'That's right. Nice firm grip on his arm and then —'

'*Oof.*'

'Element of surprise, see,' Julia said as she extended a hand to where Greg lay sprawled on the floor.

'Quite so,' Mr Lawrence observed. 'Someone else, then.' More hands went up. 'Someone a little —' When his eyes roved the circle, Isabel suspected he was looking for someone rather less eager. She crossed her fingers it wouldn't be her. 'Perhaps you, miss.'

The headmaster indicated Geraldine.

'Go for it,' Julia said as Geraldine got to her feet.

To Isabel's mind, Julia was enjoying Constable Gregory's discomfort a little too much.

'That's it,' their tutor said encouragingly as Geraldine took hold of Greg's arm. 'Remember, you are using his bulk against him. It is the bending of your knees and thus the lowering of your own centre of gravity that enables you to overcome his attempt upon you.'

Isabel withheld a laugh. Julia's attempt hadn't simply overcome the poor man but completely floored him. But she supposed that was rather the point.

'Imagine he wants to have you against your will,' Vera Mayfield said.

'Can't picture that being an issue,' someone else called out.

'You don't have to get angry –' Mr Lawrence ignored them to assure Geraldine – 'you simply need to think quickly and remember what I've shown you.'

With that, Constable Gregory was once more on the mattress, and there was a round of applause.

'Perhaps,' Isabel whispered in an aside to Julia, 'it's as well Elowen couldn't get the night off work.'

Julia nodded. 'I was thinking the same thing.'

'But it's a good turnout. Shows you how worried women have been all this time – about defending them- selves, I mean. It's a shame Alma couldn't make it. When she telephoned to let me know, she sounded genuinely disappointed.'

'There's always next time.'

'Indeed.'

*

A few days later, after the second of the twice-weekly lessons arranged with Mr Lawrence, Isabel was approached by a woman introducing herself as Harriet Seldon.

'I wondered,' Harriet ventured, 'whether you'd be interested in learning what my husband taught me about defending myself. He's gone overseas with the army. I don't know where he is, but his last letter said he was safe and well and getting a suntan. Anyway, before he went, he showed me how to make a weapon from pretty much anything I can get my hands on. He was very thorough and used to set me little tests – to be sure in his mind, I suppose, that, while he was away, I'd be safe.'

Isabel smiled. 'Your husband clearly cares for you deeply.' Until she'd met Vincent, she'd genuinely doubted such a thing was possible.

'Oh, he does, yes.'

'And although you must be proud of him, you must also miss him terribly.'

'Oh, I do.'

'So, yes, do tell me, what sort of thing did he teach you?' The simplicity of Mr Seldon's advice to his wife left Isabel in no doubt as to its value for the rest of them. 'Would you be willing to show us?'

'I would, yes.'

And so it was that a couple of evenings later, back once again in the drawing room at Fairlight, Harriet Seldon lined up an unlikely set of objects and proceeded to demonstrate, using Julia – who had volunteered to be the invader creeping silently into the house – how she would defend herself.

'You, woman,' Julia shouted as she burst through the door, brandishing an egg whisk as though it was a revolver and narrowly avoiding tripping over someone's bag of knitting, 'against the wall.'

With that, Harriet grasped the floor mop, charged the pretend intruder and mimed thrusting the end of the handle into his stomach. 'The important thing,' she puffed as Julia affected to double over in pain, 'is not to leave it at just the one strike but, while he's crumpling forward, to get him over the back of his head. Do it hard enough,' she went on to explain, swinging at Julia's skull but stopping short, 'and he'll collapse all the way down to the floor, which is when you grab his weapon or kick it out of his reach.' Obediently, Julia sprawled on the floor and groaned. 'Then you sit on the small of his back and tie his wrists with whatever you can get your hands on – apron, tea towel. Strip torn from the hem of your underslip. Anything that's –'

When Harriet was interrupted by someone knocking heavily at the front door, Isabel froze.

Around her, the room fell still.

'Open up!' a man's voice called from the veranda.

Heart pounding, Isabel sent Julia an imploring look.

Thud, thud, thud.

'Mrs Nance!' came the voice, louder this time.

'Quick, everyone,' she hissed. 'Get knitting. And try to act naturally.' *Try to act naturally? When she, herself, was scared half to death?*

When Julia darted from the room, Isabel went to stand and listen at the partly open door to the hall.

From behind her, someone attempted conversation, 'So, this weather we've been having. Not been too bad for the time of year, has it?'

'And as for the price of fish these days,' another chipped in, knitting needles clicking. 'Getting beyond *my* purse to afford.'

Above their deliberately raised voices, Isabel strained to hear what was going on at the front door.

'From the drawing room, you say?' she heard Julia remark. 'Golly, how remiss of me. I moved a chair earlier . . . happen I disturbed the blind. I'll see to it straight away. And thank you for coming all the way up here to let me know.'

Isabel turned and glanced towards the window; they were showing a light? The caller was the ARP warden? Relieved beyond measure, she exhaled heavily: better the ARP than the Home Guard come to apprehend them for treason.

Hearing the front door close, she threaded her way between the women on their assortment of chairs and lifted aside the corner of the curtain to find the bottom batten of Julia's blackout blind resting on top of an ashtray. Such a tiny sliver of light had caught the attention of the ARP? It seemed hard to credit.

'Have you put it right?' Julia asked when she returned, her look one of relief.

Isabel nodded. 'I have. The gap can't have been more than a quarter of an inch at most – certainly not enough for any light to have been seen from the village.'

Julia was of like mind. 'I was thinking the same, which

suggests that, for some reason, tonight, Doddy Phillips deliberately extended his patrol to come up here. But why? Apart from that time back at the beginning of the war, when the ARP were checking everybody's blackout arrangements, I don't reckon he's bothered traipsing up here even once. So, why start now?'

'I'm surprised he made it up here at all,' Mrs Mayfield remarked with a laugh. 'Must have taken him an age to get up that hill.'

'So,' Isabel said, unable to picture Doddy Phillips but guessing from the comments that he was elderly, 'is it possible someone saw everyone traipsing up here and was suspicious enough to send him up here on the off chance? Or did he somehow genuinely see the chink of light?'

Julia shrugged. 'I don't know. Common sense says it was just coincidence. For all I know, perhaps he does come up on patrol from time to time and tonight, of all nights, we just happened to be showing a light.'

'Pound to a penny,' Geraldine said, 'now he's caught you breaching regulations, he'll make a point of coming up more often.'

Isabel shuddered; that was all they needed. 'Then we must all be extra vigilant.'

'Especially,' Geraldine said, 'since the ARP have the right to come in and check premises they merely even suspect of not complying. And of course, there's always the risk of a fine, especially once you've had a warning.'

'Either way,' Julia picked up again, 'I say we carry on. But, as Isabel says, remain alert.'

To distract herself from their close shave, Isabel looked

about the room and, adopting a jolliness she didn't particularly feel, said, 'Yes. We carry on. So, ladies, where were we?'

'Mrs Seldon had just thwacked Mrs Nance with the floor mop,' someone said. 'And was about to tear a strip off her underslip so as to tie her up.'

'Ooh, yes, that was it,' another agreed. 'I remember because it brought me to wondering – don't they train them in the German army how to fight back?'

'They do,' Harriet said, returning to stand where she had been earlier, somewhat shaken, nevertheless. 'But, same as Mr Lawrence has been showing us with his Japanese business, when an intruder sees it's a woman in the home, and not a man with a gun, he likely lets down his guard because he's not expecting her to fight back. That's why you can't afford to hesitate. You've got to strike first.'

'What else have you got there?' Isabel asked, her hand still trembling as she gestured towards the floor at Harriet's feet.

'Puddin' basin,' Harriet replied as she bent to lift Julia's hefty pottery mixing bowl. 'If you can lift one of these when it's full of figgy puddin' batter, then you've likely got the strength to throw it at his skull. If you're not a particular good shot, rather than throw it and miss, you can swing it at the side of his head. Then, while he's still reeling from the shock, you grab something else and thwack him with that. Once he's out cold, tie up his hands.'

'But what if he comes in when you're upstairs, say, in your bedroom?'

Harriet didn't hesitate. 'Same idea, different object. Bedside lamp round the side of his head. Hand mirror, vase, anything with a decent weight to it.'

'*Guzunder*,' Vera Mayfield shouted, which brought the expected laughter.

'We've got a stirrup pump on the landing,' said someone else.

'That'd do real nice – if you can get to it.'

'Perhaps,' Isabel said when Harriet Seldon grew tired of holding Julia's mixing bowl, 'after this, we should all go home and put at least one suitable item in each room.'

'That's what I've done,' Harriet said. 'Granfer's old walking stick is in the hall – but not in the stick stand where it'd be too difficult to get out in a hurry. It leans against the wall. In the back porch, I've Norm's old brolly. Speaking of which,' Harriet went on, 'they're particular useful since the pointed end can be used in all manner of ways. My favourite,' she said, motioning Julia to get up from where she'd gone to sit in a chair, 'is to run at him same as with the mop and aim either at his stomach, as before, or better still, my Norm says, at his, er, crotch –'

'That'll make his eyes water,' roared Mrs Mayfield.

'– which will give you long enough to either get out of the house, or else to grab something with which to crack him over the head.'

And Mr Lawrence had been concerned about women being too delicate for his ju-jitsu, Isabel reflected. If he saw how bloodthirsty they could be, he'd blanch; frail females they most certainly were not. As to how much of what either he or Mrs Seldon was showing them would be possible, if genuinely set upon by an intruder, she wasn't sure. But, if any of this made them feel more confident, less vulnerable, then it had to be better than a plain old knitting circle.

When Harriet Seldon ran out of objects with which to whack, bludgeon or otherwise incapacitate an assailant, Isabel thanked her for the demonstration and the group of women left to make their way home, their mood buoyant as they dreamt up further ways to 'let Jerry have it'.

'It's all very well,' Julia said when the women had left and Isabel was helping her to clear up, 'but none of what Harriet showed us tonight will help us to protect others.'

Isabel frowned. 'If it's one German less to go on the rampage, then surely it's one German less to go on and harm someone else.'

'But what if a whole troop comes marching into the village?'

'We barricade ourselves in our homes and be ready with whatever we have to hand.'

'Sounds a bit like waiting to be shot, if you ask me.'

Unable to see what more they could do, Isabel shrugged. 'Then maybe you should sign up for one of the women's services.'

'I was thinking more along the lines of getting us taught how to fire a weapon.'

Heading towards the scullery, her tray laden with cups and saucers, Isabel held off pronouncing Julia daft. But ask her friend how she envisaged them acquiring said weapons and she would probably be accused of throwing up barriers, when all she was trying to do was be realistic. After all, the matter had been raised previously and dismissed as impractical. Besides, she'd been terrified enough when she'd thought that knock at the door had been the Home Guard – even though an assortment of everyday household items and a dozen knitting bags couldn't possibly incriminate them.

The following morning, though, Isabel awoke to find Julia's comment about weapons still on her mind. What *would* they do if a German platoon came marching into Slipscombe? It was all very well the government issuing leaflets urging them to stay at home, but wouldn't many people's instinct be to fight back? She wondered what the other women's groups planned to do in similar circumstances. Perhaps she should contact Lady Virginia and try to find out; she *had* said she could ask her for help. And no doubt quite a few of the women from last night's gathering would welcome the chance to do more than simply take aim with a pudding basin.

That said, she reflected as she got out of bed and stretched, it was quite remarkable how, in practically no time at all, their little group had got the bit between their teeth; even more astonishing when taking into account that their activities were being conducted in secret, and had only come about in the first place because one of the regulars in The Ship had drunkenly declared that a woman's proper place was in the kitchen. *Utter drivel*, she recalled thinking when Elowen had relayed the tale; an outdated belief only a man like Hector could continue to justify.

Well, she would prove Hector Thaxley wrong. She

would telephone Lady Virginia and see what could be done about weapons. And then she would jolly well make sure she knew how to use one.

'I've thought about this. And I've decided to make it simple for you.'

Fifteen-year-old Timothy Vye stared back at the women seated in Julia's drawing room as though he would rather be anywhere else but there; as though, Isabel thought, he couldn't believe what he'd been roped into doing.

'That's very good of you,' Isabel said in a bid to encourage him. Poor lad: he had to feel as though he was talking to a room full of grandmothers – a nightmarish prospect for any adolescent.

'There are so many different aircraft – British, German, Polish, Italian – you couldn't possibly remember them all. Even *I* get stuck on a few, and I've got the spotter cards. Anyway, I'll show you the common ones you really ought to recognize.'

It had been at the suggestion of Timothy's aunt, their own Mrs Vye, that this evening the women were being shown how to identify aircraft. As Isabel had remarked to Julia, even being confident of telling the RAF from the Luftwaffe might calm a few nerves every time a squadron of them flew overhead.

'So, first up,' Timothy said, 'we have the markings.' He held up two sheets of paper. 'This one,' he said, waving the drawing in his right hand, 'is the roundel you will see on our own RAF aircraft. With one or two exceptions you needn't worry about, the centre is red, the middle ring is white, the outside one dark blue. If you see this, it's one of ours.' Around her, Isabel noticed the women nodding their understanding. 'This one,' he said, waving the other drawing, 'is the black and white cross used by the Luftwaffe. The Germans go in for all sorts of markings on their planes, and some of the earlier ones look a bit different to this. But, if you see a black and white cross, it's one of theirs.'

'That's nice and clear,' Isabel complimented him.

He blushed the colour of beetroot.

After that, he proceeded to pass around playing cards printed with aircraft recognition drawings: Supermarine Spitfire; Hawker Hurricane; Boulton Paul Defiant.

'The Defiant,' he said of the latter, 'is the easiest of all to recognize because it's a two-seater with a gun turret. They're used to intercept German bombers but they're old now and a bit slow.'

From there, he showed them German aircraft: Messerschmitt Bf 109 and Bf 110; Dornier; Stuka. The latter, a dive-bomber, Timothy described with open admiration. When he went on to mention the Heinkel He 111, Isabel shivered. According to the newspaper boy that morning back in September, it was the type of aircraft that had bombed Warbone Gate – without which occurrence she wouldn't be sitting there now.

Another meeting Isabel organized featured a lesson given by Edna Price – who, although now teaching younger children, had once been a language mistress in a private girls' school – the idea being for everyone to learn one or two German phrases that might be of use for dealing with a parachutist or downed German airman.

'*Hände hoch*,' Isabel overheard Julia practising the next morning as she stood feeding towels through the wringer. In her heart, she hoped none of them would ever be close enough to a German soldier to command *hands up*.

'*Macht schnell*,' she heard her urging Elowen when she wanted her to get a move on.

What particularly pleased Isabel was the ease with which the women seemed to adopt various elements of their new-found knowledge.

On the way to the chemist's one morning the following week, she spotted Mrs Harburton coming out of the greengrocer's, in one hand, her wicker shopping basket, in the other – and despite the day having dawned crisp and bright – a tightly furled gentleman's umbrella. Barely a minute later, coming along the opposite pavement, she spotted the doctor's wife, Mrs Locke, identically equipped. When the two women exchanged the merest of nods, Isabel couldn't resist a smile.

'Miss Smith,' Mrs Locke greeted her when she drew level. 'I must say it's lovely to see the sunshine.'

'Isn't it?'

'By the way, I really must thank you.'

Isabel frowned. 'For?'

'For giving me back my spirit. To be honest, it was my husband who pointed it out. Not surprising, I suppose, considering the area of medicine that fascinates him most is that of the human mind. "Eleanor," he said to me just the other morning, "since you've become involved with this knitting circle, you've been so much brighter." And while he clearly doesn't know the half of it, I do believe he's right. I feel less . . . jumpy, less overwhelmed. Dare I say, bolder. And that's all down to you, dear.'

Isabel beamed with delight; what a lovely thing to be told. But accepting praise – deserved or not – had always made her feel a fraud. *Remember what happened to Narcissus, Isabel; always seeking the adoration of others.* How she'd longed to snap back at her mother that it took one to know one.

'Mrs Locke, I'm flattered. But I don't think *I* can take credit for *that* –'

'My dear, don't do yourself down. You've given me quite the boost. And I doubt I'm the only one who feels this way.'

Yes, Isabel reflected as she turned to head home, the effect their little group was having upon the ladies of Slipscombe was heart-warming. Seemingly, by the simple act of putting herself out there, not only was *she* redis-covering capabilities she thought long-since lost, and rebuilding her own confidence, but she was bringing about a similar transformation in others, too. And it was a discovery that brought her genuine joy.

16

After the bombing of the south coast city of Southampton on Sunday evening, heavy overnight raids were last night carried out over Bristol . . .

'Quickly, dear.' At the breakfast table, Edna Price motioned Isabel to turn up the volume on the wireless.

. . . widespread damage reported. Eyewitness accounts suggest that the attack, which started at around six thirty yesterday evening, commenced with waves of bombers dropping parachute flares and incendiaries on the old part of the city and the industrial areas around the docks. This was quickly followed by relays of further aircraft laden with high explosive and oil bombs. Much of the city is still alight and casualty numbers are expected to be high. Also last night—

Isabel snapped off the wireless. Across the room, Edna Price shot to her feet.

'We must go straight to Mr Lawrence at Foxbeare. He has the details of the children's families. I know one or two of them have telephones — as do some of their places of work. As best we can, we must try to establish whether there are casualties.'

'And when news does start coming in,' Elizabeth observed, 'it would be better if we four were all in one place.'

Picturing the aftermath of the raid that had devastated Petty France, Isabel recalled her desperation not only to know that the people who mattered to her were safe, but also how hard it had been to get reliable information. With that in mind, she turned to Elizabeth. 'If what happened in London is anything to go by, the telephone lines are likely to be down, and possibly telegraph services, too.'

At the table, Elizabeth withdrew her napkin from her lap and rose to her feet. 'Isabel's right. But while it might be difficult for people there to get word out, at the very least, we need to establish which areas of the city have suffered.'

Edna Price nodded. 'But while we're trying, we must carry on as normal. The children must not sense anything amiss. Lessons must continue.'

'Of course.'

'And if it turns out that any of them have lost family,' Edna went on, apparently unaware that, as she did so, she was wringing her hands, 'we'll need to talk to the families they're billeted with here, in the village.'

'I suppose it is always possible that our part of Bristol is all right,' one of the other teachers commented. 'From what that newsreader said, it would appear to be the city centre that bore the brunt.'

'Which is why we need to get down to Foxbeare and start trying to find out as quickly as we can,' Edna said. 'In case we are all worrying for nothing.'

When the peal of the telephone echoed around the hallway and made them all jump, Isabel dashed to answer it.

'Yes, Mr Lawrence,' she said, 'they're heading down to you now.' After a pause, she went on, 'No, like you, we've heard only what was on the wireless.'

When the teachers hastened upstairs to prepare to leave, Isabel wished she could be of help. But what could she do? What could anyone possibly do to lessen the women's fears?

'Perhaps,' Julia said, 'until there's proper word, one of us should be here at all times in case the telephone rings.'

Isabel agreed. Being forced to wait for news was an agony all too familiar to her: the gnawing in the stomach; the wretched feeling of powerlessness as hours passed without word and turned into days. Even just remembering the feeling rekindled the darkness that had enveloped her and the anguish that had shredded her nerves as she'd traipsed anywhere and everywhere for news.

'Inspector Childe,' she blurted. 'He might be able to help.' When she looked up, Julia was regarding her blankly. 'Surely, he must have a counterpart in Bristol.'

'It's a pretty big city. More than one police station. Besides, won't the authorities there already have their hands full — be too busy to stop and find out any information for him, I mean?'

'Very possibly,' Isabel said, darting through to the hallway, nevertheless. 'But I don't know how else to help.'

Having dialled the number for the constabulary, Isabel clutched the receiver, cursing the continued ringing tone and willing someone to answer it.

'Inspector Childe, please,' she said when a voice finally answered. 'It's Isabel Smith, in connection with the raids overnight on Bristol. I'm hoping he might be able to establish something of the situation there for the schoolmistresses and the children.'

In moments, the inspector was on the line. 'Miss Smith, good morning.'

'Good morning, Inspector, thank you for speaking to me. I do hope you won't think this a nerve, but everyone here is quite desperate for news of Bristol.'

When the other end of the line remained silent, she prayed it was because he was trying to come up with a way to help.

'Alas,' he eventually said, 'the contact I once had in the city has recently retired, but that needn't prevent me from placing a call anyway. You say the areas in question are Redlees and Cuckham?'

'That's right.'

'And should I learn anything, how do I get news to you?'

Isabel paused to think. 'Telephoning Foxbeare would be best. But I know they were intending to try and call anyone they could think of, and so you might find the line engaged.'

'Then when I have word, I will go directly there.'

She'd known he would try to help. 'Thank you, Inspector. I am truly grateful.'

'Miss Smith, let us hope I am able to be of some use.'

When the rest of the morning slipped by without word from Foxbeare, Isabel felt she could no longer wait about on tenterhooks; she had to learn what had transpired.

'Everyone worrying for their families is bad enough,' she said to Julia as she stood, pulling on her mac. 'But the two of us sitting here, waiting for word, when they might already have learned that all is well, would be madness.

I'll go down and see them. At the very least, by now, the inspector might have gleaned something.'

When she arrived at Foxbeare House, Isabel's first impression was that they might indeed have been worrying for nothing; small voices chanted the two times table; from the basement kitchen came the clanking of cooking pots and the smell of vegetables boiling. Hoping it wasn't all merely a front for the sake of the children, she went to the room Mr Lawrence used as his office, tapped on the open door and peered in. It was empty.

When she turned back, Elizabeth was coming in through the front porch, her countenance rigid, her greeting flat. 'Isabel.'

'Elizabeth, I came to see whether there is any news. I asked Inspector Childe whether he might try to get through to someone there, but I don't know whether —'

'Please, not in here.'

For Elizabeth, Isabel's concern appeared to be the final straw, the young woman's face puckering, tears starting to roll down her cheeks. Swiftly, Isabel took her arm and guided her back out through the front door.

The moment they were beyond sight of windows, she asked, 'Have you heard something, then?'

Elizabeth shook her head. 'Very little. But Inspector Childe has just been to see us. He was eventually able to speak to someone at the City Police Station in Nelson Street, which has apparently escaped undamaged. He hopes to be updated as the day goes on. But what he learned is not good.' When Elizabeth paused to fish about in her coat pocket for a handkerchief and then blow her nose, Isabel smoothed a hand back and forth over the young woman's shoulder. 'The destruction is far more widespread than the news bulletin suggested. Buildings in the centre of the city are still burning, as are many of the factories around the docks. Areas to the south-east were badly hit, too – Barton Hill, Knowle, Temple. Clifton, on the other side of town, as well. Apparently, the glow from the inferno can be seen from as far away as Barry, on the Welsh coast.'

Isabel swallowed hard and lowered her hand to Elizabeth's sleeve. It wasn't the outcome for which she had prayed on the walk down. 'I'm so sorry you must continue to wait for word. I know what torture it is.' With no way to reassure the young woman, she felt lost. However, as she also knew, making light, or offering false hope, didn't help. 'Do you have *any* news of the children's families? Or your own?'

Once again, Elizabeth shook her head. 'Word is slow to arrive from anywhere. But when we learned from the ARP post that little Tommy Clements' house had been hit – he's such a lovely little boy – I'm afraid I started to cry. I couldn't help it. So, I took myself off for a moment. Apparently, the Clements' home was hit by a lone aircraft, presumed caught by the ack-acks. There's no word yet as to his mother and his grandmother. I pray they went to a shelter, but it will be a while before we hear. If they . . . well, if they didn't survive, then it might even be days before we know for certain. And his father's at sea with the Royal Navy. Whatever happens, though, we mustn't let the children see us upset. They're more perceptive than we give them credit for.'

'Is there anything I can do? Anything at all?'

Wearily, Elizabeth mopped her eyes. 'Thank you. But I don't think so. All any of us can do at the moment is keep going and hope that what Inspector Childe has managed to find out is true, and that Redlees and Cuckham – where most of our children live – got away lightly.'

'I will certainly pray for it.'

'It's not knowing that's so unbearable,' Elizabeth went on.

'Yes,' Isabel said softly. 'Would you like me to stay with you? I'm happy to, if it will help.'

Elizabeth raised a weak smile. 'You're very kind, but no, I'll go and splash my face with water and then I must get back to my classroom.'

'Of course. But please telephone if you need us.'

'I will.'

Once Elizabeth had gone back inside, Isabel tugged wearily at the collar of her mac and drew it up against the dampness, before setting off back along the driveway. All war was terrible, she thought, as she tried to dodge the earlier rain still dripping from the trees. On that point there could be no debate. But the worst part had to be the loss of innocent lives, and the deaths of those trying to keep them safe. A close second was waiting around for news – and the time it took to arrive.

Hands thrust deep into her pockets, she plodded along miserably. To feel so powerless was awful. But, while she waited, perhaps to be of use later on, she would offer up thanks for the foresight shown by Mr Lawrence and his dedicated schoolmistresses in evacuating everyone to the countryside in the first place.

In raids carried out in and around London over the weekend, the newsreader on the wireless announced, *it is estimated that in the region of one hundred thousand incendiaries and five hundred tons of high explosive bombs were dropped. Early reports are that more than three hundred people were killed, with more than twice that number seriously injured. Outside of the capital —*

'Forgive me,' Julia said as she switched off the set on the way past. 'I know we shouldn't bury our heads in the sand, but there is only so much bad news a person can take.'

A few days on from the news of Bristol, Isabel felt the same way. It was gut-wrenching, having to watch as the teachers jumped at the sound of the telephone bell or braced themselves for the next bulletin on the wireless — steeling themselves to listen when they would clearly rather not. Just as bad was the way that every time a newsreader mentioned further raids on London, her own insides tensed, her thoughts immediately going to the people for whom each successive nightfall brought another trek to a public shelter or their nearest underground station, where they could do little but wait and pray to be spared. Despite winter being around the corner, she suspected few people genuinely believed the threat of a German invasion had truly gone away; of late, the number of punishing Luftwaffe raids had increased dramatically, meaning she couldn't be the only person who felt Hitler was building up to something even more catastrophic. In some instances, especially when attacks were far away, the continuing raids had even begun to lose their capacity to shock; but for Fairlight's connection to the people of Bristol, it had almost become a case of *Oh, no, which poor place have they hit now?* But once every town and city had been flattened and there was nowhere left to bomb, what then? To Isabel's mind, this latest round of raids simply made the likelihood of the Germans arriving *more* inevitable.

In the wake of the attacks on their own city, from the moment the schoolmistresses left Fairlight each morning until the moment they returned at night, they kept up a front, every ounce of their strength given over to maintaining an appearance of normality for the sake of the children. The wider school family had not got away unscathed, each of the teachers having at least one pupil with a relative either seriously injured, unaccounted for, or lost. With the situation regarding some of the pupils' homes uncertain, at best – at worst, one of complete destruction – Mr Lawrence had agreed that those directly affected would remain in Slipscombe until such time as some degree of normal life back in Bristol could be assured. For the teachers, the decision to tell the youngsters nothing of what had transpired in the meantime weighed heavily.

'As if a day spent teaching six-year-olds wasn't exhausting enough,' one of their number confessed to Isabel one evening, 'the need to appear relentlessly jolly while bearing the burden of knowing what awaits two of the pupils in my care is starting to feel beyond me.'

Elizabeth agreed with her. 'It becomes harder with

each passing day. Every night, I pray to our Lord for the strength to continue, for, while it is difficult for me, it will be worse for dear little Jenny Cole when she learns from her grandparents that she no longer has a mother.'

To Isabel's dismay, Saturday morning's post was to bring further distress for Elizabeth.

'Is everything all right?' she risked enquiring when she saw the young woman turn pale.

Hands trembling, Elizabeth set down the letter she'd been reading. 'It's . . . well, no, not really. It's from Aunty Irene —'

'Tea,' Julia said, clearly arriving at the same conclusion as Isabel and getting swiftly to her feet. 'A fresh brew. Strong and sweet. Maybe with a nip of something in it.'

'She writes that my cousin, Dennis, has been killed. I didn't realize this but, apparently, after those raids back in the summer, a few of the larger companies with premises in the centre of Bristol set up a sort of informal fire watch. A few weeks back, dismayed to have been refused enlistment — because of his epilepsy — Dennis volunteered to join them. On the night of this last attack, it was his turn on watch. When the incendiaries fell, he was caught on a roof, right in the middle of it all, and was lost.'

'I'm so sorry,' one of the other women said. 'How old was he?'

Why, Isabel wondered, was the deceased's age so often the first thing people enquired after? Was it how they measured the scale of the survivors' loss? Did losing someone young make the grief more deeply felt than had he been elderly? Or was it the other way around?

'Similar to me,' Elizabeth replied. 'Thirty-four, perhaps?'

'Here,' Julia said as she set down a cup and saucer. 'There's something in it for the shock.'

Seemingly unaware of what she was doing, Elizabeth Anderson raised the cup to her lips and took a sip. When she resumed speaking, her voice was barely a whisper. 'He was engaged to be married. He only proposed back in the summer. I was there when he did it. His fiancée's a nurse. She lives a couple of doors down. Oh, dear Lord, that poor, poor girl.'

Isabel stared into her lap. When war was first declared, and men had started receiving their call-up papers, their families' greatest fears had been that they would be sent overseas, memories of the carnage of the last war still fresh in so many of their minds. As it was turning out, this time around, those serving at home were not necessarily any safer, with casualties on the home front steadily beginning to mount.

'Does she say where in the city he was on duty?' Edna Price ventured to ask.

Elizabeth's eyes ran back over the page. 'All she writes is that, after his supper, he went back into town. More than that, she doesn't say.'

'Is there anyone you would like to telephone?' Julia asked Elizabeth.

'Thank you but no, I don't think so. Perhaps in a day or two. For the moment, it's probably better that I write.'

'Well, if you need anything,' Julia went on, 'you just say.'

Unable to find a single word she thought might help, Isabel got to her feet and started clearing the table. This last week, witnessing the teachers' distress as they waited for news, and seeing Elizabeth's shock this morning, had reignited her own feelings of grief; even now, she could feel the rawness of it twisting her insides; she recalled losing the battle to hold back tears.

Noticing Julia regarding her, she gestured with her head to the stack of plates she had collected. 'I'll take these through.'

'We might have been right to evacuate the children when we did,' one of the other teachers said as Isabel left the table, 'but being here, out of harm's way, makes me feel guilty – not just at being safe but also for being spared the horrors.'

Isabel knew what she meant; no matter the untold good the teachers were doing by being there when the children's parents could not, the woman's sense of duty was telling her she'd abandoned those who had no choice but to stay – especially those risking life and limb to help keep others safe. It was a feeling she knew well – had wrestled with herself, many, many times. But what could she do?

Distractedly, she pressed the plug into the scullery sink and turned on the tap. If she hadn't had all the confidence knocked out of her, then with the outbreak of war, she might have trained to become a nurse or perhaps have learned to drive an ambulance – at any rate, she might now have been of some use. If nothing else, had Hector not prevented her – on the supposed grounds that volunteering alongside 'shop girls, fishwives and washerwomen', as he'd put it, would be unseemly – she might at least have joined the WVS. Instead, here she was, not just without a skill to her name, but living comfortably out of harm's way in the comparative safety of Devon. Moreover, by deceitfully accompanying Vincent on a picnic that afternoon, and heeding his insistence that she take cover in the nearest shelter rather than return home, not only had she escaped almost certain death but, while those around her went through the upheaval and trauma of being bombed out, their lives in disarray, she had been spared that ordeal and even been handed a fresh start – albeit not the one she and Vincent had planned. It was the element of deceit on her part, indeed, her continuing dishonesty, that gnawed at her conscience the most: solely as a result of her duplicity, she was safe when others weren't – Elizabeth's cousin a case in point.

Turning off the tap, she pushed back the cuffs of her blouse, plunged the first of the plates into the hot water and began to scrub. At the sight of the lilac ribbon turning darker about her wrist the wetter it got, she swallowed the lump in her throat. As she had so often reminded herself, dishonestly come by or not, to squander the chance that had fallen at her feet, when others could only dream of getting away from the suffering, would be indefensible. She owed it not just to the memory of Vincent but to the family now facing life without him to ensure that, from his tragic loss, there came at least *some* good. And if all she could do to that end was attempt to ensure the safety of others by covertly pressing on with Slipscombe's Women's Guard, then that was what she would do.

'Lovely to see you, my dear.'

'Lovely to see you, too, Lady Virginia. Please, won't you come through to the drawing room.'

It was late November and, as Isabel had recently arranged, Lady Virginia was making what she termed a 'flying visit' to Fairlight.

'From what you said on the telephone, it would seem you and your merry band have made good progress.'

Isabel smiled. 'It doesn't always feel that way – especially given that we operate in secret – but, yes, I think we have.'

'You're the first group in the county, certainly to my knowledge, that has been able to organize lessons in ju-jitsu.'

'While I should like to claim that we make the best of what we have at our fingertips, the truth is that we simply struck lucky.'

'One and the same, my dear. Endeavour generally does bring its own rewards. Now, my secretary tells me you wish to discuss the matter of firearms.'

'I wouldn't say that I *wish* to,' Isabel replied, and motioned to Lady Virginia to take a seat. 'Like most of us, I imagine, I should prefer not to have to think about them at all. But, as one of our number correctly observed, were any one of us to encounter a lone invader, we could probably put up a decent fight, whereas, faced with a platoon of Germans marching down the street, it would be a different story, our safety resting entirely in the hands of the Home Guard. But that assumes a suitable number of them happened to be in the village at the time. Many of them are farmers and fishermen, whose jobs during the daytime spread them far and wide.'

'So often the case in these remoter parts,' Lady Virginia observed. 'When I try explaining that to the authorities, however, their response is always the same. "Devon is a low-risk area." Even when I suggest, as I have, time and again, that to bolster those defences might simply be a matter of permitting women to enrol – the likelihood of them being available during the daytime generally far greater – I come up against the same argument, merely repeated with even greater disdain.'

'After my experience with Colonel Harling, it doesn't surprise me.'

'As to weapons, well, as you might guess, this isn't the first time the matter has exercised women situated as remotely as you are here. For my own part, I have begun to make a nuisance of myself by bending the ear of anyone in power. Frustratingly, even on the question of a woman's right to membership of the Home Guard in the first place, I see no sign of them yielding, let alone permitting us to bear arms. It's maddening. Not only are their views on women more suited to the last century but they are so desperately entrenched.'

For Isabel, the continued intransigence of the authorities

was disappointing. While she was still unsure whether she, personally, would be able to pick up a weapon and use it to kill another human being, she wouldn't mind knowing how to go about it. She also felt that, for those women who *would* be prepared to fire at the enemy, the opportunity should at least exist for them to do so.

'Then what –'

'*Nil desperandum*, my dear. Being denied the official right does not signal an end to the matter but *will* require that you be creative.'

Isabel tried to ignore her fresh feeling of unease; they were already walking a tight line.

'How creative?'

'Picture yourself, alone in the house, when you see the envisaged platoon of armed Germans marching up the road. Picture also that, under the stairs, there is your father's rifle – or perhaps his old service revolver.'

Isabel did her best to picture such a thing. But, even in all her years married to Hector, she'd never so much as seen a gun. 'All right . . .'

'How would you feel, knowing that you had never taken the chance to learn how to use it?' Unexpectedly, Isabel saw Lady Virginia's point. 'In the short term, I believe our aim is best served by educating and training women with what's available. Attempting to gain the right for a woman to bear a weapon, when we first need her to be legally able to join a home guard, seems to me like putting the cart before the horse. And I fear that to allow the one issue to become confused with the other will do little to progress either. Rather, it simply leaves us not only unarmed but unprepared and vulnerable – the worst of all worlds.'

Isabel relaxed. Lady Virginia's way of looking at the matter made perfect sense. Moreover, it was an argument for which she could see herself winning support among fellow members.

'But how do we go about becoming trained to use those weapons we might already have in the house? Only, if opinion in The Ship is anything to go by, the men of Slipscombe are opposed to women even picking up a gun, let alone learning to fire it.'

'I don't doubt it. Some men still don't think women should have been given the vote – are set against what they see as even the slightest blurring of the traditional boundaries between the sexes for fear it constitutes the thin end of the wedge. Don't get me wrong, I'm all for men being men. But the notion of equality between the sexes is contentious – divisive, even – because while women have everything to gain, men feel they have everything to lose. And since they also currently hold most of the power . . .'

Unsurprisingly, Lady Virginia's remarks brought Hector to mind; in getting to know Vincent, she'd come to appreciate that her husband hadn't kept her down solely because he was a bully, but because he also feared what a degree of independence might do for her – that she might see through his bluster and challenge his decrees. How many times in a week did he snap *I will* not *tolerate insubordination. I will* not *have you question my authority*. Regrettably, in that regard, the die had been cast early on, when she'd submitted to his will because she knew no better; because she'd been conditioned to defer and obey; because he was the man, and women did what their husbands told them. It seemed to her now that even mothers were complicit, raising their daughters to be dutiful wives.

Realizing that Lady Virginia was regarding her, she tried to recall what they had been discussing. 'Forgive me,' she said. 'I was deep in thought.'

'I could tell.'

'So, what do you suggest we do?'

'On the matter of women being allowed to join the Home Guard, I'm urging each group to write to their MP. I would request that you and your members do the same.'

'Our MP. Yes, we can do that.'

'Between you, come up with a letter. Have everyone write their own copy of it, sign it and send it off. If they all arrive at his office at once, so much the better.'

'Yes, I see the value in that.'

'As to getting you and your members some lessons in the use of firearms, well, I usually find that the men who take least issue with women learning to shoot tend to be farmers. Do you happen to know any?'

Isabel laughed. 'Not personally, although my friend Julia — you might recall meeting her last time — knows pretty much everyone for miles around. I'll see if she can join us perhaps.' She rose from her seat, keen to seize the moment.

'John Drewe, Endacott Farm,' Julia said when Isabel brought her in and put the question to her.

'On the Lassiters' old estate?' Lady Virginia asked. 'Much of it sold off back in the twenties to cover death duties?'

'Very possibly.'

Lady Virginia appeared thoughtful. 'If so, I might have a *quid pro quo* – might be able to trade favours.'

When Julia frowned, Isabel grinned. 'Might we leave it with you, then?'

'Absolutely.' Getting to her feet, Lady Virginia went on, 'You know, my dear, please don't take this the wrong way, but you have rather exceeded my expectations. When we first met, I wasn't sure you had the staying power. But I couldn't be more delighted to have been wrong. With little more than grit and imagination, you've shown how much can be done to help women stop feeling so powerless. In fact, it occurs to me that I could use your help.'

Isabel frowned. '*My* help?'

'Seeing what you've achieved here moves me to redouble my efforts to get women elsewhere to follow your lead. On more than one occasion, though, it's been pointed out to me that I come across as somewhat aloof and dictatorial. You, on the other hand, Miss Smith, come across as . . . well, as . . .'

'Ordinary?'

'I was going to say approachable.'

'I'll take that as a compliment.'

'As it was intended. So, what do you say? Would you come with me to a couple of the places I've been meaning to get to – talk to the women there, explain how you've managed to do what you have, with very few resources?'

Put on the spot, Isabel had no idea what to say. 'Um . . . well . . .'

'She'd love to.'

Under Julia's pointed glower, Isabel shrugged. 'I suppose there's no harm in giving it a try.'

'Excellent. That's the spirit. Let's get you fixed up with a sympathetic farmer for some rifle training first, see how that goes, and take it from there.'

'All right.'

'Jolly good. Well, lovely to see you again, dear.'

Goodness, Isabel found herself reflecting as she showed Lady Virginia out. As if the task of setting up the Slipscombe Women's Guard – in secret, to boot – hadn't felt momentous enough, the thing now seemed to be taking on a life of its own.

Closing the front door, she turned back into the hall. Be that as it may, since what she needed at times was a bit of a push, perhaps being forced to keep up with the idea's surprising expansion – in particular, this latest turn of events – might be no bad thing.

'Right, then, er . . . ladies. Gather round as best you can and watch closely.'

For a November afternoon, the weather was bright, although, for Isabel's taste, a tad too chilly to be standing about at the edge of a field. Having ventured into the antiquated women's clothing store in the village, she'd found and purchased a pair of slacks – the only ones in her size.

'We don't normally stock *extra small*,' the proprietress had said. 'No call for it.'

On Isabel, even the extra small size had been roomy. She was glad of the socks, too, which, at Julia's suggestion, she'd bought from the agricultural merchant's.

'Look for an "M" in youths' sizes,' Julia had told her. 'Get a couple of pairs like farmers wear, and you'll find them thicker and warmer. And they'll wash and last better than anything you'll get from a women's clothier.'

Needless to say, Julia had been right. So far, inside her new wellingtons, her feet were the warmest part of her body.

Barely a quarter of an hour previously, along with ten other members of the Slipscombe Women's Guard, she had been collected from outside Skinner's Garage by a farm lorry driven by John Drewe's yard lad, Brian. They'd bumped along the lanes to Endacott Farm, cursing the cold draughts but laughing as well. If nothing else, Isabel had thought as she'd looked around at the pink noses and rosy cheeks, getting away from the village was already fostering a kind of team spirit – a sense that, while for all of them this was going to be a new experience, they were in it together.

'Now,' John Drewe began. 'This –' he held up a rifle; to Isabel, it looked frighteningly large – 'is a P14 Enfield .303 calibre rifle. It's been around for decades. It's what your fathers would have used in the last war. It's the one I'm showing you because it's the one you're most likely – at least, your husband or grandfather or uncle or whoever – is most likely to have at home. It's called point three-o-three because that's the size of the ammunition it uses.' He reached into a box on the ground and held up a cartridge. 'This,' he said, 'is what it fires.' As the women leaned forward for a better look, John Drewe handed the cartridge to the nearest woman, who happened to be Julia.

'Christ,' she muttered, turning it over on her palm. 'It's

a darn sight bigger than I was expecting. I'd always pictured a gun having little round bullets.'

Isabel had been thinking the same thing; a piece of ammunition as lethal looking as this made it impossible to mistake the weapon for a toy, which was how she'd previously persuaded herself to approach the afternoon's lesson.

Turning to Alma, standing on her other side, she handed her the cartridge. 'Glad you could make it this afternoon, by the way. I wasn't sure you would be able to.'

Alma grinned. 'Miss the chance to learn how to fire a rifle? Not for all the tea in China.'

When each woman had examined the cartridge, John Drewe continued. 'Five cartridges go into a clip.' One by one, he loaded them. 'This clip,' he said and held it up for them to see, 'is what goes into the rifle.' When each of the women had practised loading a clip for themselves, he went on, 'Now for a few more of the basics.'

Having shown the group how to operate the safety catch and withdraw the bolt, he passed the rifle to Mrs Mayfield.

'Lummy, that's heavy,' Vera said as she accepted it from him.

'Bit less than five bags of sugar.'

'Forgotten what a full bag of sugar feels like,' Julia whispered to Isabel.

'Five bags, though,' Isabel whispered back. 'That's weighty.'

'Still, if it turns out I'm not much of a shot, I could always use it as a cosh.'

Isabel laughed. 'Whereas I doubt I'd even manage that.'

When the rifle was back in John Drewe's hands, he lectured them about safety. 'Unless you intend killing the enemy, don't ever even *point* a loaded weapon at another person. Can anyone tell me why?'

'It might go off accidentally,' Geraldine piped up.

'Exactly. While you're waving it around, it might go off.'

'Because you might not *think* it's loaded but it might be,' another of their number suggested.

'Because the safety catch thingy might be broken.'

'Correct. Too many people die in accidents with guns because someone failed to observe the most basic principle. So, remember, unless you need to fire at the enemy, what's the golden rule?'

'Never point a weapon at another person,' the women chimed.

'Right. That way, if something's amiss with the weapon, or you're mistaken about it being loaded and it goes off, you won't *accidentally* kill anyone.'

From the corner of her eye, Isabel noticed Julia's odd expression. Recalling then how she'd lost her husband, Jago, to an accident with a gun, she whispered, 'Are you all right?'

Julia nodded stiffly.

'Right, then,' John Drewe picked up again. 'Now you all understand that much, we're going to learn how to load her.'

To Isabel's mind, the procedure looked surprisingly simple: safety catch forward; withdraw the bolt; clip of cartridges on the charger guide; load into the magazine;

close the bolt. Ready to fire. But, when her turn came to step forward and have a go, she was shocked to discover that, not only did she have small hands but weak fingers, too. And that was without considering the fact that, as John Drewe pointed out, they might not always have any-where to rest the weapon while loading it. Eventually, she managed it but was sorely disappointed by the length of time it had taken. Indeed, when all the other women had finished their turns, she asked if she could have another go. To her relief, second time around, she fared a little better.

'Happen you've got yourself worked up over it,' John Drewe observed.

He was probably right. She did get into a flap quite easily these days.

From there, they learned how to use the sight to aim at a target.

'Thank goodness there's something to help,' Julia mumbled when Geraldine was first to take a shot.

'Make sure you're happy before you squeeze the trig-ger. And remember,' John Drewe warned, 'I do mean *squeeze* the trigger. You want your muzzle steady when you fire, not moving all over the place because you've pulled or snatched at the trigger instead of squeezing it.'

'*Squeeze*,' Geraldine whispered as she did just that and fired the gun.

Even though they'd been warned to put their fingers in their ears, the noise of the blast from the rifle as it fired the cartridge made every single woman start – Geraldine included.

'Christ, my poor ears,' Mrs Vye muttered as she shook her head.

'No wonder my old dad was deaf,' Vera agreed.

'Now, unfortunately, on account of the shortage of ammunition,' John Drewe continued when Geraldine had fired the five cartridges in the clip, aiming at a target pinned to a bale of hay, 'you've got only the one clip each. And trust me, I know that's nowhere near enough. That you've even got that many is down to your Lady Virginia. So, like I say, make sure you've properly aligned the sight with the target before you fire. You've only got the five shots.'

If ammunition was in such short supply, Isabel reflected, it hardly seemed worth the palaver of learning to shoot. After all, what if, the day they needed to fire in earnest, no one had any ammunition at all? Or there were only two cartridges left in the clip? She supposed it was a problem for another day – perhaps one to raise with Lady Virginia; if she'd managed to get this ammunition, maybe she could get her hands on more. She wouldn't put it past her.

All too soon Isabel's turn came and, resting the weapon on top of the low wall as the others had done, she moved the safety catch forward and withdrew the bolt. This time, it moved more easily – perhaps, she decided, because she had been standing with her hands in her pockets, and they were rather warmer than for her previous attempts. She loaded her single clip of cartridges into the magazine and closed the bolt. Then she lowered herself to the height of the rifle on the waist-high wall, adjusted her stance and stared through the sight; heavens, the target seemed miles away. Remembering what she'd been told about operating the trigger, she drew a breath, held it in her chest and squeezed. Smoothly, a little more. Smoothly . . .

Boom. Jolt. Ringing sound.

Flood of relief.

She'd done it. She'd fired a gun.

Her five precious shots taken, she heard a round of applause from the others.

'That, if I might say so, miss, is very nice shooting.'

She looked at John Drewe in disbelief and then squinted at the target. 'Really?'

'You certain you've never used a rifle before?'

'Until this afternoon, I'd never even set eyes on one.'

'Well, in an ideal world, you'd practise at least a couple of times a month to keep your eye in. But if you try and remember what you did there, you'll be fine.'

Rejoining the others, Isabel was struggling to believe what had just happened. Such a shame Hector would never know; for once, he might have been speechless.

'Maybe I should have brought my spectacles,' Mrs Harburton said as she crouched against the wall.

'That's good,' John Drewe said encouragingly. 'Now remember –'

Boom. Mrs Harburton reeled backwards. 'Was that me? Only, I wasn't ready.'

'You'll be all right now,' Isabel assured her. 'Now you've got the first one out of the way, you know what to expect.'

After a lengthy pause while she got comfortable, Mrs Harburton fired again. 'Did I hit it?' she looked back to ask.

'Off to the right,' said Julia. 'Try again.'

Neither of Mrs Harburton's next two shots troubled the target either.

'Come on, Milly,' Mrs Vye urged her friend.

As Mrs Harburton readied herself, though, Isabel gasped: in the long grass in front of the target, something moved. *Boom.* Four sandy-brown feet flicked up into the air and then dropped back down out of sight.

'Race you for it,' Julia shouted. But Mrs Vye was already through a gap in the wall and running across the grass. Seeing the head start she had, Julia gave up.

When Mrs Vye returned and held up her prize, Isabel looked away; it was one thing to eat rabbit but quite another to see one so newly dead it was still twitching.

'That'll help with tomorrow's supper,' said Mrs Vye. Catching sight of Mrs Harburton, she said, 'Though, course, if you want it, Milly . . .'

Milly didn't.

Not long after that, the lesson came to an end and, while the rest of the group was climbing into the back of the lorry, Isabel stopped to speak to John Drewe.

'Thank you for your time and your patience. Our complete cluelessness must have had you wanting to tear your hair out, but I think even being able to simply handle a rifle has been of tremendous help. Perhaps, now, if it came to it, we'd be less terrified to have a go.'

'I daresay. Though let's hope it never comes to that.'

'Indeed. Tell me,' she went on, 'do you know Lady Virginia well?'

'Hardly at all. More knew *of* her in the days of the Lassiters.'

'I see. Well, I hope she made it worth your while. You must be a busy man.'

'Suffice it to say, I've been put in touch with someone in need of ewes to build up his flock, someone apparently willing to pay well for decent animals.'

'And you have just the creatures?'

'Happen I do. I also now have the name of the man down at County responsible for issuing equipment. Which is proper handy since there's a thing or two I could do with to make life easier. Getting a bit long in the tooth, I am, now.'

Isabel laughed. 'Aren't we all? Anyway, thank you again for your time. This afternoon has been most enlightening.'

Enlightening in surprising ways, Isabel reflected, as she accepted a hand up into the back of the lorry and looked around at the animation on the faces of the other women. Unlikely though it was, this afternoon, with everyone feeling similarly out of their depth, and through not ducking out of the chance to do something that had initially terrified her, she had regained something of the belief and optimism she'd had that year in Lausanne – when the world had seemed filled with promise. Had it not been for the indecent haste with which her mother had subsequently married her off, Isabel suspected some of that confidence and belief might have lingered. Had she managed to cling to even a fragment of it, she might not have wasted so much of her life browbeaten by Hector but have found the courage to challenge him about his affair and seek a divorce. But life was filled with 'what ifs' and 'if onlys'. And nothing was more certain than that the clock couldn't be wound back. From today, though, she would make certain to remember how she felt right now – euphoric, validated – and to have more faith in her own abilities. After all, if she could load and fire a rifle, what else might she be capable of doing?

Struck by the notion that Vincent would be proud of her, she slid her fingers into her sleeve. When they didn't meet his ribbon, she pushed them further. With a quick glance at the other women, animated and jolly, she pushed up the sleeve of her coat and unfastened the cuff of her shirt: nothing.

Stiffly, she rebuttoned her cuff and adjusted her coat sleeve. Clearly, her ribbon had fallen off; she'd noticed only yesterday how badly frayed it had become.

Catching sight of Julia regarding her quizzically, she managed a smile. Not so long ago, the loss of Vincent's ribbon would have left her inconsolable; this afternoon, despite her shock at finding it gone, she felt surprisingly calm. It might have been her only remaining physical connection to Vincent but, having lately come to realize that he would always be in her heart, her need for the comfort of it had faded. Furthermore, if it had fallen off while she'd been taking her turn to shoot at the target, it would seem gloriously fitting. After all, it was Vincent who had opened her eyes to what was possible, had given her back her self-belief; because of him, she knew now that she could do anything she set her mind to – and fully intended to continue to prove it.

'Is it just my imagination, or is there even less food here than I'd manage to put together for an ordinary Sunday lunch?'

Isabel surveyed the array of dishes spread out on the kitchen table. 'No, I think it's simply a case that, in your desire to make an extra effort for Christmas, you're more aware of just how many things we've been unable to get this year. I mean, last Christmas, although we all knew rationing was coming, we hadn't had to cope with it yet. What's more, with the war then barely four months old, we didn't face the shortages we do now, either.'

Hands on hips, Julia sighed. 'Maybe not. All the same, as Christmas spreads go, this one does seem miserly.'

Isabel continued to study the dishes. 'You're being too harsh on yourself. The parsnips look good. You did well with those – not just in having the foresight to sow the seeds last spring in the first place but by succeeding in growing them so large. *I* wouldn't have known where to start. And they've roasted beautifully. The cabbage, like-wise, was huge.'

'It's a savoy. They usually grow big. I don't mind admit-ting I'm real cross about the sprouts, though. I felt certain they'd be big enough in time, but they're still only the size of marbles, so there was no point even picking them.'

'No matter, we have the carrots you managed to buy. And the goose fat has crisped up the potatoes nicely. Anyway, if we don't get it all through to the dining room, our problem won't be so much the quantity as that we've let it get cold.'

As Isabel was slipping her hands into a pair of Julia's oven gloves, Elowen arrived.

'I've lit the candle in your table centrepiece, Isabel. It looks pretty, brings a bit of cheer to an otherwise gloomy day.'

Isabel smiled. Given Fairlight's windswept situation, her hunt for evergreen foliage had quickly proved frustrating. But the outhouse had eventually yielded a couple of strands of ivy – complete with cobwebs and drowsy hoverflies – and the ancient and gnarly yew tree, which always reminded her of an old crone huddled with her back to the gales, had provided a couple of sprigs of greenery – albeit entirely devoid of berries. Even as she'd been cutting it, and apologizing to the tree for the theft, it hadn't been lost on her that yew was generally associated with death – hardly Christmassy, but it had been either that or go without.

'What didn't help,' Julia whispered, as she and Isabel returned from ferrying the first of the dishes to the dining room, 'is that, until last week, I'd overlooked the fact that I'd be having to cook for the teachers. I'd assumed *they'd* go down to Foxbeare for Christmas lunch. I'd forgotten their rations are registered here and that, resourceful as she might be, the poor old school cook couldn't possibly magic up four extra dinners – just as she wasn't able to put on a meal for the children billeted out with families.'

Julia's remark sent Isabel's thoughts to Malcolm Baker; at least the Bales seemed the type of people who would make the day as festive for the child as they could. And she'd heard from Elizabeth that most of the children's families back in Bristol had managed to send their little ones a present or two.

'No,' she agreed, somewhat distractedly, nevertheless.

When Julia carried the platter bearing the goose into the dining room, the teachers applauded in appreciation.

'My, that's a good size bird.'

'Look at the lovely golden colour of that skin.'

'It's cooked nice enough,' Julia said once she'd set it on the table, 'but there's nowhere near as much meat on a goose as a turkey.' No, Isabel reflected, there was probably only half the amount; as Julia had confided earlier, stretching it to feed the seven of them was going to require some adept carving. 'Still, I'm always minded that what it lacks in quantity, it makes up for by having juicier flesh than other birds – *and* a richer flavour.'

'Definitely,' Edna Price agreed.

'Moot, anyway,' Julia went on, reaching for the carving knife and fork, 'since, when it came to getting a turkey, the butcher said there was no chance whatsoever. Goose, on the other hand, was off ration, and to be had relatively easily.'

'It smells divine,' Elizabeth remarked. 'And we're all hugely grateful for your effort.'

'Right, well,' Julia said when she'd eventually coaxed

the last of the flesh from the carcass, 'since there wasn't
an onion to be had anywhere, and since the young sage
bush in the garden was lost to those early frosts, Isabel
has very cleverly made stuffing with celery and parsley
instead. But, since it took every breadcrumb we could
muster, I'm afraid there's no bread sauce.'

'For goodness' sake, Mum,' Elowen exclaimed. Seated
at the other end of the table, she waved a hand in apparent exasperation. 'Stop apologizing. You and Isabel have
worked wonders. So, sit down and let's all tuck in. As
you always used to point out when I was little, *worse where
there's none.*'

Yes, Isabel reflected, the longer the war went on, the
truer that particular adage became: the Christmas pudding she'd made a couple of weeks back might owe more
to apple and grated carrot than the traditional dried fruit,
there might be no mince pies for tea later on, no Christmas
crackers, either – their jokes and paper hats a tradition she
had to confess she wouldn't miss – and their glasses might
contain water rather than wine, but the women around
the table there today were not just safe from harm but
about to enjoy a hot meal. As for her own situation, well,
she might not be spending Christmas with Vincent, as
she'd hoped back at the beginning of September, but she
wasn't having to endure it with Hector and his impos-
sible-to-please parents. That particular life – no, that
particular *existence* – was now firmly behind her. And so,
if for no other reason than that, she would offer up her
thanks and try to look to the new year with hope.

*

'I'm not sorry, you know.'

'Not sorry about what?'

'To see the back of nineteen forty.'

'I can't say *I'm* sorry, either,' Isabel agreed.

It was now New Year's Eve and, against her better judgement, Isabel had allowed Julia to persuade her to go out for a drink in celebration of the fact. It was nothing glamorous: the blackout boards at the windows of the snug bar at The Old Ship Inn made the diminutive room feel as though they were at a wake, but the fire was crackling, and their fellow drinkers sounded in good spirits.

After a second wartime Christmas, of necessity celebrated even more frugally than the first, the mood in the wider village remained as might have been expected: families missed loved ones doing their duty away from home; uncertainty about the enemy's plans persisted, albeit now largely as an undercurrent to what had become the more pressing daily business of simply getting by.

'Rotten from start to finish, that's what it was,' Julia picked up again. 'Well, 'til you turned up. Although even that was rotten for you.'

'Yes and no,' Isabel replied. Aware that Julia seemed not just tired but on the verge of becoming tipsy, she carefully removed the half of cider from between her friend's fingers and put it back on the table: better safe than spilt on her skirt. 'I'll admit to spending more than half of the year trying to get up the courage and see my way clear to leave Hector —' At the thought of her husband, she tensed. She wasn't necessarily free from him even now; just because a private investigator hadn't turned up at their door, it didn't mean one still couldn't. But, as Julia had continually pressed her to, she had taken to ignoring the possibility and living each day as it came. 'I'll also admit these last few months have brought me more pain than I could have imagined possible, but I'm still glad I met Vincent. He brought me hope, let me dare to dream. Left to my own devices, I don't for one minute imagine I would have found the courage to simply walk out of Warbone Gate and go into hiding. Besides, had I not been on a picnic with him that afternoon, I would almost certainly have been killed by that bomb.'

'Close shave.'

'Quite. That I survived, only for Vincent to be lost, still leaves me feeling cheated, though. And I suspect it always will.'

'Only natural,' Julia agreed. 'Even now, all these years on, *I* still feel cheated out of a life with Jago. Although, I will say, it does eventually get easier.'

'I hope you're right.'

For Isabel, her own state of uncertainty existed in layers. On a daily level, she wasn't sure what to do about the Slipscombe Women's Guard, finding ways to maintain the women's readiness and enthusiasm proving tricky, the generally dank weather not doing much to help. On the level above that, she worried about her financial situation; Julia wouldn't entertain accepting rent from her, claiming that the billeting allowance for the teachers, alongside the economies created by preparing meals for all of them at the same time, and Elowen's contributions from her wages, were just about keeping them afloat.

'We're all right,' Julia had stressed just that morning, 'as long as no catastrophe befalls us.'

Isabel's greatest worry, however, had become what she was supposed to do in the longer term. Viewed in that light, the situation with the war was largely academic; hostilities or peace, despite a growing drive to make something of herself, she simply couldn't picture the future; her circumstances felt so far beyond her to resolve that she didn't even talk about it to Julia any more. After all, if she couldn't work out for herself what she was going to do, why would Julia have any more success?

'Elowen's really good with the customers, isn't she?' she said, distracting herself from Hector by watching Julia's stepdaughter at work behind the bar. 'Not everyone could be so bubbly and bright all evening.'

'Takes after her dad,' Julia replied, her look a distant one. 'He was just one of those people who never let anything get him down. He could be hot-tempered, I'll own to that. If someone wound him up, he'd put them straight in an instant. Next minute, though, he'd be back to larking about with them. Life and soul, he was. Ellie has much the same way about her. We've had our moments – her and me – these last few years especially. But I couldn't feel any more strongly for her had she been my own flesh and blood. And I doubt there's many in my shoes as could claim that.'

'No.'

'Tell me, ever wish *you'd* had children?'

Isabel stared into her lap. Over the years, her childlessness had aroused all manner of emotions, few of them helpful. 'Children were the only reason Hector married me. Once the great love of his life, his do-no-wrong Audrey, had married the wealthier of her two suitors, he took no interest in replacing her in his affections. But he did badly want sons. Like most men, I suppose, he craved a legacy. Had I given him children, our relationship might have turned out differently – although I doubt by much. Once Audrey had become a divorcée, he would still have taken up with her again, he just wouldn't have been able to accuse me of being worthless. Even in his eyes, being the mother of his progeny would have given me some degree of standing.'

'Yes, yes, but what about you?' Julia persisted. 'Did *you* want children?'

'Of course I did. And I never for one moment imagined I wouldn't have them. Girls got married and nature gave them babies. When they still hadn't come along after two or three years, I supposed something was amiss but, by then, I'd begun to feel relieved – especially since Hector, who really didn't want me physically anyway, simply became exasperated by what he saw as the amount of effort involved in continuing to try.'

'But all that troubled water is long under the bridge.'

'It is,' she said, deciding to leave it at that.

'With a bit of luck, you'll never have to set eyes on the man again.'

God willing. 'No.'

'Which brings me back to what I was saying about not being sorry to see the back of nineteen forty,' Julia picked up again. 'All told, it was quite the year. Losing my last two guests. Fretting about Pasco and his shenanigans . . .

my brush with the law once he got caught and jailed. Bankruptcy constantly nipping at my heels.'

'You never told me things were *that* bad.'

Julia shrugged. 'They weren't, really. The cider's making me exaggerate. Grim, maybe. Dicey, certainly. And without the teachers being billeted on us, then by now I would be worryingly closer to the bottom of my savings. D'you know what, though?' In response to her friend's question, Isabel shook her head. 'The one thing that saved me from going quietly mad was the preparedness committee. You'd think going a while without guests would come as a respite, wouldn't you? Well, let me tell you, it didn't. I was so overwhelmed by the gloom and the worry of it all that I was struggling to even get out of bed in the morning. According to Elowen, I was snappy and irritable and there was no reasoning with me.'

To Isabel, it did sound as though Julia had endured quite a year – as she herself had. Although, in her case, most of what had befallen her had done so in the last quarter of it. Even the worst of the war had happened in the last three months. Indeed, there were reports again just this morning that London in particular had been subjected to yet more incendiary attacks, with bombs being dropped by the tens of thousands, the resulting and widespread fires causing further dreadful loss of life. It was all so awful, so truly, truly awful.

When she raised her head, it was to see Julia taking a long slug of her cider.

'You know,' she said, 'you might not want to drink that quite so fast.'

'Or,' Julia replied, gesturing to Isabel's empty glass, 'since they're about to call for last orders, we could get you another one of those and you could keep me company. We could be merry together.' As Julia then raised her head to stare across to the bar, Isabel watched her straining to see. 'Ellie? Love?'

When Elowen turned to see what her stepmother wanted, Isabel signalled with an exaggerated shake of her head that she should ignore her. At that same moment, from the adjacent public bar came a roar of laughter.

'It's that loudmouth Derry Long and his cronies,' Elowen lowered her voice to explain as she came to clear Isabel's glass. 'Sorry – you didn't want another, did you? Only, I'm just popping through to lend a hand in the public.'

'No, thanks. We're about to head home.'

'Right you are. Then just be careful, the pair of you.'

'Do I know Derry Long?' Isabel asked as Elowen opened the door to the public bar and, from beyond it, a scruffy individual caught sight of them.

'Lad, lads,' he bawled. 'There's two of them women – you know, them that thought they could set up their own Home Guard.'

His remark made her flinch.

'Derry Long, pipe down,' Elowen called firmly in his direction and closed the door.

'Since you ask,' Julia said when peace returned to the snug, 'Derry Long is a mouthy smallholder with a short fuse, a grudge against women and a liking for the strong liquor he brews in an outhouse. In other words, a lazy good-for-nothing whose wife walked out on him some years back. If you ask me, the woman deserves a medal for putting up with him as long as she did.'

'I see. And he hasn't been called up?'

Julia shook her head. 'When we were all registered on that census at the start of the war, despite his smallholding producing nothing but a couple of pigs each year, he somehow got himself put down as a farmer. As a result, ever since, he's been in a reserved occupation. When the call went out for volunteers to join the LDV, though, he was one of the first to sign up. To no one's surprise, in next to no time, he was put on notice for arriving late on patrol . . . or else for showing up drunk.'

'Goodness.'

'Suffice it to say, while the man might be all bluster, he's still best avoided.'

'I see.' By now beginning to feel weary, Isabel longed to head home. Perhaps she would go and find the Ladies' and then persuade Julia it was time to leave. 'Can you point me to the –'

'Far end of the bar. Through the door. Ladies' is on the right. Don't go out into the yard, that's the Gents'.'

'Thanks.'

To Isabel's dismay, as she was leaving the Ladies' a couple of minutes later, Derry Long was returning from the yard, the pair meeting face-to-face under the dim light of the tiny back porch.

Recalling Julia's advice, she raised a polite smile and gestured to the door to the snug. 'Excuse me.'

When, instead of moving aside, Long took a step

closer, she teetered backwards, her shoulders ending up pressed against the cob wall.

'You women,' Long said, pointing a finger in her face, 'soon got put in your place, didn't you? Women's home guard, my arse. Women? Allowed guns? Never.'

As he leaned even closer, she was on the point of shoving him when he unexpectedly reeled away to leave her exhaling in relief.

'You can be sure the day will come, though,' she said, sufficiently rattled to forget Julia's advice to ignore him. 'You just wait and see. Then who will be left to eat his words, hm?'

'*You can be sure the day will come*,' Long mimicked. 'Stuck-up cow. It'll never happen. Never. The law will see to it. Still,' he went on, the expression on his face one of pure hatred, 'what do you expect from a house full of women with no man to keep them in check? Tedn't natural. No, what you all need is husbands to keep you in the kitchen, where you belong.'

Reminding herself that trying to reason with a fool, let alone a drunken one, was only ever a lost cause, Isabel wondered afresh why she was even *attempting* to hold a conversation with the man. He was barely coherent.

'Excuse me,' she said stiffly, fingers trembling as she reached for the door handle.

Back in the snug, she stood for a moment to compose herself. Julia was right: the man was nothing more than an odious fool.

When Isabel arrived back at their table and sat down, Julia frowned. 'You all right?'

'Yes.'

'Sure?'

Irritated at having let the man get to her, Isabel shook her head. 'I bumped into Derry Long.'

Julia laughed. 'Like I said, best approach to that sorry individual and his ilk is to ignore them. Don't take the bait.'

Isabel sighed. 'I know. But I'm afraid I did. I couldn't stand there, listening to him ranting on about us needing husbands to keep us in the kitchen.'

'Look,' Julia said, placing her hand on top of Isabel's in a gesture of sympathy. 'Forget about him. He's not worth troubling your head over.'

'I'm sure you're right. But since he clearly saw my posters that time, and hasn't forgotten we tried to set up a home guard, he's left me wondering what would happen if he ever found out we've done precisely that? I wouldn't even put it past him to watch us, try and catch us out, purely for the satisfaction of seeing us *put in our places*, as he would probably have it. It only needs someone to suspect we're up to more than knitting when we get together – for someone to start a rumour – and you can be sure he'd be first in line to report us.'

'Issy, listen,' Julia said. 'You're blowing it all out of proportion. Truly. Derry Long hasn't got it in him to see beyond the end of the day. Put him out of your mind.'

Isabel let out a weary sigh. 'You're right. Sorry, I'll try.'

With that, the sound of the door latch and the feel of a draught rushing under the blackout curtain signalled the arrival of someone into the front porch, the head that subsequently poked around it taking Isabel by surprise.

'Inspector Childe,' she said and raised a smile.

For a second or two, the hubbub of conversation in the snug quietened and several of the remaining drinkers made to head home.

'Good evening, Isabel, Julia.'

'Evening, Inspector.'

'If you wish to get warm here by the fire,' Isabel said, 'we are about to leave.'

'Not on my account, I hope.'

Again, Isabel smiled. 'No, of course not.'

'Care to pull up a chair and join us?' Julia asked. 'There's still just about time.'

'A kind invitation, for which I thank you, but I'm on my way home and only looked in to check that Mr Nott is closing up.'

'Tell me, Inspector,' Isabel said as she got to her feet and reached to the peg for her coat. 'Do you stay up to see in the new year?'

'More often than not, I've found myself on duty, and so I've had no say in the matter.'

'I suppose not, no. Well, Happy New Year anyway.'

'And a Happy New Year to you. Might I enquire how you're getting home?'

'Since we're both rather tired, somewhat slowly, I imagine.' She reached for Julia's coat and scarf. 'And making the most of the fresh night air.'

'Would you perhaps accept a lift? My motorcar is outside, and I should prefer to know you've arrived home without incident.'

To Isabel's mind, the timing of his offer couldn't have been more fortuitous. 'That would be tremendously kind of you. But only if you're sure it's no trouble.'

'None whatsoever. Please, take your time. I'll go and bring my car around to the front door.'

Through a stroke of less fortunate timing, as the two women went to leave through the blacked-out porch, the door to the public bar opened and, from where he was swaying on a stool, Derry Long spotted them.

'Yeah, that's it, slope off home, the pair of you, back where you belong.'

'Oh, go and take a long walk off a short pier,' Julia shouted back.

'So much for ignoring him,' Isabel muttered.

By the time the Inspector pulled up in the lane behind Fairlight, she was simply grateful to be home.

'Tell me . . .' Julia turned to address the Inspector as she tried to poke the key – until Isabel took it from her – into the lock of the back porch to let them in. 'Are you available for a spot of first footing in a bit? You know, make sure the first person over my threshold this year is dark-haired . . . so as to bring me good luck?'

'I think I'm rather too grey now to fulfil the requirements of that particular custom.'

Julia grinned. 'Darkest there'll be in this house tonight.'

With a groan, Isabel went ahead of her friend and opened the door to the scullery. 'My apologies for bringing you to the tradesman's entrance, Inspector.'

'I am more than used to it.'

Whereas Isabel felt weary, Julia appeared to be bene-
fiting from a second wind.

'Nightcap, Inspector?'

'Kind of you to offer, but I ought really to head home.
I might be off duty now, but I do need to remain available
in case I'm needed anywhere.'

Please, Isabel willed her friend, *just let the poor man go home.*

'Pah. You're too sensible.'

'Mrs Nance, I daresay that's true.'

'Thank you for seeing us home,' Isabel said. 'I'm sorry
it has taken you out of your way. Please, allow me to see
you out.'

Back in the porch, Harrington turned towards her.
'Isabel, is everything all right? Only you seem . . .
preoccupied.'

Isabel gave him a brief smile. 'Everything is fine, thank
you. I'm just tired.'

'All right. Well, goodnight, then.'

'Goodnight, Inspector.'

Watching as he disappeared into the darkness, Isabel
turned the key in the lock and made her way cautiously
back through the unlit scullery. Alerted by the clink of
glassware, she headed to the drawing room, where she
found Julia pouring whisky.

'Here.'

'Do you think that's wise?' she said, waving away the
crystal tumbler Julia was offering in her direction.

'Wise? There's a war on.'

'You've already drunk the best part of three halves of
cider – and the strong stuff, too.'

'Takes more than that to incapacitate *me*.'

'That's as maybe. But following it up with a whisky is going to give you the very worst of headaches. Still, it's your funeral.'

'Precisely. Come on, Miss Prim 'n' Proper. Just this once, let your hair down. We made it through the year. Jerry might not have come for us yet but there's no telling he won't. And then, well, who knows?'

Some long time later, hearing the front door opening and closing, and the sound of the blackout curtain being dragged across, Isabel turned towards the mantle and squinted at the hands on the clock. If it was that late, no wonder she was tired.

'I'm surprised you two are still up,' Elowen observed, arriving in the doorway and unwinding her scarf from around her neck. After hanging her coat up, she moved to stand, hands on hips, in front of her stepmother.

'Alf Nott finally let you come home, then?' Julia observed as she looked up to meet her stepdaughter's stare.

'As you might imagine,' Elowen said, 'not only were folk harder to shift this evening but there was more than the usual amount of clearing up to do. And before you ask, yes, on this occasion, I did stop for a drink with the Notts. Seemed only polite.' Turning to Isabel, she went on, 'By the way, did I hear Derry Long giving you trouble?'

Isabel shook her head. 'Just expressing his opinion about a woman's place.'

'Sad old fart.'

'Elowen Nance, you're not so big that I can't still wash your mouth out with soap.'

'Mum, many's the time you've called him worse.'

'Truly,' Isabel continued, 'it was merely a lot of hot air.'

'Only, if you ever think he knows about your home guard, or indeed, threatens trouble of any sort, I've plenty stored up you could use against him. One of the benefits of working behind the bar,' Elowen went on with a laugh, 'is that, get a pint of rough inside them, and the silly sods forget I'm there – forget I hear every word they say.'

'I thought you only work the snug?' Julia perked up to remark.

'Usually, yes. But if Mr Nott has to fetch in a new barrel or go out to bring something in from the store, I'll pop through to help out.'

'You seem very proficient,' Isabel observed.

'Thanks. Took me a while to get into the swing of it but I quite enjoy it now. Anyway, one thing I've recently learned about Derry Long is that he's diddling the Excise men.'

'Do you know how?' Isabel asked. As Elowen had just suggested, having dirt on Derry Long could indeed be useful.

Elowen sank on to the arm of the settee. 'Well, you know the red diesel that farmers and the like can get without the tax on it, but ordinary folk can't have?'

Although she didn't really, Isabel nonetheless nodded.

'What about it?' Julia asked.

'Well, what few people know is that it's only the normal

stuff with red dye added to deter those folk with a legal entitlement to it from selling it on.'

It was the first Isabel had heard of such a thing, and she was intrigued. 'So –'

'Derry Long and his cronies have found a way to wash it.'

Julia frowned. 'Wash it?'

'That's what they call it but, when I overheard the different things they've tried doing to get the dye out, I'd say what they're actually doing is filtering it.'

'Do you know how?' Isabel asked.

'Through bread.'

'*Bread?*' Isabel and Julia chorused.

'In particular, the brown sort. The denser the better.'

'And it comes out clean?' Julia asked. 'With all the red gone?'

Elowen shrugged. 'Never seen it done but, according to them, the folk they sell it on to don't complain.'

'Goodness.' Unexpectedly, Isabel felt a weight lift from her shoulders. Should Derry Long ever find out they'd gone ahead with their women's guard, and choose to make trouble, she now had something she could hold over him. Granted, for the information to be of any real use, she would have to resort to blackmail but, well, as she seemed to find herself thinking quite often these days, *needs must.*

'You should tell your Greg,' Julia said. 'First thing tomorrow morning, you should tell him what you've just told us.'

'Or perhaps,' Isabel said, 'we should hold on in case

the man ever threatens trouble over the home guard. Although, of course –' with a sudden appreciation for Elowen's position, she changed tack – 'not if you feel obliged to tell PC Gregory.'

Elowen shook her head. 'Can't go running to him every time I hear of something stupid going on.'

'I say we shop him, pure and simple,' Julia announced. 'If Pasco got done for defrauding Customs and Excise, Derry Long should too.'

'To be fair,' Elowen said, shifting her weight on the arm of the settee, 'Uncle Pasco's downfall was of his own making. He was caught red-handed and had no choice but to admit to black marketeering. It had nothing to do with Derry Long.'

'I still say the man belongs in jail.'

'He does,' Isabel agreed. If there was one thing she couldn't stand, it was people who worked the system for their own gain. It was what Hector had done, albeit by wheedling his way out of being appointed to positions that didn't suit him – or making sure he was promoted into those that did – purely by calling for a favour from someone he knew. 'And, in time, we can see that's where he ends up. However, I still say that, where men like him are concerned, it never hurts to have something in your armoury, just in case.'

'Hey, look,' Elowen suddenly said, sliding off the arm of the settee and indicating the clock. 'Two minutes to midnight.'

'And since it's unlucky to toast the New Year with an empty glass,' Julia added, getting up and going towards the drinks cabinet, 'both of you, come on, come and get a finger of whisky.'

When the little clock set about chiming the hour, the three women raised their tumblers.

'Cheers,' Elowen said. 'Happy New Year.'

'Good riddance to nineteen forty. Welcome in, nineteen forty-one.'

'Happy New Year,' Isabel echoed before downing her whisky in one go. And *this* year, I'm going to start as I mean to go on.'

19

Spring 1941

'You know, I've started to think that if we're to keep all of our ladies enthused about the women's home guard, we're going to need new ways to hold their interest.' When Isabel glanced at Julia, walking beside her, she found her looking thoughtful.

'I must admit,' Julia eventually replied, 'at times, it does rather feel as though we're running out of steam. But what sort of new ways did you have in mind?'

Isabel sighed. 'That's what I've been trying to decide. Given our general lack of resources, and that we're having to operate in secret, it's tricky.'

It was a pleasant morning at the beginning of April, and Isabel and Julia were traipsing back up the hill after yet another largely futile shopping trip to the village: none of the yarn in the wool shop was suitable for the lightweight sweater Julia had been hoping to knit to see her through the summer; Isabel had been dismayed to find there still wasn't a single pair of stockings to be had anywhere. Furthermore, at the chemist's, she had been aggrieved to learn that, since it had apparently been advertised in every newspaper and women's magazine as excellent for treating hands chapped by household

307

detergents, they had been unable to procure a further stock of petroleum jelly.

When Julia slowed to a halt near the top of the hill and paused to catch her breath, Isabel turned to look back over the bay. This time last year, she'd known nothing of Slipscombe Sands; instead, having met Vincent a couple of times, and started to get to know him, she had begun to wonder about the possibility of a different life for herself. In none of those early visions had she pictured ending up alone in Devon – certainly not doing something as bold as running Slipscombe's women's equivalent to the Home Guard, even if she was doing so covertly.

But here she was.

'After all of your efforts,' Julia said as she picked up her shopping basket and the two continued on their way, 'it would be a shame if the thing was to fold.'

Isabel sighed. 'It would. After all, no one can know what Hitler is really intending. Just because he didn't invade last summer, when we were all expecting him to, it doesn't mean he won't. In fact, that could be precisely what he'd planned.'

'For us to take our eye off the ball?'

'Perhaps. After all, just this last week, we're told he's invaded Yugoslavia and Greece. And what about poor old Bristol again? Those raids on Good Friday were devastating. Why do that, if not to bomb us into submission? What's more,' she continued as facts to support her argument lined up in her mind, 'in the post office the other day, Geraldine overheard Captain Richardson suggesting that training for the men's platoon is becoming *more* rigorous, not less. She also said – and don't ask me how she knows this, but she does have an ear in the most unlikely of places – the Home Guard has recently been told they are to man roadblocks day and night now, *and* to have guards permanently stationed at key locations. Although, what those are, out here, in the middle of nowhere, I can't imagine. Geraldine also says that Captain Richardson has been training his men in how to make grenades and mortars from anything they can lay their hands on. All of which leads *me* to believe that, regardless of popular opinion, or what's printed in the newspapers, the War Office clearly doesn't think the threat of invasion has gone away at all.'

'All right,' Julia said as they crossed the stretch of grass in front of Fairlight. 'Then if you still think Hitler's going to invade, shouldn't the women's guard simply continue to stand by, as the preparedness committee does?'

'Of course we should. But you come to the meetings. You see how hard it is to keep the women's attention when all we do is go over the same old ground, time and again. It's different for you. Your preparedness committee has practical tasks to carry out, like checking the wells once a month and seeing that the emergency first-aid supplies are still useable, updating the list of empty houses and so on. The women's guard doesn't have that. There's only so many times I can check we all remember how to load a rifle, certainly without actually having one with which to practice.'

'I suppose you could mount patrols,' Julia suggested as she eased her feet out of her lace-ups. 'Oh, what I'd give for a new pair of sandals. My pair from before the war are far too tatty to wear outside now. But have *you* seen any in the shops?'

Isabel shook her head. 'I haven't. But since it's not something I can afford, I haven't really been looking.'

'I can't afford a new pair either, but that doesn't stop me craving them.'

'I can't begin to describe how badly I long for some stockings, though. I used to think that to be able to wear a pair of slacks, with no one to disapprove, would be liberating – and I suppose, if it were possible to buy a nice-fitting pair of ladies' socks to wear with them, it might not be so bad. But since all I've been able to get are scratchy woollen pairs in men's sizes, I find myself longing to be back in a skirt and stockings. And please don't suggest I do as Elowen does and go bare-legged. Unlike *her* legs, *mine* no longer stand scrutiny.' In any event, more greatly concerned by the direction of the war than by shoes she couldn't afford and stockings she couldn't find, she went on, 'You started to say something about patrols.'

'I did?' Julia stood upright and stretched. 'Oh, yes, but only as a result of seeing the pillbox back there, and thinking about how, almost the instant war was declared, they came in a great rush to build the things, getting everyone up in arms about spoiling the views, and yet I've never seen a single one of them put to a minute's use. Once the Home Guard was set up, I supposed *they* would man them, but apparently that's not their job.'

'That's something else Geraldine told me. According

to Captain Richardson, manning more than the odd one or two of them leaves him short-handed for more important duties.'

'*More important duties?*' Carrying her meagre purchases through to the pantry, Julia scoffed. On her return to the kitchen, she switched on the wireless. 'I mean, if you were Hitler, where would *you* invade? One of the harbours down to the south, where all manner of boats would be standing by to put out and thwart you? Or some quiet sandy beach up here, where you could come ashore in your droves – maybe even set up proper camp before anyone even noticed?'

Julia's remarks gave Isabel pause for thought. 'One would hope someone, somewhere, would spot their approach and alert the authorities, so that they didn't make it ashore in the first place.'

Alert the authorities. Yes, but, as Julia had just pointed out, along this stretch of coast, no one was on watch at all. So –

Hearing the newsreader on the wireless mention London, she paused, mid-thought, to listen.

. . . the raids, on Easter Sunday, are believed to have been the heaviest so far. An estimated seven hundred German bombers carried out the attacks, which started just before nine o'clock in the evening and continued until shortly after five o'clock the following morning. The number of those killed is estimated to be in the region of one thousand, with twice that number injured, many seriously. Eight hospitals are reported to have been damaged. The areas worst hit included the docks and industrial areas to the east of the city, and the West End, where offices, homes and shops over a wide area

were destroyed. The Houses of Parliament and St Paul's Cathedral also received hits.

'Dear God,' Julia whispered.

'Clearly,' Isabel muttered under her breath as she swiped at the tears of anger welling in her eyes, 'Hitler's not going to stop until he's brought us to our knees – until he can just walk in over the ruins.'

'It would seem to be that way, wouldn't it?'

'In which case,' Isabel went on, 'we simply can't let our efforts with the women's guard go to waste. We have to find ways to be more useful. When we were walking home, you mentioned the pillboxes – and how they're never used. So, as I was about to say before that news report came on, what if *we* were to man a couple of them?'

'Man the pillboxes,' Julia repeated, her expression suggesting she was giving the idea some thought. 'Could work.'

'Of course it could,' Isabel said. 'If the likes of Derry Long can go on patrol, so can we.' With the idea growing in appeal, she tried to picture how it might be brought about. Under different circumstances, she would speak to Captain Richardson and discuss the women taking turns at filling shifts, in rotation with the men's unit; with the way events in the war had moved on, there might be a chance that, despite the colonel having been against the idea of a women's group *last* year, he might now acknowledge that they could perform a useful service to the village, thus easing the burden on the thinly stretched men's platoon. It wasn't beyond the realms of possibility.

Regrettably, there was an obstacle: to even raise the matter with either of them would require that she disclose her group's existence – with no idea how the revelation would be received. She sighed; if the colonel had just been able to see beyond his narrow and traditional view of the world then, by now, they might already be working together.

'Cup of tea, while you think about it, then?' Julia asked. 'Only, I recognize that expression on your face – you know, the one you adopt when you've got the bit between your teeth. If you don't fancy tea, I can make you a cup of coffee.'

Out of her friend's sight, Isabel allowed herself a wry smile; one of the few things she missed about Warbone Gate was Hector's expensive coffee, the so-called instant stuff that came in tins barely recognizable as the same drink. 'Tea's fine, thanks.'

'Then I'll get the kettle on.'

'And then, yes, you're right. I'm going to sit down and work out how we might go about your idea of mounting patrols. I mean, obviously, it will be contentious – we women, taking matters into our own hands and patrolling, just like the *men's* Home Guard? How *dare* we? Whatever next? But,' she said with an insouciant shrug as she went to the dresser to fetch two cups and two saucers, 'it won't be the first time we've put some man's back up. We've incurred the wrath of the authorities before. And we didn't let that stop us. No, the situation simply calls for us to continue being wily and astute.'

*

'Goodness, it's chilly.'

'I'm sorry, it is, rather, isn't it? But, once we get set up, we can take it in turns to walk about and keep warm.'

It was one night the following week and, in her bid to establish whether her idea to mount cliff-top watches was even feasible, Isabel had decided to postpone putting the idea to Captain Richardson until after she'd given it a go; if she went to him beforehand, she risked setting in motion a chain of events from which there could be no going back. However, if she went to him with the news that – despite what he would see as their lack of skills, experience, or proper training – a trial run with a small group of women had shown the task to be well within their capabilities, and explained that the aim would to be work with his men's unit but as a separate entity, then surely he would at least be obliged to hear her out. Until this evening, it had seemed a promising way forward; tonight, though, she was beginning to think that even *hoping* the idea would be well received had been naive. However, since she had already approached Geraldine and elicited her help, she'd decided to plough on and give it a go. After all, if the trial run proved a success, she didn't *have* to tell the captain. As long as they continued to be discreet, she supposed they *could* mount the patrols on their own.

'Golly, yes,' Geraldine had gushed when Isabel put the idea to her. 'Count me in.'

'The prospect of a two-hour watch, commencing at midnight, doesn't put you off?' Isabel had checked. With the mornings already growing light shortly after five, if the enemy *was* going to arrive under cover of darkness, she considered they would need to do so well before then.

'Not at all,' Geraldine had replied. 'I'm a night owl anyway. It's rare for me to retire to bed before two.'

'Here,' Isabel said now, unfolding one of Julia's deck-chairs and setting it on the concrete floor of the pillbox situated just down the slope from Fairlight. 'There's just about room for this. We can take it in turns to sit there with the blanket while the other keeps watch. I should imagine staring into the darkness is going to require a good deal of concentration, meaning we'll need to give our eyes a rest after a while anyway. So, how about we start with fifteen minutes each and see how that goes?'

'Sounds about right.'

'In the shopping bag is a flask of cocoa for later and a couple of sandwiches – but only with the merest scraping of jam, I'm afraid.'

'No matter. The sugar from even a little jam will keep us going if we flag.'

'Precisely.'

'So,' Geraldine said as she settled into the deckchair, 'in the event that we actually spot a German vessel – or, if you believe the government's warnings about the risk of enemy parachutists, have the misfortune to come face-to-face with one of those – what do you propose we do?'

From where she had been trying to acclimatize her eyes to scanning the darkness, Isabel lowered Julia's field glasses back down to the ledge of the embrasure.

Geraldine's point was one to which she'd already given a good deal of thought.

'If we spot one of their craft trying to come ashore, it will simply be a case of making an urgent report. If, as you mooted, we encounter parachutists, even a lone one, we're unlikely to be able to actually apprehend him. For a start, he'll most likely be armed. And we're not.'

'Not currently,' Geraldine agreed.

'So, my thought is that, assuming we're in this pillbox here, one of us will run back up the slope to Fairlight and telephone Sergeant Edworthy in the police house.'

'It would be quite something, wouldn't it,' Geraldine went on, 'if we did spot Germans? The Home Guard would have to eat their words then.'

'They would.' Heartened by Geraldine's eagerness, Isabel returned to scanning the darkness only to quickly let out an irritated groan; spotting anything with the binoculars wasn't going to be as easy as she'd thought. 'I don't think this is going to work.'

'Why? What's up?' Struggling up from the deckchair, Geraldine joined Isabel at the embrasure.

'Julia's field glasses aren't up to it.'

'Ah.'

Isabel passed them to Geraldine. 'Here, see for yourself. It's all just black.'

'To be fair,' Geraldine said, sounding to Isabel as though she was grinning, 'field glasses or no, everything looks black at night. After all, an enemy boat is hardly likely to show a light, is it? If they're planning to come ashore, one imagines they'll do so by stealth.'

'I suppose.' Isabel took the field glasses back. Geraldine's observation might be accurate but didn't help her to feel any less frustrated.

'I say we keep watching anyway. There's still a chance you'd spot movement. Or maybe even hear it.'

Hoping Geraldine was right, Isabel brought her elbows to rest on the concrete ledge and resumed scanning the expanse of darkness. Apart from the gentle buffeting of the breeze, the only other sound was the gentle *slop . . . hush, slop . . . hush* of the swell folding lazily on to the beach below. She sighed. Vincent would have loved Slipscombe. Although would he? Or, had he, like her, been more of a town mouse than a country one? In their time together, they had never discussed anywhere but London, neither of them ever mentioning either the countryside or the coast. In fact, with so many months having now passed, it was hard to remember what they *had* talked about; at the time, so much had seemed possible and yet, it was apparent now that their plans had only ever existed in the vaguest of outlines. Considering how matters had turned out, perhaps that was no bad thing; given that she was now trying to consign the whole short but glorious affair to the past, perhaps its dream-like vagueness would eventually make it easier to recall with fondness and gratitude.

Continuing to rest her elbows on the ledge, she swept the binoculars from left to right across the horizon. Then she ranged them back in the opposite direction, this time over the surface of the sea. She hadn't truly been expecting to see anything, but it was disappointing, nonetheless.

'Would you like to take a turn?' she asked over her shoulder.

Geraldine got to her feet. 'I would.'

Once satisfied that her companion was settled with the binoculars, Isabel lowered herself into the deckchair. 'Do you think this is mad?'

'Nope.'

'Truly?'

'Having second thoughts?' Geraldine asked.

'I have second thoughts about everything. More and more as time goes on.'

'It's the war,' Geraldine replied. 'Received opinion would have it that a thousand little worries are a good thing since they distract from the bigger ones. But whenever I stop to think about it closely, I'm struck by the sheer lunacy of it and find myself questioning the point of anything. If it's our destiny to live under Nazi rule, then why fret over whether it's too soon to plant maincrop potatoes in my little patch of garden, or which of two skirt patterns will be most serviceable for the summer?'

'I think you're right,' Isabel replied as she tried to stave off a yawn. 'When one frets over the petty, it's for the distraction, isn't it, the sheer banality of it preventing one toying with drowning oneself purely to bring an end to all the uncertainty.'

'Couldn't drown myself anyway. I'd have to —'

When Geraldine stopped mid-sentence, Isabel stiffened. Then, taking care to move slowly and quietly, she got to her feet. 'What is it?'

Backing away from the opening, Geraldine lowered her voice to a whisper. 'I thought . . . I heard something.'

Isabel edged closer. 'What sort of thing?'

'Rustling. In the bracken.'

'Rabbits, perhaps?' *Please, God, let it be rabbits.*

Geraldine shook her head. 'Too loud.'

'Sheep?'

'Too big.' Geraldine crept back to look out.

'Too big to be a *sheep*?'

'And sheep,' Geraldine whispered, 'don't carry torches.'

Unable to believe they might be about to encounter a German on their very first watch, especially without first sighting a vessel, or hearing enemy aircraft, Isabel felt along the wall to where she'd propped the dummy wooden rifle fashioned for them by Mrs Harburton's nephew. Curling her fingers tightly around the barrel, she lifted it silently from the floor.

'How many of them?' she hissed.

'Pretty certain it's just the one. Quick – you go and telephone.'

Isabel's feet seemed stuck to the ground. 'I can't leave you alone.'

'But you said the plan was to –'

'I know. Stay there.' With that, she slipped through the lookout's narrow entrance and pressed herself hard against the concrete wall, her heart thundering so loudly she feared it would give her away. *Stay calm*, she reminded herself. *You have the element of surprise.* Hearing the rustling drawing closer, she leapt away from the wall. '*Stehen sie still.*'

The circle of light from the prowler's torch fell to the ground, where it illuminated a pair of muddy brown boots.

She pointed the wooden rifle. '*Hände hoch.*'

'Do what? Daft cow. I'm no German.'

From behind her, Geraldine lunged to retrieve the torch and turn it upon the interloper's face. 'Derry Long. What are you doing up here at this time of night?'

Hands trembling, Isabel lowered the dummy rifle. That the prowler should be Derry Long made her only partially less afraid than had he been a German.

'I could ask you two daft bats the same question.'

'Except that,' Geraldine said, as she directed the beam of light back at Derry's face, 'I asked you first.'

'I can be wheresoever I like. It's you who's got no right being *in there.*' With a finger, he jabbed towards the pillbox. 'That's for the army, that is. Not women. You could have killed me.'

Isabel held up the dummy rifle. 'With a wooden cut-out? I don't think so.'

'Besides,' Geraldine said. 'Why aren't you on patrol with the Home Guard?'

'Not that it's any of your business but it ain't my turn.'

'Not true.' The authority with which Geraldine spoke made Isabel turn to regard her. 'You forget, there's a copy of the rota in the library. And every night, before I lock up, I check it to see who's on duty. And you, Derry Long, are rostered to be on the roadblock at Coach Path Cross.'

Long's momentary silence confirmed to Isabel that the man had been caught in a lie.

'I swapped.'

'With whom?'

'That's Home Guard business. And none of yours.'

'Oh, for goodness' sake,' Geraldine went on, 'get back to manning your roadblock and we'll forget we saw you.'

'I've told you, I've changed nights. I'm on me way 'ome. What's more, I'll move on when I'm good an' ready and not a moment sooner. And then, come morning, I shall be down the constabulary to report the two of you for . . . for trespassing on government property and . . . and . . . for 'personating the army.'

When Isabel tensed afresh, Geraldine merely sighed.

'Quite how you intend to show that two women, dressed in their ordinary clothes, and barely a hundred yards from one of their homes, could possibly be mistaken for soldiers, I can't imagine. But I should like to be there when you try.'

'And for having weapons,' Derry belatedly added. 'Weapons women can't have.'

This time, it was Isabel who laughed. 'We haven't any weapons.'

'So you say.'

'For heaven's sake, Derry, go away.' When Geraldine held Derry's torch towards him, he snatched it from her hand, made a vulgar gesture and then turned to shamble in the general direction of the zigzag path.

'*Now* we have a problem,' Isabel said once Long had ambled out of earshot. 'I just know it. Ever since we crossed paths one night in The Ship, he's been waiting for a chance to make trouble for me.'

'Oh, let him try,' Geraldine remarked. 'We're not doing

anything wrong, and he knows it. He's simply trying to distract us from the fact that he's bunked off from Home Guard duty.'

'Perhaps. Anyway, shall we call it a night?'

'Maybe we should.'

'Here,' Isabel said once she'd folded the deckchair and was holding out the dummy rifle. 'Take this. If nothing else, *should* you be accosted by an invader on your way home, you can at least use it to whack him about the head.'

'Thanks. I'll bear that in mind. Sleep tight, then.'

'You, too.'

As she headed wearily across the grass to where Fairlight loomed up in the darkness, Isabel knew she was unlikely to sleep a wink; Derry Long's threats had her rattled. But then it occurred to her: rather than stew over the possibility that he might go on to cause proper trouble for them, why not turn the tables on him? After all, if he was still messing about with red diesel, then he was the one breaking the law. And perhaps now would be a good time to remind him of the fact . . .

She could tell this was the place. Even before she sidestepped the open gate, rotting on its hinges, and went up the uneven path, where ankle-high grass was growing up through the clay tiles, she knew this had to be the dwelling Julia had described.

'Do I want to know why you're asking where Derry Long lives?' Julia had asked in response to Isabel's enquiry when they'd been washing up after breakfast.

'You don't,' she had replied.

'Fair enough.'

Despite Isabel's concerns last night, she had slept surprisingly well and awoke this morning to find that, while she'd been asleep, her resolve in relation to Derry Long had only hardened. The man needed putting in his place and, since she held the perfect trump card, why not use it? Now that she was on his doorstep, however, she had cause to question her sanity. It was one thing to come striding down here, her dander up, but quite another to actually confront him.

Still in two minds, she cast her gaze about the bungalow. In the ivy coiling its way up the right-hand side of the porch, insects were buzzing; in a thick and dusty cobweb to her left, a moth had met a sticky end. Was she crazy? Perhaps. But she was also incensed.

Inhaling deeply, she raised the knocker. As she hit it hard against the door, she was left to watch as flakes of black paint fluttered to the ground.

After waiting for what she considered a polite amount of time for anyone inside to respond, she rapped again. Having got up her courage, it would be just her luck for the man to be out.

She was on the point of turning away, when the door was snatched open.

'What the ruddy hell?'

Instinctively, she took a step backwards. Derry Long was clad in a navy-blue workman's overall, the top half folded down to his waist to reveal a greying vest bearing an almost perfectly circular brown stain.

'Good morning,' she said, struggling to conceal her

nausea. At least, she thought, as she watched him scratch his ribcage, he had the grace to look uneasy.

'What business you got, coming here?'

'I've come to check whether your threats last night were genuine or merely a lot of hot air.'

Finally, he stopped scratching. 'Do what?'

'I've come to check whether you are still intending to go to Sergeant Edworthy this morning, to report your concern that we are impersonating the army.'

Long frowned. She hadn't meant to bamboozle him; that she appeared to have done so was a bonus.

'Aye, I shall be down to see him, by the by.'

She had him. Now to swoop. 'I can't talk you out of it? Only, I should hate for you to look foolish.'

'No,' he said, moving to close the door. 'I shan't look foolish. I know what you women are doing. And it's against the law.'

'Very well. Then I have just two words for you.'

Long's expression turned to one of puzzlement. 'Eh?'

'Red diesel. Specifically, the washing of it. Now *that* is against the law.'

She didn't think she'd ever seen a grown man's face pale so quickly.

'Don't know what you mean.'

She fought the urge to laugh. 'And yet, we both know that you do. However, if you leave us women to go about our business free from mockery and threat, then I suppose I *might* eventually forget –'

The door slammed with such force that the knocker bounced against it and the glass in the transom rattled.

As she edged her way back out through the gate, the sensation washing over her was one of relief. It was so long since she'd stood up to a man that she'd forgotten how it felt. Better still, while Derry Long would loathe that she was now the one wielding the power, he would almost certainly leave them alone. She'd never genuinely proposed telling Harrington about the sorry individual and his diesel-washing anyway, not because she had no proof but because she'd decided not to risk courting retribution – if not from Long himself then one of his cronies. No, better, for now at least, to simply hold on to what she knew, just in case, and, in the meantime, to enjoy the satisfaction of having put the man in his place.

20

'I thought that went very well. They seemed genuinely enthused, wouldn't you say?'

Seated with Lady Virginia in the back of her motorcar, Isabel nodded. They were returning to Fairlight from the village of Twincombe, where a group of women had expressed a desire to know more about setting up their own women's home guard.

'If the number of questions they asked is anything to go by then, yes,' Isabel said. 'They seemed most keen.'

'I hope you didn't mind me suggesting they contact you for further help.'

'Of course not. In these awful times, we must all do what we can to help one another.' Since she, herself, had been grateful for help when she'd been getting Slipscombe's group together, it was right that she aided others in the same position. Moreover, it was all good practice at recovering her confidence and becoming more certain of her abilities: if, at some point, she was to completely stand on her own two feet, she was going to need to be markedly more forthright than she had been as Mrs Hector Thaxley. That said, if Germany won this wretched war, who knew what she would need to become to get by? She glanced sidelong at her companion. 'Lady Virginia, might I ask you something?'

'Absolutely.'

'What do you think is going to happen in the end? In the war, I mean.'

Lady Virginia pursed her lips. 'That's rather a big question, isn't it?'

'I ask only because I'm not sure how much of what we read, and what we hear reported on the wireless, is reliable or to be believed. I might have left London behind, but I do try to keep up with events there – indeed, with the war as a whole. But lately, the news is so grim and so frightening, I'm beginning to think we're not going to win. Those air raids just after Christmas were bad but this last month seems to have been so very much worse. Every few days, there's a raid we're told is the costliest yet – sixteen thousand incendiaries one night, twenty-five thousand a few days later. Then, last week, estimates of more than a hundred thousand of them dropped on the East End alone – and that's without all the HEs, and on top of the destruction already wrought. Every time I listen to a report, I find myself wondering how much more the country can take.'

'The answer to that, my dear, is a very great deal indeed. It has to.'

'Even with so many dead each time? With the loss of hundreds of ordinary people who are simply doing their best to stay safe and to get by? Not to mention the deaths of firemen, ambulance drivers, policemen, ARP wardens.' All of them, she thought, people like Vincent, simply intent on helping others.

'There can be no question of it. Not only do we owe

it to those already lost, but the alternative is simply too ghastly to contemplate. No, we keep going. We all just keep on, one breath at a time.' When Lady Virginia reached to squeeze her hand, Isabel felt her throat constrict and feared she might cry. But she mustn't — not in front of this formidable woman. 'But we don't have to do it alone. We do it by tackling our fears together, through practical means, as you have done in Slipscombe, and as the ladies of the various towns and villages in the south of the county are doing. We band together. And when we come up against an obstacle, we find a way around it — or over or under it — whatever it takes. No matter the news from our cities and our ports, we soldier on.'

'So, it's your belief,' Isabel started to say and then paused briefly to quell tears, 'that, ultimately, we *will* win?'

'I am certain of it. We did last time, and we will again now. We are not the aggressors. We have right on our side. But we must all do our bit. And keep doing it until good has prevailed.'

'Yes.' If only she could be as strident in her belief as Lady Virginia. And if only she could be of more use. 'Ah,' she said as she recognized the last stretch of lane before Fairlight, 'we're here.'

'Indeed. And once again, I must thank you for both the clarity with which you explained what you've been doing, and your candour in relation to the difficulties you have encountered. I could tell that the latter, in particular, was greatly appreciated. If the women of Twincombe succeed in getting their own home guard off the ground, it will be in no small part down to you. So, forget what we women are always told about pride and, on this occasion, take credit for a job well done.'

When Lady Virginia's driver stopped the motorcar at the rear of Fairlight and got out to open the door, Isabel's thoughts were in a whirl. Setting aside for a moment her wider concerns about the direction of the war, in Lady Virginia's opinion, this afternoon, she had made a difference. She had spoken to a group of strangers; she hadn't, as she'd feared beforehand, felt overwhelmed. Neither had she tripped over her words or been stumped by their questions. So, perhaps, in future, whenever she doubted herself and questioned her ability to do something, she would cast her mind back to this afternoon and draw strength from what she had done. Furthermore, no matter how awful the atrocities being committed in this war, she would simply keep putting one foot in front of the other and doing the right thing, drawing one breath at a time. As Lady Virginia had pointed out, they really had no other choice.

'So, you and Miss Marshall didn't have no trouble keeping watch last week, then?'

It was now later that evening and, as Isabel set about unfolding the deckchair in the beam of torchlight proffered by Vera Mayfield – her watch companion for the next two hours – she shook her head. 'A slight scare for a moment, but it turned out to be nothing.'

'Bet that got your heart racing,' Vera said as she flapped open the rug.

'It did, rather. Anyway –' anxious not to be diverted to

the matter of Derry Long, Isabel hastened on – 'are you happy for me to take the first turn while you sit down for a quarter of an hour or so?'

'One of the reasons I'm up here, love,' Vera replied with a laugh. 'For a sit-down and a bit of peace and quiet.'

'Well, it's good of you to volunteer, especially as I know you have to make an early start in the mornings.'

'That's the other reason I'm here,' Vera chuckled. 'So that, come morning, I can claim entitlement to a lie-in.'

'Well, thank you, anyway. I feel it's important we at least give our experiment a little longer. If, after a couple more nights, these watches prove either impossible to keep up or else appear to serve no purpose, I'm not too proud to admit to having made a mistake.'

'More than can be said for most.'

In the darkness, Isabel smiled. Just as she liked and admired Geraldine, she had come to enjoy conversing with Vera Mayfield, finding her direct manner of speaking refreshing. In fact, she was rapidly coming to think of both women as friends. 'You keep warm for a moment and then we'll swap.'

After barely two minutes spent scanning the coastline and the sea, though, Isabel lowered the binoculars to rest her eyes. But, as she went to retrieve them from the ledge, she fell still. Was that movement down in the bracken again? Suspecting Derry Long of mounting a prank, she held her breath and listened more carefully: yes, there it was – the crisp and steady crackle of someone tramping their way up through the brake. Unlike last time, the disturbance was much heavier – as though the culprit didn't fear being heard. Carefully returning the binoculars to the ledge, she felt about for the dummy rifle. Her fingers finding the smooth wooden form, she folded them around the barrel and leaned further into the embrasure to peer out.

'What is it?' Vera whispered and levered herself up from the deckchair.

'Not sure. Stay there.' If this was Derry Long, she would make him regret it. Raising the wooden rifle, she pointed it out of the opening. '*Halt! Wer geht?*' Her fury, in that instant, meant it was the only German phrase she could remember.

'Isabel?'

'*Elowen?*'

'Yes. Me and Greg.'

'What on earth –'

Two shadowy figures drew closer.

'Sorry,' Elowen called up to her. In the darkness, Isabel heard PC Gregory clear his throat. 'Mum did tell me you were going to be out here again, but I forgot. We were just –'

'I offered to walk Elowen home from The Ship when I came off duty.'

Hands still trembling, Isabel put down the dummy rifle and went out to see them. 'Thoughtful of you,' she said to him, her heartbeat beginning to slow.

'In fact, it was my idea to come up through the cove,' PC Gregory went on. 'If I'd known you were up here, I wouldn't have suggested it.'

'It's all right,' Isabel said, the tension from being on

high alert beginning to drain from her limbs. 'At least it shows I was vigilant.'

When Elowen and Greg wished them goodnight and set off towards Fairlight, Isabel turned to hear Vera stifling laughter.

'Next time, those two might want to choose their courting spot more carefully.'

For the next hour or so after that, Isabel and Mrs Mayfield took turns to keep watch.

'Can I be honest with you, love?'

'Of course. Please do say what's on your mind. Always.'

At the embrasure, Vera returned to scanning the horizon with the binoculars. 'Don't get me wrong, even though it's the men that's got us into this war, I'm all for women doing their bit, howsoever they choose. And you and Julia, both of you, I hold in the greatest esteem. You don't take no nonsense. And I like to think I don't either. Speak as I find, me. But – well, blow me. What's that . . . right . . . there?'

Isabel scrabbled to her feet. 'What is it?' Grabbing the pair of Julia's opera glasses she'd brought just in case, she joined Vera.

'Good Lord, I do believe it's a . . . you know, one of them submarine thingies.'

Isabel stiffened. 'Where?' Lowering the opera glasses, she followed the line of Vera's finger; trust the moon to have gone behind a cloud the moment they needed it.

'Directly in front. Chest height. Here, try these.'

Accepting the field glasses and directing them to where Vera was pointing, Isabel picked out a long dark shadow, her heart leaping at the sight of it. 'Golly, yes.' She thrust the binoculars back at Vera. 'Keep an eye on it. I'll go and telephone Sergeant Edworthy. I'll be no more than a couple of minutes.'

Her dash back up the slope to Fairlight left her panting for breath, the shock of what she'd seen making her fingers tremble almost too much to turn the knob and open the door. But, once inside, she eased it quietly shut behind her, drew across the blackout curtain and, rather than switch on the overhead light, felt about for the hall table and turned on the lamp. In its soft glow, she stood, trying to recover her breath while scanning the list of numbers pinned on the board above the telephone. Unable to stop her hand shaking, she dialled the number for the police house.

'I'm so sorry to call this late,' she whispered fiercely. 'But this is Isabel Smith from Fairlight. I've been watching the coast with Mrs Mayfield, and we've spotted a submarine. In the bay. Black.' *Black?* What a ridiculous thing to say; in the darkness, everything looked black. 'Yes,' she replied to a question from the other end of the line. 'We both saw it. I've left Mrs Mayfield to keep an eye on it.' After a further short pause she answered, 'Yes, she's still there.'

The receiver quietly replaced, she switched off the lamp, held aside the curtain just sufficiently to reach the door handle and then let herself back out. Hurtling down the grassy slope to the pillbox, she gulped down great breaths of the cool night air.

'I've just this second lost sight of it,' Vera hissed.

'Bother. But you know . . . where you last saw it?'

Beside her, Vera nodded. 'Oh yes. I know right where he was. If it wasn't for the fact that it's the sea we're talking about, I could pin a cross to the exact spot.'

To his credit, Sergeant Edworthy arrived in a matter of minutes.

'So,' he said, arriving to prop his elbows on the ledge and raise a weighty-looking pair of field glasses to his eyes. 'Where's this submarine?'

'Plumb centre,' Isabel replied, thinking as she did so that she didn't like his tone.

'Square on,' Vera added.

In silence, the two women watched Sergeant Edworthy scan left and right, slowing once or twice as he did so.

'But you can't see it now.'

'Just as Miss Smith was returning from telephoning you, I lost it. I can only imagine it went back under the water.'

'Couldn't have been a dolphin?' the sergeant asked as he continued to scan. 'Word is there's a couple of pods shown up again this last week. Or maybe a seal?'

'Not like one I've ever seen. Far too long. And it kept too still.'

Alongside Vera, Isabel agreed. 'No. If it was anything else at all, I would say the upturned hull of a boat – but that wouldn't have remained motionless in the water, either. Whatever it was, it wasn't bobbing about in the waves. In fact, they were washing over it.'

'See any people?'

'None.'

'Any other vessels? Anything go out to rendezvous with it? Or come ashore?'

It was Vera who replied first. 'I was fixed on the shape. Couldn't see any wider than that.'

Isabel could have kicked herself; her only thought had been to alert the authorities. 'I regret to say I didn't stop to look anywhere else.' Perhaps that should be a new area of training for them – observation and reporting. She would have to give it some thought.

Alongside her, the sergeant manoeuvred himself upright. 'Well, ladies. Whatever it was, I see no sign of it now.'

'No.'

'But I'll file a report, even so. And you did the right thing in alerting me. But if I were you, I'd go back to your homes. Get some sleep – especially you, Mrs Mayfield.'

Unseen by the other two, Isabel frowned. The moment Vera reported having lost sight of the thing, her own conviction had begun to waver; without anything to corroborate their account, why would anyone believe them? In Sergeant Edworthy's mind, they were simply two middle-aged women, with no better way to spend the small hours than growing cold and tired in a draughty lookout. No doubt, privately, he had them down as batty.

When he'd bid them goodnight, and urged them afresh to go home, Isabel waited until she considered him beyond earshot before saying, 'He didn't believe us.'

Beside her, Vera was folding the rug. 'Not for a moment. But I know what I saw.'

'Me too. But what can we do? Something was there.

Then it was gone. And what else but a submarine could just vanish like that?'

'An ordinary boat would have sailed away. I'd have seen it go.'

'All we can do, I suppose,' Isabel went on as she folded the deckchair and leaned it against the wall to collect later, 'is watch out in the village for any strangers. Although, if anyone did come ashore from it, I shouldn't think they'd hang around.'

'Frightening thought,' Vera said as the pair started across the dewy grass.

'Yes.' And one which, Isabel realized, if she was to stand any chance of getting to sleep at all, she was going to need to cast firmly from her mind.

Isabel stiffened. After more than seven months, it was ridiculous to tense at the rap of the door knocker, she knew that. But she still hadn't entirely managed to free herself from the fear of Hector finding her. Besides, as she had so often pointed out to Julia, better safe than caught.

This morning, there being only her to answer it, she went to the drawing room window where, peering around the curtain, she stiffened afresh: the inspector? And in uniform?

She hurried through to the hall.

'Inspector Childe.'

It was the morning after Isabel's watch with Vera Mayfield and, much as she had expected, her sleep had come in fits and starts and been riddled with unsettling dreams. As a result, already this morning, she was feeling crotchety and tired.

'Miss Smith, good morning. Don't worry. I don't come bearing bad news.' Evidently sensing her disarray, he went on, 'One of the unfortunate downsides to my job is that whenever someone opens their front door to me, as often as not, they turn pale.'

Recovering her composure, she smiled. 'Yes, I suppose so. Anyway, won't you come in? Although, if it's Julia you were hoping to talk to, I'm afraid she's out.'

Once in the hallway, the inspector removed his cap and ran a hand over his hair. 'Actually, Miss Smith, it's you I've come to see.'

Stiffening at the disclosure, she gestured him through to the drawing room. When she sat in one of the armchairs, he took the one opposite.

'It's on the matter of your ladies' group.'

She exhaled in relief. Of course – their sighting of the submarine; for a moment, she'd wondered whether it might have to do with Hector, or her change of identity. But no, of course, he was there to check what they'd seen. Perhaps other sightings had been reported. Better still, maybe someone else had actually apprehended a German.

'Is there more news?' When his expression displayed momentary confusion, she continued, 'Of the submarine we saw?' How brilliant would it be if an invader *had* been caught? Dear old Sergeant Edworthy would have egg on his face then; she knew he hadn't believed them – at the very least, he'd considered them mistaken.

'No further word, no. Although it is in that connection I'm here.'

Despite feeling suddenly cold, she strove not to show it. 'All right.' Perhaps he'd simply come to tell her to keep up the good work.

'Since this is a little delicate, I feel I should perhaps start by saying that, given the restrictions placed upon women generally, especially their activities on the home front, let alone the fact that, of necessity, your operation here in Slipscombe has been clandestine, I feel you have done tremendously well to organize and inspire your ladies into such a committed group. I, for one, would not wish to be in the shoes of any German who, accidentally or otherwise, startled one of your members. I am also fully aware that it was me who put you in touch with Lady Virginia in the first place.'

Isabel's unease deepened; he appeared to be paving the way to saying something he knew she wasn't going to like.

'And I'm not sure I ever properly thanked you for the introduction. She was such an inspiration.'

'A redoubtable woman, yes.'

'Indeed.'

'The blame is also mine for failing to keep more of a . . . well, *a watch* on the way your group has developed – the direction it has, of late, begun to take.'

Blame? She'd known there was something to his tone. Was it possible Derry Long had been stirring up trouble – maybe even concocted lies about what they were doing? If so, he clearly hadn't believed she would disclose what she knew about the red diesel. Well, as he was about to find out, she was a woman of her word.

'Has there been a complaint made about us, Inspector?'

That the suggestion appeared to take him by surprise left her glad she hadn't gone as far as to mention Long by name.

'Complaint? Nothing that has been brought to my attention.'

'Then please do tell me what I've done wrong. I shan't hold it against you.'

'Very well. Then the situation is this. While we will never know for certain whether what you and Mrs Mayfield saw last night was, or was not, a submarine, the balance of probabilities makes such an occurrence unlikely. Unless further sightings come to light, we shall never know. The problem that arises from your observing and reporting is that, had it not been Sergeant Edworthy on duty last night – had your report been taken at face value by a more junior officer – all hell could have broken loose. Aircraft could have been scrambled, ships diverted to investigate. And all on the say-so of two well-meaning but untrained ladies observing and reporting off their own bat.'

Isabel shifted in her seat. 'You're saying we got carried away.'

'No, I'm not saying that. I will be the first to accept that if it *was* an enemy submarine which, through an inadequate system of patrols by any other body, without you and Mrs Mayfield would have gone unnoticed, then the situation must be remedied post-haste. Indeed, I have already raised the matter with Captain Richardson and secured his agreement to pass my concern up the chain of command.'

'Captain Richardson knows about us?' The discovery was an unwelcome one; as far as she'd been aware, neither he nor the colonel had known of her group's existence.

Reading her alarm, Inspector Childe continued, 'Please, don't look so worried, I didn't tell him who had reported the sighting, simply that one had been brought to our attention by a credible source.'

She exhaled in relief. *Credible source.* At least he'd taken their report seriously. Moreover, if it had uncovered a gap in defences, then they had been of *some* use.

'But you've come to ask us to disband,' she said. Inside, she felt close to tears.

'Not disband, goodness, no. You have done far too much for the morale and the spirits of the ladies of Slipscombe for me to suggest so draconian a step. No, that would be a terrible waste.'

Despite his protestation, she sensed he was merely trying to soften the blow. 'Then what *do* you wish us to do?'

'Scale back your activities. I fully understand that won't be what you want to hear. If nothing else, there will be the resulting loss of face. I also know that, when it comes to Slipscombe's Home Guard platoon, concerns as to the extent of *their* effectiveness are not entirely without merit. But it should not fall to you and your ladies to plug the gaps.'

Isabel gave a dismayed shake of her head. 'So, when you say scale back —'

'Cease your watches. Hold off broadening your activities further, and direct your energies instead to what you were doing at the beginning – giving women advice and training on how to defend themselves in their own homes.'

In some respects, Isabel felt as though a burden had been lifted from her shoulders. She started to grin. 'We can do that, Inspector.'

'There's no reason why you can't still hold regular meetings –'

'Continue to hold our weekly needlework groups . . .'

'Your needlework groups, yes, enabling you to ensure no one has forgotten what they've been shown, and to perhaps discuss any new concerns arising.'

'That sounds like sensible advice.'

'It also occurs to me now that you might become elected to the preparedness committee, so that you have formal means to raise any concerns from your members.'

'Your idea continues to improve.'

'It relieves me to hear that. Now, while I have no wish to rush away, I regret that I have another call to make.'

Isabel rose to her feet. 'Then thank you for coming to speak to me personally. I'll show you out.'

'And if I don't see you before, I shall hope to see you at the next preparedness meeting, such that I might propose you for election.'

'Thank you, Inspector. I'll discuss your idea with Julia.'

When Harrington left, Isabel closed the door and stood for a moment, unable to decide whether she felt incensed or relieved. Last night, their sighting of the submarine – for she knew, without a shadow of a doubt, that's what it had been – had left her feeling vindicated, the idea of mounting watches shown to be worthwhile.

Unfortunately, it was also true that, with the new direction of their activities, she had indeed begun to feel out of her depth. Clearly, the inspector had thought long and hard before coming to see her, and had planned his approach so that she might, as he'd put it, *scale back her activities without losing face*. Now she would have to show the same respect to her members. She would have to assure them that, by not expanding their undertakings, they were not watering down the organization, nor losing any of its worth; the shortcomings their activities had exposed in others were to be addressed. It was simply that, from now on, they would attend more directly to protecting what they valued most: the safety of their families, themselves and their homes. And if anyone suggested that, as women, they were back where they belonged – at the stove or the kitchen sink – well, then they were free to disabuse them of that notion in whatever manner they saw fit.

21

Isabel shot upright. The spluttering noise she'd assumed to be part of her dream now appeared to be the engine of an aircraft – one flying far too low and heading straight –

She hurled herself sideways. Fingers laced across the back of her head, she pressed her face into her pillow and held her breath. The picture above the bedstead rattled against the wall; on the side table, her wristwatch clinked against her water glass.

The noise cut out. She braced for an explosion.

Scuffing, dragging.

Silence.

Raising her head, she gasped for air. The aircraft had missed them – probably by no more than inches. But wait – *aircraft*. There would be a pilot, possibly injured and in need of help.

Or German and getting away.

She leapt out of bed. *Capture the pilot before he escapes.* Reaching to the chair for her dressing gown, she thrust an arm into a sleeve and felt about with a foot for her slippers. *Slippers? For heaven's sake, woman, you'll need shoes.*

With that, someone pounded on her door. 'Issy. Quick.' It was Julia. 'An aeroplane's come down in the field. A German one. *Quick.*'

She shouted back. 'On my way.'

After pulling her door open, she hurtled along the landing and down the stairs. A couple of steps short of the bottom, her mackintosh came flying towards her.

'Put it on,' Julia yelled. 'It's windy.'

Throwing off the dressing gown she'd just tied around her waist, she pulled on her mac, at the same time forcing her feet under the straps of her shoes and wincing as the leather snagged at her bare skin. 'You saw it come down?' she called towards Julia's departing back. 'The plane?'

'Here.' Rolling towards her over the tiled floor of the back porch came one of several sharpened broom handles they'd taken to keeping by the door. 'And bring that torch.'

She reached to the shelf. 'Got it.'

'Quick, then. They could be getting away.'

They? Light-headed from dashing about so soon after waking, she directed the dull beam of torchlight straight ahead, illuminating the hem of Julia's coat, flapping as she ran up the path.

By the time she made out the stone wall at the bottom of the garden, Julia was already over the top and extending a hand back towards her. In her haste to climb over, she caught her knee on a jagged flint, the pain excruciating. 'Christ,' she hissed, landing heavily in the grass on the other side. She glanced ahead to see the beam of light from Julia's torch picking out the tussocky turf. On the wind came the smell of engine oil.

'Here!' Julia shouted back. 'It's here.'

As Isabel stumbled towards her friend's voice, she heard the clump of feet catching up to her.

'Mum!' It was Elowen. 'Mum, stay back. It could explode.'

'Bombs!' Isabel yelled. 'There might be bombs.'

'*Crazy woman*,' Elowen screamed in exasperation. 'Anything could happen.'

Ahead of them, the flickering beam of Julia's torch picked out a dark tail rudder, and on it, German insignia.

'It's not a bomber,' Julia shouted. 'It's a fighter plane – a Messerschmitt.'

'It could still explode,' Elowen bellowed back.

Lungs fit to burst, Isabel stumbled to a halt alongside the aircraft; its undercarriage had scoured a shallow trench, the fuselage embedded in the earth.

From further along came a metallic grating sound and the canopy over the pilot slid open. A voice called out. The words sounding like *nicht schiessen*; she darted forwards and aimed her torch down into the cockpit. The next utterance, although heavily accented, she understood.

'Please. Don't shoot.'

In the light of her torch, the pilot looked barely old enough to be in uniform, let alone flying an aeroplane, his complexion deathly pale, a bloody gash on his right temple. Squinting into the beam of light, he dangled a revolver between forefinger and thumb and then tossed it on to the grass.

'Quick,' she directed Elowen. 'Pick it up. Keep it away from him.'

With the sharpened end of her broomstick, she motioned to him to get out. Beside her, Julia was yanking the belt of her raincoat free from its loops.

'Surrender,' the pilot muttered. 'Surrender.'

Isabel nodded vigorously. The lad was terrified. 'Get out. We won't shoot you.'

With some difficulty, the pilot clambered from the cockpit on to the wing. As he went to step from there down on to the grass, his legs buckled beneath him.

'Keep aiming that at him,' Julia directed Isabel as she threw aside her own broom handle and moved to haul him up. 'Keep pointing it,' she urged as she pulled the pilot's hands behind his back and set about binding his wrists with her belt.

Behind them, shouts rang out and more powerful beams of torchlight lit up the pasture.

'We're only handing him over,' Isabel said, yet to regain her breath, 'to Inspector Childe. No one else. Not to anyone . . . from the Home Guard. I won't see him mistreated.'

To her relief, Julia agreed. 'If the Home Guard was the only authority in the county, I still wouldn't hand him over to them.'

With that, a braying crowd closed in around them.

'Stand back! The lot of you.' The forcefulness of Isabel's command brought an astonished silence. 'The pilot has surrendered. We are only handing him over to Inspector Childe.'

'So, keep back,' Elowen yelled with a wave of her pike. 'I'm warning you, don't test me.'

Despite a rumble of discontent, no one challenged them.

'Thank you, Miss Smith, you can put that down now.'

When a warm hand attempted to unclamp her fingers from her staff, she swung round to see Inspector Childe. 'You too, Miss Nance, Mrs Nance. Sergeant Edworthy and I will take the pilot to the constabulary, where he will be treated as a prisoner of war. You have my word that he will be given water and first aid.'

In that moment, as the magnitude of what they had done sank in, Isabel thought her knees might crumple beneath her. 'First aid, yes . . .'

'Constable, guard the aircraft. Do not let anyone near it. The rest of you, go home. Captain Richardson is alerting the Ministry. Tomorrow morning, they will almost certainly send a team to question the prisoner. So, go on, all of you. Go back to your beds.'

When Sergeant Edworthy led the pilot away, the crowd jeered but parted to let him through.

Inspector Childe turned to address them. 'You, too, ladies. You've shown immense bravery but now, please, all three of you, go home. Get warmed up. Should the authorities wish to speak to you about the incident, I will telephone to arrange a time. Come on, allow me to see you safely across the field.'

Back in the kitchen, moments later, the women found Edna Price stirring a saucepan of cocoa, and Elizabeth setting out cups and saucers on the table.

'We thought you'd welcome something to warm you up,' Edna ventured.

Pulling a chair out from under the table, Isabel collapsed on to it; of all the feelings she had at that moment, being cold wasn't one of them.

'We were watching from upstairs,' Elizabeth said. 'Not that we could make out very much in the darkness.'

Julia slumped heavily on to the adjacent chair. 'Never thought I'd get to detain a German.'

When Edna placed a cup of cocoa in front of her, Isabel simply stared at the tiny bubbles glistening on its surface. 'They would have lynched him.'

'If we hadn't got there first, or Inspector Childe hadn't turned up, they would certainly have given him a rough time of it.'

'And he was just a boy.'

'As so many of them apparently are,' Elizabeth said. 'Nothing more than conscripts following orders.'

Isabel shook her head in dismay. 'He looked terrified.'

Beside her, Julia agreed. 'He did. I'll give him that. But, for all we know, he'd just shot down a couple of our boys sent up to intercept the squadron of bombers he was escorting.'

'Makes me wonder where those bombers were headed,' Elowen said. 'Or where they'd just been.'

'There's a terrific glow in the sky to the north.' The observation came from Edna. 'I pray it's not Bristol again.'

'There's an orange patch to the south, as well,' Elowen said. 'Plymouth, I shouldn't wonder.'

And that was why, Isabel thought, as she continued to stare into her cocoa, war was so evil. The young man they'd spared from an angry mob, as well as being somebody's son, was also a killer – probably fresh from helping to ensure Hitler's latest bombs reached their intended targets, destroying homes and businesses and murdering ordinary people. Seven months ago, Vincent had been just such a casualty; were it not for his quick actions, she could have been another.

'I think,' she said, feeling the welling of tears, 'I'll take my cocoa upstairs.'

'Why don't the two of you do the same,' Elizabeth suggested to Julia and Elowen. 'And please, don't feel, any of you, that you must get up and make breakfast for us. We're more than capable of fending for ourselves.'

Slowly, Julia got to her feet. 'It's real kind of you to offer, but no. You have to go to school just the same. The least I can do is send you off with a proper breakfast inside you.'

Bidding the others goodnight, Isabel went upstairs. In her room, she crossed to the window, drew aside the black-out curtains, and stood staring out into the darkness. She supposed she should feel proud; they had apprehended a German airman who might otherwise have slipped away into the night. That said, she couldn't imagine he would have got very far; even had he found somewhere to hide his uniform, he would have needed different clothes. Even in civvies, he still would have stood out as foreign; in London, few people gave anyone different a second thought but, around here, they eyed strangers with suspicion. Sooner or later, he would have been apprehended.

Was it wrong, she wondered, as she continued to stare out, that, despite his being the enemy, she was glad he was safe? Shouldn't she hate him for what he had probably just done? What did it say about her that her relief at having ensured his safety was greater than her hatred of him for being German? Men like him had killed Vincent. Men like him were the reason she was alone in Devon and not starting a new life in London with the loveliest man she had ever met.

Absently, she got into bed and pulled up the covers. For the first time since the air raids that had destroyed Warbone Gate, she'd come face-to-face with the sharp end of war. And all she could think was what a mess the world had become. What an all-round, bloody awful mess.

22

'Oh, good morning, madam. My name's Ivan Sedwell and I'm from the *North Devon Crier*. No doubt you read our newspaper. We are, after all, the area's leading purveyor of news.'

It was the afternoon following the German aircraft incident and, in her sleep-deprived state, Isabel was in no mood for salesmen. She was so tired, she hadn't even remembered to check the caller's identity through the window before answering the knock at the door.

'I'm sorry,' she said tersely, 'Fairlight Guest House is closed at the moment and so the owner has no need of advertising.'

His approach evidently well honed, Sedwell took a step closer, one of his grubby shoes coming to rest on the threshold. 'Forgive me,' he said. 'I'm not here to sell you advertising. On the contrary, I am interested in the Messerschmitt that came down last night in the field behind you. I'm given to understand some of the residents from this abode apprehended the pilot, and I should very much like to talk to them – interview them, if you will, for a front-page article. My editor thinks the story will be of great interest to our readers. Perhaps,' he went on, opening the flap of the leather satchel he wore slung across his body, 'you would introduce me to those involved. I'm given to understand they were women.'

353

Isabel looked him up and down. Alongside him was an older man with a case over his shoulder that she supposed contained a camera –

She stepped sharply backwards. She couldn't be in the newspaper. New name or no, other than having a few more wrinkles, no doubt brought on by the worry, her appearance was unchanged, leaving her instantly recognizable. No, the last thing she needed was her face in print. That said, if Julia wanted to talk to the man, that was down to her; it was probably preferable that her version of events made it into the local newspaper, rather than have the Home Guard – worse still, Derry Long – take credit or spin a yarn of their own.

'Well,' she said, 'I would have to ask the proprietress. She might be busy.'

'Then would you enquire of her, please? I am more than happy to wait. Or even to come back later.'

'Stay there. I'll go and talk to her.'

The front door closed firmly behind her, she stood for a moment in thought. If Julia *was* interested in recounting what had happened, she would need to press upon her the importance of leaving her out of it. And she would have to ask that Elowen do the same.

'*North Devon Crier*?' Julia said when Isabel found her and explained. 'Not the *Slipscombe Courier*? You couldn't have misheard him?'

Isabel frowned. 'No, he definitely said *North Devon Crier*.'

'Fair enough. As long as it's not the *Courier*.'

'So, you'll talk to him, then?'

'Chance to be in the news for the right reasons for once? "Local heroines capture enemy pilot." I can see the headline now. "It was nothing, claims modest guest house proprietress." Why not? Chance to show the place in a good light this time. *And* it'll be one in the eye for the Home Guard. Silly old duffers.'

'I should probably tell you he has a photographer with him.'

'Show him into the drawing room, then, and I'll go and comb my hair.'

'All right. But promise me you'll make no mention of *my* part in it. If he asks whether it was just you and Elowen, you have to say the two of you acted alone.'

'If you're sure that's what you want.'

'It's not necessarily what I *want*. But having hidden away down here all this time, I'd be foolish to risk someone spotting my photograph in the newspaper and showing it to Hector.'

'Very well. Although, who you think would recognize you from a blurry black and white photograph in a north Devon newspaper, I can't imagine.'

'Well, I'm sorry if you think I'm being ridiculous. And I'm also sorry that, on my account, you might now need to lie –'

'Stuff and nonsense.'

'– but I can't take the risk.' Her statement, while boldly made, did however raise the question of when *would* she be able to take the risk? How long *could* she continue to remain secreted in north Devon – especially without any form of income?

'Go on, then,' Julia said. 'Bring him in. I'll give Elowen a shout. She'll *definitely* want her picture in the paper.'

At the front door, Isabel bade the men enter. 'Please wait in here,' she said, directing them to the drawing room. 'I doubt she'll keep you waiting very long.'

'Thank you, Mrs er . . .'

'Smith,' she said briskly. 'Miss Smith.'

'Thank you, Miss Smith.'

Once Julia and Elowen, suitably tidied up, were in the drawing room, Isabel closed the door behind them and crept away to listen from the stairs and reassure herself as to the tone of the interview.

'How do you do, Mr Sedwell?' she heard Julia greet the reporter.

From her perch on the third stair up, Isabel found herself reflecting upon her situation generally; the reporter showing up had certainly made her stop and think. When she'd first arrived at Fairlight, Julia had told her she could stay there for as long as she wanted – but everyone said that sort of thing to a friend in their hour of need. Did Julia still feel the same way now, seven months on? Even if she didn't, and it became necessary for her to leave, where would she go? Where was 'home'? The only person for whom she would have contemplated going back to London had died – which rather prompted the question of where on earth *did* she belong?

At that moment, a burst of laughter from the drawing room made her realize she'd stopped listening.

'I wasn't afraid at all,' she heard Elowen say. 'I work behind the bar of a public house. If I can keep the peace among a bunch of inebriated locals, a lone pilot doesn't bother me in the least.'

How different, Isabel thought, must the world look to Elowen right now: war aside, she had the whole of her adult life ahead of her – not to mention two separate pay packets.

Hearing further laughter, she returned her attention to the drawing room. The tenor of the discussion suggesting proceedings were coming to an end, she got to her feet and crept on up the stairs to continue listening from the landing.

'We can go up through the garden to it,' she heard Julia explain above the sound of the drawing room door opening. 'There's a police constable posted up there at the moment, but he knows us. He won't mind.'

As the conversation drifted through to the kitchen, before eventually fading from earshot, Isabel allowed herself to relax a little; she had avoided getting drawn in. Her secret remained safe. On the pressing matter of her future, however, she was no closer to having a long-term plan now than she had been when she'd run away in the first place.

'From the reports I've read, these last few nights' raids have been even worse than those back in March.'

'And those were bad enough. I heard from a woman with family down in Plymouth how some of the factories that were bombed were on fire for days.'

It was a Sunday, a week or so after what the women of Fairlight had come to call 'the Messerschmitt incident', and Julia had extended an invitation to Harrington to once again join the household for lunch. Not surprisingly, as they tucked into Julia's rabbit hotpot with dumplings, broad beans and a few very tiny carrots – the latter harvested from the 'Dig for Victory' patch got up together the previous November by the schoolmistresses – the discussion around the table centred upon the devastation recently unleashed upon Plymouth.

'I've read the same,' Harrington remarked. 'Apparently, this time around, the Luftwaffe didn't confine their attacks to the naval yard. Whole areas of the city centre were destroyed. Even the Guildhall, which was serving as an ARP post, suffered a direct hit.'

'I heard the same happened to a public air raid shelter,' Elowen joined the conversation to say.

Harrington's expression remained solemn. 'I believe so.'

'Makes me feel proper guilty sometimes,' Julia confessed. 'Plymouth, Bristol, both being bombed to destruction. And here we are, with just one aircraft come down in a cow pasture, and a pilot all too willing to simply give himself up.'

'You're still doing your bit.' The observation came from Elizabeth who, to Isabel's eyes, seemed genuinely grateful. 'It's thanks to the people of Slipscombe that we have a refuge from such attacks – that the children know safety and, without wishing to sound too theatrical, will have the chance to know adulthood.'

Sobering but true, Isabel decided. When the matter under discussion had first turned to the Messerschmitt, she had deliberately kept quiet. Everyone at the table knew she had been the one to confront the pilot and order him out of his aircraft. So far, though, no one had questioned why she wasn't in any of the photographs in the *Crier*; they could hardly have failed to notice her absence – there was a copy, folded so as to display the headline and accompanying picture, in almost every room in the house. By rights, she should have been ready with a reply to the inevitable enquiries but had yet to come up with anything even remotely convincing: *I was feeling under the weather; my hair was a frightful mess; I detest having my picture taken.* All pathetic. *I'm lying low: when my lover was killed helping in an air raid, I absconded from London and allowed my husband to think I'd died during a direct hit on our home by an HE.* Now *that*, she *could* make sound convincing. Whether anyone other than Julia would ever speak to her again afterwards, or whether she would forever be ostracized by the entire population of the village, she could only guess. And that was without the risk that someone would then go to the authorities. No, she would just have to hope that if anyone did eventually ask, she could convince them she'd declined the opportunity solely because she was shy.

The enquiry came sooner than she'd hoped.

'I was wondering, Isabel,' Harrington said when the meal was over and the teachers were clearing up, 'whether you might like to accompany me for a short stroll? Earlier this morning, I was minded it might rain and so I drove here, depriving myself of the walk home. But I'm at an age now where I find gentle exercise after a meal beneficial to my digestion.'

His last remark made Isabel laugh. *'At an age?'* Now

that he'd raised the matter, she found herself once again curious to know what that was – late forties?

'I certainly no longer qualify as young.'

'Few of us do,' she said. 'But yes, I should enjoy a stroll – if you don't mind waiting while I fetch a jacket.'

'Not at all. Please, take your time.'

'Rather than head down to the village,' Harrington said, as Isabel stepped outside a few minutes later and closed the front door, 'I thought we might find it more pleasant to go towards Lively Point.' Belatedly, he glanced at her shoes. 'If you don't mind the lack of a proper path.'

Lack of a proper path. Of late, those few words had come to sum up her entire existence. It was a thought that made her wonder whether the man knew more about her than he let on. But how could he? And from whom? Since it wouldn't be from Julia, she would attribute the notion to a guilty conscience, and apply herself instead to enjoying the walk.

For late April, the weather was surprisingly warm, the breeze, from the south-west, lacking the rawness of the north-westerlies that had persisted throughout most of March, and which had made walking something to be endured rather than enjoyed.

'The bright yellow is very striking,' she remarked of the gorse growing along the bank.

'In this part of the world,' Harrington said, 'it flowers year-round. Even in January, it's possible to see the odd little bloom.'

'Now you mention it, I remember seeing some.'

'It's at its most prolific from around about now, though.

Come along here on a warm day in July and the scent will be unmissable.' When she looked at him, he went on, 'Strongly reminiscent of coconut. If you're here in the summer, I recommend you come along to see for yourself.'

'If I'm here, I shall do that.' *If she was there?* As things stood, where else would she be? 'Those mounds of pink flowers are pretty, too.'

'Thrift,' Harrington said as they left the tarmac lane and headed towards the rough path through the stand of bracken. 'Also called sea pinks.'

'I like the way it grows right at the edge of the cliff – as though marking it out as dangerous.'

'I would never have thought of that but yes, it does, doesn't it?'

When they emerged from the bracken on to the springy turf, she remembered the last time she had come in this same direction; on that occasion, she had been grappling with the likelihood that Vincent was dead. More than six months ago now, that would have been. And while it was true that, whenever she stopped to recall what she had lost, she felt the same twisting pain, she also knew that very little of the woman who had gone to sit on that bench over there still remained; the physical distance between Slipscombe and her old life in St James's really had helped her to shed the shackles and regain some of the spirit that two decades of marriage to Hector had stripped away.

Noticing that Harrington was leading them towards that same bench, she said, 'Do you think we might continue straight on? I've never ventured all the way to the point, and I should quite like to see it.'

'Of course.' With a change of direction, they walked in silence until he said, 'I couldn't help noticing your absence from the photograph in the *Crier*.'

When he turned towards her, she met his look straight on. 'I had no wish to steal the limelight. It felt right that Julia and Elowen, as locals, should take the credit.'

'Incredibly magnanimous of you.'

She laughed. 'Old-school upbringing. Of equal truth is the fact that I have yet to see a single photograph of myself that I actually like.'

'Whilst I believe you might genuinely feel that way,' he said with a kindly smile, 'I really don't know why.'

'Seldom does one see oneself as others do. Nor do we regard ourselves with the same compassion we afford other people.'

'Perceptive.'

'Hm.'

Fractionally, she relaxed. If he didn't believe her reason for not being in the newspaper, at least he wasn't sufficiently concerned to press her on the point. But then, as a police inspector, doubtless he was quick to get the measure of a person; he wouldn't be much good at his job if he couldn't tell the difference between a hardened criminal and someone choosing to conceal a few personal secrets.

With the spine-like ridge of Lively Point stretching ahead of them, they continued across the soft turf.

'It was you who approached the aircraft, though, wasn't it?'

'I felt compelled. He was a German. I was cross.'

'Cross because he was a German?'

'Because he was the enemy.' When a gust of wind whipped across the promontory, she reached to flatten her skirt against her legs. 'But then I saw him, stared into his eyes, and was shocked that he was so young.'

'His identity papers gave his age as twenty-two.'

Twenty-two; he could have been her son. 'He looked utterly terrified. But also relieved, too.'

'He certainly appeared thankful to find himself in a police station. He was also quite proficient in English.'

'Goodness only knows what he made of my schoolgirl German.'

'You did well.'

'It was strange but, once I'd looked into his eyes, my anger completely dissolved. All I was left feeling was pity.'

'Soldiers on the front in the last war often report feeling something similar.'

'I recall hearing the same. But then that angry crowd came hurtling towards us and my anger turned on them. I couldn't be sure they wouldn't harm him.'

'There are always those who will want revenge for the loss of loved ones.'

'By rights, I should have felt the same way. The Luftwaffe bombing of London last September cost me dearly. Terribly dearly – changed the course of my life. But I couldn't take it out on that poor soul, sitting there in his crashed plane. He didn't order the air raid that night – didn't even drop the bombs.'

'Messerschmitt pilots fly escort duties.'

'I realize that. Faced with those villagers, though, I felt this surge, this . . . this sense that it was my duty to keep the poor man safe until you arrived.'

'I understand you made it plain he was only to be handed into my custody.'

'You were the only authority I trusted to be fair.'

Just short of the point at which the headland dropped precipitously down to where the waves were crashing over the dark and jagged rocks, they came to a halt.

'Would you like to know what happened to him – the pilot?'

She shook her head. 'All the while I don't know, it can't haunt me.'

'There's nothing to haunt you. The Ministry will have questioned him about his missions, and he will now be held as a prisoner of war. He will be treated with dignity.'

'Good.'

'I say again, you did well. Coming down in the darkness as he did, he could easily have slipped away. As I understand it, opportunities to talk to German pilots have been few and far between. You were brave and remained calm. And I think it important you know that. I could have arrived to find him shot in the head or run through with a bayonet. You were a credit to your sex. You were a credit to your country. And, for what it's worth, if you say you sighted a submarine that time, I believe you. To my mind, the only unanswered question is whether it was one of our own or one of theirs.'

'You know,' she said, 'I'm glad we came on this walk. You've made me feel . . .'

'Proud?'

'Not proud, no. But perhaps vindicated – that my efforts these last months haven't been a waste of time.'

'You can afford to be proud as well, you know. Pride isn't always the sin it's made out to be.'

'Lady Virginia said something similar. But the head-mistress at the school Julia and I attended couldn't have disagreed with you more. "Humility and modesty always". That was the edict by which she ruled over us.'

'As time moves on, attitudes change.'

'They do. You know,' she picked up again, 'talking to you has also helped me to find some sort of . . . well, peace, I suppose. A sense that, while some madman in a foreign land has set half the world's populations against one another, those sent to carry out his dirty work are people, just the same as us, with loved ones and homes. And I find the recognition brings me a sense of forgive-ness for the fact that I am where I am.'

'Isabel,' Harrington said, 'that you can find it within yourself to show compassion, despite the circumstances of your loss, is quite singular, and something I hope will enable you to live on, free from the shackles of bitterness and recrimination.'

She smiled. 'I hope so, too.'

'Tell me,' he said, bringing his gaze back from the hori-zon. 'Should we turn back? Or would you like to walk a little further?'

'I should probably turn back. But thank you for asking me to stroll with you. You've helped me to put one or two things into perspective.'

'Then I'm glad.'

When they turned inland, Isabel allowed herself that moment of pride; the young Isabel Walcot had been endowed with spirit and spunk and, as it had turned out, the only thing necessary to rekindle that fire, even twenty years on, had been an unfettered supply of air. Vincent had reawakened the embers slumbering within her; all she'd had to do from there on was keep them alive. And while the inspector's praise was welcome, of greater importance was her own belief that she wasn't useless. And whatever the future held, from that knowledge she would draw strength.

Continuing to smile, she cast a glance at Harrington. And, yes, from here on in, she might even allow herself the occasional moment of pride, as well.

23

On the night of the tenth of May, the newsreader stated in his precise manner, *in the most intense German air raids to date, an estimated five hundred Luftwaffe bombers dropped incendiaries and high explosive devices over a wide area of the capital. In Westminster, damage was caused to the Houses of Parliament, Westminster Abbey, St James's Palace and Piccadilly. Extensive damage was also caused to areas of Mayfair, Soho and Knightsbridge. In the city, damage was widespread in Marylebone, Holborn and Waterloo. To the east of the capital, where areas had already suffered significant damage in previous raids, bombs fell on an area from Elephant and Castle to Bermondsey and Greenwich. St Thomas's Hospital is also reported to have been hit. The main railway termini are closed, as are several bridges across the Thames. Casualties are expected to be significant. Elsewhere in the country . . .*

Sitting at the table, amid the remains of breakfast, it was Isabel who spoke first. 'Do you think this is ever going to end?'

Reports of repeated raids on places such as Bristol and Plymouth were difficult enough to hear but, for Isabel, it was the continued attacks on London that made her come over cold. She supposed it was because, for twenty years, it had been her home, and she knew the places behind the names. Added to that was the continuing rawness arising from her own experience of an air raid: she could still hear the crump of bombs exploding, feel the ground trembling beneath her feet; could still visualize the aftermath, taste the acrid smoke that made the back of her throat burn, and feel the terror of not knowing whether the most important person in her life was still alive.

'In my opinion,' Julia said, 'for what little *that* counts, Hitler won't simply give up. More likely, he'll try and pound us into submission so that he doesn't so much have to fight his way on to our shores as simply stroll in over the wreckage.'

Isabel studied her friend's expression. 'Then what would have been the point of all those bombs? Why go to all that effort to just take over nothing but ruins?'

'Maybe he thinks it'll be easier to impose his ways on a country that's already on its knees.'

Isabel hung her head. In front of her on the table, her plate bore the burnt corner of a crust from her piece of toast. Feeling ashamed to have left it uneaten when, elsewhere today, people would be homeless and hungry, she picked it up and put it in her mouth; it tasted bitter. It felt fitting.

'There can't be much of London left,' she said.

'Well, one thing's for certain, you won't be going back there now.'

'No.' Julia was right; her life in London was behind her. But then she had no desire to go back there now anyway. It might have been where she'd spent twenty years going about the routine of daily life, but it had never really been her home – certainly not in the sense that Fairlight was Julia's. 'No,' she said. 'There's nothing left for me in

London. Besides, with the benefit of distance, it's clear now that what I inhabited there wasn't a life anyway but an existence, a regimen of simply passing one day after another after another.'

'Well, I've said it all along, but I'll say it again,' Julia replied as she hauled herself up from the table. 'You're welcome here for as long as you want. I know it will never feel like your home —'

'I already feel more attached to Fairlight than I ever did to Warbone Gate. There might be a war on, but I have a freedom here I've never felt anywhere else.'

Julia looked back at her. 'Well, good, because none of us knows how or when we're going to come out of this war. Nor what life will look like when we do. But, until that day comes, you're here. One way or another, we'll get by.'

'Then in that case,' Isabel said, and got to her feet, 'shall I wash up the breakfast things or, since it's Monday, and that's wash day, shall I go and strip the beds? Only, since I still can't properly pay you for my keep, you are duty-bound to accept my labour.'

'You go and top-to-bottom the teachers' beds. My hands are already wrecked from perpetually being in the sink — no sense ruining yours as well.'

Without Julia and her kindness, Isabel thought, as she trotted up the stairs to the first landing, she would have been utterly lost. Instead, she was merely borderline desti-tute. Continuing up the second flight of stairs, she scolded herself. No, she was *not* destitute; people leaving the air raid shelters in the East End of London these last mornings were destitute. *She* had a small income from her trust; that it wasn't enough to allow her to pay for rent as well as food and to keep herself in essentials didn't make her destitute. Unlike many this morning, she also had the security of knowing where she would be sleeping tonight, as well as the companionship and support of friends. So, what she had to do now, it seemed, was sit down with Julia and think how she might go about earning a wage. And yes, that might mean going to make beds in the old folks' home or standing behind a counter wrapping shoppers' purchases and taking their money. But she was alive. She was healthy: she had the use of her brain and her limbs. And while, if it was easy, she would have done it by now, the time had come to put that mind, and those limbs, to paid work.

'Whoa, slow down there, young lady. You're going to do *what?*'

Lowering the knife she'd been using to peel potatoes, Isabel turned to watch as Elowen calmly repeated the same words she'd used to Julia seconds previously.

'I'm going to join the Women's Auxiliary Police Corps.'

'Since when?'

'Since just now, when I handed my application to Inspector Childe.'

Julia's stance didn't change. 'So, this was *his* idea?'

'No, Mum, it was –'

'Your Greg's, then.'

'For heaven's sake, Mum, no. If you'd let me get a word in edgeways, I'll explain.'

Julia moved to lean against the dresser. 'Well, go on, then. I'm all ears.'

'I'm nineteen now.'

'I'm well aware.'

'And at nineteen, lots of girls are already doing something for the war effort. What's more, according to Inspector Childe, the government is soon to start registering *women* for conscription, as well as men.'

'I've heard the rumour,' Julia replied stiffly. 'But as far as I know, it's just that – a rumour.'

Elowen ploughed on regardless. 'Well, anyway, when I asked him what age he thought conscription might start, he said perhaps twenty-one, but it could be as low as eighteen.'

'And it might not.'

'No,' Elowen agreed. 'It might not. Either way, I've no mind to be told to go and work in a factory – or to be sent down the dockyard. Nor do I hanker after joining one of the services, where I would most likely end up as a lackey to some handsy old bloke who thinks he's God's gift to women.'

In awe of Elowen's resolve, Isabel asked, 'So, what will you be doing in the police force?'

Julia sent her a glower. 'Did you know about this?'

'I didn't. But I am interested to hear more.'

'Then since at least *you* seem interested, Isabel,' Elowen began again, 'I will tell *you* that there's no guarantee I'll be accepted. Women can apply to join once they turn eighteen but, apparently, most applicants are upwards of twenty and have experience of doing something more useful than serving breakfasts or pulling pints.'

'Don't be so quick to put yourself down,' Isabel said. 'If *I* was in charge of recruitment, the fact that you went out, under your own steam, and got work in order to help out here, would tell me that, as well as showing initiative, you've held down two jobs, seven days a week, when some people don't even do one.'

'Isabel, you're not helping.'

'Actually, Mum,' Elowen interjected, 'Isabel's right. I hadn't looked at it like that. I must write down what she said for when I have to go for an interview.'

'Now just hold on,' Julia said, tossing aside the tea towel she'd been clutching. 'I haven't agreed you can do it yet. And until you tell me what it is you'd actually be involved in, I'm not even moved to consider it.'

Now it was Elowen's turn to glower.

Able to sympathize with both parties, Isabel decided to risk weighing in with advice. 'Look,' she said, 'why don't the two of you go through to the parlour and discuss this calmly. Julia, your concern not to see Elowen decide something in haste is understandable, but many's the time you've told me she's a sensible young woman. And perhaps you, Elowen, could try to understand that, for your stepmother, your announcement has come out of the blue, and is therefore something of a shock.'

'I'm not doing it on a whim,' Elowen countered. 'It's a thought I've had for a while.'

'Then both of you go through, sit down and explain to each other how you feel while I get on with supper.'

With an irritated shake of her head, Julia mumbled something that sounded to Isabel like, *All right, bossy boots.*

When the two women nevertheless went through to Julia's parlour and closed the door, Isabel sighed. Young women today were being presented with opportunities to do things that, even as recently as two or three years ago, would have been unthinkable. She could only hope that whatever this police job involved, Julia would warm to the idea – or at least not forbid Elowen to go ahead. As she, herself, knew all too well, these were exceptional times, requiring equally exceptional sacrifices.

As it transpired, when the two eventually emerged from the parlour, Julia seemed largely mollified.

'If I'm accepted,' Elowen explained to everyone over supper a while later, 'Inspector Childe said I'll most likely have to go to Exeter to start with, where I'll get some training in working in the office but also the chance to assist male constables with female criminals. The inspector also said that next time he has a vacancy here, he can request that for the duration of the war, the position goes to a WAPC.'

'What does your young man think?' Elizabeth Anderson enquired.

'He's all for it, thinks I'll be good at it. He also thinks it will be somewhere for me to . . . how did he put it? Oh, yes, to invest my energy.'

The younger of the teachers around the table looked impressed; the more mature Mrs Edna Price looked doubtful.

'My dear, I wish you well. Times have certainly changed from my day.'

'They've changed for all of us,' Elizabeth said. 'More in the last two years than at any time in the last twenty, I'd say.'

'Anyway,' Elowen went on, 'I've put in my application. And Inspector Childe is going to write a testimonial. That way, he says, with the need for women on the force being so great, I might not even have to go for an interview. Which would be good news.'

When Elowen looked directly at her, Isabel smiled. 'I'd wish you good luck, but I don't think you'll need it.' It was quite glorious to witness Elowen's blossoming.

'Thanks for stepping in earlier,' Julia said as she and Isabel were putting away the last of the serving dishes and saucepans a while later. 'Sometimes, we can both be a bit too bull-headed for our own good.'

'But you're reconciled to her decision?' Isabel felt it necessary to check.

'I am. Like you said, it just came out of the blue. She never thinks to ask first, or even to let me in on what she's planning – just swans in and presents the thing as a *fait accompli*.'

Isabel laughed. 'Remind you of anyone?'

'Oh, ha-ha. I might have known whose side *you'd* be on. Seriously, though, no matter how much she's grown up this last year and a half, it's still hard to stand by and watch her spreading her wings.'

'I can only imagine.'

'Despite wanting her to have the freedom to decide her own course through life – the sort of freedom you and I never had – it's hard, feeling abandoned.'

'It's because you've done such a good job with her.' When Julia frowned, Isabel went on, 'But trust me, having been the mother figure to her that you clearly have, even once she leaves, I doubt she'll stay away. No matter what she does, and where she goes, I guarantee you won't lose her – not forever.'

'You'd better be right about that.'

'I am.'

'Course, it doesn't help that I envy her both her youth and her freedom.'

With a pat of Julia's shoulder, Isabel agreed. 'So do I.'

'It might be an awful time to be alive –'

'But perhaps a strangely good one, as well.'

'Yes. Tell you what. Want to come through to the parlour for a little nip of something? In a while, that drama series is on the wireless – *At Home With the Somebody-or-Others.* You know the one – the awful family that's always at each other's throats. Happen that's why I like it.'

Isabel regarded her friend doubtfully. 'Well –'

'Oh, come on with you. We'll have a giggle.'

'Very well. But *only* a nip. I know what you're like.'

'Right this way, madam.'

Perhaps, Isabel thought, as she followed her friend through to her parlour-cum-office, with a nip inside her, and with Elowen having already raised the matter of employment, she might finally discuss with Julia ideas for how she, too, might go about finding her own way into the world of work.

The envelope Julia had just collected from the doormat bore handwriting that Isabel recognized as Ronnie's. It was a sight that made her falter; she still felt guilty about being unable to let their friend know she hadn't perished in the air raid on Warbone Gate. Her sole consolation came from reminding herself that she was withholding the information for Ronnie's own good – because she still didn't want to put her friend in a difficult position.

It was the morning after Elowen's revelation about the WAPC job, and Isabel was shaping the last couple of dumplings for the vegetable and lentil hotpot she was preparing for that evening's supper. Inwardly, she despaired at having to make dumplings with so little suet because they always came out rather dense. But, in common with most women now, she was long past the stage of bemoaning the latest food shortages and well aware of the truth in the saying *worse where there's none*; dense or not, her make-do dumplings would help to fill everyone up when the stew, by itself, was unlikely to.

Rubbing the flour from her hands, she glanced across to where Julia was now leaning against the dresser reading Ronnie's letter. Despite her growing desperation to know what their friend had to say, she took care to keep her tone casual as she enquired, 'So, does Ronnie have any news?'

In distracted fashion, Julia nodded. 'Uh-huh. Although, before I share it, I should probably read all the way to the end.'

'Fair enough.' Since Julia was clearly in no mood to be rushed, Isabel carried the mixing bowl and cooking implements she'd been using through to the scullery to wash up.

'Right, then.' Julia's remark, moments later, made Isabel turn off the tap, dry her hands and return to the kitchen. 'Now I've got the gist of it, I think it best I let you read it for yourself.'

'Would I be wise to sit down?'

When Julia shrugged, Isabel sat down anyway. Then she placed the letter on the table, smoothed out the folds and drew a breath.

Dismissing Ronnie's opening pleasantries with the merest of glances, she directed her eyes to the longer paragraphs further down the page.

Yesterday, I saw Elspeth Wade, an old friend, whose husband had recently bumped into Hector. This morning, reflecting upon what she told me, I felt moved to pass on her news.

Sadly, despite what Elspeth termed 'extensive enquiries' on Hector's part, it seems Isabel is still unaccounted for. However, when Hector attempted to obtain a declaration of her death, he was advised that, despite events strongly suggesting she was indeed lost in the bombing of their home, without her remains having been recovered from the ruins, the law requires that he wait for seven years after she was last known to be alive before applying to have her declared dead. As I later remarked to Ralph, since Hector is already living with the Deacon-Jones woman anyway, I don't suppose the wait will unduly trouble him.

When Isabel paused to look up, she was surprised to see Julia grinning.

'So, for once, Ronnie's letter brings you *good* news.'

Clearly, Isabel thought, she had to be missing something. 'On what basis?'

'Well, if, as it seems, Hector's intent is no longer to find you but to have you declared dead, then why would he keep trying to find evidence that you're actually still alive?'

'Hm.' She supposed Julia had a point.

'The situation also suggests,' Julia continued, as she picked up Ronnie's letter, 'that you can stop worrying about Hector discovering your new name because, even if he has learned it, it clearly hasn't enabled him to find you. Instead, maybe now, you can relax a little in the knowledge that by changing your name and leaving London, your audacious plan has worked. You really have escaped from under his nose.' After a momentary pause, Julia continued, 'And in light of that, you might also want to accept that, despite losing Vincent and ending up here, in Devon, the time has come to get on with your life.'

To Isabel's surprise, a long-standing fog seemed to lift, the view before her unexpectedly clear. As Julia said, not only had she foiled Hector's attempts to find her, but it suited him to think her dead; forget her and move on. And surely *that* gave her licence to do the same. In which case, from this point on, she would do as she hadn't so far dared: put Hector firmly to the back of her mind and live each day as it came. She would refuse to waste another second of her time fretting about him finding her. She wouldn't go so far as to abandon caution altogether, but she *would* do as she'd spent the best part of twenty years longing to do – and as she'd hoped to do with Vincent – and make up for lost time.

Dearest Ronnie. Perhaps, one day, she would be able to thank her for the part she'd inadvertently played in spurring her on to look towards a future that was now free from resentment, humiliation and fear.

*

'With the weather finally improving, and everywhere no longer just a single shade of grey, you must think the place looks very different.'

Isabel nodded. 'Very different, yes. On a sparkling jewel of a morning like this, I can see why people holiday here – or used to. Well, apart from the pillboxes on the headland,' she went on to remark, as she looked up and spotted the one just beyond Fairlight. 'And those coils of barbed wire on the dunes.'

'Not long now and there will be more, along here, by the esplanade, which means I shall almost certainly have a near riot on my hands.'

'People will complain about the spoiling of the view?'

'*And* about not being able to go on the sands – especially with summer almost upon us.'

It was a couple of days after Elowen had broken her news about applying to join the Women's Auxiliary Police Corps and, quite by chance, as she'd been leaving the chemist's, Isabel had walked straight into Inspector Childe, with whom she was now chatting. That he seemed in no rush to get back to his work was pleasing; she always enjoyed conversing with him. He had such a lovely manner, coupled with which, when he offered a point for consideration, he seemed genuinely interested in her response.

'Isabel, forgive me, but do you have a moment?' When she evidently appeared surprised, he hastened on, 'I have something I should like to put to you.'

Why, she wondered, had her heart started to race? What might he have found out about her? She didn't *think* she had cause to worry, but the idea that he had somehow discovered her secret – that she was neither single nor in Slipscombe for quite the reason she'd made out – was hard to bury. However, until she knew otherwise, on that front, she would keep her powder dry.

'How intriguing.'

'Might I suggest we go and sit over there on the bench?' When he pointed to the pavement bordering the grassy esplanade, she glanced across; the seat was sufficiently public that, whatever he had in mind to say, it clearly wasn't going to be particularly personal in nature. 'We can go into the station if you prefer. However, if what I should like to propose is of no interest to you, then at least this way, I won't have made you traipse all the way there purely to turn me down.'

Now her heart really was racing. 'Goodness. The intrigue deepens. And in which case, yes, perhaps it had better be over there.'

Once seated a polite distance from one another on the little wooden bench – thoughtfully angled to best take in the view over the bay – Isabel rested her handbag on her lap and determined to wait.

After a momentary pause, Inspector Childe turned towards her.

'Miss Smith – Isabel – I feel an explanation is in order. When I mentioned the arrival of the better weather – and also when we were walking together on Sunday – I was hoping to discover whether you intend to remain here in Slipscombe for the duration of the war, or whether you have plans to leave us.'

Recalling her surprise when, after Sunday lunch, he had invited her to accompany him for a walk — and given her anxiety as to why her movements should be of interest to him — she reminded herself to exercise caution. 'I do not currently have forward plans.'

'I see.'

Almost immediately, she regretted sounding so formal, so *rehearsed*. Time, perhaps, for a grain of honesty. 'In truth, I have nowhere else to go. The place where I lived in London was destroyed by an HE —'

'I remember you saying.'

'— and in any event wasn't mine.'

'Ah.'

There. That was better. 'The few relatives I have are all distant and leading their own lives.' So far, so good: none of what she'd said constituted a lie.

'As is so often the case.'

'I suppose so. But Julia continues to be extraordinarily kind and goes to great lengths to stress that I may remain at Fairlight for as long as I wish.'

'Which would seem both fortunate and generous.'

'It is. *She* is.'

'I sense, though, that you fear outstaying your welcome.'

'I do fear taking advantage. More so because my income is meagre and leaves me unable to contribute as I would wish. Just lately, my circumstances have certainly been occupying my thoughts.'

'Then forgive me for asking in such a fashion, but have you considered taking employment?'

Why did she smell a rat? Had Julia, after their discussion

the other evening, said something to him? While it was hard to believe she would have, the coincidence felt simply too great for it to be otherwise.

'As it happens, just recently, I was talking to Julia about that very possibility. Unfortunately, having just been on the receiving end of Elowen's news –'

'Ah, yes,' he said and raised a hand in confession. 'I'm afraid that's rather down to me.'

'– I joined Julia in a nightcap, with what ensued turning into rather a lot of reminiscing and giggling and considerably little by way of serious discussion. But yes, I have been contemplating seeking employment. Sadly, my greatest impediment in that regard is that I have no particular skills.'

When he started to smile, she once again smelled a rat. 'Then I wonder whether I might make a suggestion?'

'If it's more respectable than some of Julia's last night, please, go ahead.'

'County has given me permission to employ a female clerk.' Isabel's spirits sank; clearly, he had missed the part where she'd said that she didn't have any skills. 'I was hoping they would allow me to train young Elowen as a WAPC, but they were keen to have her get up to speed in Exeter. On the positive side, they *have* agreed to allow me a part-time female clerk – four hours a day, five days a week. And I thought of you.'

'Goodness.' She couldn't think what else to say.

'You wouldn't become a sworn officer – wouldn't be in uniform – but the position will be properly remunerated.'

Properly remunerated. There went her pulse again.

When he paused, seemingly to gauge her response thus far, she urged herself to remain calm. After all, what did she know of clerical work – in a police station, at that? When he didn't continue, she drew a breath. 'What would the duties entail?'

'The usual administrative mixture. Answering the telephone –' answer the telephone: she could do that – 'filing paperwork –' she could manage that, too – 'typing reports –' Ah.

'I'm afraid I haven't typed a word since attempting to learn when I was about fifteen.' Why hadn't she tried to keep her hand in? Now she might miss out on what sounded like the ideal opportunity.

'I'm sure you would soon get back up to speed. You strike me as conscientious.'

'Oh, I am, I am.' *Calm down.*

'I also happen to believe you more than capable of answering the telephone and taking messages. And, when it comes to doing the filing, the only skill required there is remembering the alphabet.'

When she noticed him grinning, she laughed. 'That's probably the one thing that *hasn't* changed from when I was taught it.'

'I sense,' he said, 'that you're hesitant. And I do wish you weren't. You're precisely what the station needs.'

'I'm flattered you think so. But I'm . . . what I mean is, the position sounds to be one of some responsibility.'

'I won't make light of it. Record keeping and administration are key parts of the smooth running of the entire station.'

'Of course.'

He turned more fully towards her. 'Isabel, what can I say to convince you?'

Part of her needed no convincing whatsoever; the other part felt considerably less gung-ho. 'You do realize that I've never been out to work before. I mean, I couldn't even supply you with a reference.'

'Personal recommendation carries far greater weight. Especially coming from an inspector.'

'I see.' *Could* she do it? It was all very well vowing to dismiss Hector from her thoughts but could she, in good conscience, let Harrington vouch for her while ignorant of the almighty secret she was keeping? Was her personal situation even relevant?

'I should also probably point out that, once this war ends, in all likelihood, so will the job.'

And so, she imagined, would a great many other things. 'I suppose so.'

But that did put the opportunity in a more favourable light, make it easier to convince herself that she would be doing this for the war effort and to get him out of a fix – rather than simply taking advantage to earn some much-needed money. Besides, a few days in, she might turn out to be completely useless at it, and he might ask her to leave.

'All right. Then how about this?' he said. 'What if you were to come along for a week's trial? Paid, of course, but with no obligation on either side to take it any further than that?'

In Harrington's look, Isabel read nothing but warmth

and sincerity. While he had no way of knowing it, the favour he would be doing her amounted not solely to offering possible financial salvation but also another step towards the much-needed fresh start she'd been promising herself. How much he really knew about her situation, she couldn't tell – and it might be better that she never found out. Either way, surely, this was the chance for which she'd been hoping. She had no dependants; she had no commitments. But until she was able to pay her own way in the world – at least to some extent, in notes and coins – true independence would always evade her.

Unwittingly, she sighed. This cruel and wretched war might have robbed Vincent of his life, and her of a future with him but, just lately, she had begun to wonder whether perhaps he was somehow watching over her. After all, here she was, not just reunited with her dearest friend in a safe and tranquil part of Devon but presented with the chance to strike out and stand on her own two feet. And throughout all those years of suffering under Hector's control, wasn't that what she'd craved – a chance to live by the efforts of her own hands?

In that moment, despite having no idea whether by taking up the inspector's offer she would succeed or fail, the way ahead seemed not only clear but the answer to twenty long years of prayers.

'Then I have just one question,' she said, glancing up to meet the inspector's inquisitive look.

'And that is?'

'When would you like me to start?'

Author's Historical Note

The story of *Isabel's War* draws to a close at the end of May 1941. At this point in the events of the Second World War, unbeknown to the people of Britain, Hitler had come to realize that a successful invasion of the British mainland would be too great a test of his military capabilities, the recognition leading him to focus instead upon his grander plan to invade and defeat the Soviet Union.

This new invasion plan, code-named Operation Barbarossa, was launched on 22 June 1941, the consequence being that, with many Luftwaffe attacks diverted away from Britain, the threat of invasion gradually began to recede. The war in Europe would last a further four years, with great hardship and sacrifice still to come, but for people across Britain, especially in the towns and cities of southern England, the summer of 1941 saw their long-running fear of a German invasion finally fade from their thoughts.

He just wanted a decent book to read ...

Not too much to ask, is it? It was in 1935 when Allen Lane, Managing Director of Bodley Head Publishers, stood on a platform at Exeter railway station looking for something good to read on his journey back to London. His choice was limited to popular magazines and poor-quality paperbacks – the same choice faced every day by the vast majority of readers, few of whom could afford hardbacks. Lane's disappointment and subsequent anger at the range of books generally available led him to found a company – and change the world.

'We believed in the existence in this country of a vast reading public for intelligent books at a low price, and staked everything on it'
Sir Allen Lane, 1902–1970, founder of Penguin Books

The quality paperback had arrived – and not just in bookshops. Lane was adamant that his Penguins should appear in chain stores and tobacconists, and should cost no more than a packet of cigarettes.

Reading habits (and cigarette prices) have changed since 1935, but Penguin still believes in publishing the best books for everybody to enjoy. We still believe that good design costs no more than bad design, and we still believe that quality books published passionately and responsibly make the world a better place.

So wherever you see the little bird – whether it's on a piece of prize-winning literary fiction or a celebrity autobiography, political tour de force or historical masterpiece, a serial-killer thriller, reference book, world classic or a piece of pure escapism – you can bet that it represents the very best that the genre has to offer.

Whatever you like to read – trust Penguin.